everything you know

mary beth bass

The orange sun burst between two buildings, blinding Joe for a second. He shaded his eyes and looked around. The detainee tower was straight ahead, just to the right of the setting sun. If he stayed reasonably clear of it he'd be able to avoid the Masevo, he hoped, and if he kept it in his sightline he wouldn't get lost. Emma was somewhere in the city. He was sure of it. And he was sure the vision in the water meant he had to reunite her with her family, wherever they were. He just had to find the tunnel and Emma before the Masevo.

Joe's clothes and shoes had dried in the wind and his jeans had shrunk until they were uncomfortably tight. The air was getting cooler as the sun sank lower. He wished he had a jacket.

The outskirts of the city were dotted with small houses fronted by little walled gardens. The architecture was a strangely appealing mix of modern and medieval, as if Frank Gehry had designed house-sized castles made of steel and stone. A few gardens had flowering vines that climbed over white walls. Joe heard laughing. He saw a few winged kids flying and playing above their yards…

everything you know

mary beth bass

www.BOROUGHSPUBLISHINGGROUP.com

EVERYTHING YOU KNOW

Digital edition created by Maureen Cutajar

ISBN 978-1-941260-96-8

For Sam Bass, who is and always has been the hero of his own life.

ACKNOWLEDGMENTS

If you are a reader of acknowledgments—and you must be if you are reading this now— you know that a book never comes to life through the efforts of a single person. The miracle is that it happens at all, but that is a story for another day.

I am grateful every day for the unbroken support of my super-agent extraordinaire, Miriam Kriss. She never lost faith in me or in this book, and that in itself is a little bit of a miracle.

Without Chris Keeslar's masterful, sensitive editing I never would have been able to tell the story I wanted to tell with this book. And since these are acknowledgments and you've come to these pages of your own free will, I'm going to say what I'm really thinking and not pretend to be cool, or reserved, or erudite, or anything other than what I actually am. I'd need a new, bigger, more powerful language to be able to sufficiently thank Chris for sticking by me as a writer when the possibility of ever selling anything or completing anything seemed all but hopeless. I am forever, forever grateful.

Thanks always to Suzanne Collins, Laura Toffler-Corrie, Sharon Struth, C. C. Hunter, Kassy Tayler, Maggie Stiefvater, Joanna Novins, Laird Sapir, David Bass, Rebecca Bass, Ben Bass, Sam Bass, the gifted and fabulous Romance Writers of Southern Connecticut & Lower New York (COLONY), Romance Writers of America, the amazing team at Boroughs Publishing Group, and especially cover artist Anne Cain, who captured what I wanted to say with a single picture.

And thanks to you, reader of books and acknowledgments!

CONTENTS

everything you know

mary beth bass

Part One

There was a listening fear in her regard,
As if calamity had but begun;
As if the vanward clouds of evil days
Had spent their malice, and the sullen rear
Was with its stored thunder laboring up.
—John Keats

PROLOGUE

"To start," said the voice coming from everywhere and nowhere, "it's been two months? Since your wife's death?"

Glad of the dark, the man answered, "Not quite."

"I'm sorry."

"Yes," the man said.

"You will turn yourself in, then."

"That's been arranged," the man said. "I don't need a reminder. You should know that."

"Tomorrow."

"What?" the man said. "Surely not tomorrow. I was promised time. I need—"

"That allowance has passed."

"And if I refuse? I'm not the only one with something at stake. Remember that."

The voice was stern. "Threatening me is unwise. *You* should know that. Turn yourself in to us tomorrow or your children will be executed."

There was no arguing. The voice went silent and the man was alone.

From out of the shadow of silence, a soft-throated chorus began. These were the truly dangerous ones, these whisperers, these misguided purveyors of the truest-seeming lies. Like the voice that came before, they wanted him. They'd waited for him. His wife had kept him from falling, and now she was gone.

No matter what happens, never give in.

And yet, their new song couldn't be mistaken. There was no escape.

The boy in the next room sang a different song. It was the man's son, and he sang with a voice of honey and daggers. He sang a song of the making of the two worlds, of the beauty of life, of indefatigable hope. He sang for his dead mother, for he would not believe she was dead. He did not know he should cry for her.

The man would cry for her. Then he would do what must be done.

CHAPTER ONE

March, fifteen years later
Warwick, New Hampshire

She was sweating under her breasts and in her armpits. Her scalp crawled with imagined flies, all fluttering wings and rushing feet. Her heart pounded so hard she was sure she was having a heart attack.

Emma Mathews closed the classroom door behind her and walked as fast as she could without breaking into an attention-grabbing all-out dash. She'd had something like this panic attack every afternoon for the past two weeks, with horrible physical symptoms no matter what kind of soap she used or how much deodorant she put on. All she wanted to do was run.

Until today she'd been able to stay in class. Bouncing in her seat, the fingers of her right hand drumming on her thigh, she fake-listened as Mr. Kochenderfer read from *The Canterbury Tales.* Staring straight ahead with her arms plastered to her sides, Emma had ignored the irritated sighs from Heather Sapienza and Heather's cadre of acolytes, and the taunts from Kyle Sparks about her supposed drug use. But today was different. Today it was either pretend she was about to throw up or run crazily from the room. All she had to do was make it to the girls' bathroom in the next corridor. If she was lucky it would be empty and she could turn off the lights, block the door with a garbage can, and wait for the thing to pass.

"Mathews. Hey, Mathews," Kyle had whispered. "I know you can hear me, you little freak. Your tits are blushing."

Emma had counted the seconds between the times Mr. Kochenderfer pushed up his sliding wire-framed glasses. Twelve. Seven. Ten.

"Mathews," Kyle whispered again. "Hey, Mathews. Do me a favor, will you? Please? It won't take long."

Five. One. Four.

"When your teeth fall out," he continued, "and they will. Sorry. It's an unavoidable consequence of that shit you're taking."

Two. Eleven. Four.

"When your teeth fall out," Kyle repeated, leaning close and enunciating every syllable. "I want you to blow me."

Emma whipped her head around and sneered at him. He grinned. In a bizarre flash Emma remembered Kyle sharing his cupcake with her in first grade after she'd dropped hers in the dirt. She turned back to Mr. Kochenderfer. Three. Six. Five.

"And don't forget, Mathews," Kyle whispered over the end of *The Nun's Priest's Prologue*. "Spitters are quitters."

Emma stood up. "Mr. Kochenderfer," she said. Her voice and her legs were shaking so it didn't even sound like a lie. "I'm going to be sick."

Kyle snickered.

"Go," the teacher said, nodding in the direction of the door.

And then she'd left the classroom, angry that Kyle thought she was leaving because of him. As if he wasn't going to peak in high school and die a fat, lonely, bitter old man.

Emma run-walked toward the bathroom. She'd read about panic attacks online. Fight-or-flight response. That's what one of the articles had said. But Emma didn't have an impulse to run from anything. No, the overwhelming compulsion that made her sweat and shake and want to scream at the top of her lungs was to run as fast as she could *toward* something.

The problem was, she didn't know what that something was. If it was dangerous. Or awesome. Or if it existed at all.

Laughing voices exploded in the next corridor. Emma dropped her head and crossed her arms. Floor tiles flecked with grey and red slashes flew beneath her feet as she marched, eyes down, toward the bathroom.

The giggling voices hushed then disappeared. Emma sprinted for the end of the hall. As she turned the corner, her face, her whole, open-mouthed face, was suddenly, violently, buried between two warm, sweet-smelling breasts.

"Hey!" the angry voice belonging to said breasts shouted, and strong hands pushed Emma away.

She caught herself before she fell on her butt, and looked up. Stacy Keeler, flawless, flushed and pissed, glowered.

"Watch where you're going."

"You didn't see me, either," Emma sputtered. "Unless you *wanted* me to face-dive into your bra. We bumped into each other."

Stacy stared at Emma like there were no appropriate words in any known language and turned to Isabel Peccant. Emma's heart gained fifty pounds. It had been four and a half weeks since her forever best friend Izzy Peccant stopped responding to her texts and started hanging out with Stacy. When Emma confronted Izzy at Pop's Clam House in what had been until this tragicomical, ego-leveling incident, the humiliation zenith of Emma's brief existence, Izzy confessed that she'd been bored with their friendship for a long time.

"Well, now I totally forget what I was saying," Stacy said.

Izzy blushed. "Doug's party," she said.

Stacy smiled and nodded. "Oh, yeah." And just like that, Emma disappeared again.

Everyone knows elementary school friendships fall apart in middle school when the ruthless architecture of the cool and the hopeless, apparent since kindergarten to any halfway-observant human, is forged in iron and blood. At the beginning of sixth grade Emma and Izzy had watched in horror as girls devoured each other and soft, unathletic boys retreated to places where their new invisibility wouldn't be noticed. No one but Emma and Izzy had remained friends through junior year. Now Izzy shot her a furtive, sympathetic glance, then followed Stacy into the library.

Emma stood motionless, her stomach unraveling, aware of every inch of her skin. Before Izzy friend-dumped her, Emma's outsider status hadn't mattered. She didn't need the affection or the admiration of five or ten or five hundred girls. She and Izzy spoke their own language of ridiculously important and importantly ridiculous things, absurd-genius nothings irrelevant outside their circle of two. No one else needed to know why the bright orange scarf was so hilarious or why listening to a song like "How Soon is Now" a hundred times was still not enough. When she and Izzy read *The Perks of Being a Wallflower* in ninth grade, they wrote their own "Dear friend" letters and embroidered the lyrics to "Asleep" by The Smiths on matching jean jackets. Izzy was the reason Emma found and loved The Smiths and Morrissey. Now, somehow, Izzy was finding new orange scarves and new sad songs with Stacy. Stacy Keeler had replaced Emma.

Replaced. The verb was benign but the reality of the situation struck Emma's heart like a flaming torch. And if that sounded dramatic, fuck it. It was the tiny things that killed people. *And if you don't know this, then what do you know? Life is a pigsty.*

The urge to run, which had fallen away while Emma was making face-contact with perfect Stacy's perfect breasts, roared back ten times worse than before. Her hands itched. Her legs shook. Her mouth was dry. Did she have a rare disease? Was she allergic to something in Mr. Kochenderfer's classroom? Was she *crazy?*

Would she have to take medication? Go to a hospital? Leave school?

"Emma?" Mr. Norway came out of his office. "Are you all right?"

No, Emma wanted to say to the guidance counselor. I'm not. I think something's wrong with me.

"Yeah," she said, "I'm fine. I just..." She looked at her white-toed bright green sneakers. "Never mind." She sighed then raised her head. "I ran into Izzy and Stacy." Shrugging, she added, "Literally."

He nodded sympathetically. "Oh."

"I have to get back to class," Emma said, leaning toward the bathroom.

Her heart still pounded and her scalp still crawled but the urge to run diminished in Mr. Norway's calming presence. He was the nicest teacher in the school. He knew every student, noticed everything and judged nothing. Emma was almost three when her family moved to Warwick from Portsmouth. Mr. Norway was the first person her parents met. He'd introduced them to a lot of people, including his closest friend, Agatha Moore, who'd died last year. She'd helped Emma's dad get his job at the university and babysat for all five Mathews kids when they were little.

"If you have a minute," Mr. Norway said, "I'd like you to do something for me. I'll give you a pass."

The sweat pooling between Emma's shoulder blades and around her ribcage was making her shirt stick to her skin. "Sure," she said, tugging gently at the light fabric. "What do you need?"

"This is Joe Castlellaw," Mr. Norway said. He pulled a kid from the open office door behind him like a reluctant rabbit out of a magician's hat.

"Joe," Mr. Norway said. "This is Emma Mathews."

A tall boy, around her age, with long eyelashes and coffee-ice-cream skin glanced at her then looked away. The sun coming through the Diversity Club's rainbow mobile made his thick dark hair look indigo blue.

"Joe moved here from Wolfeboro two weeks ago," Mr. Norway said. "Today is his first day at Henry Dearborn High School."

"Oh," Emma said.

Joe Eyelashes glared over her head. Curious, Emma turned but there was nothing there except for a few *Spring Fling!* posters on the wall about the upcoming freshman dance. Emma reached into her pocket for her lip balm then remembered she'd lost it. Her mouth was still dry and her lips, which weren't her best feature to begin with, were probably peeling like a zombie's. Subtly she scraped any dead skin back into her mouth with her teeth.

Maybe hot boys from Wolfeboro were into girls with zombie lips.

Not likely.

"Hey," she said.

"Hey," he grunted, barely audible, before looking away again.

Awesome. Another arrogant asshole to grace the school with his exalted presence. Well, at least she didn't have to worry what he thought about her sweaty tank top. Or her zombie lips.

"Joe couldn't get here earlier," Mr. Norway continued, smiling kindly at Mr. I'm-So-Amazing-Don't-Look-at-Me. "So if you don't mind…"

Joe shifted his weight and exhaled. He was still glaring at the freshman dance posters as if their very existence offended him. Emma grabbed the chance to look at him again.

Even if he was a douche, Joe Castlellaw was wicked cute. Wiry and strong, his chest and shoulders filled out his black tee shirt just right and his dark hair curled above his collar. Maybe she'd judged him too quickly. Maybe he was nice. Maybe it didn't matter. She wasn't always nice herself. Emma tried to catch his eye but Joe dropped his gaze to the floor and glued it there, probably wishing he could dive in and swim away.

"Would you mind?" Mr. Norway asked.

"What?" Emma said, turning. Apparently the counselor had been talking while she was mentally swooning.

"Would you mind showing Joe to Mrs. Eyre's class?" Mr. Norway said.

"Uh, sure. Come on," Emma said.

Joe Castlellaw was staring hard at her chest, like he couldn't look away, then he raised his head and gazed directly into her eyes. Emma felt calmer. Her skin and her scalp and her legs— *everything*—felt normal. And the urge to run that had faded when Mr. Norway asked her if she was all right disappeared completely.

Joe resumed his intense examination of the opposite wall. In a spectacularly epic fail, Emma tried to bite back a grin at the sight of the sweet place between Joe's jaw and his ear. What would it be like to kiss him there? Would he like it? Would he kiss her back in the same way? Would he kiss her mouth? The inside of her wrist? The palm of her hand?

Oh, no. Was she that girl? Was she really *that* girl, thoughtfully unhappy about something real and true until a hot boy looked at her and then it was all sappy songs and unicorns, and all the dragons in the world were pink and breathed cotton candy instead of fire?

Joe gazed at Emma again, slightly longer this time, right out from under those gorgeous black eyelashes.

Oh my God, she *was* that girl. If Emma hadn't felt like Gene Kelly in *Singing in the Rain* right then, she would have been vomiting in self-disgust. And, awesome, she'd gone from age-appropriate, real-life–appropriate depressing songs to movie musicals old enough to be shown in a museum.

"What the hell is wrong with me?" Emma whispered.

Mr. Norway winked.

Oh, no. No. No. No. No. No.

Face-flaming a thousand shades of red, Emma muttered something about Mr. Norway not understanding. She backed away and smashed her hip on the guidance office doorknob. Joe's cheeks darkened. He might have grinned slightly.

"Come on," Emma said, none too nicely, leading him down the hall. She paused and touched her face to see if it was warm. It was, which meant she was still pink, and maybe even splotchy. Perfect. She didn't want to look at her chest, which also reddened when she was really embarrassed, or at her beloved Smiths *The World Won't Listen* tank top that suddenly seemed much too small.

"Where are we going?" Joe asked.

Was that concern in his quiet voice? Was he worried she was going to lead him astray or forget her task?

"This way," Emma said. She pointed. They started walking again toward Mrs. Eyre's AP history class.

Joe passed her. He stopped at the corner where the old building connected with the new one. Emma pointed again.

"Did you like Wolfeboro?" she asked. She couldn't stand the silence any longer, and she wanted to hear more of his deep, lush voice.

"I guess," Joe said, still staring straight ahead and walking fast.

"We don't have a lake like you do," Emma said. "But we do have awesome hiking and bike trails. Do you like to hike or mountain bike? I have a bike."

I have a bike? The skin on her face tightened. Why didn't she just invite him over for animal crackers?

Joe stopped. Emma looked at her shoes.

"Sometimes," he said, a terrible hint of a smile in his voice.

Anxious to obliterate her I-have-a-bike announcement, Emma gestured to the book in Joe's hand. "What are you reading?"

"Samuel Beckett plays."

"Are you an actor?" Emma asked.

"No. I like reading."

That soft, low voice was mesmerizing. He gazed unsmilingly at her again with those serious eyes, and something slowly opened in Emma's chest. Like a small door, or a casement window "opening on the foam of perilous seas in faery lands, forlorn." She wanted to hum but smiled back at him instead.

"I like to read," she said.

Joe eyed her, flipping through the pages of his book with his thumb, making a noise like mechanical insect wings.

"But I really love music," Emma continued. "My sister Maude loves to read. She's obsessed with poetry and flowers. I have four brothers and sisters, which is, obviously, a lot. Do you have any brothers or sisters?"

Joe shook his head. The movement visibly shifted the air as if they were under breathable water. Emma's chest contracted, and then the school, the hall, the lockers, and Joe vanished.

CHAPTER TWO

Cecilia Castlellaw kept talking as she scrubbed the last few dishes in the sink. The apartment had a dishwasher but she didn't use it. Thin light from the overhead fixture shone on the drying silverware.

Finishing his homework at the small kitchen table, Joe had paid attention to his mother at first. Now her singsong monologue hung in the air like inane pop music in a supermarket. She was afraid. Like always. Afraid his real parents would find him and want him back. Afraid he might get in more trouble for what he'd done when Sean Bolton locked that freshman in a locker at his old school. Afraid he'd get sick and have to go to the hospital. But mostly his mother was afraid someone would discover his freak-secret and take him away from her and she'd never see him again.

Her goldfinch voice pierced the rushing water and fell between the cracks of Joe's brooding thoughts. The events of his first day at Henry Dearborn High School ran through his head like a nightmare gone viral. And Emma Mathews. She was a nightmare, too. Though it hadn't started out that way.

At the end of their meeting that morning, Mr. Norway led him to the waiting area of the guidance suite. Joe's first class was AP American history. He would have been happier starting the day with his Shakespeare elective, but he'd already missed it and anything was better than staying in the apartment for one more day. He and his mom had lived in shitty apartments before. Hell, they'd hardly lived in any other kind, but Joe felt more trapped in this one than he had anywhere else. He'd ridden his bike past the school every afternoon and all through town over the weekend. It didn't help, but he had to do something.

Mr. Norway opened the suite door and stuck his head into the hall. Joe waited. Like always. He was always waiting for someone else to make decisions for him, to tell him what to do, where to go, what to think. He opened the book he'd brought to school and read the introduction.

"Emma?" Mr. Norway said. He stepped into the hall, leaving Joe in the waiting area.

The counselor sounded genuinely interested in whomever he was talking to. There had been good teachers in every school Joe attended but none were as smart and compassionate as Mr. Norway seemed. When they'd met that morning Joe had almost confided in him. But maybe his mom was right to be afraid about his secret being revealed.

"Are you all right?" Mr. Norway asked the unseen student.

A girl's defiant, embarrassed voice answered, "Yeah!" And the feeling Joe had been trying to crush every day since they moved here two weeks ago roared up like a fucking kraken. Hope. Fucking *hope*. The irrational, sweet, determined-to-exist feeling that this time, in this new place, something would work out. It was an emotional morass that always got him into trouble. A belief in possibility when there was no such fucking thing.

"I'm fine," the girl said. Clearly not fine, and a terrible liar. "I just..."

What? Joe thought, as if whatever she said might hold a lifeline for him. Want to go somewhere? Be something? Understand fucking anything? Keep talking, he thought, please keep talking. The girl's bright voice reached inside him. It stroked and fed the kraken. Made Joe long for something better.

"Never mind," she said, the brightness falling from her voice.

Right, Joe thought. Right. Never mind. Never mind.

"I ran into Izzy and Stacy," she said. "Literally."

Joe killed the kraken.

"Oh," Mr. Norway said in his painfully empathetic way. It made Joe murderously angry. What was the fucking point of anyone being nice or reaching out?

"I have to get back to class," the girl said.

"If you have a minute," Mr. Norway said, "I'd like you to do something for me. I'll give you a pass."

Thudding apprehension drilled Joe's feet to the floor.

"Sure," the girl said. Her airy voice swung in and out of his ears like music, like kisses, like the sound of the ocean. "What do you need?"

Joe felt dizzy.

"This is Joe Castlellaw," Mr. Norway said. And before he could stop it, the guidance counselor's hand was grabbing his—when had he moved so close to the freaking door?—and Joe was dragged into the hall.

"Joe," Mr. Norway said, smiling. "This is Emma Mathews."

And there she was, the girl with the voice.

Defiance, hope, embarrassment, curiosity, sweetness, sorrow, and anger were all there in bright colors and beautiful contrast on her face. She was wearing a black tank top even though it was snowing, and her silvery-blonde hair fell like swan feathers over her bare shoulders. She smelled like flowers and like sweat, which, horrifyingly, gave him the beginnings of an erection. He stared immediately over her head and thought of nothing, nothing, nothing, nothing, nothing.

"Joe moved here from Wolfeboro two weeks ago," Mr. Norway said. "Today is his first day at Henry Dearborn High School."

"Oh," she said.

Don't come closer, Joe begged silently. He started making new words from the letters in the existing words on the *Spring Fling!*

poster behind her. She turned around to see what he was staring at. He glanced at her. Mistake. She was slowly sucking her lower lip into her mouth. *Fuck.* Freshman, Spring, Fling, March, Thursday. Hm… Martyr, Giant, Fruit.

"Hey," she said. Her voice reached into his skin. It felt like she kissed him.

"Hey." He could hardly grind out the one syllable, but he couldn't help stealing another glance. Then more words. Thrum, Death, Data.

"Joe couldn't get here earlier," Mr. Norway said, smiling kindly at him. Why was he so fucking *nice*?

"So if you don't mind, Emma," Mr. Norway said, "would you show Joe to Mrs. Eyre's classroom?"

Emma, Joe thought, repeating the name to himself. Her name was Emma. He shifted his weight and exhaled. Sprite, Uncle, Rare.

She was watching him. He could feel it. He couldn't look at her. Not now. Not in front of Mr. Norway. Not at all if he wanted to get through this day in one piece.

"Would you mind?" Mr. Norway asked.

"What?" Emma said. At last she turned and faced the guidance counselor.

Gratefully, like a drowning man pulled from the waves, Joe gazed hard at Emma Mathews. Like he had to take something from her in order to keep breathing.

She was sweaty. It was fucking March in fucking New Hampshire and she was sweaty. Her Smiths shirt clung to her breasts and sweat gleamed on her pale pinkish skin. Like candy, that's what her skin made him think of. He wanted to lick down her throat and between those breasts and taste her salty skin. He definitely had an erection now.

"Would you mind showing Joe to Mrs. Eyre's classroom?" Mr. Norway repeated.

"Uh, sure. Come on," Emma said.

She was talking to him. She was probably looking at him. Joe ripped his eyes away from her breasts and looked into her eyes, dark, dark blue, like the place where the ocean meets the sky at night. Emma gazed back at him, chill and serene. And happy; something about looking at him made her happy. He was sure of it.

A warning voice flared but Joe flicked it away, sending it scurrying to the floor of his soul. He looked at the poster. Maybe she liked him. Maybe she'd be interested in him. Maybe they could talk. Maybe they could kiss. Maybe she'd let him see those breasts.

He couldn't resist. He peeked at her again. Happy, yes. Something about looking at him made her happy. Which seemed to confuse her slightly. Good, he thought. She was smart and cautious and didn't expect everything to be easy.

"What the hell is wrong with me?" Emma whispered.

Joe turned away, grinning slightly. Mr. Norway winked at her.

She blushed and said something, backing away from Mr. Norway and knocking into the office door. Joe should have felt bad but instead he felt a rush of exhilaration. She liked him enough to be embarrassed about it. He grinned to himself.

"Come on," Emma ordered. She walked down the hall.

He followed her, watching as she touched her cheek and threw her hand down as if it were on fire.

"Where are we going?" he asked when she paused.

"This way," Emma said. She pointed.

He walked past her, hoping she'd catch up. He wanted a chance to see her face without seeming like he was looking directly at her on purpose. He stopped at the corner. She pointed again, but she still didn't say anything. Maybe he was wrong, maybe this was all in his head. He walked faster.

At last, when he had almost given up, Emma asked, "Did you like Wolfeboro?"

Like Wolfeboro? He didn't like *anything*. Except for her, apparently. Which probably wasn't going to end well for either of them.

"I guess," Joe said. He stared straight ahead and kept walking.

"We don't have a lake like you do," Emma said. "But we do have awesome hiking and bike trails. Do you like to hike or mountain bike? I have a bike."

He smiled to himself and stopped walking. *I have a bike.* How cute was that? He looked at her. She looked at her shoes.

"Sometimes," he said, imagining mountain biking with her. He'd have to be able to keep his secret though. That might prove almost impossible if she really did like him back.

Apparently anxious to erase her adorable I-have-a-bike announcement, Emma gestured to the book in his hand. "What are you reading?"

Joe turned the book over so she could see the cover. "Samuel Beckett plays."

"Are you an actor?" she asked.

"No," he said. "I like reading." He almost never told anyone, especially a girl, anything he genuinely liked or was important to him. He looked at her again, trying to say with his eyes what he couldn't with words.

She smiled back, and Joe felt his heels lift slightly from the floor. She smiled at him and he was able to control it. Which was in itself a tiny miracle.

"I like to read," she said.

He watched her, flipping through the pages of the book with his thumb, concentrating on staying fixed to the floor.

"But I really love music," she added. "My sister Maude loves to read. She's obsessed with poetry and flowers. I have four brothers and sisters, which is, obviously, a lot. Do you have any brothers or sisters?"

He shook his head. And just like that, everything turned to shit.

Emma opened her mouth and gazed unsteadily around the hall like she was drunk. Was that why she was so sweaty? Was she wasted or something and he just hadn't noticed?

"Are you all right?" Joe asked.

Clumsily, Emma lowered her head and stared at her shoes. She didn't answer him.

"Uh," Joe said, "I can probably find my way to class if you have something else to—"

"The old woman is running as fast as she can," Emma interrupted, lifting her gaze and staring fixedly into the empty hall. "She's terrified. I don't think she's going to make it."

"What?" Joe said. "What are you talking about?" He turned around. "What old woman?"

"The winged little boy fell down twice," she said. "The baby girl in the white dress and the tiny red shoes is screaming."

Ice congealed in Joe's stomach. It wasn't possible. Emma couldn't have seen any of his mother's strange paintings. His mother never displayed them *anywhere*. The only time they'd ever been out of the house was when he'd stupidly brought the gruesome triptych for show-and-tell in second grade. No one ever let him forget about it. Years later, in a class on monsters in Greek mythology in middle school, when Joe was still tiny and skinny and afraid of everything, a girl brought up the painting of the explicitly naked half dragon, half woman chasing the two children. *Dragon faggot* pounded in Joe's ears every time a bigger kid beat him up on the way home from school. But that was in Wolfeboro. And it was five years ago. Emma couldn't possibly know about that.

"The dragon," Emma said. "She has a woman's face. And enormous breasts. She's furious. And she's flying straight for the boy and the baby girl."

"Is this a joke?" Joe said, his skin crawling with skinny metal teeth. "Because it's not funny."

"The tree swallowed the little girl," Emma whispered.

Joe felt nauseated—and more sorrowful than angry. Because he was pathetic.

"Blood," Emma said. "So much blood is gushing from the tree. Over the exposed roots and onto the ground."

"Okay," Joe said. He'd had enough. "Was that fun for you?" He leaned close to Emma's still stoned-seeming expression. "Because it *sucked* for me."

"Why are you looking at me like that?" Emma snapped in a flawless melody of bitchy indignation.

"I don't know," Joe said, fury and sorrow at war in his mouth, thrashing like dying snakes in his blood. "Why don't you tell me?"

"I have no idea," she said.

"Whatever," Joe said. Done. Done. Done. Done with Warwick. Done with school. Done with hoping to ever fit in anywhere. And fucking *done* with Emma Mathews. "I can find my own way to class."

* * *

His mother's uncharacteristic silence in the kitchen made Joe look up from his tangled thoughts. She was leaning against the counter with her back to the empty sink. She brushed a strand of faded red hair behind her ear.

"Do you miss Wolfeboro?" she asked.

Joe laughed. "No," he said. "I don't."

She scrunched her face into a rueful smile.

When he was two years old, Joe's biological parents abandoned him in a dumpster behind a church. His mom found him, dirty and crying, and took him home with her, never telling anyone what she had done. He had no real birth certificate, no real social security number. He rarely saw a doctor but had sufficient vaccination records to make it seem as though he did. Somehow his mother had forged identity documents for him, and she paid for everything in cash. He was constantly, painfully aware how odd this all was, how different his life from everybody else's. He'd never invited anyone over. Even in elementary school.

"I'm going to bed," his mother said and smiled at him for real this time. "Don't stay up too late," she added, mussing his hair.

"I won't," Joe said, smoothing it.

She grabbed a notebook and drawing pencils then went to her bedroom at the end of the hall.

Joe stretched his legs under the table and scratched the scars on his shoulder blades. When his mom found him he'd had two enormous growths on his back. Sometimes Joe thought his bio-parents abandoned him because they couldn't afford the medical bills to fix whatever was wrong with him. Sometimes he thought they were drug addicts. Sometimes he imagined they were the victims of a terrible crime and when he was old enough and strong enough he would avenge them. Most of the time he was just angry. About everything.

His mom had the growths removed by some shitty doctor when Joe was still really little. He didn't remember it. He had huge scars. Joe hated them for a long time. When he was younger he refused to take off his shirt even when he was swimming, but now he didn't really care. Although he still never took off his shirt in front of anyone.

He got up from the table and opened the flimsy, shit-plastic blinds. The moon was bright enough to ride his bike into town. It wasn't even eight o'clock. Stacy Something in AP history had given him her number.

"I'm going out," he shouted to his mom in her bedroom.

"Where?"

"To that clam house."

There was a pause. Joe knew how to drive but his mother wouldn't let him get a license until he was eighteen and no one could take him away from her.

"I'll take my bike," he added.

"Okay," she said.

Joe ran down the common-hallway stairs two steps at a time.

CHAPTER THREE

Emma had ridden her bike up to the waterfall in Richardson Park after school. Still sweating but less frantic, she got home after six and took a shower. Her wet hair was cool against her shoulders as she went into the kitchen to set the table.

Her mother looked up from the stove. "What's the matter?"

Everything, Emma thought. "Nothing," she said.

She took a red tablecloth out of a drawer in the old breakfront. Mom had soul-piercing laser vision, but Emma didn't know how to say what she wanted to say or if she was ready to know the answers, whatever they were.

"Does he have to be right there?" Emma asked, pointing to her little brother Sandy who was lying on his stomach doing his math homework in the middle of the floor of the small kitchen. Without waiting for an answer she stepped over him.

"What's seven times three?" Sandy asked.

"Figure it out, Sandy," Mom said.

"Twenty-one," Emma whispered.

"Don't help unless you're planning to take his multiplication test for him, Emma," Mom said, not turning from the pot on the stove. "Elizabeth! What did Daddy and I say about not texting when you're doing your homework?"

Elizabeth was eleven and perfect—except for the excessive texting, apparently. She was poised and self-possessed, like an ideal girl or a daughter on a TV show. Elizabeth matched her gum with her nail polish and made more friends every year than Emma had at all.

Emma shook the tablecloth high over the table and watched it slowly settle down, casting a red shadow on the floor. Sandy's math sheet turned scarlet. He gazed up at Emma and smiled.

"Cool," he said.

Emma grinned and shook the tablecloth up again.

"Did something happen in school today?" her mother asked, taking a pitcher of orange juice out of the refrigerator and handing it to Turner who had just walked into the room.

"*No,*" Emma said. She dropped silverware onto folded napkins.

"Time to clean up, Sandy," Mom said. "You can finish your homework after dinner."

He jumped back as a spoon landed on the floor near his hand. "Hey!"

"Sorry," Emma said. She brushed the spoon on her jeans. "Five-second rule."

Maude came in from the greenhouse carrying a large blue vase filled with paperwhites and forsythia. She'd turned fifteen yesterday. Mom and Dad got her an especially pretty, very old book of Shelley's poetry. She was thrilled and carried it around all day.

"Maude, honey," Mom said, "that looks beautiful. Where did you find them? I thought the paperwhites were dead."

"You have to know where to look," Maude said, placing the vase in the middle of the table.

Maude was beautiful. Not in a Photoshopped way or in a specious *everyone is beautiful* way, but like a princess in a fairy tale. Maude had a kind of beauty people sometimes imagine but rarely get to see. Dad read Keats to all the kids when they were little—because that's what babies love most, he'd teased later: nineteenth-century Romantic poetry. A line from one of the poems echoed often in Emma's head, "Heard melodies are sweet, but those unheard/Are sweeter." Maude looked like an unheard melody.

"Is Izzy hanging out with Stacy Keeler?" Mom asked. "I saw Izzy's mother at Stop and Shop this morning and she told me Izzy and Stacy were going to the movies this weekend."

Emma pretended not to hear. She shifted a plate so the pictures of peaches were at the top and the cherries were at the bottom.

"You could invite both of them over after school some day," her mother continued, ignoring Emma's feigned deafness. "Izzy hasn't been here in a while."

"I met that new boy," Maude said.

Emma exhaled in relief. Now Mom would turn her laser vision on Maude and Emma could think about the panic attacks and her hallucination—or whatever it was—without being the subject of her mother's ever-watchful eye. Maude had only ever had a few friends and none of them were close. Emma's count-on-one-hand number of friends had never concerned her parents, but unlike Emma, Maude didn't seem to need close friends. She was self-sufficient. Solitary and self-contained. And *that* was what alarmed Mom.

It was too late to change her younger sister now, Emma thought. More than any of them, Turner included, Maude was unalterably herself. Mom could carry the ocean in her arms more easily than she could change Maude's mind.

"Because Mr. Norway liked my story about the girl with invisible skin," Maude said.

"What?" Emma asked, just realizing her sister was talking to her.

"My story about the girl with invisible skin," Maude repeated.

"Oh," Emma said. "Cool." Last January Maude published an intense, bizarre story in *Echoes*, the school literary journal.

"I thought," Maude said, "and Mr. Norway did too, that because his mother is an artist he might like my story."

Everyone was sitting down except for Mom and Dad. They were still bringing food to the table.

"Who might like your story?" Emma said. She wasn't hungry at all. She must have said something, something bad, to Joe in school today. After she zoned out or hallucinated or whatever Joe practically snarled at her, and then he left her alone in the hall. A spoonful of applesauce plopped onto Emma's plate. She stuck her finger in it and licked it off. Turner huffed and gave her a disgusted glance. Emma made a face at him and mouthed, *Don't you ever get tired of being perfect?*

Turner ignored her. Of course.

A little too late Emma heard Maude sigh and mutter, "Never mind."

"Wait," Emma said. "Wait. I'm sorry. I wasn't listening. Ask me again."

Maude shook her head and her black hair swung like a bell. "It doesn't matter."

"Yes, it does," Emma said. "Tell me. I'll listen."

"That new boy," Maude repeated softly. "Mr. Norway said you met him."

Emma sucked in a mouthful of air and pushed back from the table. The sweating and the racing heart and the compulsion to run returned with a vengeance. Mom and Dad stared at her.

"Yeah," she said. She took a huge swallow of orange juice. "I did. I showed him around school a little. He seems okay." Emma cut her chicken into cubes of dead flesh and tried to make her heartbeat slow.

"Can I have a bite of your applesauce?" Sandy asked.

"Sure." Sweat poured down Emma's back and between her shoulder blades. She scraped her applesauce onto Sandy's plate. "Have all of it. I'm not hungry."

"Thanks." He made a smiley face in the applesauce before he ate it.

"Don't play with your food, Sandy," Mom said.

"But I like to."

"I know, sweetie," Mom said, "but you're making a mess."

"No, I'm not," Sandy said. "See? I'm licking it off."

"I have to show Maude something," Emma said.

She stood up quickly and knocked over her chair. Splotches shaped like handprints bloomed on Turner's face. *Really?* Emma thought, righting the wooden chair, ready to jump out of her freaking skin again. Turner sat rigidly, watching her. She made another face at him. What kind of a seventeen-year-old is only embarrassed about someone *else's* behavior? Turner needed to screw up a little. A colossal mistake might make him slightly more human.

"Elizabeth can do the dishes even though it's my night," Turner said to Mom and Dad. "I need to talk to you about something important after dinner."

"I have homework," Elizabeth protested.

"We all have homework, Elizabeth," he said pompously.

"Fine," Elizabeth said. "But Sandy's not a baby. He can help me."

"I want to help," Sandy said.

Emma pulled Maude into the hall.

CHAPTER FOUR

Joe turned his bike into the Pop's Clam House parking lot. Stacy Whatever vaulted over the porch railing and came to meet him. The pretty, brown-haired girl he'd met earlier with her followed. Joe thought the girl's name was Lizzy or Izzy.

"A bike," Stacy said, eyebrows raised but kind of smiling. "Cool." Warwick was more affluent than other places Joe lived. Almost every kid had a car or unlimited access to one.

"This is how the other half lives," he said, arms outstretched, grinning back at her. He came to a stop beside both girls but stayed on his bike.

"What did you think of your first day at Henry Dearborn High?" Stacy said. "Ready to kill yourself yet?" She grinned at Lizzy-Izzy, who blushed.

"Not yet," Joe said, riding slowly around them. "I heard it gets better."

"Yeah," Stacy said, laughing. "It gets better."

An open-topped Jeep blasting terrible music and crammed with kids and a barking golden retriever pulled into the parking lot.

"Seriously," Stacy said, pointedly ignoring the Jeep now emptying, clown-car style, of kids, who strode up to the restaurant like they owned the ground they walked on. And maybe some of them did.

"Did you find all your classes?" Stacy continued. "Meet all the cool kids?"

Joe supposed he should flirt back and say something like, *I met you*, but he didn't.

"I did okay," he said, still slowly circling the two girls.

"Are you hungry?" Stacy asked. "Do you want to get something to eat?"

He didn't have enough money for much more than a soda, and he certainly didn't have enough to treat Stacy and her friend. "Nah," he said. "I just ate."

Laughter burst from the porch. Stacy rolled her eyes. "*That joyful noise*," she said, "is most of our illustrious football team." Her tone was dismissive but she gazed softly at one of the boys, who grinned cockily back at her.

Izzy—that was the friend's name—watched Stacy for a second then turned to Joe. "Most of them are okay," she said.

A short, round, curly-haired boy around thirteen or fourteen walked out of the restaurant by himself. The kids on the railing turned in unison. Halfway down the steps the boy dropped his backpack and took off his sweatshirt, a wine-colored hoodie with GRANITE STATE written across the front. The railing boys scoffed then returned to whatever they were talking about—all except for one kid in a baseball cap and plaid shorts who watched intently, grinning as the younger boy dug through his enormous black and blue backpack.

"Boomer," the watching kid shouted to the golden retriever barking in the Jeep. "Come here, buddy."

The curly-haired boy glanced at the dog then returned to his backpack, both hands cradling something deep inside. From the reflected light on his face Joe guessed it was a phone or an iPod. The kid put in earbuds. He didn't notice Baseball Cap sneak over to the wooden steps and snatch the hoodie. Joe leaned forward and felt Stacy's hand on his arm.

"Leave it," she said. "Kyle's not a bad guy. He won't do anything too terrible. If you interfere it will be worse. For Puccini, I mean."

Joe raised his eyebrows.

"Phil Puccini," she said. "That's the fat kid's name."

By this time Boomer had leapt out of the Jeep and crossed the parking lot. Kyle rubbed the dog's ears. "Good boy. That's a good boy."

Kyle tugged Phil's hoodie over Boomer's head and pulled his front legs through the arm holes. The railing boys hooted.

Phil turned around. "Hey! That's mine."

"It is?" Kyle said innocently. "Uh-oh. Boomer thinks it's his. You'll have to catch him."

The dog was running in circles and wagging his tail.

Joe cycled to the porch.

"Come on, Kyle," Stacy called out, laughing. "Give it back."

"What?" Kyle said, cupping his hand to his ear. He pulled a raggedy tennis ball from the pocket of his shorts. "Is this your ball?" he asked the dog, tossing the ball and catching it in one hand. "Is this your ball?"

Phil grimaced, chewing his lips, refusing to cry. Kyle grinned at him then tossed the ball across the length of the parking lot.

Boomer took off. Joe followed, pedaling furiously.

"Ooooh *shit*," one of the railing boys shouted. "It went in the river."

Joe sped past the dog, slid into the half-frozen mud on the edge the river, and jumped off his bike.

"Come here, boy," he said, squatting, arms open in the retriever's path. He caught Boomer before the big dog splashed into the water after the ball. "That's a good boy," he continued, pulling the hoodie off the dog, who hadn't stopped wagging his tail. "Good boy."

"What the hell, dude?" Kyle said as Joe pedaled back to the restaurant, Boomer trotting behind him.

"You're an asshole," Joe said. He turned the bike hard, coming within inches of Kyle's feet. Still standing in the middle of the steps, Phil Puccini's round face was flushed and tight.

Joe got off his bike, shook out the hoodie and handed it to Phil. "It didn't get wet."

"Thanks," Phil said.

A red Honda pulled into the parking lot and a woman called from the driver's side window, "Phillip, honey. Let's go. Daddy's waiting. Come on."

"Yeah, Phillip," Kyle teased. "Daddy's waiting."

Phil got into his mother's car. Joe got back on his bike and turned to Kyle.

"Seriously?" Kyle said, laughing, looking over Joe like he was made of wet paper. "You wanna come at *me*?" He cocked his head at the porch filled with now-silent football players. "Because I borrowed some little faggot's faggoty shirt? It was a joke, dude."

"Do you wanna come at me?" Joe echoed quietly. "Because you're the raging asshole in every town who picks on smaller kids whenever..." He dropped his bike. "I don't know. You tell me. What *is* so weak and sad about your sorry-assed self that compels you to do something so pathetic?"

Kyle strode up to him but Joe didn't move. Joe wanted to hit him. He couldn't wait to hit him. He wanted to pound his fists into Kyle's cocky over-privileged face until his hands hurt.

"Cops!" the porch chorus warned as a red and silver Warwick police car slowly rolled into the parking lot.

"You're lucky, asshole," Kyle spat at Joe, shaking his head from side to side and backing away.

"Yeah," Joe said, glancing at the cop car now stopped a few feet away. "I'm lucky. But," he added, leaning toward Kyle to whisper. "I'm not the one running away."

* * *

The swinging kitchen door shut behind Maude. Mom and Dad were lecturing Elizabeth about spending too much time texting her friends and not enough time doing her homework.

"What?" Maude whispered.

"I think there's something wrong with me," Emma said.

"Are you sick?" Maude asked. "If you are you should tell Mom and Dad."

"I'm not sick," Emma said. "I don't think so anyway."

"What is it then?" Maude said.

"Let's go outside."

"It's freezing," Maude protested. "And Mom and Dad don't like it if we go outside after dark without telling them."

"Please," Emma said. "I'm sweating." She tossed Maude her green jacket.

Maude caught it. "Sweating?"

"I told you, I think there's something wrong with me," Emma said. "Please come outside."

"Okay, okay," Maude said. She put on the coat and followed Emma onto the frozen grass.

"Climbing tree?" Emma said.

"Are you serious?"

"Please," Emma said. "I feel like I'm going to jump out of my skin."

"Emma," Maude said, "maybe you should tell Mom and Dad. You're acting really weird."

"No!" Emma said. "No. I just want to tell you for now. Please, Maude." Her hands were visibly shaking. She curled her fingers into her palms.

Maude sighed. "Only if you promise to tell Mom and Dad something's wrong *tonight* if I ask you to."

"Okay," Emma said.

"Pinky swear," Maude said. "Or I'm going back in the house."

"Pinky swear," Emma said.

She ran to the big old maple tree Turner had named Ozymandias when they were little. Maude followed. Emma glanced at the house. Through the window she saw Mom and Dad follow Turner into the living room. Elizabeth and Sandy were doing the dishes and dancing, probably to some lame song Elizabeth loved. No matter what songs or artists Emma introduced her to, Elizabeth had terrible taste in music. Loving those songs and those bands was like purposefully choosing to eat dirty shoes instead of hot pizza, or so it seemed to Emma whenever she scrolled through Elizabeth's appalling music library.

Sandy was singing into a wooden spoon with his eyes closed.

"Why do you think there's something wrong with you?" Maude asked when she and Emma were both in the tree.

Emma locked her ankles together under the rough branch. "Every afternoon for like two weeks," she said, "I start sweating like it's June in gym class and all the doors are closed. I feel like my scalp is literally crawling with hundreds of bugs and my heart beats really, really, really hard."

"Okay," Maude said, moving to jump out of the tree. "You're telling Mom and Dad right now."

"That's not all of it," Emma said. She grabbed her sister's leg and took a huge, deep breath. "I feel like I'm missing something. Or I'm separated from something. Something important. Like medicine. Or a machine I need to keep breathing. And then all I want to do is run to the missing thing. But I don't know where it is. Or what it is."

Maude paled. She sat up straighter and stared into the woods at the edge of the yard.

"Have you ever felt like that?" Emma asked.

Maude shook her head. "No."

"You looked like you have," Emma said. "You looked like you knew exactly what I was talking about. This isn't the time for your silvery tower of privacy, Maude. If you've felt something like this, *anything* like this, maybe there's a toxin in the house. Or our family has some genetic disease. Maybe it's not just me," she added.

"I haven't, okay?" Maude said. "Not exactly, anyway."

"What do you mean, not exactly?" Emma asked.

"Girls!" Dad's voice broke through the cold hush of the night. "Get out of that tree and come inside."

CHAPTER FIVE

"In a minute, Dad," Emma called to her father who was standing in the open front door.

"Now," he said.

"Okay," Emma said. "We're coming." She turned to Maude. "What do you mean not exactly?"

"I *always* feel like I'm missing something," Maude said. "I always feel like I'm severed from something necessary."

Emma pressed her spine into the bark of the tree. Sometimes Maude seemed much older than she actually was, or it seemed her younger sister wasn't any age at all, that she'd been alive forever, always exactly the way she was now, at this moment. Emma didn't know if Maude ever had a crush on anyone—anyone flesh and blood, at least. Maude seemed to love some boy who lived in her head or in the pages of a book.

Emma tapped Maude's shoulder. "Who do you talk to in the woods?"

Maude gasped.

"I'm not going to make fun of you," Emma promised. "I'm the last person who should make fun of someone for doing something weird."

Maude's mouth quivered. "I can't tell you."

"I won't tell anyone," Emma said. "I promise. And besides, I know you want to tell me."

Maude played with the silver buttons on her jacket pocket. "I can't."

"I know you're talking to someone imaginary," Emma said. "You can't be talking to someone invisible. I won't make fun of you, I swear. Who do you imagine?"

"He's not imaginary," Maude said in her thoughtful voice.

"Okay," Emma agreed. "Who do you think he is?"

"My soulmate."

Emma felt a thud in her chest like someone punched her. "Who is he?"

"I don't know," Maude said. "Not yet, anyway. Although, I thought I saw him today, outside the greenhouse."

Emma shivered. "For real?"

"For a second," Maude said nodding. "Then I looked harder and there was no one there."

"What did he look like?" Emma asked.

"I don't know," Maude said.

"What do you mean, you don't know?"

Maude turned away.

"I didn't mean to hurt your feelings," Emma said.

"You didn't," Maude said.

"Yes, I did," Emma said. "You look like you're ready to cry."

"I'm never going to fit in," Maude said. "I am never, *ever* going to be like everyone else. I am never going to know the right thing, or the wrong thing, to say. Or how to make people like me." She bit her cheek and made a noise like an abandoned kitten. "I wish Mom would homeschool me. I really do. I can't stand Dearborn anymore."

"Wouldn't Mom drive you crazy?" Emma asked. "Oh my God, what would she teach you? If you don't know what to say to regular people now, you'd never know after a semester with Mom."

Maude sighed. "I guess you're right. I just wish I felt like someone else was like me."

"No one else is like you, Maude," Emma said without a trace of mockery. "You're beautiful and—"

"Stop it."

Emma wrapped her arms around her chest and watched her sister stare down at the grey-green blades of grass sticking out of the dusting of snow below the tree. Moonshine glittered in Maude's hair like drops of water in a midnight stream. Maude was so beautiful, but she didn't have any real friends, and she was seriously imagining a soulmate in the woods. She seemed utterly unprotected, like she was the girl with invisible skin from her story.

"I'm sorry," Emma repeated.

"Forget it," Maude said.

"Today in school," Emma said, "I saw something that wasn't there. Really saw it, like I was transported somewhere else."

Maude took her hands out of her pockets. "What did you see?"

"I felt like I lost my sense of place," Emma said. "For a second or a few minutes, I don't know how long, I wasn't in the hall in school. I was in a forest and it was fall. The ground felt soft under my feet. I could smell the damp leaves and cold air. White mushrooms were growing out of the dirt at the base of a huge gnarled tree."

"Has anything like that ever happened to you before?" Maude asked.

Emma took in a mouthful of air that made her teeth feel cold. "Kind of. I forgot about it until today. I was really little and I was at the mall with Mom. Some woman was trying to get Mom to try on perfume—you know how crazy she is about artificial smells. Anyway, I was crying and Mom picked me up, and all of a sudden I remember being in the woods instead of the mall." Emma shivered. "There was something scary or sad about it." She shook herself. "A freak from the cradle, I guess." She made a face.

Maude didn't smile.

"Anyway," Emma continued, "the same kind of thing happened today. Only this time there was blood, or something like it, on one of the mushrooms." For an instant Emma felt she might break down and cry, but she smiled broadly at Maude instead. "Then the mushroom turned into the white toe of my sneaker. So maybe I was just seriously daydreaming. I don't know. Weird, huh?"

Maude nodded. "What does this have to do with the new kid?"

Emma leaned back so hard she bumped her head against the tree. "What makes you think it has anything to do with him?"

Maude just looked at her. "You almost fell out of your chair when I said Mr. Norway told me you met him. Two minutes later you're dragging me outside and up into this tree."

Emma crossed her bare arms over her chest. She was starting to feel chilly for the first time in two weeks. "I think I said something while it was happening," she admitted. "The vision or the hallucination or the daydream or whatever. Something strange. To Joe. That's his name."

Maude nodded. "I know."

"He was being really nice," Emma said, trying to sound calmer than she felt. "I mean *really* nice. He was kind of flirting with me."

"He was?" Maude asked.

"Kind of," Emma said. She inhaled swiftly, remembering Joe's intense gaze and his beautiful eyes.

"What do you mean 'kind of'?"

"I don't know," Emma said. "He didn't say much. He hardly said anything, actually, which of course made me talk way too much."

"How do you know he was flirting with you?" Maude asked.

Emma felt hot. "He was looking at me."

"Looking at you?" Maude snorted. She jumped out of the tree and started back for the house. When Emma jumped down and followed she added, "You don't have to tell me any more if you don't want to. I'm too cold to stay outside any longer."

Emma stopped walking. "Joe Castellaw looked at me like I was someone important. Like he needed me. Like he *wanted* me."

"Oh," Maude said quietly.

"And then I screwed it up," Emma said. "I must have said something while I was having my little hallucination, something mean or stupid because he got mad and left."

Dad was waiting in the open front door. "Please don't go outside at night without telling us," he said when Emma and Maude got back to the house.

"We were just in the tree," Emma said.

"You could have fallen." He locked the door behind him.

"Sorry, Dad," Maude said, taking off her coat.

As Emma walked upstairs she suddenly envisioned Joe Castlellaw rapidly pedaling his bike up the hill from town. Joe's dark curling hair was blown back in the wind and his ears were pink from the cold. The expression in his fierce, gorgeous eyes was furious.

CHAPTER SIX

Joe rode into town after school the next day, hoping he'd run into Kyle and his band of merry assholes.

He rode aimlessly up and down the picture-perfect, tree-lined streets, tormented by thoughts of Emma Mathews. How had she known about that painting? And why couldn't he stop himself from longing so, *so* hard to kiss her? Emma had fooled him into thinking she liked him and then hyper-dramatically mocked him for his mom's strange painting. Bitchy and mean. Joe was so not into that kind of girl.

But, all of his dreams last night were about Emma. He couldn't get to her. She was screaming for him to find her and every time he thought he saw her she disappeared. And then, *then* something happened that hadn't happened in forever. Dream Emma found *him*, and she wrapped her soft arms around him and kissed him. For a long, long time. And Joe woke up with his—

"Sorry!" Joe screeched to a halt before he crashed into Mr. Norway, who was getting out of a car.

"Are you all right?" Mr. Norway asked.

"Am I all right? I almost hit you. Are *you* all right?"

"But you didn't hit me," the guidance counselor said calmly. "So I am all right. No harm done." He closed the car door. "How are you adjusting to Warwick?"

Joe walked his bike onto the sidewalk in front of the hardware store where Mr. Norway was waiting. The front window of the hardware store, which had been in business since 1897 according the plaque on the wall, displayed ancient mechanical beavers slowly chopping at fake fallen trees.

"Fine, I guess," Joe said. He straddled the bike. "Nice car."

Mr. Norway beamed and patted the silver hood. "It was a present," he said, smiling. "A long time ago."

"What kind of car is it?" Joe asked.

"A 1962 Alfa Romeo."

"It's sweet."

"Thanks." Mr. Norway glanced at Joe's bike. "Where were you going in such a hurry?"

Joe reddened. "Nowhere."

Mr. Norway smiled. It wasn't a condescending smile.

"I'm coming from somewhere," Joe admitted.

"Ah."

Mr. Norway stood for a moment without saying anything more. Joe wanted to talk about Emma, about what she'd said, about how terrible it made him feel, and about liking her anyway. More than he'd ever liked anyone. But he didn't.

"My book is in," Mr. Norway said at last, pointing to Once Upon a Time, the bead-curtained, incense-scented bookstore connected to the hardware store and partially obscured by the slow-moving beavers.

"What is it?" Joe asked, glad his voice wasn't shaking.

"What is what?"

"Your book." Joe sat back on the hard bike seat.

"Oh." Mr. Norway laughed. "It's a book of poetry by a poet named Stanley Kunitz. The new science teacher Mr. Spencer recommended it." He smiled and shrugged. "I'm not much of a poetry reader but I'm trying to expand my outlook in my old age."

Joe grinned and pressed his toes into the sidewalk. "I like Stanley Kunitz a lot," he said, happy to be talking about something he understood. "'How shall the heart be reconciled to its feast of losses?' That's from *The Layers*. It's one of my favorite poems."

Mr. Norway raised his eyebrows but just smiled.

"Do you know Emma Mathews?" Joe blurted. Then he shrank from the absurdity of the question. Mr. Norway had introduced them.

The counselor smiled. "I do. Yes."

"She said something yesterday," Joe said. He tried to ignore his throbbing heart and the sick tremor in his stomach, but he didn't know how to finish his question.

Mr. Norway put his hand on Joe's shoulder. "Why don't you ask her about it?"

"I don't know how." Joe grabbed his thighs, which were starting to ache from balancing on the bike.

"Emma is a good girl," Mr. Norway said. "She's had her share of difficulties, too. Try talking with her."

"Okay," Joe said. "Thanks."

"You're welcome." Then Mr. Norway walked into the bookstore, shouted hello at the long-haired woman who ran it, and closed the door.

Joe started riding again. He'd only made it a few blocks before his stomach leapt as Emma came out of the office supply store. She was eating something from a paper bag. Joe rode in front of her and accidentally surprised her. She dropped the bag. Jelly beans scattered all over the sidewalk.

"Sorry!" Joe got off the biked and brushed the jelly beans into a pile then scooped them into the bag.

Emma knelt in front of him. "Er, I'm not going to eat them now," she said, laughing.

He handed her the bag anyway.

"Thanks," she said.

"Sorry," he said again.

"No worries," Emma said. "I haven't heard any dire news about a jelly bean shortage, so I think I'm safe. I can get more."

"Have you ever heard any of the stories in my mom's paintings?" Joe blurted before he lost his nerve. "They're dark fairy tales."

"I don't think so," Emma said. "But I know a lot of stories." She pulled a lock of hair across her chest then tossed it back over her shoulder. "We didn't have a TV until I was ten. My parents are a little odd."

She rolled her eyes and stared down at her feet. Joe noticed she was wearing the same white-toed, bright green sneakers she was wearing the day before. Her eyelashes made tiny shadows on her cheeks. Liquid heat flared in Joe's stomach and poured down his legs.

"Maybe I heard your mom's stories somewhere," Emma suggested. "We went to a lot of puppet-show-organic-food-story-festival things when I was little. Maybe I heard something then. Did your parents ever take you to one of those festivals where people dress their kids in fairy costumes and sell hand-dyed wool and things like that?"

"No," Joe said, trying to look casual when he felt like everything in the world depended on Emma seeing who he was and liking him anyway. "I don't know who or where my dad is. And my mom…" How could he say his mom found him when he was a baby and never told anyone? How could he tell Emma what he looked like, what he *was* like as a baby: freakish, ugly, and deformed? Joe's scars itched suddenly. He crushed the impulse to scratch at them until they bled.

"I guess it doesn't matter." He kicked a jelly bean he'd missed into the street and watched it get crushed under the wheel of a car. "Never mind."

"Never mind what?" Emma said. "Didn't I answer your question?"

"Yeah," Joe said. "Sorry about the jelly beans."

"Did I say something weird yesterday?" Emma said. "I think I zoned out or something when we were in the hall."

"Zoned out?" Joe repeated. "You were talking the whole time."

"I was?"

"Yes. You told me the entire story of one of my mom's paintings in vivid, dramatic detail."

"How could I say anything about one of your mom's paintings if I've never seen any of them?" Emma asked.

"I don't know," Joe said, suddenly angry again. "That's why I asked. How can you say something and not realize you're speaking? Were you wasted?"

"No!" Emma said.

"What then?" Joe said.

"I told you. I don't *know*."

Joe got back on his bike and swore under his breath. "Forget it."

Emma stepped in front him. She was inches from his face. He could see her lacy black bra strap under her green tank top and he smelled the fruity sugar candy on her breath. He wanted so much to kiss her, even though he was angry at her and she was equally angry with him. He wanted so much to kiss her, here, now, on the mouth, in the middle of the sidewalk under the chilly March sunlight, and keep kissing her until everyone else went home to bed.

"Why would I lie to you?" Emma asked. "At least you know what happened yesterday. I have no idea what I said. Or why you're so upset. Why ask me about it if you aren't going to accept my answer? You left me in the hall without any explanation at all." She was shouting, and a silvery sheen of sweat gathered at the base of her throat. "Whatever I did yesterday, I'm sorry! Okay?" She stomped around him. "I'll see you in school."

"Wait."

Joe grabbed her arm. For a second they both just looked at his dark hand on her bare pale wrist. Did she feel what he felt? A jolt of peace and happiness in the place where his skin touched hers. As if right there, in that small space, everything was okay.

"You don't remember anything?" he asked.

Emma exhaled and closed her eyes but didn't pull her arm away. For a crazed moment Joe imagined that his touch was the only thing keeping her from falling apart.

"I'm sorry," he said, gently squeezing her wrist.

She opened her midnight blue eyes. Joe could hardly stop himself from sighing.

"I'm kind of sensitive about my mom," he explained. "She's not like other moms. She's not even like other painters. I hate it when anyone makes fun of her."

He almost told Emma about bringing the gruesome, beautiful painting she'd described in the hall yesterday for show-and-tell in second grade. How one little girl cried and the rest of the class laughed. How his teacher pulled the wood-framed triptych out of his hands and sent him to the principal's office telling him she would have spanked him if he was her son.

"You thought I was making fun of your mom?" Emma said.

"Why else would you bring up her paintings? Her work is strange and disturbing. She's an Outsider Artist," Joe added.

"What's that?" Emma asked.

Joe let go of her arm. The loss of connection felt as if someone were pulling out one of his veins like a loose thread from a sweater. "Outsider Art is art created outside the conventional art world, outside of schools, museums, galleries. It used to be a name that referred to art made by people in insane asylums, but now it means art made by self-taught people who are *way* out of the mainstream."

"Oh," Emma said. She held her wrist where his hand had been. "I'm sorry it seemed like I was making fun of her. I wasn't." She let go of her wrist, crossed her arms over her chest and then dropped her hands to her sides. "Yesterday in the hall, when I zoned out and somehow talked about your mom's painting, which I swear I've never seen, I thought I was in the woods for a few minutes. I saw trees and smelled the wet forest floor. And at my feet there was a mushroom covered with blood."

CHAPTER SEVEN

Just before eleven that night Emma walked down to the kitchen to sneak Oreos. She hadn't eaten anything for dinner again and now she was starving.

As she passed his door, she heard her brother sobbing. She hadn't seen him all day. She hadn't seen him since he'd been so intent on talking to Mom and Dad the night before. Emma knocked gently on his door. "Turner?"

A sound like moving chairs. "Go away, Emma."

She tried the door. It was locked.

"I said, *go away*."

Emma walked toward her own room and then came back and whispered loudly through the crack in Turner's door, "I've been in more trouble and fucked up more times than any kid in this family. Who better to talk to than me? I'm your best source."

"Go away," he said. "I don't want to talk to anyone. Just leave me alone."

She pressed her head against the smooth white paint on the wooden door. "Aren't you always telling me your schoolwork is superior to mine because you take the time to find the most relevant information from the best sources? That's *me*. I'm not SparkNotes or Wikipedia, Turner. I'm freaking primary source material!"

The door opened. Her older brother's normally perfect hair was sticking up all over the place like it had when he was little and had bedhead all the time, and his light brown eyes were swollen and red. He stepped aside and let her in.

"It was the Wikipedia reference that did it, right?" Emma said.

Turner laughed. "Yes."

He sat heavily on his bed and rubbed his face with both hands. Emma sat across from him in the reproduction Windsor chair he'd bought for himself with birthday money when he was twelve.

"I broke up with Rachel," he said, his voice cracking.

"Oh, no," Emma said. "I'm so sorry. What happened?"

"She got pregnant," he said.

"Is it yours?" Emma asked.

"Of course it's mine." He stood up. "God, Emma. Sometimes I really worry about you."

"Rachel's pregnant with your baby and you *break up* with her?" Emma asked, shocked that her brother could be so cold.

A choking sob tore from his throat. "I almost ruined her life," he said, crying. "She got a free ride to Yale. Her parents don't have money. She'd never be able to pay for an education like that on her own. I almost destroyed everything Rachel's worked for since she was in seventh grade."

"What is she going to do?" Emma asked, not exactly sure what Turner was saying.

For a minute he didn't say anything. Turner was super private about some things. Emma had no idea about what he thought or felt about something like this.

"Her parents convinced her to have an abortion," Turner said quietly.

"Are you okay with that?"

He glared at her.

"I don't understand," Emma said. "Why did you break up with her if nothing is really going to change? I mean, she's not going to have a baby now. You still love her. She still loves you, right? I don't understand."

Turner made a noise like a dying animal. "Rachel doesn't make mistakes. She doesn't deserve any of this. She didn't deserve to be pregnant with a baby she didn't want. She didn't deserve to have to have an abortion when she's seventeen. None of this was her fault. And I can't live with the fact that the fault is mine. How could I look at her knowing I almost fucked up her whole fucking life!"

"No one gets pregnant by themselves," Emma said.

"The condom slipped," he said furiously. "Okay? Are you happy now? The condom slipped and I felt it and I didn't pull out and I didn't tell her. How is that not my fucking fault?"

She watched him pace around the room. "When did all this happen?"

Turner exhaled heavily. "She had the abortion two weeks ago. I broke up with her yesterday."

"Is that what you were talking to Mom and Dad about last night?" Emma asked.

Turner nodded. "I told them about the pregnancy and the abortion. I didn't tell them about breaking up."

"What did they say?"

He stood up, opened the blinds and stared outside. "Not much. They looked scared."

"What did you expect?" Emma said. "You're the golden boy."

Turner whipped away from the window.

"You know what I mean," Emma said.

"When I told them Rachel had an abortion Mom almost cried," he said. "From relief. Not from sadness."

Emma stood near her brother. "I'm sure she wasn't *relieved*, Turner. I'm sure she was upset for both of you. You know how Mom feels about people not having kids until they're ready to be parents. How it's a sacred responsibility to raise a child, not to be entered into lightly. God, remember those mortifying birth control lectures in *middle school*? I thought Maude might actually die from embarrassment."

"There was something else," Turner added. "Something Dad said under his breath until Mom made him shut up. Something about Rachel not knowing what I am." He clenched his teeth. "What the hell does that mean, *what I am*? What do they think of me?"

"They love you, Turner," Emma said, squeezing his arm. "Everyone loves you. You're perfect."

"Shut up," Turner hissed. "I am obviously not perfect."

"You know what I mean," Emma said.

Turner sat on the bed. He was almost panting. Emma sat next to him.

"What is it?" she asked.

"Have you…?" he began then took a swift breath. "Have you ever done anything weird?"

"Yes," Emma said, lying back on the bed and fighting back laughter. "God, I'm surprised you asked *me* that."

"I don't mean have you ever done anything embarrassing. I know you have."

"Thanks." She hit him gently with a pillow.

He didn't smile. "I mean, something no one else can do."

A chill uncurled in the back of Emma's neck. She sat up. "Like what?"

"When I fell in love with Rachel," Turner said, his voice shaking, "which was the first time I saw her, in the park near the library, doing her homework and eating Cheetos without getting that orange dust on her fingers. I still don't know how she did it." He exhaled. "Anyway, the first time I saw her, I felt strange."

"Turner," Emma said softly. "Love feels strange."

"How do *you* know?" he asked unkindly.

"I don't," Emma snapped, her face hot. "Obviously. But I've listened to enough music and seen enough movies to know that you feel different."

"That's not what I mean," Turner said. "God, Emma, sometimes you're so…"

"What?" Emma asked.

"Nothing. Forget it." Turner stood in the middle of his room, curling and uncurling his fingers so rapidly Emma could see the tendons in his hands stick out. "The first time I kissed Rachel her books fell off her desk."

Emma bit her cheek to not laugh. "You're such an incredible kisser the earth literally moves? So…you're not perfect but you have superpowers?"

Turner took a deep breath. "When I was really little I used to move my stuffed animals around my crib."

Emma suddenly began to worry about her uptight genius brother. Maybe this was what happened when perfect people made mistakes; they couldn't handle it and freaked the hell out. "Oh my God, Turner. You should talk to Mom and Dad again. You're acting a little bit crazy."

"I didn't touch them," Turner said. "I moved my toys without touching them."

Emma said nothing. Neither of them spoke.

"What do you mean?" Emma asked after a moment. "Wait. Are you saying you think you're telekinetic?"

I don't know," Turner replied. "Mom caught me making my Eeyore fly around the room and she screamed at me to stop. She scared the hell out of me. I never did it again. Until I fell in love with Rachel."

"You think you *made* the books fall off the desk when you kissed her?" Emma said.

He nodded.

"Why?"

"I don't know," he said. "But I didn't try to do it, it just happened. After that, I *did* try, just to make sure it wasn't an accident or that I was imagining it. The next time I knocked over a water bottle, and after that I made her phone fly across the room."

"What did Rachel think?" Emma asked.

"She doesn't know," Turner said, horrified. "When things move it's always behind her. And her eyes are closed, I make sure. I don't want her to know."

"Is that why you broke up with her?" Emma asked. "You think there's something wrong with you and Rachel won't love anymore you if she finds out?"

Turner nodded and made the saddest noise Emma ever heard. "Something like that."

* * *

Later, after everyone else was asleep, Emma went downstairs, brought a glass of milk, six Oreos, and a banana back to her room and ate them. Mom and Dad had had a huge fight right after dinner and so she'd stayed clear of the kitchen. She hadn't heard what the fight was about, but it surely had something to do with what Turner just told her. Her parents rarely fought, but when they did it was usually because Dad thought Mom was being too hard on one of the kids. Dad walked out after the fight but came back half an hour later. He and Mom were ridiculously in love. It was embarrassing sometimes.

Emma stretched her bare toes into the cold sheets of her bed and pulled her silky blue blanket up to her chin. What if she and Turner—and maybe someday, Maude, Elizabeth and Sandy—had secret powers? Maybe when they fell in love with someone, some kind of latent magic power emerged. Emma didn't know how else to explain the fact that she'd vividly seen something that wasn't there and told a story she'd never heard before as soon as she met Joe, or that Turner thought he was telekinetic. Her brother was not the kind of person to make things up or indulge in ridiculous fantasies. He was going to Yale next year to major in international studies. Turner wanted save the world—and he probably could do it. And last night it seemed like she'd actually seen Joe furiously riding his bike up the hill when she was standing on the stairs in her house, like he was in a movie and the theatre was in her head.

Emma wasn't in love with Joe, though. She'd just met him yesterday, and half of the time they were together one of them was hurt or angry. Or, in her case, hallucinating. Joe hadn't seemed weirded out when she'd confessed her freakish vision this afternoon in town, but she couldn't be sure; his mom called and asked him to come home before he could say much. Although, he did squeeze her hand before he left.

For a second Emma thought about how nice it felt like to have Joe's hand in hers. If nothing else happened between them, she had that. An interesting, cute, mysterious boy had confronted her unfairly; she'd defended herself, and not only did he not run away or laugh at her, he'd listened and apologized. And held her hand. Maybe Joe liked her the way she liked him. She wished she knew. She wished she could slip into his head without him knowing and find out.

She wasn't in love with him. She couldn't be. She didn't know him; not really. But she did like him. Bad attitude, cranky personality and all. And she thought he might like her in return. Emma inhaled the chilly air, lightly perfumed with the flowery scent of her shampoo, and let her head sink into her pillow.

Of course, maybe she and Turner didn't really have secret powers. After all, she hadn't seen Turner move anything without touching it. And she was highly imaginative. She spent way too much of her time daydreaming. Sometimes an entire geometry class went by and Emma realized she hadn't heard a thing Mrs. Reeve said. There was only one way to find out if she really could see something that wasn't there, something that was happening right now and somewhere else.

Emma closed her eyes and concentrated on Joe: where he was, what he was thinking, what he was doing. She didn't try to make anything happen or imagine him doing anything. She just lay still and let whatever would happen come to her. Like meditation. Or listening to the same song over and over again until it hummed in her blood.

After a few minutes of concentrating Emma did see Joe. He was in his room, in his bed. He wasn't asleep, and he was thinking of her. She actually *saw* him. And she saw what he was thinking. About her. As if she really was inside his head without him knowing. Joe was thinking about her in a way she'd never thought about herself. She felt like she was watching a movie someone had made about her. She looked different in Joe's imagination. She looked pretty. And confident. Happy. And smart. Emma lay in her bed with Joe's sweet thoughts of her running through his head and hers. She felt the breath of the world on her skin, and…then she saw what he was doing.

Oh my God. He did like her. He *really* liked her.

Emma jumped out of bed, her heart pounding and her legs shaking as if she were running through ice-cold fire. This could just be her overactive imagination; after all, she'd imagined things like this before, usually involving some singer she loved, or after listening to *Spring Awakening* for the millionth time, but this didn't seem like a fantasy. Emma's vision of Joe alone in his room, thinking of her, doing what he was doing, felt immediate and real. She could practically smell the amazing scent of his beautiful skin. And she could feel the rising tension in his body as he thought of her.

Her heart still pounding, Emma unplugged her phone from its charger and turned her wrist to the moonlight coming in through her window, happy she'd used a blue Sharpie when Joe gave her his number in town today.

His phone rang four times. Emma almost hung up every time.

"Hello," Joe said, out of breath. "Emma?"

"Hey," she said.

"I was just thinking of you."

His voice was soft and rough. Emma's face burned, and a thrill ran through her whole body, leaving a trail of sparks like a necklace of fireflies. "I was thinking of you, too," she said.

"Really?" he said. "I hope you were thinking something good. I was."

Emma blushed so hard she thought smoke might come out of her hair.

"I like you," she said.

Nothing. The splinter of silence pricked Emma's heart. She heard Joe breathing and almost hung up or took back what she'd said.

"I like you, too," he said at last.

Emma smiled in the darkness of her room.

"Are you still there?" Joe asked after a minute.

Emma laughed. "Yes. Did you think I hung up on you?"

"No," he said. "Maybe. I don't know." He exhaled, and it sounded like he got out of bed. "I swear I was just thinking about you."

I know, she wanted to say. *I saw you.*

"Do you want to do something tomorrow, since it's Saturday?" he asked. "Ride up to the waterfall? I know you have a bike."

"Shut up," Emma said. "I can't believe I said that. What an idiotic thing to say."

"I thought it was cute," he answered in a half-whisper, and the sound of his voice unraveled the skin of Emma's heart and made her feel like she was flying.

"Well, do you want to?" he asked. "Bike up the trail, I mean."

"Sure," she said. "Do you want to meet at Richardson Park? The blue trail is the prettiest. It starts up the hill at the intersection of the red and yellow trails. The trails are pretty well marked, but there's a map in the parking lot if you need it."

"Yeah, all right."

"Okay," she agreed. "Cool."

"Cool. I'll see you tomorrow."

"Okay," she said. "Good night."

"Good night, Emma," Joe said.

She fell back on her bed and screamed into her pillow. She had awesome, *awesome* dreams.

CHAPTER EIGHT

The scent of the coming spring hid under leaves on the forest floor and drifted through the air like music. Last night Joe hadn't asked Emma what time she wanted to meet, but she'd texted him this morning. He was twenty minutes early, which was probably a bad idea because he didn't know what to do with himself. He'd ridden up and down the trail already. Luckily it was cool out, so he wasn't sweaty.

After he'd ridden idly around for another few minutes, Joe leaned his bike against a tree and tried to see if he could throw a rock above the canopy of naked branches. The buzz in his thighs and fingertips was about more than his intensely happy anticipation to see Emma. The scars along his shoulder blades burned, and for the first time since he was very, very little, Joe felt as though he had room for extra air in his lungs.

His rock sailed above the black trees and landed with a thud near the still-icy brook. He stepped on a thin stick to hear it crack beneath his shoe.

Everyone dreams of flying. When Joe was little he *could* fly. He remembered bumping his head on the ceiling of their first apartment in the Catskills. He remembered being fascinated that the brown spots on the inside of his Winnie the Pooh light were actually dead bugs. He'd picked out a soft, grey moth and kept it in his bed until his mother threw it away. When he'd told her he could fly she'd told him he had a wonderful imagination and maybe he'd be a writer someday. She'd drawn him pictures of a blue-haired boy with silver wings and told him the boy was his secret invisible self. Everyone had one, she'd said, like a fairy guardian who looked just like you.

The vivid flying dreams diminished and then vanished altogether as he got older and his mother grew more fearful and less fun and happy, but since Joe met Emma he'd dreamed of flying again. And then two nights ago he'd woken up with his back pressed hard to the ceiling. Dream Emma vanished from his arms and Joe floated gently back to bed. It should have been impossible, but if he kissed her today—and more than anything he wanted to—he didn't know what would happen. If he'd be able to keep his feet on the ground.

He heard Emma's bike then saw her pedaling up the hill, breaking twigs and sloshing through leaves. In the endless seconds before she saw him Joe tried to look chill, although his heart was pounding so hard he thought he might throw up. Taking a deep breath and praying he didn't look as nervous as he felt, Joe jumped off the rock he'd climbed up on and walked down the hill to meet her.

* * *

The wind burned Emma's ears as she rode toward the woods. She'd forgotten her helmet, and her hair spread behind her like wings. As she entered a clutch of trees at the base of the trail, the scent of damp leaves and living earth surrounded her. The ground was soft and wet. She had to be careful not to fall.

Joe's image had hung in the air in front of Emma for the whole ride. He was wearing shorts and his muscular legs pumped his bike hard up the hills. The vision made her heart beat faster, so as she approached the trail she tried to catch her breath and appear completely calm.

"Hey," Joe called, jumping off a rock and breaking her daydream of him like a train bursting through a painted tunnel in a cartoon.

"Hey," she said.

"Want to ride up to the waterfall?" he asked. "Can you ride up the hill?" he added, glancing doubtfully at her slightly tight jeans and ratty sneakers.

"Yes," she said, laughing. "How do you think I got here?"

"Sorry," he murmured. Then he took off up the trail.

Okay, she thought, following him closely on her bike. She didn't want to seem too girlie or silly, and she was almost embarrassed to think this thought in real time, in real, awake life, but Joe looked so staggeringly hot, his strong legs, his long, lean back, and his perfect, *perfect* butt. Thank God he wasn't following her. God, what if he did? What did her butt look like on a bike?

Joe stopped all of a sudden. He wasn't smiling and his eyes were wide and bright when she caught up.

Emma got off her bike. "Are you okay?" she asked. The air around him vibrated, as if he could touch her without moving.

"I *really* like you," he said on a single breath.

Time opened up around her head, and the air tasted like rain. Joe still wasn't smiling. His chest rose and fell in a rhythm Emma wanted to touch with her hands.

"You're so pretty," he said softly.

Emma bit her cheek, snorted quietly and looked at her shoes.

"It's true," he said. "I love your face."

Emma sucked in a mouthful of air. "I… Thank you."

Joe smiled at her, and a light went on in the middle of her world. Whatever it was that gave life and wonder to everything concentrated for one brief amazing moment in Joe Castlellaw's beautiful eyes.

He brushed Emma's hair behind her ear and leaned closer. Her heart was pounding so hard she could feel it in her mouth. He leaned back a little and put his hands on her hips. "Stand on my feet," he said.

"What?"

"Stand on my feet and put your arms around my waist."

Without another question she did what he asked. She hoped he couldn't feel that her hands were shaking. His skin was warm through his shirt and his back was hard and strong, so different from hers.

Joe laced his fingers at the small of her back and pulled her close. Then...he kissed her.

Oh, amazing! Beautiful. Indescribably sweet.

Joe's heart beat hard against hers. He felt so warm and strong it almost seemed like they were floating. Emma let go of his waist to slide her fingers into his hair and nearly lost her balance. He grabbed her more tightly and kissed her hard on the forehead, and Emma opened her eyes. To her shock, the ground was fifteen feet beneath them. They were flying! He'd asked her to stand on his feet so he could hold her up.

Emma stared. Joe's face was lovely, soft, beautiful—and terrified. She clung tightly to his waist and smiled.

Relief flooded his features and he kissed her again. This kiss, longer and more intense than the first, made Emma want to pull Joe inside her and keep him there forever. And he kept kissing her. Sometimes he pulled away just to smile at her. Sometimes he kissed her so long she thought she might die or explode. Or something else. He held her head, kissed her nose, and eventually they came down, slowly landing soft as a balloon on the ground.

* * *

"I've never done that before," Joe said, his heart thrashing in his chest. How much he wanted Emma shot like fire through his blood. What would she think of him now? Would she think he was a freak? He was, he supposed. No one was like him. Maybe it was better Emma find that out now.

"What?" she asked. "Kissed a girl?"

"No," he said, laughing. "No. I have kissed a girl. I've kissed many girls."

"Really?" she said, running her fingers up his stomach to his chest. He struggled to steady himself.

"I meant the flying." Joe couldn't keep his thoughts in order, and he was worried if he tried to explain what he was feeling—if he could even figure it out—his voice would shake or something worse. Of course, flying was cool. Who wouldn't want to be able to fly? He should be thrilled. He should be out saving civilizations or fighting crime. But he didn't know why he could fly. There were things he didn't know about himself and his past and his real parents. More than anything, he was afraid that he had done something terrible or caused some tragedy that was why his real parents—wherever they were—didn't want him.

Emma smiled and then bit her lip and walked away from him toward the half-frozen brook.

Please, say something, Joe thought.

Emma sat down on a stone studded with an arc of white quartz as if some toothy creature had left its jaw behind in the grey rock. "You can sit next to me," she prompted when he stood there like a fool, staring. She slid over; her jeans stuck to the jagged stone and strained against her thighs. "I won't bite you."

Joe exhaled and walked over. He had to get a hold of himself. It had been just a kiss. Well, several awesome kisses, but just kisses nonetheless. And if he wanted to kiss her again—which he did—he'd have to stop freaking out.

He sat next to her. She pulled him close. He *really* had to get a hold of himself. Her breasts pressed against his chest, and she kissed him, and they rose again, cradled by the air. The melting brook gurgled noisy and swift below.

"Don't tell anyone I can fly," he whispered into her ear as they landed on a circle of bright green moss on the other side of the brook.

"Why?" she asked, her dark blue eyes flashing with silver light.

"Do you know anyone else who can?"

"No." She blushed and turned away again.

"What?" he asked, following her. "Is this too weird for you? I can probably stop it. It hasn't happened since I was really little." He didn't tell her he'd woken up with his back pressed to the ceiling after dreaming of her the day they met.

"It's not too weird for me," she said.

"Why do you look scared then?"

"Do I look scared?" she asked.

He nodded. "You do."

Emma pushed the white toe of her sneaker in the dirt and kicked out a small stone. "I'm not scared," she said.

"Well, some people are scared of weird or hard-to-explain things," he said, remembering the gang of mean girls who'd chased him in the hall in sixth grade whispering *dragon faggot*.

Emma laughed. "I'm not."

He didn't smile.

She took his hand. "I'm not," she said again. "I'm more nervous about things that seem too normal. *That* weirds me out."

Joe laughed and squeezed her hand. *Then I guess you're perfect for me,* he thought but didn't say.

Emma blushed and grinned, almost like she'd heard what he was thinking. "It's not scary," she said. "It's awesome."

* * *

Joe glanced at his feet, his eyelashes ridiculously long on his cheeks. Emma wanted to tell him about her brother and Rachel, about how Turner said kissing Rachel made him telekinetic. She wanted to tell him that when she'd seen him for the first time, she'd also seen things that weren't there. Things she hadn't ever seen before. And she *would* tell him. Soon. But right now nothing—not Turner's power to move things, not her power to see things, nor even Joe's power to fly without wings—mattered as much as their first kiss. Joe Castlellaw liked her, really liked her. And she liked him, more than anyone or anything in her life. For now that was miracle enough.

He smiled, and she felt his breath in her mouth. He kissed her again and leaned into her. They stayed on the ground. The rough skin of a tree scratched against her shoulders. He pushed her hair out of her face.

Emma ran her hands up his back, and he flinched and sucked in a short mouthful of air. "Are you okay?" she asked, afraid she'd hurt him.

"Yeah," he said, stepping away. They'd landed nearby their bikes and he went to pick up his. "Yeah."

Emma gazed at him. Why was everything he did so amazing? How could she be interested in every movement he made? He grinned slowly at her. It felt as if she had the sun inside her body.

"I'll race you up the hill," he said.

"Wait!" Emma got on her bike and rode ahead. "Okay," she called over her shoulder. "I know a shortcut."

"Cheater!" he yelled, pedaling up behind her.

Emma let him pass, afraid of her own butt-on-the-bike look and more interested in watching him than having him watch her.

At the end of the trail Joe dropped his bike and ran to her, gathering her in his arms and kissing her as if it were the first kiss anyone had ever given. They floated, ever kissing, up and around the waterfall, spray wetting their faces, the thunderous sound of the falls pounding in their ears.

It was perfect. He was perfect. Emma was happy.

CHAPTER NINE

After a week of hardly being able to concentrate in school and kissing Emma in the art supply closet whenever they could sneak out of class, Joe sat at a computer in the Warwick library on Saturday and deleted a paragraph about identity, power and transgression in *Measure for Measure*. He leaned back to think about how to rewrite it when a wrinkled paper bag dropped onto the table beside him.

"I found them in my closet," his mom said. Her hair was pulled into a messy bun and there were paint splatters on her pants and fingers.

"Were you cleaning?" he asked, glancing around to see if anyone was looking. "You didn't throw anything of mine away, did you?"

"No," she said, sitting next to him and pulling her hair out of its faded denim scrunchie. "I was painting in the kitchen. I found them when I was looking for my sable brushes. The Russian ones." She glanced at the bag but didn't move it closer to Joe.

"What are they?" he asked.

"The study sketches for those triptych paintings you asked me about last week," she said, sitting straight as a ballet dancer. "The day you started school, remember? From the story you were obsessed with when you were little. The one about the tree and the female monster."

"You mean dragon," Joe said. His mother always called the dragon *a female monster*. When as a kid Joe insisted it was a dragon because it had wings and a tail and a scary face, his Mom characteristically told him the image was just a metaphor for murderous women, especially women who killed children.

"You know I don't, Joe," his mom said. "The monster could as easily be a witch like some versions of Baba Yaga or a serpent like Echidna. To insist that she is a dragon because she has wings is too specific and therefore limiting."

Joe exhaled. A couple of kids from school walked by and nodded at him. Like a two-year-old who thinks you can't see her when her eyes are closed, his mom stared at the table. She didn't look up or acknowledge the pair in any way.

"I haven't thought about that story in years," she said, pointing to the bag after the kids passed. "What made you think of it?"

Why had she brought these to the library? Joe wondered, hoping no one else he knew would come by. Why couldn't she just have given them to him at home?

His mom slapped her hand noisily on the bag and Joe jumped. "You're not going to show them to anyone, are you?" she asked, keeping her pale, paint-splattered hand on the bag. "These are private, Joe. I don't want anyone to see them. I don't want anyone to see my work. I do it for me. You know that."

"I know," Joe said. "I won't show anyone. I just wanted to see them again." He pulled the bag out from under her hand. "We're talking about tree symbolism in English," he lied, "and I remembered your story. I won't show anyone."

"All right," she said. "See you at home." She kissed him on the head and left. Joe felt his cheeks turn scarlet.

Stacy Keeler came up and sat on the edge of the table. "Hey," she said. "Have you seen Izzy Peccant? She was supposed to meet me here twenty minutes ago to work on our Italian project."

Joe glanced around the room. "Uh, no."

Stacy wrinkled her tiny nose. Joe wondered if she took her perfect face and her perfect life in stride, or if she was grateful.

"What's this?" she asked, picking up the bag.

"Drawings," he said, coloring again. "My mom's."

"Can I see?"

"Uh, sure," he said, breaking his false promise earlier than he intended.

He held still as Stacy paged through the vivid images of monstrous trees and children running from a female dragon. She smiled enigmatically and put the pictures back into the bag. "Are these illustrations for a children's book or something?"

Joe took the bag and slid it under his English textbook. His stomach leapt unpleasantly. "Uh...no. Well, not exactly. It's a story she made up for me when I was a kid."

Stacy's magazine-pretty face glowed. "That's *so* sweet," she said. "I wish my mom was creative."

Joe didn't know what to say.

"Are you going out with Emma Mathews?"

Joe blushed and his tongue felt fat in his mouth. "Uh. Yeah."

How did Stacy know? We're they being that obvious? Except for the woods, he and Emma never met out of school. And in school it was always the art supply closet, because no one ever used it. Joe still didn't trust that the thing he and Emma had would last. What if she met someone from Wolfeboro? He wouldn't seem so awesome if Emma heard what kids said about him there.

Stacy grinned.

"What?" Joe asked, feeling hot and nervous.

"Nothing. I just think you two make an interesting couple." She jumped off the table and threw her hair over her shoulder. "If you see Izzy, tell her to text me."

"Sure," Joe said.

"See you," Stacy said, cocking her head.

"Yeah," Joe said.

Joe tried to recapture his idea about *Measure for Measure* but couldn't think. He took his memory stick out of the library computer, stuffed his mom's sketches into his backpack, and left the library.

Emma was across the street. Sometimes Joe thought she had a strange sense about where he was when they weren't together. He'd told her he was going to study in the library this weekend but he hadn't told her when. Whatever the reason for her presence, he was grateful. He watched her slow stride, her half smile hidden by her hair whenever she looked down. She stopped at the corner and turned in the direction of her house, away from him.

He was about to call after her when Emma stopped in front of the town hall parking lot and turned. He watched her scan the street until she saw his face. Joe's lungs filled with air and lightness. He had to concentrate to keep from floating off the ground. The previous week had been the best of his life.

Emma ran down the street to where he was standing. "Hey," she said, her face flushed and her eyes shining with happiness.

"Hey." He leaned forward to kiss her and brushed his fingertips against the back of her hand instead. "Are you going home?"

"Yeah. Well…no. I'm just walking around," she said. "My dad wanted everyone out of the house. I think he and my mom are trying to make up about something."

He only heard part of what Emma said. He just wanted to be alone with her.

"Are you going home?" she asked.

"Yeah," he said, wishing he didn't have his heavy backpack with him.

"Do you want me to walk with you?" she asked. "I don't have to be home for a while, I'm sure."

He didn't know what to say. He wanted to be with her, just not at his house.

"I don't have to come in, if your mom is weird about people being there when she's not home," she said. "My mom's weird about everything."

Joe laughed. "I doubt that."

Emma smiled at him, and he had to stop himself from grabbing her there on the street and kissing her. Instead she kissed him, softly and sweetly on the mouth. He felt breathless as she said, "Well, most people are better than we think they are—or at least they're more complex than we want to give them credit for. And," she added, taking his hand, "I secretly think that everyone is weirder than they seem. Some people are just better at hiding it."

Joe couldn't argue with that. Wasn't he the one who'd taken her for a flight and had terrible scars on his back? Wasn't she the one who'd seen a vision of the paintings his mom painted so long ago?

They got to his apartment complex. Joe prayed his mom wasn't home as they walked up the main stairwell. "Do you want to bike to the park?" he asked, unlocking the front door.

The apartment was empty. Joe was instantly aware how dingy and small the place must seem to Emma who probably had always lived in a nice house. The dark living room smelled stale and old, like every previous tenant had left behind scent trails of what they'd cooked or drunk and how often or not they washed their hair.

Joe ran down the short hall and tossed his backpack onto his bed. "You can ride my mom's bike," he suggested when he got back. "It's old but it's okay."

"All right," Emma said. "Is this you?" She held up an eight-by-ten-inch, gold-framed photograph. "You're so serious. How old were you?"

"Second grade," Joe said, ready to get the hell out of the apartment. "It was a hard year."

"You were so sweet." Emma stroked Joe's face in the picture then returned it to the scratched end table. "No seven-year-old should have a hard year. My brother Sandy is seven. I think I'd want to kill anyone who was mean to him."

"Sandy's lucky," Joe said.

"I'm lucky," Emma said, winding her arms around his waist.

Joe pressed his cheek to Emma's neck and breathed in the sweet soft scent of her hair. She slid her fingers into his waistband at the back of his jeans and kissed him. It took all his concentration not to float up to the ceiling.

"Let's go to the park," he said, out of breath. "I don't know when my mom will be back."

Emma brushed her hair out of her eyes. "Okay."

They biked to Richardson Park in silence. Joe was happy for the exercise and for the cold spring air on his face. He rode hard and fast, turning occasionally to make sure Emma was keeping up.

She hooted suddenly. Speeding past, she zipped through the park entrance to the top of the trail hill where she waited, out of breath, grinning triumphantly.

Joe jumped off his bike and grabbed her by the waist. Panting slightly, Emma stood on Joe's feet and smiled at him. She wound her arms around his neck and they shot into the air and floated under the lace of newly budding branches. Her soft mouth explored his, and her breasts crushed thrillingly into his chest. Joe fell slowly back as if the insubstantial air was an infinitely wide bed. Emma followed, the sweet weight of her body falling onto his.

"Move up higher," he said, sucking air through his teeth as Emma repositioned herself until she was exactly where he wanted her.

"Like this?" she asked.

"Yes," he said, holding on to himself by a thread. "Just like that."

She kissed him. Her silky hair fell over his face. She kissed him.

"Don't move," Joe said, his voice like sand in his throat. "Be still."

"Are you worried about me?" she murmured against his throat. "Don't worry. I'm all right. I'm not going to fall."

"I'm worried about *me*," Joe said, trying to feel and not feel her mouth and breasts and legs agonizingly snug against him.

"Are we going to fall?"

"God!" Joe said as Emma sat up in alarm. The sudden shift in her weight almost ended everything right then and there.

"What?" she asked. "Did I hurt you? Am I too heavy?"

"No," Joe said. "No, you're not too heavy. And no, you didn't hurt me."

He should have been able to say what he was thinking, to say what he wanted to say. That he didn't want this to be over too soon, that he wanted, more than anything, to go farther, much farther than they had gone. Desire for Emma had taken over Joe's blood and his breath and his thoughts. He could hardly sleep. He wanted to know—*had to know*—that Emma liked him enough, wanted him enough, to do everything he'd been dreaming about almost since the moment he met her. But if she didn't, if she just wanted to kiss him for hours and then go home to her happy, normal family, Joe couldn't hear it right now. So instead he said what he thought all girls wanted to hear.

"You're beautiful," he whispered, drawing her face back to his so he could kiss her eyes and nose and mouth. "You're perfect. Just the way you are."

Emma smiled, sweet and blushing, as he had expected, and kissed him back.

Joe forced himself to kiss Emma without getting too into it. For a bizarre moment he wished he had a guy friend so he could brag about this superhuman accomplishment. A girl couldn't understand. Not that he would ever tell Emma something like that anyway.

She was making sweet little noises in the back of her throat. That was nice. He could do this. He could. And then someday soon he'd find a way to convince Emma to do the rest. Because if he didn't, Joe was afraid he might burst apart in a gargantuan Hulk-like explosion of flesh like the rag-and-bone dealer's spontaneous combustion in *Bleak House*, complete with thick liquor coating the walls and the shudders of repulsion from all observers.

Emma sighed softly in his ear and Joe raised them to a vertical position. He caught her weight again in his arms, and Emma ran her hands up and down the scars on his shoulder blades.

Suddenly, she drew away from him with a harsh cry. They dropped to the ground. Too quickly. Luckily it wasn't too far.

"Sorry!" Joe said, helping Emma up. "Are you okay?"

She sat on a rock and didn't answer.

Joe froze. "What is it?" he asked. "Are you okay?"

Emma's hands were shaking. She stared uncomprehendingly at the ground as if trying to recall an unsettling dream. Joe's stomach clenched. He picked up a stone and threw it at a tree. Emma slid down her rock and sat on the ground. Joe didn't know what to do. He wanted to ride home, to ride away. To disappear.

Emma lowered her head to her knees. Joe sat next her.

"Don't cry," he said, running his fingers through the ends of her hair. He *had* gone too far. He'd scared her or grossed her out. "I'm sorry," he said. "It won't happen again. I'll be more careful. I'll try to control myself."

"I saw," Emma said.

"You saw what?" Joe asked, digging the fingers of his free hand into the cold moss beside him. Was it *that* visible? Er, and shouldn't she kind of want to see it, anyway?

Emma dropped her forehead onto her hand. "It's my fault," she said. "I ignore things I don't like or understand. My dad says I can't keep acting as if…" She stopped. "As if I can pretend something bad is not real. I have to learn to face things I don't like or am afraid of. And stop running away."

Shit, Joe thought. Shit, shit, shit. He *had* blown it. And now sweet Emma was trying to find a way to tell him something she knew would hurt his feelings.

"What do you mean?" he asked, wishing for a second that he'd never met her and then instantly trying to recover from that thought.

Emma drew in a deep breath and turned, her face full of empathy, kindness, and traces of desire—which threw Joe for a loop. Did she like him or didn't she? Did she want him the way he desperately wanted her, or didn't she? Joe didn't think he could bear it if Emma liked him only a little. Or worse, just as a friend. He couldn't stand to keep seeing her at all if that were true. He'd feel like half a person. A vulture trying to mix with eagles.

"I saw you when you were little," Emma said, taking his hand before he could pull it away. "I saw you crying. I saw your mom crying. I saw what that doctor did."

Ice water shot through Joe's veins. Emma Mathews didn't just have vivid daydreams; she was psychic or something. And she knew something about him that he didn't know. Something terrifying and awful that happened when he was very young. Maybe she knew the reason his bio-parents dumped him in that parking lot.

"I'm so sorry," Emma said, rubbing her hand up and down his arm. "I can't believe someone would do that. I can't believe anyone could see something as miraculous and amazing as a baby with wings, and cut them off."

Joe jumped to his feet.

"What?" Emma said.

Joe couldn't speak.

"You didn't know," she realized, her face pale. "Oh my God. I thought you knew. I was sure you knew. I don't know how I could have seen it if you didn't remember. Oh my God, I'm so sorry. Maybe I made it up to explain the flying."

"Stop," Joe said, his head reeling. "You didn't make it up."

"But you didn't know," she said.

"My mom told me I had nasty growths on my back when she adopted me. She had them removed when I was almost three."

Emma didn't say anything.

Joe leaned back on the rock behind him and let the cold of it seep into his skin. He'd had wings? What the hell was he, and where did he come from? And how did Emma see something he didn't know about or remember?

"That story," he said, trying to keep an even tone to his voice. "The one you told in the hall, the one from my mom's painting. You still don't remember it?"

Emma shook her head.

He could hardly continue; it sounded crazy and stupid. He hated Emma. He didn't want to talk about this. Not with her. Not with anyone. He wanted to climb out of his skin and be someone else.

"It was a story about a winged little boy and a baby girl who got stuck inside a tree." He didn't feel any better for having said it. Unlike in fairy tales, speaking the words aloud changed nothing.

"I didn't see a tree when I touched your scars," Emma clarified. "Or a baby girl. I saw little-boy you crying on your stomach on a metal table with your mom holding you down. I saw a doctor with a disgusting tan face and crazy eyes cut off your wings and throw them away."

"Can we go?" Joe asked, picking up his bike.

"Are you angry?" Emma said. "I thought you knew. I wouldn't have said anything if I knew you didn't know."

"Yeah," Joe said. "'Cause that would have been so much better, you knowing I'm some kind of mutant freak and me laboring under the delusion that you think I'm human."

"Stop it," Emma said.

"Why?" he snarled. "So you can feel better? So you can pretend everything's great and normal?"

"There's no such thing as normal," Emma said.

"Yeah," Joe said. "Like you'd know anything about that."

Emma's eyes flashed. "No one is normal," she promised. "Everyone feels lost, or different. Everyone thinks no one is like them, that no one thinks like them or feels what they feel. But the truth is everyone wants the same kind of things. Everyone feels pain. Everyone wants love. Everyone fears death and embarrassment. I don't care that you had wings when you were a baby. I don't care that your mom is strange or that you don't know where you come from. No one is normal. And everyone feels alone."

"I have to go," Joe said. "Leave my mom's bike at the bottom of the steps."

"You can't just walk away every time you feel uncomfortable or embarrassed," Emma called, following him.

"Watch me," Joe said, and without looking back he pedaled off down the hill.

* * *

"Jerk!" Emma called after him. He just rode faster.

She was so angry. Too angry to cry or feel sorry for herself. Or to want to run after him and apologize. But for what? She hadn't known he didn't remember his wings or the creepy doctor who cut them off. She never would have said anything to upset him on purpose. Who was he to make all the decisions about when to stay and when to go? And what the hell was he so afraid of? Did he really think she'd care about anything anyone else thought about him—or about her? She *didn't* care. The best thing about being an outsider was the luxury of not giving a shit about what people you didn't like thought of you. People you did care about… Well, that was another thing.

Furious, Emma pedaled Joe's mom's bike down the trail and back into town, half hoping and half dreading she'd see him, but he was nowhere to be found. She rode into the parking lot of Joe's apartment building and looked up at his window. It was dark. She leaned his mom's bike against the stairs and walked home through the woods. The trees were leafless, but skunk cabbage shone in luminous green patches on the forest floor.

Maude was kneeling up ahead, a big yellow plastic sand bucket on the ground in front of her.

"What are you doing?" Emma asked.

"The soil right here is great," Maude said in her serious, soft voice, "and the ground isn't frozen anymore." She held up the bucket for Emma to see. The soft dirt inside looked like crushed chocolate cake. Maude took stones and twigs off the shovel, but she left the worms.

"Are you okay?" she asked, not looking up.

"No," Emma said.

Maude sat back on her feet and tossed her smooth black hair over her shoulder. She looked up expectantly.

"I found out something about Joe," Emma said. "And I told him."

"Was it about that kid he beat up?" Maude asked. There are no secrets in a high school or a small town.

"No," Emma said. "He told me about that. This was something else. Something he didn't know or didn't remember." She picked up a rough, triangular stone. "He was really upset when I told him."

Maude stared at her, silent.

"I don't want to tell you what it was," Emma said.

"Okay," Maude agreed.

"Is this where you come when you talk to the boy you imagine?" Emma asked; then she waited while Maude searched her face for signs of mockery or disbelief. There were none, of course.

"Sometimes," Maude admitted, tipping a last shovelful of dirt into the pail.

Emma sat on the edge of a small wooden bridge nearby. Turner had helped build bridges like this one when he was a Boy Scout. "Does he ever answer you, this boy?"

"He doesn't," Maude said, standing and brushing broken leaves off her jeans. "But I know he's there. Like I know there's air in my lungs and blood in my veins. Like I know there's a real world even when I'm asleep." She blinked and stared at the ground. "I know it sounds stupid." She eyed Emma. "I don't care."

The memory of Joe's fury and the humiliation he'd tried to hide in his voice crushed Emma's heart. She was still angry, but she ached for him anyway. It was all mixed up. She didn't know what to do. And she hated feeling confused about anything.

"It doesn't sound stupid," she said to Maude. "I hope you get to meet him someday."

Something shivered over Maude's face. "I think he can hear me," she said. "That's why I recite a poem."

Emma stood up and leaned over the bridge railing to watch the stream run over the dark, mossy rocks. From one perspective Maude seemed like a troubled, crazy girl. And maybe she was. But right now, in the cool, fading light of the late March woods, with the green skunk cabbage singing the song of spring, and especially considering what Emma knew about Joe and Turner, and about her own heart, Maude just seemed like she was trying to be herself and in the world at the same time.

"What poem do you recite?" Emma asked. She stepped off the bridge and walked over to her sister.

"'The Eve of St. Agnes,'" Maude said, picking up her bucket of dirt. "I recited a little bit of it to you once, remember? 'She closed the door, she panted, all akin/To spirits of the air, and visions wide…' It's an unbelievably beautiful poem about thwarted lovers. Her family hates him."

Emma's chest felt cold.

"We should go," Maude said then silently pointed. A huge buck stood on a ridge not twenty feet away. He was looking right at them.

"I always think it's lucky to see a buck," Maude said after it ran off.

Emma nodded. "Me, too."

Maude walked a little bit ahead of Emma. She cradled her pail of black earth close to her chest, careful not to spill any. Her sleek dark hair swung behind her, catching the last bits of light coming in from though the trees, and Emma worried that she was being reckless or irresponsible in encouraging her younger sister's imaginary-boy fantasy. Too caught up in her own problems, she let the feeling pass.

CHAPTER TEN

Emma was sitting on the couch with Sandy watching TV after dinner when her phone buzzed.

"Text from your boyfriend!" Sandy announced after taking his thumb from his mouth.

Emma felt her face flame blood red. "Shhh," she hushed, getting up from the couch and checking her phone. "He's not my boyfriend. Well, maybe he is. And how do you know, anyway?"

"I'm right, aren't I?" Sandy said a little slurrily, his thumb back his mouth and his eyes on the television. "That song plays when he texts you."

"Yes," Emma said, unwilling to read the text in front of her little brother. "But how do you know he's my boyfriend? If he even is. And I'm not saying he is," she added, feeling more and more foolish for arguing.

"It's obvious," Sandy drawled disdainfully in a perfect imitation of Elizabeth.

"I don't think it is," Emma said.

Sandy hummed then laughed at something on the TV.

Emma went up to her room to read the text—which was from Joe, whom she still wanted to be her boyfriend. If he really was her boyfriend. And if he apologized.

Heart pounding slightly, and still a little angry, Emma opened the text.

- I am a jerk.

She smiled in the dark of her room and replied. **Yes but ur a good kisser so I forgive u.**

- Is that all I am to u? A sex toy?

- Ur also an acceptable mountain biker.

- Thanks?

- I thought you knew. About the wings.

She waited, heart still pounding but no longer angry.

- I know, and maybe I did and I put it out of my head or something. I just hate being different. Or maybe I hate that people care so much about shit like that.

- I don't care about it.

A few seconds passed, and Emma had the distinct feeling Joe was trying not to say something he really wanted to say. Because of envisioning him on his bike the day they met and seeing him in his bed the following night thinking of her—and doing more than just thinking—Emma knew she could cheat and try to hear what Joe wanted to say. But she didn't.

Her phone buzzed suddenly and she jumped.

- I know. GTG and ur a good kisser too.

The next few weeks were the best of Emma's life. Everything was useless and pointless except for Joe. Nothing mattered but him. Emma was aware of the world around her like knowing it's raining when you're inside watching a movie, but she didn't give it any more thought than that. She didn't want anything but to be with Joe. And he didn't want anything except to be with her—and to do his homework, because he was a little bit Turnerish that way.

They had been going out for a month now. It was the middle of April and the weather was living up to its changeable New England reputation, jumping back and forth between winter and spring. On Mondays and Wednesdays she and Joe had study hall together after lunch. Usually Joe wanted to do homework. At first Emma just waited while he worked but then she started doing her own work. Science was actually super interesting this year—well, maybe not physics, which was still a little too hard to call interesting, but Emma had thought her dad would literally pass out from happiness when she switched her science elective from software development to environmental studies taught by cool Mr. Spencer.

Mr. Spencer. There were all sorts of rumors about him when he came to Dearborn from Boston, and he didn't look like any Dearborn teacher Emma had ever seen. For one thing, he was kind of hot. He had a pierced tongue and gauged ears. He spoke five languages, including Farsi, and he talked about famous dead writers as if they were his friends. Mr. Spencer hated what he called "the artificial separation between science and art" and talked about poetry when he talked about cell regeneration. He seemed to know everything. He was her favorite teacher. She almost felt like she could tell him about her visions and about Joe's flying. Almost.

Emma was sitting alone in study hall, going over Mr. Spencer's corrections on her fragile ecosystems paper when a thin triangle dropped onto her notebook. The sight of the folded paper caught her heart like a hook. It read, MEET ME @ THE 2ND FL ART SUPPLY CLOSET. Even Joe's handwriting made her feel goofy and swoony.

Emma stuffed her books and papers into her bag and walked up to prehistoric Mr. Raven, the study hall monitor. "I have to go to the bathroom," she told him.

He eyed her bag. "Is it necessary to bring all of your books?"

Emma shifted her weight. "I *need* my bag."

"Ah," Mr. Raven said. You could get away with almost anything from an old man teacher if he thought you had your period. He handed over the pass without looking at her.

She actually did go to the bathroom—to take out her ponytail, brush her hair and put on lip gloss. She slid a mouthwash strip onto her tongue. It was so minty it made her eyes water.

Joe was waiting outside the boys bathroom near the art supply closet. Emma stopped to catch her breath. Ever since she'd told Joe about his wings something had tightened between them. Whenever he was with her it seemed they were the only two people in the world. This had been cliché until it happened to her.

Emma tried not to grin like an imbecile as she walked up to Joe, but he saw her and smiled, and she forgot to pretend to be cool.

"Hey," he said softly.

"Hey."

He laced his fingers briefly through hers and glanced down the empty hall. "You go in first."

Emma opened the door. The scent of paint and brushes and crayons mingled into a strange perfume she knew would make her feel seventeen whenever she smelled it again, as long as she lived.

"Did I interrupt you?" Joe asked, shutting the door and pulling her close. "You looked pretty focused." He ran his warm hands up her back and through her hair. "If you have too much work I can see you later."

Emma was melting. "It's okay." The muscles of Joe's back shifted beneath her hands as she kissed him. "I read Mr. Spencer's notes. I'm not going to revise that paper until tonight."

"Good."

He smiled and brushed her hair back over her shoulders. He pulled her closer, and his warm, hard stomach pressed against hers. She kissed him again.

The doorknob turned, and she and Joe jumped apart.

"What are you two doing in here?" Mr. Spencer asked, leaving the door open behind him.

"Uh," Joe stammered. "Mrs. Eyre needed paint for a project."

Emma bit her cheek so she wouldn't nervously laugh at such a ridiculous lie.

Mr. Spencer narrowed his eyes and glanced back and forth between them. "I thought you had history third period, Joe."

Neither of them said anything.

"You realize that this is *fifth* period," Mr. Spencer said, holding up his watch for them to see.

"Cool watch," Emma said quietly. It *was* cool. She'd never seen a watch like it. It was big and bronze-looking, with ornate, intricate hands. Now, however, was clearly not the time to comment on unusual timepieces. "Sorry," she murmured.

Mr. Spencer scowled and sighed. "You can't stay in here." He gazed hard at Emma, and she felt unaccountably exposed, as if he knew something about her that she didn't. He sighed again and then grabbed a huge container of glue. "Come on," he said, holding open the door.

Emma and Joe left the closet and followed Mr. Spencer down the hall. Emma saw that the tips of Joe's ears had turned pink. She smiled at him and grabbed his hand briefly. Mr. Spencer turned. Emma stepped back, seized by the sudden, terrible notion that he was about to talk to them, here in the hall, about sex, and about waiting and being sure, and about using protection. Oh my God, that absolutely could not happen.

"Listen," Mr. Spencer began.

"I'm almost done with the corrections on my ecosystems paper," Emma interrupted. "I think it's pretty good. That site you told me about, about cranberry bogs and maple syrup, you know, the one about climate change and New England crops? Well, it was really good. I got a lot of stuff from it. I cited all the sources correctly of course," she added breathlessly.

Joe stared at her. She ignored him. She still hadn't gotten rid of her impulse to laugh.

"Good," Mr. Spencer said, still scrutinizing both of them. A student came out of a classroom up the hall. "All right," he decided, turning his attention to them again. "Go to class. But if I catch you *alone* when you're supposed to be somewhere else…"

"We understand," Joe said.

Emma nodded.

* * *

That night, Emma opened the front door and let Joe into her house. She'd invited him over as soon as she realized her parents, Elizabeth, and Sandy would be at a school thing, while Turner was at the library and Maude was babysitting. It was the first time she and Joe would be alone together somewhere private and inside.

She closed the door and led him into the family room at the back of the house. She hadn't told anyone but Maude that Joe was coming over. If anyone came home early he could sneak out through the back door.

"I can't get in trouble," Joe said.

"I know," Emma said. Joe had told her why he'd been kicked out of his other school. Even though he was defending a kid who was getting beaten up, the school had a zero tolerance policy for fighting. Joe and the jerk tormenting the younger kid had both gotten expelled. Joe couldn't make any big mistakes at Dearborn if he wanted to go to a good college. "Do you want some water or orange juice? We're not allowed to have soda."

"Water, thanks," Joe said, hands in his pockets, looking around. The small room was filled with comfortable leather furniture surrounding a fieldstone fireplace, and the wood-paneled walls were covered with academic awards for Turner and literary awards for Maude. Good-citizen awards for Elizabeth. And Sandy's drawings.

"Yeah, I know," Emma repeated, blushing as Joe realized nothing of hers was displayed. "I'm not really well represented here. If they gave awards for Still Trying to Figure Shit Out, or Best Taste in Music I'd totally dominate."

Joe smiled. "You're good at a lot of things," he said quietly and picked up one of the comic books Sandy was always drawing.

"Be right back," Emma said, her heart fluttering. She went into the kitchen.

"You have to stop worrying about what happened today," Emma said, handing Joe a glass of ice water when she returned. "Mr. Spencer is cool. You won't get in trouble."

Joe exhaled in frustration. "Just because Mr. Spencer dresses cool and likes the same music you do doesn't mean he's not a teacher. He was serious. We can't sneak into the art closet anymore."

"I know," Emma said. "I think he was going to give us a sex lecture," she added with a shudder.

"What makes you say that?"

"After I squeezed your hand he turned around and looked directly at me. I swear he was about to start to tell us to be careful, and wait, and to use a condom." She groaned and sat on the couch. "That's why I started talking about cranberry bogs."

Joe laughed and sat beside her. The tension between them fell away.

"I'm going to miss that art closet," Joe said wistfully.

"Me too," Emma said, taking his hand.

He gazed at her, his star-bright eyes so beautiful. Although Joe was hardly touching her, Emma felt something overwhelming, as if he were physically connected to her, like he was already kissing her, like he had already pulled her tightly against him. He drew closer and made a sound; it might have been her name, it might have been some other word or idea, but his voice curled around Emma's heart like it belonged there. She leaned forward and kissed him.

After a few long minutes of increasingly awesome kissing, Joe pulled away, out of breath. "Are you a virgin?" he asked.

"Are you?" Emma said, gradually adjusting to the unexpected absence of his mouth as if time had suddenly slowed.

Joe blushed.

"I just don't know why I have to be the one to answer that question first," she said.

"You don't, I guess."

"So, *are* you?" Emma asked.

"Would it matter to you either way?" Joe sounded nervous.

"No," Emma said. "I don't care what you did before. I care about what you do now." She stroked his cheek. He smiled at her and brushed his face against her fingers.

"I am a virgin," he said.

Emma smiled back. "Me, too. I've never even really kissed anyone. Before you."

"Really?" Joe said. "You're so pretty."

Emma laughed. "That was exactly the right thing to say."

He blushed again. "Good."

"I have kissed a girl before," he said.

"One girl, one kiss?" Emma said.

"No," he admitted, thinking for a second. "Seven girls—"

"Seven!"

"Hey," he said. "I thought you were all 'I don't care what you did before'?"

"I don't," she said, because it was the truth. "But I think maybe I don't want to hear about it. What else have you done?"

"Make up your mind," Joe said, laughing and blushing.

"Have you ever seen a girl naked? In real life, I mean. Not on the Internet."

"Ha-ha. And no."

"Has a girl ever seen you naked?"

He laughed again. "No!"

Emma exhaled.

"Are you finished?" he asked, leaning over to kiss her.

"Yes?"

He fell against the puffy back of the couch, realizing she wasn't. "Go ahead," he said. "Ask me anything. If I don't want to answer I won't, okay?"

Emma smiled. "Okay."

Joe stretched his arm over the cushion and twirled his fingers through the ends of Emma's hair.

"Touching through clothes?" she said.

"Yes."

"On the top and the bottom?"

He laughed. "Yes. Are you considering becoming a cop or a lawyer?"

"No," Emma said. "Under the clothes?"

He exhaled. "Yes."

"On the top and the bottom?"

"Just the top."

"You and the girl?"

"Just the girl." He walked to the fireplace and picked up a solid glass sphere with a green and gold wire tree inside it. "Almost finished?"

"Almost," Emma said, "but I don't exactly know how to ask my last question."

Joe returned the sphere to the stone mantel and grinned slowly at her. Emma felt hot. He climbed onto the couch and gently pushed her onto her back. "Do you want to know if things went as far as they could go," Joe whispered in her ear, kissing down the side of her throat, "through the clothes?"

"Yes," Emma said, running her hands up and down his back and listening to the low hum deep in his throat.

"For the girl *and* for me?" he said.

Emma nodded against his cheek as he continued to kiss her neck.

"Yes," Joe whispered, grinding his *very ready* hips into hers.

Emma sucked at the insufficient air. "I'm not ready for that."

Joe groaned and swore and pressed his forehead against hers.

She took his face in her hands and waited until he was looking into her eyes. "Not yet, okay?" she said.

He thrust his hips against hers and growled in frustration again then kissed her eyes.

"Okay," he said.

He continued to kiss her, though. Emma tried to catch her breath along with a coherent train of thought. She opened her hands and laid them on Joe's chest.

"I'm serious," she said.

He half growled and rolled off her, sitting on the far end of the couch with his hands on his knees and his legs spread apart. "Do I seem like I'm going to force you?"

"You couldn't," Emma said.

He smiled.

"What?" she asked.

"You're not the kind of girl who needs to be taken care of, are you?" he said.

"No," she agreed. "Why? Are you the kind of guy who needs to be taken care of?"

He colored and stood up.

Emma curled her feet under her legs, wishing Joe was still kissing her and wishing she didn't have to worry about going too far too soon or disappointing him. Or saying the wrong thing. "I might be the kind of girl who should think before she speaks, however."

"Yeah," Joe said, glancing slyly at her from underneath those fierce lashes. "You might be that." He exhaled. "I have to go."

"Really?" she said, way too pathetically.

"Yeah." He picked up and put back down the same sphere he'd looked at earlier on the mantel. "I would never try force you to do something you're not ready for, but sometimes it's going to be hard—"

Emma snorted and gnawed on her lower lip.

"Ha ha," Joe said. "Sometimes it's going to be *difficult* for me to stay. Unless we're doing something else. Like talking or watching a movie. On opposite ends of the room," he added.

"So what does that mean?" Emma said. "No kissing? No anything until I'm ready for everything? That's not fair either. I'm not made of stone, Joe, but you're the first person I ever kissed and that was only a few weeks ago."

"I know." He nodded. "I get it."

"So why are you acting like this?"

"Like what?" He looked angry.

"Pretty much refusing to see me or kiss me until I'm ready to sleep with you."

"That's not what I said. And it's not what I meant. Shit, Emma, you're making me sound like some kind of sex monster."

"No, I'm not," she said. "I'm making you sound selfish because that's how you're acting."

And there it was, Emma thought, the thing she should have thought through before she said. The thing she should have kept to herself. Joe wasn't being any more selfish than she was. They wanted different things, and neither of them seemed ready to compromise.

"I'm going home," he muttered.

She didn't stop him.

CHAPTER ELEVEN

As it was Saturday, Emma did her homework in the library in town the next day, hoping to see Joe. He hadn't called or texted after he got home last night and neither had she. She didn't know what to do. Why couldn't Joe just wait without making her feel bad—or punishing her by staying away? Emma couldn't talk to Turner, and she didn't know if she should talk to Maude. Fifteen was a lot younger than seventeen.

Joe never came into the library, but Emma got all her work done, which was a thing in itself. Now she had no homework to do the rest of the weekend. If he didn't text her by the time dinner was over, she'd text him. She was starting to feel weird not hearing Joe's voice, which made her feel somewhat pathetic. And she *really* missed kissing him.

Emma walked into the house around six. Dad's car wasn't in the driveway. There was no smell of dinner. Mom and Turner were fighting upstairs.

"What's going on?" Emma asked Elizabeth, who was making Play-Doh aliens in the kitchen with Sandy.

"I don't know," Elizabeth said. "Mom's mad at Turner about something."

Emma stared into the refrigerator. "Where's Dad?" she asked after shutting the door.

"I don't know," Elizabeth repeated, rolling a spike to add to her alien's tail. "He dropped me and Maude off and went somewhere."

"I got new shoes," Sandy crowed.

"Can I see them?" Emma asked.

"No."

"Why not?"

"They're upstairs. I'm wearing slippers." Sandy lifted his feet so Emma could see his Scooby-Doo slippers.

"Nice," Emma said, smiling.

Sandy grinned back then shoved his fingers into his alien's head, making its mouth unnaturally wide.

"Isn't there anything for dinner?" Emma asked, opening the refrigerator again.

"Pizza," Elizabeth said.

"When?"

"I don't know. Ask Mom. I'm supposed to watch Sandy until you get home."

"You're not watching me," Sandy protested quietly. "You're playing with me. And you're taking all the green."

"You used too much already," Elizabeth said.

"No, I didn't."

"Stop it," Emma said. "What are Mom and Turner doing?"

"Fighting," said Sandy.

"About what?"

"I don't know," Sandy said. "That part's too quiet."

"I'm starving," Emma said, opening the refrigerator a third time. "When are we getting the pizza?"

"I don't care what you think!" Turner's furious voice came muffled through the ceiling. "It isn't about you. It's about me. And Rachel. Don't pretend to want to help when all you want is to tell me what to do!"

Mom must have replied, but Emma couldn't hear her.

"No!" Turner shouted. "No. You're wrong. You don't know everything!"

A door slammed, and Turner ran downstairs. He passed Maude in the hall. "Don't talk to me, Maude," he shouted. He grabbed his car keys and slammed the front door behind him.

"What's wrong with Turner?" Maude asked, looking pale. She hated to be yelled at.

"He had a fight with Mom," Emma said softly.

"Was it about the thing with Rachel?" Maude mouthed.

Emma nodded. "I think so."

"What thing with Rachel?" Elizabeth asked. "Did Rachel break up with him?"

"Set the table, Elizabeth." Mom's voice came from upstairs. "Daddy won't be home for dinner, so set it for six."

"Why do I always have to set the table?" Elizabeth muttered. "You can't keep playing, Sandy. We're eating dinner. Take everything apart and put the colors in the right containers." She lined up the Play-Doh cans.

"Not this one," Sandy said, holding up a pink alien with chunky green teeth.

"Fine." Elizabeth spun away from the table.

"No," Mom said, coming into the kitchen as Elizabeth grabbed a bottle of soda out of the refrigerator. "Put it back."

Elizabeth grumbled something under her breath and put the soda back.

"Wait," Mom said. "Don't put it away. I'm going to dump it. I don't even know why we have it."

"No," Sandy begged. "I like it."

"Dad bought it," Elizabeth said, stomping into the family room. "I asked him to."

"I don't want you guys drinking soda."

"Mom," Emma said. "Live in the real world for once. Everyone drinks soda."

Mom poured the soda down the drain and walked out of the room. Sandy sat down and whispered to his alien. Emma pulled out a chair and sat next to him.

"What's your alien's name?" she asked.

"Marcus."

"Marcus!" Emma exclaimed, imitating Dory from *Finding Nemo*. "That's a nice name."

Sandy smiled slightly and stared down at the table.

"Does Marcus have a story?" Emma asked.

Sandy picked up his head. "Yes."

"Do you want to tell me?"

"Mmmm," Sandy said, glancing furtively at Maude, who was arranging stalks of heather she'd brought in from the greenhouse. "Can I just tell Emma, Maude?" he asked. "Is that okay? Will it hurt your feelings?"

Maude placed the heather in the middle of the table. "Of course you can 'just tell Emma,' Sandy. And don't worry," she added, "you won't hurt my feelings. I have to check something in the greenhouse anyway."

"Thanks," said Sandy.

Maude shut the back door after her.

"Okay," Emma said, "what's this secret story?"

"Well…," Sandy began.

"Wait." Emma glanced into the family room where Mom had disappeared following Elizabeth. "Let's sneak cookies. I'm starving, and I don't think Mom's even ordered the pizza yet."

"Okay," Sandy said.

Emma dumped Oreos onto a plate and poured two glasses of milk. "Okay," she said, sitting down and dunking a cookie.

"Well," Sandy said again, half of a milk-wet Oreo in his mouth. "Marcus got kicked off his planet when he was a baby."

"Why?"

"Uh...," Sandy said, wrinkling his eyebrows. "I don't know."

"Okay," Emma said. "Go on."

"Anyway. He got kicked off his planet when he was a baby and landed on a planet with nothing on it but a mouse."

"If there was nothing on the planet," Emma said, "what did the mouse eat?"

"Emma," Sandy protested.

"Sorry."

"Anyway. It was Marcus's job to protect the mouse."

"From what?"

"Bad guys," Sandy said derisively.

"Ah," Emma said.

"He made a house for the mouse, and brought him mouse food, and made him mouse toys, and played mouse games. But he missed his own planet that he could see every night in the sky."

"That's sad."

Sandy made a face. "Stop interrupting."

"Sorry." Emma put a whole cookie in her mouth.

"He made a super trampoline so he could bounce back and see his mom and dad. He promised the mouse that he'd come back very soon and that he'd bring him a present. The mouse said okay, but he was scared."

Emma put another wet cookie into her mouth.

"Marcus tucked the mouse in bed and jumped onto the super trampoline. He bounced home and came back in two days with lots of presents for the mouse."

Emma swallowed a fourth cookie and pushed the plate away. "What happened?" she asked.

"The mouse died. He froze and turned to mouse dust in his bed."

Emma sat up straighter. "That's kind of scary, Sandy."

"I know," her brother said, "but that's what happened. Hey! Did you eat all the cookies?"

"Shhh," Emma said, glancing at the family room doorway. "Sorry. I'll get you two more."

"Three," Sandy bargained.

"Two," Emma said.

"Three," Sandy insisted.

"One," Emma said.

"Okay, two."

The back door slammed open and Maude came inside, her face flushed.

"What?" Emma asked.

"I have to tell you something."

"Me too?" Sandy asked.

"No, Sandy," Maude said. "This is girl talk."

"I like girls," Sandy said.

"I know," Maude replied, "but this is just for girls."

"That's totally unfair, you know," Sandy said. "Mommy always says there's nothing that's just for boys or just for girls."

"Well, this is just for girls," Maude said, and she gave her brother a severe look.

"Fine," Sandy said. "But you are totally unfair." He went into the family room with his alien.

"Come into the greenhouse with me," Maude said to Emma.

Emma grabbed her jacket and followed her sister out to the greenhouse. When they got there, Maude pointed through the window.

"Look."

Turner was sitting on a bench at the edge of the woods, between the compost heap and the tool shed. His head was hidden in his hands and his car keys sat beside him. Above his head, a dirt-caked glove, a green watering can and a deflated purple ball floated in circles. The ball rose and fell as if it remembered bouncing on the driveway and didn't know it was broken now.

"I don't think he knows it's happening," Maude whispered. "He got in the car and then got out again, slammed the door and went over to that bench. He hasn't looked up or anything."

"Joe can fly," Emma admitted, the muscles of her stomach tightening until she felt she was made of stone. When Maude stared at her, Emma whispered, her voice dry, "I'm serious. The first time he kissed me he asked me to stand on his feet. When I opened my eyes, we were above the trees on the waterfall trail."

"Are you sure you were *flying*?" Maude asked. "Are you sure you're not just excited about the kissing?"

"Maude," Emma said, kicking a clump of dirt across the floor. "I'm not insane. We were flying."

Her sister sat on an overturned bucket. "Do you think I'll have a secret power when I kiss someone?" she asked quietly.

Emma smiled and sat on the floor next to her. "I don't know. Did you ever have any especially weird dreams when you were really little? Or did you ever think you could do something impossible?" She stretched out her legs. The dirty white toes of her sneakers reminded her of that bloody mushroom in her vision. A flash of sadness rose up in her chest. She'd text Joe as soon as she and Maude talked to Turner. "Turner and Joe both said they remembered being able to do stuff when they were little."

"Could you?" Maude asked. "Do anything special when you were little."

Emma shook her head. "No. But I always found people right away when we played hide and seek."

"That's not much of a superpower," Maude said.

Emma leaned against the pole that supported the glass roof. Maude stood up and looked out the window at their brother.

"Is that stuff still in the air?" Emma asked.

Maude nodded. "Let's go talk to him."

"Wait," Emma said, standing up and brushing the dirt off her jeans. "Don't startle him. The watering can might fall on his head."

Maude quietly opened the greenhouse door. Turner raised his head. The glove, the can and the flattened ball crashed down beside him, and he jerked as if someone had thrown them. He didn't look at the objects, though. Maude and Emma went outside.

"I don't want to talk to anyone," he said. "Could you guys just leave me alone?" He picked up his keys and stood.

"We have to talk to you," Maude said.

"I don't want to talk, Maude. Okay? I'm fine. I'll be fine. I just want to be alone." He stomped off toward his car.

"You were making things fly above your head," Emma called.

Turner spun. "Fuck you, Emma."

"I'm not kidding," she said. "Maude saw you first and came to get me."

Turner stood, his arms sticking out oddly as if he didn't know what to do with them.

"It isn't just you," Emma added, glancing at Maude.

"Well?" Turner prompted when she didn't elaborate. "Who else is it? Can you do something freakish? Can Maude?"

"I think I'm telepathic," Emma said quietly.

"What does that mean?" Turner asked, the angry muscle in his jaw flickering like a dying light bulb.

"Sometimes I know what people are thinking," Emma said. "And sometimes"—she blushed at the memory of seeing Joe fantasizing about her—"I can see what people are doing when I'm nowhere near them."

"Have you always been able to do that?" Turner asked.

Emma shook her head. "No."

"Well," Maude said. "She was *awesome* at hide-and-seek."

Emma kicked Maude's foot. Turner made a face.

"What the fuck does that mean?" he said.

"Nothing," Emma replied. "Maude's just jealous because she doesn't have a secret power yet."

Maude reddened and turned around.

"I'm sorry," Emma said. "I didn't mean it."

"Yes, you did," Maude said. "Or you wouldn't have said it."

"I didn't mean to hurt your feelings," Emma corrected.

"I know," Maude said.

"Can we *stop* this?" Turner asked, his eyes on fire. "Aren't you guys worried about it? Don't you want to know why this is happening? Why we can do this stuff? What it means?"

Maude gazed meaningfully at Emma, who said, "It isn't just us."

"What do you mean?" Turner asked. "Can Elizabeth or Sandy do something?" He sat back on the bench. "I thought it had something to do with coming of age or falling in love." He looked up. "Are you going out with someone?"

Emma nodded.

"Who?"

"Joe Castlellaw."

"Who the fuck is Joe Castlellaw?"

"He's new," Emma said. "He just moved here from Wolfeboro."

"The one who beat up that kid and got kicked out of school?"

"I guess," Emma said.

"You guess?" Turner repeated, his face white. "Emma, I swear you've never had a rational thought in your life. Rachel's brother told me this guy also tried to beat up Kyle Sparks in the Pop's Clam House parking lot."

"That's mean," Emma said. "And Kyle Sparks is an asshole."

"Just because you don't like him doesn't make him an asshole," Turner said. "He's the president of your class."

"So what?" Emma snapped. "Kyle Sparks is a complete and utter douche. And if you were thinking clearly you'd realize that I might have a very good reason for believing that!"

"Joe Castlellaw can fly," Maude inserted.

There was a long silence. Turner sank back onto the bench.

"When he kissed Emma," Maude continued, "they flew to the treetops in the woods."

"Is that true?" Turner asked.

"Just because I've never had a rational thought doesn't mean I can't tell the difference between fantasy and reality," Emma said.

"Does what's-his-name know about you or me?"

"He knows about me," Emma said, "kind of. I think he thinks I'm just really intuitive. I haven't told him about you yet."

"Has he always been able to fly?" Turner asked, his voice oddly high, as if he couldn't quite believe what he was saying.

"He thought he dreamed it when he was little."

"Did you think you could do anything strange when you were little?" Turner asked Maude.

"No," she admitted again. "But I've never kissed anyone, either," she added, quiet embarrassment coloring her voice like blood in water.

"Do you trust Joe?" Turner asked Emma.

"I kissed him, didn't I?" Hot indignation burned her skin.

Turner rolled his eyes. "That doesn't mean anything."

"It means something to me," she said.

"Sorry," he replied. "You're right. So...Joe. You trust him."

"Yes," Emma said.

"Ask him to come over tomorrow. Mom and Dad are taking Elizabeth and Sandy to the movies."

"Do you think we should keep this a secret from Mom and Dad?" Maude asked. "Maybe they know something."

"Yes," Turner said, standing up. "Mom..." He stopped and steadied his voice. "All Mom cares about is that I go to Yale and we just keeping living our perfect little suburban lives."

"I think we should tell Mom and Dad," Maude said.

"Well, I don't," Turner growled. "At least not until we talk to Joe."

CHAPTER TWELVE

Joe's stomach turned over as he walked up Emma's driveway the next day. She'd sounded strange on the phone last night. She wouldn't say why she wanted him to come over, just that she needed to tell him something. Joe was terrified she wanted to break up with him.

The air was chilly but the sun was warm on his back as he stood on the brick steps in front of her house. He lifted the dragonfly knocker and dropped it. After a minute, Emma opened the door. She was wearing a fitted pale blue shirt that made her look so good Joe had to take a breath. Her silvery-blonde hair poured over her bare shoulders and her shiny earrings glittered like raindrops on her neck. Joe sucked the spring air through his teeth.

"Hey," she said and smiled shyly at him.

Maybe she didn't want to break up. Maybe things were okay. Joe had no idea how to bring up their fight. Emma hadn't mentioned it at all when she called. He wanted to be respectful of what was important to her, but *this* was important to him, dammit. Shit. How did normal people do anything, get along? Work things out?

"Come on in," Emma said. She closed the door.

A shockingly beautiful girl came into the narrow hall. She was smaller than Emma, with black hair and piercing blue eyes. The girl was followed by a tall, slim guy with a ferocious, serious expression.

"This is my sister Maude," Emma said. For some perverse reason the thread of jealousy in her voice made Joe happy. "And this is my brother Turner."

Joe nodded at both of them. "Hey."

"Let's go into the living room," Turner suggested.

Turner definitely had the air of a guy accustomed to being right and getting his own way.

Emma laced her fingers through Joe's and led him into the smallish living room filled with plump, fake velvet, wine-colored furniture and chrome tables. It wasn't as cozy as the family room in the back of the house, but maybe it was better they were in a different room today. Joe sat on the couch next to Emma. Turner sat on a chair near a loudly ticking grandfather clock.

"That's a cool clock," Joe said after a few minutes of awkward silence. "At the Old Manse in Concord, Massachusetts, there's a clock that's been keeping time in the same room since the American Revolution."

Emma's pretty sister Maude beamed at him. "Hawthorne and Emerson both lived at the Old Manse."

"Yeah," Joe said, blushing a little. "I know. I've always wanted to go."

"'I have a bike,'" Emma mouthed to him.

She slipped her hand under his thigh, and he smiled at her. A string of pleasurably painful fire trailed through his blood, and Joe realized he would probably cave in two seconds if he was ever tortured. Emma had now touched him once, in front of her shy sister and fierce brother, and here he was ready to kiss her. More than kiss her, which was apparently a freaking problem.

"So," he said, exhaling and sitting up straighter on the squishy couch. "What did you want to tell me?"

Turner's phone vibrated. He looked to see who was calling and turned pink at the top of his cheeks, just below his eyes. "Just a minute," he said. He walked into the adjacent dining room. His image was reflected in the glass case of the clock.

"Oh," Maude said, jumping up. "Mom asked me to move the clothes from the washer to the dryer. Don't talk about anything without me."

She ran out of the room. Joe leaned over to Emma and kissed her, temporary impasse be damned. Emma sighed in what sounded like relief, so he kissed her more thoroughly.

He pulled away after a few moments and smiled at her just to see her smile back. "Détente for now?" he asked.

She laughed. "Détente."

Turner was still on the phone, pacing in the dining room. Emma slid her arm behind Joe's back. He moved to kiss her again but something in the clock cabinet caught his eye. At first he thought it was the pendulum or the natural workings, but then he realized that it was a reflection. A bowl of colored glass balls was floating above the dining room table, following Turner's path.

Joe turned to Emma. An expression of horror bloomed in her eyes, and it wasn't about the floating bowl. It was—

Something unfurled inside Joe's chest. He almost lost his balance. He felt like he was running, but he was still sitting on the couch. Someone taller than he was gripped his hand so painfully he cried. He panted and looked at Emma. She took his face in her hands. He pushed her away and stood up.

Turner was off the phone; he and Maude were in the doorway between the living room and the dining room. Joe was still running—no, he was being dragged through a forest by an old woman he almost recognized, like a forgotten word on the tip of his tongue. There was a baby, a baby girl, in the woman's arms. She was crying. The woman was trying to quiet her. She kept glancing back.

Hurry, she whispered to Joe. He felt her spit wet his cheek.

She stopped abruptly at a tree and put him into it. He was going to fall. Where was his *zino*? What was the woman doing?

The woman screamed. Joe felt like he was melting, like he was melting into the tree. He cried for Zino. Why wasn't he coming? Why wasn't he coming to help them?

The wood opened further. The woman put the baby girl, Edoro, into the tree. Before the tree surrounded him completely, Joe looked up and saw a pretty young woman with a fierce expression and enormous grey wings flying toward them. Then the tree swallowed him. There was more screaming. Terrified screaming. And blood. Then silence.

Joe opened his eyes. He was lying in a crumpled ball on a beige carpet with giant red and purple geometric shapes. Emma, Maude, and Turner were all kneeling around him. He sat up. Emma was white. Maude and Turner looked terrified.

"It's okay," Joe said. "It's okay. I'm fine."

"It's not okay," Emma said, gazing wildly from Maude to Turner and back to him again.

"What happened?" Maude whispered.

"Someone killed a baby girl," Emma said, choking on sobs. "And that little boy, that little boy with the wings and the blue hair, I think it was you," she said to Joe. "The old woman pushed you through the tree. She tried to push the baby through, but the woman with wings grabbed the baby and she got stuck. The baby girl was torn in half."

Emma groaned and ran from the room. Joe followed, only to hear her violently vomiting in the bathroom. He pressed his fingertips against the panels of the door, his heart pounding in his throat and the scars on his shoulder blades hot and stinging. Emma turned on the water. Maude and Turner came into the hall and stood behind him.

"Are you okay, Emma?" Maude asked, knocking.

The door flew open. Emma's face was wet and her eyes were wild. "*That's* what I saw in the hall when I first met you," she said to

Joe, her voice shaking. "But I didn't know what it was. I didn't see all of it."

"What do you mean?" Turner asked.

Emma sat on the toilet and pushed her damp hair off her face. No one said anything.

After a moment, Joe spoke. "I already told you," he said. "My mom told me strange stories and dark fairy tales when I was little. Our house was filled with paintings of monstrous trees and dying children until she threw them all away." This was a lie. His mom didn't throw any of her work away. But he didn't want Emma to see those paintings. He didn't want anyone to see them. He would burn them. He backed up against the wall in the hall.

"I don't have the same kind of normal, happy family you do," Joe said. "I told you that. I didn't know any other kids until I went to kindergarten. I didn't know anyone else at all. It was just my mom and me. Forever."

"We're not normal, either," Maude said. "You saw what Turner can do, didn't you?"

Turner reddened.

"There's something else," Emma said. "After the woman pushed you through the tree, a man came. He moved you through another tree and left you crying in the woods."

Joe stared at her. "I've gotta go."

"Wait!" Emma cried out, following Joe down the hall. Turner and Maude were behind her.

Joe spun around. "Listen," he said, his voice thin but measured. "I don't know what's going on exactly, and I guess you wanted me to come over so we could talk about...I don't know...so we could talk about *being different*, but I can't stay. I have to go."

"Don't you want to know?" Turner asked. "Don't you want to know why this is happening?"

"Of course I want to know," Joe said. "But what do you think? Do you think we're gonna put our heads together in your living room and come up with the answer? Nothing that's happened to me since I met Emma makes any fucking sense."

Emma sucked in a mouthful of air.

"I don't mean it like that," Joe said. "Shit. I don't know what I mean. But I do know that staying here and talking to you—any of you—is not going to help. I'm going home."

CHAPTER THIRTEEN

That night, Joe went in to pick up a pizza while his mom sat in the car. His ears were ringing and his heart throbbed like infected flesh. He tried to disappear, to fool himself into believing that he didn't exist and that nothing was real. If only that were true.

Stacy and Izzy were sitting outside the Pizza Oven, sharing headphones and singing loudly together.

Stacy burst out laughing when she saw him. "Izzy *loves* this song," she said.

"Shut up," Izzy snapped, but her eyes lit up and she looked prettier than she usually did.

"What's up with you, Joe?" Stacy asked, scrunching up her beautiful face and scrutinizing him. "You look like a hot zombie."

Izzy laughed. Joe felt like he was going to fall over.

"Typical shitty Sunday," he said. "You know," he added weakly.

"Are things okay with you and Emma?" Izzy asked. When Stacy arched a perfect eyebrow, Izzy added, "She's not as high maintenance as you think," to her, as if she were selling Stacy a used car with one or two minor problems. "She's reactive. And sometimes—well, *often*—she says things she shouldn't. But she's funny and smart. And loyal," Izzy added, blushing slightly.

"No worries," Joe said, hoping he sounded better than he felt. "Things are fine between Emma and me."

Stacy took a sip of her energy drink. "Emma *is* sweet," she agreed. "In her own quirky way."

Izzy beamed at Stacy like she'd just come up with the solution to reverse climate change; she seemed half in love with the girl. Joe guessed most people were. Stacy Keeler was most people's idea of perfect. Just not his.

"Do you want a garlic knot?" Stacy asked Joe, holding up a thick white plate. "They're a little cold but they're awesome."

"No, thanks," Joe said. "My mom's waiting in the car and I have to get the pizza."

He cringed as Stacy and Izzy leaned over to check out his mom. She was staring straight ahead, her straggly hair hanging in her face, a deer-in-the-headlights look in her pale eyes.

"Hey, does your mom volunteer at the museum?" Izzy asked. "I think I saw her once when I was there for an NCL thing."

"Yeah," Joe said. "Sometimes. She's an amateur painter." He hoped Stacy didn't remember seeing his mom's sketches in the library that day. "But she works from home as a medical transcriptionist," he added, as if that piece of information would explain the messy hair and vacant expression.

"My mom used to volunteer at the museum," Izzy said. "Now she volunteers at the thrift shop."

Joe smiled stiffly. "I've gotta go," he said. "See you in school tomorrow."

"See you," Stacy said. Izzy grinned at him and put Stacy's headphones back on.

Joe's mom chattered idly at him in the car on the way home, and in the apartment, and while they ate. Joe listened and responded appropriately. The pizza sat like a wet shoe in his stomach. He'd tried to ask if she knew anything about his real dad, but even saying, "I have a question," brought on something like a panic attack in her and Joe had to make up a question about the history of Outsider Art so she could talk herself out of it.

After dinner his mother sat on the couch and opened a shiny blue hardcover with a one-word title in raised gold lettering. She sighed and blew on her orange blossom tea.

"I'm going to read on the steps outside," Joe said, walking toward the door with his biology text and a notebook.

"Isn't it too dark?" his mom asked, glancing up at him.

"The parking lot light is close to the steps," he said. "It's brighter out there than it is in here."

"Do you need a jacket?"

"I'm warm enough."

Joe sat on the white-painted steps and laid the book and notebook beside him. His stomach churned as he took his phone out of his pocket. It didn't matter that no one could see him calling Emma, he was totally self-conscious about what he looked like and sounded like sitting in the harsh shine of the parking lot light.

The shaking sensation in his stomach expanded to his skin as Emma's phone rang several times.

"Hello?" she said.

Joe inhaled quickly. The scent of wet asphalt and garbage and cold spring air filled his mouth.

"Hey, Emma," he said. "It's Joe."

"I know," she said.

"About today—"

"That vision with the baby and you was so horrible," Emma interrupted.

Joe's clenched his teeth. "I saw the baby girl. And I saw an old woman. We were running. I didn't see what happened to the baby." He shivered, trying not to remember the screams and the blood. "The old woman put me in a tree and I moved through it. I don't remember anything else."

"You were crying and the man picked you up," Emma said. "He put you in another tree and moved through it with you. The next thing I saw was you crying on the ground and the man walking away."

Joe dug his fingers of his left hand into the soft wood of the steps and pressed the phone to his cheek. Was the man his father? Why had he left Joe alone in the woods? And what happened to the baby girl? It was all so impossible to believe, and more impossible not to. Joe stared into the parking lot. The couple with the little black dog they dressed up in costumes pulled into their spot. Joe watched them take the dog, who was wearing a red sweater, out of the car. The car lock clicked and beeped, and the couple walked into their apartment.

"Tell me about your mom's paintings," Emma said.

"What?" Joe said. "Why? What do my mom's paintings have to do with anything?"

"She must know something. You said the paintings were all about murdered babies and monstrous trees. It can't be a coincidence."

"Are you saying my mom had something to do with all of this?" Joe asked. "You don't know her. You can't say that. She's strange but she's not violent. Or cruel. You don't know her."

"Joe," Emma said. She sounded sympathetic. It would have been easier if she was angry then he could have been angry back. It was so much fucking easier to be angry.

"Joe," Emma said again, and something cracked inside him. He heard it, like a shell of bone breaking away from his heart or from some part of his brain. Emma felt it too, he knew she did, and somehow that made things better.

"I saw that baby girl torn apart inside that tree." Emma stopped and caught her breath. "I don't think your mom had anything to do with it. You don't have to ask her anything. You don't have to tell her anything. But maybe if we look at the paintings together we can figure something out. You want to know what happened and why, don't you?"

"Of course I do," Joe said, his voice strained. "I don't have any of the paintings—I don't know what she did with them—but I do have the sketches. They're studies of what became the painting. I'll bring them to school tomorrow."

The hanging silence seemed to dissolve and recreate all the muscles in Joe's arms and legs.

"Are you okay?" he asked.

"No," Emma said. "But neither are you."

The sadness in her voice pulled Joe out of himself and across town to wherever she was. He felt a little bit better.

"I have to go," she said.

"Okay," he whispered. "See you tomorrow."

She hung up the phone, and Joe sat on the steps until his mother called him in.

CHAPTER FOURTEEN

Mondays Emma didn't see Joe until the end of the day. He gave her the sketches and said he'd come over after school to talk about them. He hardly looked at her.

All day Emma tried to make herself believe none of it was real, that she'd somehow imagined it because of her telepathy, or whatever the hell it was if it was fake, but since she met Joe she'd lost the ability to lie to herself. And last night on the phone it seemed something happened to him. At the time, Emma thought he'd broken or dropped something. She'd thought she'd heard a cracking sound, but later she realized she'd somehow felt it. She didn't know what to do. She was tired and overwhelmed. She wasn't ready for this. Whatever it was, she wasn't ready for it.

An unfamiliar car was in the driveway when Emma got home from school. In the pink haze of the setting sun the car was the color of pond scum, but at a second glance it morphed into a retro St. Patrick's Day green.

Emma entered the house and slammed the front door behind her. Two faces snapped to attention in the living room.

"Sorry," Emma said sullenly, stopping in the doorway.

Her mother smiled. "That's okay, honey."

Mom's hair was brushed and shiny. She was wearing lipstick and eye makeup and PTA–meeting-ready, super-volunteer-mom clothes. WTF? Did Mom even own clothes like that?

"This is…" Her mom's mouth moved as if she were saying a name but no sound came out. Or maybe Emma didn't care enough to listen. Certainly neither Mom nor the smiling man in the corner seemed to notice.

"There's a developer trying to buy Concordia Park," Mom said. "He wants to build McMansions on the land. Mister"—the name slipped away again—"has taken up a petition to stop it. Although," Mom added, smiling almost flirtatiously at the stranger, whose pale, liquid-soft features made Emma think of important causes and no girlfriends, "apparently the developer is smart enough to offer something back."

"Oh," Emma said, trying to find an escape hatch in the monologue.

"He's offered to donate a considerable amount of money to the schools, and to set up a scholarship fund for all eligible town kids." Mom turned to smile again at Mr. Squishy-Face.

"Uh," Emma said, "nice to meet you." She didn't look at the man and zipped out of the room before her mom could say anything else she didn't care about.

"Will you check the chicken, honey?" Mom called airily after her—like Emma checked chicken every day. Whatever that even meant.

"Okay," Emma shouted back from the door between the kitchen and family room.

Joe had texted her on the walk home: His mom needed him to help her with something after school and he wouldn't be able to come over today. Emma realized Joe didn't want to come back to her house. Not yet, anyway. Maybe it would be better if she looked at the sketches without him first. She'd decided to show them to Maude. Maude knew about art and poetry and symbols, so maybe she'd be able to help. Maybe this was all just some freaky nightmarish story Joe's mom told him when he was little that had zapped into her head.

"Where's Maude?" Emma asked Elizabeth, who was frantically texting from a chair in the kitchen.

"I don't know." Her sister muttered something else at the screen, her face a stiff mask of concentration.

"What's going on?" Emma asked.

"I can't tell you," Elizabeth whispered in a froggy voice. "It's private."

"I don't mean with your stupid friends."

Elizabeth's head popped up, her brown eyes shiny and sharp.

"Sorry," Emma said. "They're not stupid. I meant, what's going on with Mom and the weird hair and the lipstick and the man in the living room?"

"I don't know," Elizabeth repeated impatiently, her fingers poised above the phone and her lips moving while she silently read a particularly long, vehement message.

"You can get in trouble for mean texts, you know, Elizabeth," Emma warned. "I hope you're being careful."

"I...am not...mean," Elizabeth said, separating every bit with an emphatic breath. "I am helping. I'm saving the situation. I didn't make it."

"Okay, okay," Emma said. "Do you know where Maude is?"

"I told you already. I don't know."

A sizzling pop sounded, and the scent of chicken came from the oven.

"What does 'check the chicken' mean?" Emma asked.

"I don't know," Elizabeth said, not looking away from her phone. "Make sure it's not burning or something."

"Oh," Emma said, feeling stupid.

"Emma." Her sister spoke in the slow, steady voice she reserved for babysitting Sandy or showing off for unfamiliar adults. "Would you please leave me alone? This is important and I can't concentrate with you asking so many questions."

"Sorry," Emma said, trying not to smile. "I'll go."

She went and opened the oven door. The chicken was white and dead-looking. It wasn't burning, but it didn't look edible. She slammed the door.

"The chicken looks fine," she called out toward the living room, staring absentmindedly through the window over the sink. The sun fell between black branches. Red light spread like spilt blood behind the unfamiliar car.

"Thanks, honey," Mom called back.

What was up with her? She never dressed up for anyone, not even Dad.

Emma walked back to the living room. Her mom beamed at her, all shiny red lipstick and smooth hair.

"Yes, honey?" Mom said expectantly, like she had all the time in the world to listen to her oldest daughter.

"Nothing," Emma said. "I was just wondering…"

Inside Mom's glossy, brain-dead face a second face quivered as if trying to get out. This face, while clearly still her mother's, was pale and unsmiling, with no makeup and stringy hair.

"I mean," Emma continued, shaken, "did…did you want me to do anything else?"

"No thanks, honey," Mom sang back, all bright colors and empty thoughts again.

The man in the corner spoke. Mom's other face appeared for a second like a changed channel. Emma heard her mother breathe out something, but the words fell apart in the air. And the man looked different somehow. Maybe Emma wasn't paying attention before. He was sort of handsome in a young-ish, Morrissey-ish kind of way. Emma's fingertips felt cold.

The man smiled slowly and softly at her. He was hotter than Morrissey and younger than she'd thought, she realized. Emma smiled back. She felt suddenly pretty. Joe thought she was pretty.

"Emma." Mom's voice sliced through her ear. "Would you set the table for six?"

"Uh," Emma said, glancing at the man in the corner who looked so nice. Maybe he could help her understand what was going on. "Sure."

Her mother stood up. "Thank you, honey."

"Uh, you're welcome."

Turner's car pulled into the driveway. Emma opened the front door and went outside, hoping Maude was with him.

She was. She was waiting for Sandy to get out of Turner's car.

"Hey," Emma said, running up to her sister.

Maude smiled. "Hey."

Turner stopped and stared intently at the strange, green car. He glanced at the house then opened the passenger door and took something out of the front seat. "Let's go in through the back," he said, grabbing Sandy's hand.

"Why?" Sandy asked.

"Because the path is muddy and someone's here. Mom won't want the floor to get dirty."

"Okay," Sandy said. "What's that?" he added, picking at Turner's fist.

"Nothing," Turner said, pulling his hand away.

"Can I see it?"

"No."

"Is it a ball?" Sandy asked, trying to peek between his brother's long fingers.

"Yes," Turner said impatiently.

"Can I see it?"

"No! Leave me alone, Sandy!" Turner snapped, shoving the thing into his pants pocket and going inside.

"How's your hero project coming?" Maude asked, leading Sandy away from Turner and into the yard.

"Really great," Sandy said. His hero project was a comic book he'd made with a half-man/half-shark hero.

Emma caught up with them. "Joe gave me his mother's drawings," she said to Maude.

"What?" Maude asked, but she wasn't looking at Emma or Sandy; she was staring at the house.

"Joe gave me his mother's drawings," Emma repeated. "What are you looking at?"

Maude dragged her attention from the living room window, fixing her eyes to Emma's only when they were face-to-face. For an instant, a shimmer of air just at the surface of Maude's skin swelled and contracted like a gossamer heart. "Why did Joe give you his mother's drawings?" she asked.

"I thought they could help us figure out what's going on," Emma said. "Are you okay?"

"Yes," Maude said, still distracted. "How could his mom's drawings help?"

"What is *up* with you?" Emma asked, craning her neck to see if Mom was doing something odd in the living room with the Morrissey dude.

"Nothing," Maude said, and she shook herself, tossing her silky black hair over her shoulders. "Nothing. I was just thinking about something in the poem I'm reading now."

"What?" Emma said.

"It's a line." Maude paused. "A beautiful line in 'The Eve of St. Agnes' when Porphyro is trying to convince Madeline to run away with him. Do you want to hear it?"

"Uh, okay," Emma said.

"'Hark!'" Maude crooned in her lovely, airy voice, "''Tis an elfin-storm from faery land/ Of haggard seeming, but a boon indeed:'" She smiled at Emma. "Isn't that beautiful?"

"Er, yes," Emma said. "It's beautiful. Will you look at Joe's mom's drawings with me? I thought maybe you could see something in them that I wouldn't notice."

"Sure," Maude agreed, her face still flushed from reciting the line from the poem. "Where are they?"

"I'll go get them," Emma said. "Wait for me on the bench under the climbing tree."

"Okay." Maude walked off for the bench.

Emma went inside to get her backpack. Morrissey was back to the squishy-faced man. He was listening intently to Mom, who hadn't moved from her perch on the edge of the couch. It looked like his eyes were on her, but Emma glanced again and it seemed that his attention was fixed on Maude outside. Then for a flash, like a subliminal message in an old commercial, he became a sixteen-year-old boy.

As Emma walked by, he smiled at her. Mom watched him like a dog waiting for a door to open. Emma went outside. A part of her knew it was weird for someone's face to change but something about the man in the living room made her feel that everything was okay. She felt oddly happy when she saw him, actually, and after the stress of the past few days odd happiness was a relief, and she welcomed it.

Emma sat on the bench next to Maude and opened the drawings on their joined knees like a treasure map. They were beautiful in a strange way. Maude said they were like something by Edvard Munch. She told Emma about a beautiful Munch painting of a vampire with long red hair and a swallowing mouth.

In one of Joe's mom's drawings, inside the milky-brown body of a blue-haired little boy, a thread of light quivered like a translucent nerve. Emma ran her finger over it. She felt an opening and a breath of cool air, as if a tiny, invisible cavern waited beneath the surface of the paper. The vibration from the light entered her skin like a gentle poison, and she heard an unfamiliar voice. A man was speaking hurriedly to someone. A little boy was singing to a baby who was babbling back at him. A woman told them to be quiet and wait. The man continued; his low, beautiful voice blooming in Emma's ear as if he were speaking from inside her head.

Once you, Sfodro and Edoro are safely in the Otherworld, wait for me. If the Masevo follow you, contact me immediately.

Emma felt the woman nod as if she herself were nodding and listening.

The man sighed and picked up one of the children—the boy—and kissed him. The boy laughed and squirmed and said he didn't want to be quiet anymore because it was boring.

The Aythentia cannot ever find my children, Edafio, the man said. *Do you understand what I'm asking of you?*

Emma felt the woman nod, and the scene switched:

The man, his heart broken, was clutching the weeping boy to his chest. He kissed the boy a hundred times and placed him on the ground in a forest. The boy cried and raised his arms and begged to be picked up again. Emma had seen this before, yesterday when Joe remembered.

A young woman with thin red hair and an expression of ferocious solitude in her pale eyes knelt on the ground next to the crying child. The boy had pale, pale blue fuzz for hair and gray wings folded inward so that they looked like giant larvae on his back. She picked him up and seemed to love him instantly, the way a mother or a father can instantly love a newborn or adopted child, the way love can be *yes* at first sight. The way, even now, Emma knew she loved Joe.

The man reappeared without the woman seeming to notice him. He held his hands above her head and a series of images like pages in a children's book fell into the woman's waiting brain. She kissed the little boy and spoke softly to him, carrying him down the hill and out of sight.

Emma looked up at Maude to share her vision of the little boy and the baby girl and the broken-hearted man, but her sister wasn't paying attention to the drawing or to Emma; she was staring at the living room window with an expression of dazed wonder.

"Are you okay?" Emma asked, touching her knee.

Startled, Maude jerked slightly. "Yes," she said, glancing at Emma before looking at the house again. "Yes. I am okay."

Emma held the drawing tighter against her lap and leaned forward. "What the heck are you staring at?"

Maude sighed and smiled slightly at nothing, gazing straight ahead as though there were someone else right there. She turned slowly. "Did you see anything?" she asked Emma.

"No," Emma said emphatically, scanning the yard. "What do you see?"

Maude colored slightly. "I meant in the drawings. Did you have a vision or something?"

"Oh," Emma said. "Yeah. I did." But Maude's attention was already back on the house. "I'll tell you about it later, though. When you're not so enamored of the freaking living room window."

Her tone was harsher than she intended. Maude didn't even notice. Maybe this was how Maude felt whenever she was trying to confide in Emma and Emma wasn't listening.

No wonder Maude didn't like it. It sucked to feel invisible.

CHAPTER FIFTEEN

The next day after school Emma wandered though French's, the office supply store, waiting for Joe. He didn't want to talk about anything in school so she'd agreed to meet him here. French's was the only store in town that let kids walk around unattended. Every other place was terrified of shoplifters. That was the thing about the suburbs, people were always terrified. They drove giant cars as if they lived in a war zone and needed literal tons of protection. The police logs were filled with entries for FRIGHTENED PERSON. People who had nothing to be afraid of were afraid of fucking everything.

Emma pushed what she had to tell Joe to the back of her head. Maude had gone straight to her room after dinner. She never asked Emma about the drawing or the vision or anything. Emma felt unexpectedly alone with all of this. It seemed the more she knew about Joe and the mystery of their powers, the less she understood. What and where was the Otherworld? Who or what were the Masevo? And where was Joe's father now?

And why was Maude ignoring her? She spun the rack of idiotic, sappy greeting cards made by local artists and swore under her breath.

"Emma?"

The voice felt like a soft kiss on her ear. Its familiar sound made her both sleepy and happy, like when she was really little and passed out in the car. Her dad carried her to bed and her feet never touched the ground.

She turned around to see the guy who looked like Morrissey.

"Hey," she said.

"Hey." He smiled. "You have something on your face," he said, in a voice like clean sheets and summer air.

He brushed his thumb over Emma's mouth. Her spine dissolved into butterfly wings and she closed her eyes. She felt *awesome*, like she was in warm water she could breathe in. Maude would love to be able to breathe underwater. Maude was awesome. Everything Emma knew and loved about Maude danced in front of her closed eyes like visible, animated secrets. Emma felt her mouth move. Maybe she was talking. Or singing. God, she hoped she wasn't singing. Then Joe's beautiful face flashed in front of her. She was *so* in love with him. He was like her other half, like in that song, "The Origin of Love" from *Hedwig & the Angry Inch*. Joe was part of her. And she was part of him.

Emma took a deep breath and felt a tiny jolt, as if she just realized she was falling and caught herself. When she opened her eyes, Morrissey-dude was still smiling at her. Did he go to Dearborn? Maude should definitely meet him.

"See you," he said, and left the store.

"Bye," Emma said, watching him leave. She sucked in air through her teeth. He'd smelled good, like boyish flowers, if that were possible. The door closed behind him with a sound like a gasp, and a wave of guilt crushed Emma's chest.

"You're lucky Joe isn't here," Izzy Peccant's voice piped through the cloud in Emma's head. "You were practically kissing that guy. Who is he?"

"I don't know," Emma said. She only been drunk once—with Izzy, actually—and this is how she'd felt the next day, slow and thick on the inside. "A friend of my mom's. I think."

"A friend of your mom's?" Izzy repeated. "He looked barely sixteen."

"Well, he came to our house yesterday to talk about open space," Emma said. "I wasn't kissing him, I was talking to him. Did it look like I was kissing him?"

"Yes."

"Well, I wasn't," Emma said. "Maybe it just looked that way from where you were standing."

"Maybe," Izzy said dubiously. She flipped through some neon-colored poster board.

"What are you doing?" Emma asked. She was anxious to forget about the stranger. God, what if Joe *had* been here?

"I need a tri-fold for my Italian project."

"Oh," Emma said.

"Remember when we had that secret club in Richardson Park?" Izzy asked, breaking the moment of awkward silence.

"Yes," Emma said. In third grade she and Izzy had invented a secret language. They'd left notes for one another in certain trees and under specific rocks all over town. They'd even made a map that gave every place in town an alternate identity.

"Do you ever sometimes look for a note anymore?" Izzy asked, scrunching her face and glancing up from a lime-green poster board.

"Sometimes," Emma answered. She felt suddenly sad. Being with Joe was amazing but Emma really missed Izzy. She missed talking to her. She missed hanging out with her. In the months since Izzy friend-dumped her for Stacy they had hardly spoken, except in the halls. There they'd only been polite.

Izzy smiled. "I think Joe Castlellaw is perfect for you."

"Thanks," Emma said.

Izzy blinked and pushed her bracelets up her arm. The intricate web of scars was hardly visible anymore. Emma was the only person who knew Izzy cut herself, and she only learned after Izzy already stopped. At the time Emma blamed Izzy's parents for forcing their daughter to be exactly like everyone else, but now she wasn't so sure. Izzy seemed so much happier now that she was best friends with Stacy. Maybe Izzy had wanted to be like everyone else and be popular all along.

Emma rubbed the toe of her sneaker on the thick grey carpet. Izzy just stood there.

"So...," Emma said. "What's up? Is your family still going to North Carolina this summer?"

Answering the question, Izzy clicked backed into the girl she had become, the girl who fit in, who wore the right clothes and listened to the right music and crushed on the right boys. Emma smiled and tried to listen, keeping her eye on the door for Joe as Izzy chattered on in that lazy, half-growl/half-baby voice that Stacy and all the other popular girls had perfected in eighth grade. Izzy kept talking, rolling her eyes and moving her hands excitedly but Emma realized she wasn't hearing anything. Instead she suddenly saw Izzy crying in her room with music blaring in the background so her parents wouldn't notice. Floating all around her were images of Stacy looking beautiful, laughing with her boyfriend, swimming with her sisters.

Oh, Emma thought with a flood of prickling empathy. Now she understood. Here was one thing Izzy couldn't handle or fix on her own.

She took Izzy's hand. "Let's go outside." She pulled her onetime friend out of the store.

"Where are we going?" Izzy asked nervously.

"To the park," Emma said, glancing up the street for cars. "No one will be there now. We can sit in the treehouse."

"I don't want to sit in the treehouse," Izzy said, pulling away. "And there are tons of little kids in the park."

"Then sit and talk with me here," Emma said, pointing to a bench honoring her old babysitter and Mr. Norway's best friend, Agatha Moore. Agatha had been the first female selectman in Warwick and a member of the garden club for fifty years. Dad and Mom, but especially Dad, was so sad when she died, even though she seemed a thousand years old.

Izzy crossed thin arms and glared at her stubbornly. "I don't want to sit."

"You obviously want to tell me something," Emma said.

"No, I don't," Izzy replied, slipping her foot in and out of her very cute shoe.

A Jeep filled with noisy, bad-music-loving seniors screamed past. One of the kids in the car was Stacy's boyfriend, Doug. Emma watched Izzy's delicate features chill.

"Kyle Sparks drives way too fast," she said after a moment. "His parents let him do whatever he wants." The Jeep disappeared around the corner and Izzy sighed. "Didn't Turner break up with Rachel Revere?" she asked, turning back to Emma and talking in a normal voice again. "I saw them outside the auditorium the other day. He was holding her hand, but they both looked really upset."

"I don't know what's going on with them," Emma said. "Things have been shitty at my house. Turner won't talk to anyone about it."

"Why not?" Izzy asked.

"Didn't I tell you…? Oh yeah," Emma said, remembering. "We weren't really talking then."

"We haven't been talking too much at all," Izzy said softly. "Since I started hanging out with Stacy."

"That's not my fault," Emma said.

"I never said it was."

Izzy sat on the bench, blocking Agatha's plaque. Emma climbed up on a big rock nearby and pulled her knees to her chest.

"Did you draw those smiley faces on your sneakers?" Izzy asked, pointing to Emma's shoes.

"No," Emma answered, looking at her shoes and smiling. "Joe drew them because I look at my feet all the time."

Izzy smiled and bit her lip. "That's sweet."

Why don't you just *tell* me? Emma thought. But her friend didn't.

"So, what happened?" Izzy asked, watching two old people have a fight in front of Pop's Clam House across the street.

"When?"

"With Turner and Rachel."

"Oh," Emma said. Where was Joe? Would he find her out here? She'd been watching the door at French's but he hadn't shown up. "Turner got Rachel pregnant."

"Oh my God," Izzy said.

"Rachel had an abortion and Turner broke up with her."

"*He* broke up with *her*?" Izzy said.

"It's a long, crazy, only-in-the-Turnerverse story," Emma said.

"Why didn't you tell me?" Izzy asked.

"You started hanging out with Stacy," Emma said. "I started hanging out with Joe." Where was he? Had something happened? Had he seen her with that kid in French's?

"I'm in love with Stacy," Izzy said in a voice like a crushed flower.

"I know," Emma replied.

"How did you know?" Izzy asked.

"You never stop talking about her. And just now, when you said Joe was perfect for me, I realized you wished Stacy liked you."

Izzy's lip quivered. "I can't help it," she whispered. "I've never liked a girl before."

"You've never really liked anyone. Not *that* way. Have you?" Emma asked.

"No," Izzy admitted. "Not really. Maybe I just didn't want to like a girl."

"Izzy," Emma said, "just because your mom thinks—"

"It's not about my mom!" Izzy said. "I'm not like you, Emma. I don't want to be different. I don't want to stand out. I want to be like everyone else. I don't want people I don't know to hate me!" She leaned back, out of breath.

"Maybe you just have a girl-crush on Stacy," Emma said. "She's pretty and popular, and smart and nice."

Izzy rolled her eyes. "It isn't a girl-crush. I had a girl-crush on you."

"You did?" Emma asked, flattered and weirded out at the same time.

"Yes. But I never liked you the way I like Stacy."

"Hey!" Emma said.

"Well, you didn't like *me* that way, did you?" Izzy asked.

"No. But…"

"Emma," Izzy said, throwing a magnolia petal that had fallen on the bench at her. "God. Stop being so needy. Joe likes you. You don't need me to like you."

Emma crushed the petal with her toe, leaving a wet smear on the grey stone.

"Anyway," Izzy said, standing up. "It's useless. Stacy's not gay. She loves Doug even though Doug's stupid. And I can't tell her because she'd never want to hang out with me again."

"Maybe she would."

Izzy rolled her eyes again. "Would you?"

"Yes," Emma said. "I stayed friends with Pete Martin even after he told me he liked me."

"Out of pity," Izzy said. "You didn't want to hurt his feelings. I don't want that. I don't want a pity friendship."

Emma smeared the crushed petal more into the ground.

"Don't tell anyone," Izzy said.

"I won't."

"I mean it," Izzy said. "No one. Not even Turner. And certainly not Joe."

"Why not Joe?"

"He's friends with Stacy," Izzy said.

"Okay," Emma agreed.

"Well," Izzy said. "I'd better go." She smiled at Emma. "Thanks."

Emma smiled back. "You're welcome."

Izzy and she were friends again. That was something.

CHAPTER SIXTEEN

Joe stood outside the big bay window of French's Office Supply, half-excited, half-terrified to hear what Emma had to say. Had she actually discovered something just by looking at his mother's sketches? Joe had been around them for years and never saw anything beyond a kind of gruesome beauty. But Emma had seen his memory of running with that woman in the woods. Maybe she'd see something in the drawings Joe had never noticed.

Another question surfaced: Could the man Emma saw in her vision be his real father? Was he still alive? If he was, why hadn't he ever tried to contact Joe?

A woman with two little kids and a baby in a stroller came up the street. "Can you get that door for me?" she asked. The kids wrapped their arms around her thighs and stared shyly at Joe.

"Sure," he said. "Do you need help with the stroller?"

"No, thanks." She backed through the door with the little kids dangling like monkeys from her legs. "I can get it."

"Okay," Joe said.

As the woman bumped the stroller up the single step behind her, the pink-faced baby woke and smiled droolingly at Joe. He smiled back and glanced into the store. Emma stood in the center aisle, talking to a guy around her age, maybe a tiny bit older. She was flirting with him. The guy leaned close to Emma and ran his thumb over her mouth. Emma closed her eyes then grinned and blushed and talked rapidly to him, while the guy, who looked like a brainy punk rock star, listened and smiled.

Joe stepped back.

The guy came out of the store. He stopped when he saw Joe, and for a second his features shimmered as if he were underwater looking up at the sun.

"Hey," the guy said. He started to walk past Joe then turned around and stared so hard that Joe felt physically invaded. He moved closer, and Joe stood up taller.

In the broad daylight the guy looked less like a teenage rock star and more like an ordinary teenager. He was shorter than Joe, thin and intense, with straight, light brown hair and blue eyes.

"Do you want something?" Joe asked, when the kid just stood there staring at him. He did *not* get a good vibe from him, and not because he'd flirted with Emma. Maybe it was because his mom was so paranoid, or maybe it was because he'd spent so much time observing other people rather than interacting with them, but Joe always knew when someone was dangerous. This guy was dangerous, and the longer he just stood there staring the angrier Joe became.

"You're Sfodro Vatic," the guy said at last.

"Uh, no," Joe said. "I'm Joe Castlellaw."

The kid smiled and his cocky face went slack for a minute. Maybe he was wasted. Whatever he was, and whoever he was, Joe just wanted him to get the hell out of his face.

"Sorry," the kid said, in the least-convincing apology Joe had ever heard. "I thought you were someone else."

"Who are you?" Joe asked, trying hard to stay cool and only partially succeeding.

The kid didn't seem to give a shit how Joe acted. "Gryphon Venti."

"Do you go to Henry Dearborn?"

"No," Gryphon said. "You're Emma Mathews's..." He hesitated, as if he couldn't think of the right word. "You're her boyfriend."

"So?" Joe said, feeling his composure drain away. He kept seeing the kid touching Emma's mouth and Emma grinning back at him.

"That explains a lot," the boy said.

Joe raised his fist to hit Gryphon Venti in his douche-y face, but something happened. In place of Gryphon's face, Joe saw a succession of other faces: Sean Bolton begging Joe to stop hitting him, Sean's mother crying hysterically, his own mom's face when she picked him up at school that day.

Gryphon turned away and walked down the street. Joe started to follow, but the sleigh bells on French's door chimed and the sound of Emma's voice softly arguing with another girl spilled onto the sidewalk. Joe retreated into the alcove of the drugstore. He watched Emma and Izzy Peccant walk to a small park bench at the far end of the street.

When he looked back for Gryphon, the kid was gone.

* * *

After Izzy left it was only a few minutes before Joe called Emma's phone. He apologized for not showing up. He said his mother wouldn't let him out of the house and he'd sneak away as soon as she went to bed. They would meet in the greenhouse at Emma's at eleven. Joe's voice sounded weird, but he said his mom was right there.

Emma walked home. She stood at the screen door. Dad was in the kitchen talking on the phone. He glanced at her, and his hurried smile shifted into a concerned-Dad face. Caught under the microscope—her least favorite place to be—Emma dropped her gaze, but when she looked up again Dad was holding his hands to his eyes like pretend binoculars, the way he did when she was little and he helped her look for what was making her sad. He smiled then returned his attention to his conversation on the phone.

Emma made a decision. "Hey, Dad, can I talk to you about something when you're done?" she asked, walking into the kitchen and opening the refrigerator. Maybe he would understand. Maybe there was a family history of strange phenomena. An old psychic aunt. A telekinetic great-great-grandfather. Something easy that would explain everything.

He nodded.

Emma grabbed a raspberry yogurt smoothie and glanced into the family room. Sandy was sitting on the floor frantically coloring a monster in the comic book he was working on. Elizabeth was on the computer. Turner was sitting on the couch doing homework. *Why is everyone in the family room?* she wondered. Turner hated to work with other people around.

"Hi, honey," Dad said, hanging up the phone and clearly changing his mind. "I'm a little busy. Can whatever you want to talk about wait until after dinner?"

Dad never said no if any of them wanted to talk. Not meeting Emma's gaze, he washed out a coffee mug in the sink then rubbed his face with both hands.

"Who were you talking to?" Emma asked.

"No one," Dad said. "Someone from the university. I'm going to take a few vacation days. I needed to arrange for someone to cover my classes."

Emma licked off her cold raspberry-yogurt mustache. "Are you okay? Your face looks funny."

"I'm fine," he said.

"You're lying," Emma argued. She smiled so he wouldn't be pissed, but he didn't seem to notice. The plastic smoothie bottle was freezing her hand. Emma put the smoothie on the table and breathed hot air onto her palm. "Is Mom okay?"

"Mom's fine."

A low hum like a song she couldn't quite hear resonated from the floor and from the ceiling, falling like snow around Emma's ears. "Do you hear that?" she asked.

Dad turned his head and listened. "Hear what?"

"It sounds like someone singing," Emma said. "But I can't tell what song it is. Did Elizabeth leave her speakers on in her room again?"

"No." Dad crossed his arms and leaned against the counter.

Emma listened. The song dissolved like salt in hot water. A new sound replaced it, a sound Dad could surely hear: Maude pacing in her room, loudly reciting that poem, "'…and half anguished he threw thereon a cloth of woven crimson, gold and jet—'"

"That's your fault," Emma said, raising her head to indicate Maude's room above the kitchen.

"What?" Dad asked, his voice thin and distracted.

"It's nothing bad," Emma said. "I just meant Maude reciting poetry so loudly in her room. You guys didn't exactly prepare us for life with regular people." She took a huge swallow of smoothie. It dropped into her throat like chilled glue.

"When does Maude recite poetry?" Dad asked, his voice still strained.

"Can't you hear her?" Emma said. "She's upstairs reciting 'The Eve of Saint Somebody.'"

Dad's shock thumped hard into Emma's chest, but then a sound like animals fighting came from the front hall.

"What the hell?" Emma said.

Dad pushed her into the family room and closed the pocket door Emma hadn't seen since she was little. He was on the other side.

"What the hell is going on?" she asked.

Turner was standing in front of Sandy, listening to the terrible noise. "Where's Maude?" he said.

"In her room," Emma answered.

Elizabeth sat beside Sandy, who had started to talk to himself, and put her arm around him.

"I thought she was with you," Turner said.

"Why would she be with me?" Emma asked.

Turner pushed Emma out of the way and grabbed the pullout handle on the pocket door, but the door wouldn't open. He pulled on it and kicked it. It didn't move. "Shit!"

The fighting noise grew louder; then a huge crash like breaking glass silenced everything.

CHAPTER SEVENTEEN

Five hours passed. Turner couldn't open the door or break any of the windows. Their phones and computers didn't work, and there was nothing but silence in the rest of the house.

Finally, Dad's footsteps sounded in the kitchen. The door flew open.

"Is everyone okay?" he asked.

Elizabeth, who had fallen asleep next to Sandy, sat up and burst into tears. Dad picked her up, even though she was eleven years old.

"What happened?" Emma asked. "Where were you guys? What was that noise?"

"Where's Maude?" Turner asked.

"She's okay," Dad said, kissing the top of Elizabeth's head.

"What do you mean 'she's okay'?" Emma said. "What happened?"

Mom came into the room. She looked like she was going to fall.

"Is she asleep?" Dad asked, putting Elizabeth down.

Mom nodded.

"What the hell is going on?" Emma said.

"Don't swear," Dad answered softly.

"Don't *swear*?" Emma repeated. "Why is Maude sleeping? What the hell just happened?"

"Are you guys okay?" Mom asked Sandy and Elizabeth.

"What happened?" Sandy asked, waking up. "What was that noise? Why was it so quiet for so long?"

"Don't worry, sweetie," Mom said. She glanced at Emma. "It's over."

"How can you *say* that?" Turner asked, his eyes burning.

Mom gave Turner a ferocious look and he was quiet. "Emma," she said. "Take Elizabeth and Sandy into the kitchen." She stopped talking and bit her lip to keep it from trembling. Emma had never seen her mother cry. "It's only ten thirty. Tripoli's is still open. Order a pizza," Mom added. "Daddy and I have to talk to Turner."

"No," Emma said. "You have to tell all of us."

Turner gave her a pleading glance. Mom and Dad were silent.

"Fine," Emma said. Turner would tell her anyway. She grabbed Sandy's hand. "You order the food, Elizabeth."

No one ate dinner except Sandy. Maude stayed asleep upstairs. All Mom and Dad would say was a man they knew a long time ago had tried to take Maude but they'd stopped him. No one said anything else. No one said, "That's crazy." No one said, "Call the police." No one said, "Stop lying."

Emma watched Mom and Dad stare into the center of the room, their faces impenetrable and their food untouched. Emma had always hoped that in an emergency she would be miraculously able to save the day, even though she was afraid of confrontation or drawing too much attention to herself. But, of course, since this was real life and not a movie Emma sat still and scared. No brilliant ideas came to her; no useful, secret powers manifested themselves seemingly out of nowhere. Her sister was almost kidnapped, her beautiful, sweet, delicate sister, and her parents sat there, promising that everything would be okay.

This is bullshit, Emma thought, and tried to stand up. But something held her thighs to the chair and what felt like an invisible fist stopped her mouth when she tried to talk. She glanced at Turner. He was feeling the same thing. Were they just too scared to speak? Was she really the giant baby she feared she was? Was Turner? He couldn't be. She knew he wasn't. So what was happening?

* * *

It was after 11:00 when Joe's mom finally fell asleep. He crept out of the apartment and rode his bike to Emma's. The lights were still on downstairs so he parked it on the street and sneaked into Emma's backyard. She was waiting in the dark greenhouse.

"Can we go somewhere else?" she whispered when Joe opened the door. "I'm afraid my parents will catch us."

"What are you so afraid of?" he asked, biting his tongue before he added something like they wouldn't be doing anything they couldn't do on the street in broad daylight; she'd made *that* clear that last time he kissed her.

Emma looked stricken. As if she'd heard what he was thinking. Joe was too pissed off to care whether she had or not. He still had images of the boy from French's in his head. The boy she'd flirted with.

"The Lowrys next door are on vacation," she said. "We can talk on their front porch." Without waiting for him to answer, Emma pulled Joe out of the greenhouse and into the warm night.

"I met Gryphon Venti," Joe said, sitting on the wooden steps of the neighbor's porch. He hadn't meant to say anything, or at least not right away. He'd meant to ask her about the drawings, or if she'd ever heard of Sfodro Vatic, but Gryphon's name fell out of his mouth like rotten food.

"Who's Gryphon Venti?" Emma asked.

That made him angry. He stood up and cracked his head on a hanging plant. Geranium petals fell into his hair.

"Are you okay?" Emma asked. She brushed the blood-bright petals off his head.

"I'm fine," he said, pushing her away.

"What are you mad about?" she asked.

"I saw you today with Gryphon Venti at French's. My mom didn't need me to stay. I just didn't want to see you."

Emma sat down again. She didn't respond to his implied accusation but she didn't look guilty either. She stared across the grey yard as if trying to remember something.

"Who's Sfodro Vatic?" Emma asked after a long time.

A chill ran through Joe. "I don't know. I was going to ask you."

Emma stood up.

"What?" Joe said. "What are you thinking?" He followed her onto the footpath. "Did you see something when you looked at the drawings?"

"I heard something," Emma said, her voice distracted. "When I touched the boy in the drawing."

"What?"

"I heard a man's voice. He was telling someone—a woman—to take Sfodro and Edoro somewhere…" She hesitated.

"Take them where?" Joe said, patience bleeding away.

"He said to take them to the Otherworld and wait for him, and to tell him if they were followed."

"What the fuck is the Otherworld?" Joe asked.

"I don't know," Emma said.

Joe wanted to run away. All his life he'd wanted to know the truth about himself and where he came from, and now he fucking didn't want to hear it. Not in front of someone. Not in front of Emma. He felt the skin lining his throat break apart. He didn't want to know.

"I saw him," Emma said quietly. "The man."

That she was so clearly trying to spare him was infuriating. He wanted her to see him. He wanted her to know him. But not like this. Not when he had no control over himself.

"It must have been after the baby girl was killed," Emma said. "He was so sad. He kissed the little boy and then put him on the ground. A woman came and picked the little boy up."

"Then what happened?" Joe asked, his voice stuck like a finger in his throat.

"She left with the little boy."

Joe walked to the end of the path and kicked a rock across the dark street. He wished Emma would just leave. She didn't.

"Someone or something came to our house tonight and tried to kidnap Maude," Emma said.

Joe turned. "Is she okay?"

"I think so," Emma said. "She was still sleeping when I left." She came over to him and added, "It's all connected." Her voice was strained as if trying to hold together something delicate and dangerous. "The story underneath your mom's drawing. Maude. Sfodro Vatic. Gryphon Venti."

"I thought you said you didn't know him," Joe said, appalled how fast jealousy shot back into his heart, despite everything that was going on. God, he was such a fucking *girl*.

"I don't," Emma said. "But his name made me think that everything was connected. And it's not over."

"What does that mean?" Joe said.

"I don't know."

"That's helpful," Joe sneered. "Did you invite me over to tell me that you don't know anything? I saw you with Gryphon Venti. You practically kissed him in French's. I guess that's what happens when you're afraid *we'll* stop kissing."

"That's not fair," Emma said. "And it's not true. If you're looking for a way to persuade me to go farther with you that is *not* the fucking way to go about it." She walked down the footpath toward the sidewalk. "I have to get back inside. My parents are still freaked out, and I want to make sure Maude is okay."

Joe felt like he had a monster in his chest. He wished he could tear his ribs apart. "Wait!"

He ran after Emma. She looked into his eyes and Joe felt like he had when she'd looked at him in the hall that first day at school, grateful, happy, and amazed that someone he liked, someone he wanted and wanted to be with felt the same way about him.

"I'm sorry," he said.

"It's okay."

Joe kissed Emma's forehead, keeping his body a few wavering feet away from hers. "Hey," he said, inhaling the subtle scent of her shampoo. "How come you're not sweaty anymore? Now that it's warmer outside you stop sweating?"

"Shut up," she said, playfully pushing him away. "I don't know why I was so grossly sweaty last month. But I'm glad it stopped."

"I thought the sweatiness was wicked hot," he whispered.

"Argh!" she said. "You really are a weirdo, aren't you?" But she pulled him closer and kissed him on the mouth.

Thank God, Joe thought as all the tension that had been circling his chest like a snake relaxed. Thank God he was kissing Emma again. She hummed sweetly into his mouth then pulled away.

"That little boy," she said. "The blue-haired little boy…"

At first he didn't know what she was talking about. The only image in his brain was of her kissing him and letting him kiss her, and where he wanted his hands to go. Then blue hair rang in his head like an alarm. He hadn't just *seen* the terrible thing that happened to the baby girl. He'd been running with the old woman, clinging to her hand. It wasn't a vision for him. It felt like a memory.

"Is your real hair blue?" she asked. "Do you dye your hair brown?"

He nodded.

"Why didn't you tell me?" she asked.

He snorted, shame and fury in his blood. "You think that's the missing piece that ties it all together? My hair?"

"That boy was you," Emma said, standing straighter so the thin moonlight slashed her exposed collarbone. "The baby girl," she said. "The baby girl was your sister. And the man who left you in the woods was your father."

It was his turn to push her away. "How the fuck do you know that's true?" he said. "Maybe you're just crazy." He knew he was acting like an asshole but couldn't stop himself. He didn't want to be that little boy. He didn't want that memory to be his.

Emma stepped back. "Ever since I met you, I've been able to sometimes hear what people are thinking or see what they're doing. I saw what you saw," she added, "in the living room. Remember? I saw what happened to that baby. I saw your father kiss you before he put you, crying, on the ground. I felt what he felt when your sister was killed."

So much crowded Joe's throat that he didn't know how to get it all out. "So who was the woman who carried me out of the woods? Was she my mom now? Was she my real mom, my biological mom? Where the fuck is she now, then?" *Why didn't she ever try to find me again?* he thought but didn't say.

Emma crossed her arms over her chest then dropped them and pressed her palms to her thighs. "I don't know who or where your real mom is. As soon as he realized that the woman in the woods would take care of you, your dad dropped images into her head. She didn't see him. She didn't know he was there. Everything happened without her knowledge."

"What were these images?" Joe asked, curling his fingers so tightly into his palms he thought his skin would break. He couldn't control his emotions. He felt insane.

"Images of people taking you away from her unless she kept how she found you a secret," Emma said.

"Why did she tell me she found me, then?" Joe shouted. "If she had to keep how she found me a secret, why didn't she just let me think I was her natural-born son?"

"I don't know," Emma said, "but your dad wanted to protect you and your sister from someone."

"Well, he did a pretty shitty job, didn't he?" Joe snarled. "She died."

"I know," Emma said. "I saw. Your father obviously got there too late. He was heartbroken. You didn't see him—"

"I'm leaving," Joe said. He couldn't think straight.

"Stop acting like such a baby," Emma shouted, "and listen to me. Whoever was after you before, whoever your father was trying to protect you from…they must be still out there!"

CHAPTER EIGHTEEN

Emma's mom turned on the light in the greenhouse. Joe got on his bike and rode off without saying anything else. Emma walked back to her yard, walked past her mom, went in the house and upstairs.

"Thank God," her mother said. She followed Emma into her room. "I thought…" Her hair was stringy and her face grey. She didn't ask Emma any questions about where she'd been or who she'd been talking to, or why she was outside in the neighbor's yard after midnight. "Don't worry," she added, sitting next to Emma on the bed. "Everything will be okay. I promise. Nothing like that will happen again."

Emma got up and walked over to the dark window. She didn't speak.

"Daddy and I made sure of it," Mom continued, coming over to stand next to Emma. She pulled her hair in front of her shoulder and let it all slide through, drawing her fingers away long after there was no more hair in her hand.

"What *did* happen?" Emma asked, concentrating on the milky black moon shadows spread like an open hand on the soft green lawn.

"Daddy and I want to tell you together," Mom said. "It's complicated." She flipped her hair back over her shoulder.

And then Emma saw her mother as she really was for the first time. Light poured out of her fingertips when she moved and her hair had no color at all. It was hollow, like polar bear fur, catching the splash of moonlight at the foot of the bed.

"I'm sorry for lying," Mom said. "For keeping the truth from all of you." She shifted her position. Her hair floated over her shoulders as if it had a life of its own.

Emma didn't say anything.

"I know it's hard to understand," Mom said. "But we wanted you to have a normal life."

Emma felt like she was floating, like the cord of understanding that held her to the ground and showed her what to believe was severed. She stared at her mother's face.

"You were relieved Rachel's parents convinced her to have an abortion," she said quietly. "You were afraid the truth about who, or *what*, we really are would get out. Weren't you?" God, she should have been more sympathetic when Turner told her he broke up with Rachel. She should have talked to him about it more. He'd been a wreck. She hadn't asked about Rachel since the night he'd told her they broke up. When had she become so appallingly self-absorbed?

Mom's skin paled to a silvery green, but she said nothing.

"Do you know Turner is telekinetic?" Emma asked, suddenly so, *so* angry. "Did you know I'm telepathic?" She almost told her mother about Joe but something made her stop. "How could you believe we'd never find out that there was something different about us?"

"We were going to tell you soon," Mom said, her skin pink and normal again, her hair still skinny tubes of light.

Something cracked above Emma's head, and something Mom had done to keep her from moving where she wanted or saying what she wanted broke away like sheets of hot ice. "You did something weird every time you took us to the doctor," Emma said. "And you wouldn't let anyone else cut our hair."

"We did our best, Emma," her mom said. "You haven't begun to experience the full extent of your power yet. Every *Sacerian* can hear thoughts."

"What is the Otherworld?" Emma asked.

Mom gasped. "This is the Otherworld," she said. "It's how Sacerians refer most often to *Pali*. Pali, or the Otherworld, is the world we live in now. Here, in New Hampshire. *Saceres*, or the Commonworld, is where we're from."

Emma stood up and kept Joe at the back of her mind. "Can you hear my thoughts?" she asked.

"Of course I can," Mom said.

"But not all the time."

"No," Mom agreed. "Not all the time."

Turner came into the room. He looked different. "I cut my hair," he said after Emma had been staring for a minute.

She reached out and touched it. It looked like Mom's. Tiny sparks glittered at the freshly cut ends, and dark light shone in every strand.

"It's after midnight," Mom said, gazing in something like wonder at her son. "Go to bed."

"I'm not going to bed yet," Emma said. She walked outside, leaving Mom and Turner alone together.

* * *

Joe sat up in bed. His heart was pounding. For a second he thought he might throw up. Splintered images poured like blood out of the back of his head.

He was in bed with Emma. She was beautiful and sweet. Spiders and black water came out of her mouth. She kept saying his name. He got out of bed. Emma turned over. Her back was riddled with small clean holes, out of which crawled hundreds and hundreds of people, naked and crying, melting on his floor.

He was in the woods, running away from something. A man laughed and shot him repeatedly with a curling silver gun. The bullets entered his body, knocking him to the ground and spreading a sickening heat through him, stiffening his arms and legs. Still, he got up and ran, the man still chasing him. He reached a door and couldn't open it. The man laughed. The floor opened. He fell through and landed on a wet floor. A girl lay dead at his feet, her throat cut—

Joe shook himself and got out of bed. He put on pants and a shirt. Careful not to wake his mother, he went to the bathroom in the narrow hall. The moon hung in the corner of the window, white and glaring like a blind eye. He splashed water on his face and brushed his teeth.

It was long past midnight. The dream image of Emma had all but disappeared. He couldn't remember what had scared him so much, but a feeling of terror stuck to him. How could he fight an enemy he'd never seen? Who was his father? And why would anyone want to kill children?

Joe lay down and rested his hand on the hard muscles of his stomach. He'd screwed up with Emma again, walked away when he was upset. Again. He had to try harder to stick around when he was scared or angry, or both. Joe took a deep breath and stared at the ceiling's dull, sprayed-popcorn surface. Sweet images floated above his head. Emma smiling at him. Emma walking away, her hair swinging behind her like a white bell. She turned and called him to her.

* * *

Emma left Mom and Turner inside. Outside, the moon hung in the sky like a bright marble with a smoky eye and mouth.

She bent down to tighten her sneakers. Her hair fell over the tops of her shoes, partially covering the smiley faces Joe had drawn on the white toes. She stared hard at the black ink drawings; one winked shyly, the other stuck out a long tongue. Her heart swelled. She almost tied the ends of her hair into her shoelaces.

Shoes secure, Emma threw her hands over the lowest branch of the sprawling maple climbing tree. The bark scraped her skin, tearing open a few mosquito-bite scabs. Gross. She was glad Joe had never seen her bare legs. As she climbed, more than once she thought she felt an ant or worse crawling up her arms or legs.

She found the branch she wanted, fat and smooth and free of little shoots. Straddling the branch, she leaned against the thick trunk of the tree and saw the Milky Way draped like frosted breath between the upper branches. Emma brushed her hair out of her eyes and stared as the stars came into view. Turner had taught her the constellations when she was obsessed with Greek mythology in fourth grade: Regulus in Leo, Castor and Pollux, fiery Arcturus and the Great Mother Bear. Ralph Waldo Emerson, whom Dad loved almost as much as he loved Keats, wrote, "If the stars should appear one night in a thousand years, how would men believe and adore; and preserve for many generations the remembrance of the city of God which had been shown! But every night come out these envoys of beauty, and light the universe with their admonishing smile."

How did she know that whole quote? It's not like she'd memorized it. She closed her eyes and the lines ran through her head once more, and she saw her dad twelve years earlier, sitting at the edge of her bed, reading Emerson's *Nature* to her when other kids her age were listening to *The Dumb Bunnies* or *Frog and Toad*. Saw it like it was yesterday.

Emma turned to the house. Turner's light was still on but she knew he'd fallen asleep. Mom and Dad's light was on but they weren't going to sleep at all. They were watching her.

Cautiously, Emma stood up and pressed her back to the tree trunk. She closed her eyes and opened herself to the world around her, and when the buzz of the world was under her fingernails and blowing through her hair, she called out to Joe.

Emma!

Emma turned sharply and almost fell out of the tree.

Come inside.

"Maude?"

If you're talking or thinking, I can't hear you, Maude thought, *but I know, I* know *you can hear me. Come inside.*

Emma climbed down as fast as she could and ran to the house. Inside the front door the sounds of the universe stopped and she felt safe. Suffocated, but safe. She kicked off her sneakers and ran up the green carpeted stairs. Outside Maude's room she felt more than heard her father pull her mother back.

Maude was sitting on the bed when Emma walked in.

"Oh my God," Emma said.

CHAPTER NINETEEN

Don't say it. The command was on Emma's sister's tongue, dancing in the front of her brain, but Maude didn't speak.

Like most girls, Emma loved and hated really beautiful girls. She wished she was one, or would grow into one someday, but she knew that would never happen. Although Emma believed in the kind of beauty that comes from within—the beauty everyone possesses—there was mystery and a different energy in the kind that could be touched. The beauty Maude possessed before, visible to a covetous world but disregarded by those who couldn't see past her ferocious oddness, had melted away like a dying song. This new beauty, perfect and pure in a way Emma had never seen, was almost hard to look at. It had weight and substance, and a power beyond inviting envy or desire.

"What…?" Emma began. "What happened?"

"One of the actors who came to school for Shakespeare's birthday today was a kid from another school," Maude said. "His chin was receding, he had bad skin—really bad, like Mike Clark bad—and his hair was messy and woolly like old dog fur."

"Maude," Emma said, "I don't need the history of the world. What happened to *you?*"

"This is what happened." Maude turned to the window. Light floated around her like the scent of unseen flowers. "He gave me a dress and told me I'd be reading Juliet. I was really mad. I didn't want to play Juliet. I wanted to play Viola. I don't care about Juliet. That play is a one-idea story. I wanted Viola."

"Maude," interrupted Emma.

"He gave me the dress and the script…"

Maude stopped talking. Emma tried to wait patiently for her to continue. When she couldn't wait any longer she asked, "Do you think what happened tonight was your fault?"

Maude turned slowly from the window. "He had beautiful, *beautiful* eyes," she said. "Like the beast in *Beauty and the Beast*. He was sad. He needed me. He needed me to read for Juliet and wear the dress. He needed me."

"What happened after you put the dress on?"

"I don't know," Maude said in a small voice. "I felt weird. Slow and soft. Like I wasn't real. We did the reading. People clapped. Tucker Winslow kissed me. He was Romeo but we weren't doing a kissing scene. Melissa Sapienza said I looked cute but I knew she hated me. And then it was lunch and I hung out with the actor kid from the other school. He was *so* sweet, Emma. You can't imagine how sweet he was. Really, not fake sweet or stupid sweet, but smart and lovely and poetic. He even quoted Shelley to me. Then he apologized for being a dork." Maude stopped and stared blankly at her overstuffed bookshelf.

Emma sat still and thought for a moment. She thought of old stories of dresses soaked in poison. But Maude didn't look poisoned. She looked *revealed,* and impossibly beautiful, as if the contents of her soul had spilled out onto her skin and shone from her hair and from her eyes.

Maude turned back to her. "He's my boy, Emma."

"What?" Emma said.

Maude seemed unable or unwilling to add anything else. Emma bit back a demand for more information. This new beauty gave her beloved sister a fragility Emma was afraid to disturb. She wanted to ask, Why would the boy you think is your soulmate make you do anything you didn't want to do? What was in that dress, and what did it have to do with what happened tonight? Had the boy Maude thought was her soulmate tried to abduct her?

Emma sat on the bed and held Maude's ancient Pooh Bear. The old bear had one shoe-button black eye, one grey cotton-leaking eye hole, and a purple stain on his stomach where Elizabeth had left him on top of an open marker. Emma bit her cheek and squeezed the stuffed bear close to her chest. "What happened tonight?" she asked in as calm a voice as she could manage.

"The actor kid came to our house and asked me to go home with him," Maude said. "He waited while I thought about it. He's not ugly. He changed his face. He's beautiful and smart and fierce."

"How did he change his face?" Emma asked, remembering Morrissey-dude in the living room and at French's. "And where does he live?"

"He lives in the Commonworld," Maude said.

"Did he tell you what the Commonworld is?"

Maude nodded.

"How did he change his face?" Emma asked, a chill dragging up from the base of her spine and spreading out like wings over her shoulders. "Does everyone from the Commonworld have powers?" Hadn't her mother said something like that? "Is that why I'm telepathic and Turner is telekinetic?"

Maude nodded. "But Gryphon said everyone in the Commonworld can read thoughts."

"Gryphon *Venti*?" Emma said.

"Yes."

"The kid I met in town?" Emma said. "The one from the living room with Mom?"

"Yes," Maude said.

"How did he change his face?" Emma asked. "He looked a little like a young Morrissey when I saw him."

Maude smiled. "I bet that worked for you."

"Obviously." Emma grinned. "And I guess whatever he did worked for you too."

"He didn't have to do anything for me," Maude said.

"How did he change his face?" Emma asked again, worried Maude was going to get all quiet and not confide in her.

"Gryphon is a *Teknasma*, a Mask," Maude said. "If a Mask is physically near enough to a person, he can make them believe he is someone or something else. He makes you see him the way you need to…in order for him to get what he wants from you. But he has to be close enough."

"But if everyone in the Commonworld can read thoughts," Emma said, "don't people know what he's doing?"

"A Mask taps into what people feel," Maude said. "What they want, what they're afraid of. All of us are vulnerable or susceptible to something."

"How did you know he didn't use his Mask power on you?" Emma asked.

Maude took a deep breath but didn't say anything.

"Well, how do you know?" Emma said.

"Because he didn't," Maude said quietly. "Because he showed me his real face, not something that would fool me. Because *Eynosyndeo*—Soulmates—are always true."

"Maude," Emma implored, terrified that something bad was going to happen to her beautiful, delicate sister. "How can you be sure he isn't trying to trick you?"

"I'm not weak or stupid, Emma," Maude said in a gentle unwavering tone. "Just because I'm strange and don't have any friends except for you, just because I love poetry and I know how to grow flowers doesn't mean people can push me around or make me do something I don't want. Gryphon is my Eynosyndeo, my Soulmate. I know it. There isn't anything else to say."

"Okay," Emma said, and she meant it.

Maude sat in a chair near the window. Her long black hair fell past her shoulders.

"Did you kiss him?" Emma asked.

"You can't ask me that."

"Yes, I can," Emma said. "I told you about Joe."

"But I didn't ask you," Maude said.

"You're really not going to tell me, are you?"

Maude smiled and shook her head. "No."

"Then I know you did," Emma said.

"You're free to think what you like."

Emma groaned.

"I'll tell you how a Mask's power works, if you want," Maude offered.

"Only if it's kissing power," Emma said.

"Shut up." Maude shook her head. "I won't tell you."

"No," Emma said. "I want to know."

Maude stood and walked over to sit beside her. "It was so cool," she said. "He asked me to think of people I admired and then, right in front of me, he just turned into them."

"Oh my God," Emma said. "That is cool. Who did you think of?"

"Shelley and Keats." Emma rolled her eyes, but Maude didn't care. "What was so awesome is there are no photographs of Shelley or Keats, obviously. There are several paintings and drawings of Keats, but only a few likenesses of Shelley. So in order to become each of them, Gryphon accessed my memories of the paintings and became a composite of them all." Maude covered her face with her fingers, her mouth showing through like blood or candy. "It was *amazing*." She lay on the bed. "Literally amazing."

Emma smiled at her. Maude beamed back, and Emma stretched out beside her.

"Did he actually change into them for a second?"

"No," Maude said. "A Mask doesn't actually change at all. It's not like a shapeshifter. A Mask knows what image you'd be most susceptible to, and he or she becomes that in your eyes, the way your brain fills in the image of what it thinks it sees. Like that night we were walking home and we thought a Mylar balloon was a rabid raccoon. Remember? You screamed."

"I don't remember screaming," Emma said.

"You did. Like a banshee." Maude smiled. "Anyway, a Mask tricks you into thinking you see something different. He reflects what you want back to you. And Gryphon is very, very skilled. He's the best Mask anyone has seen in a long time."

Maude snuggled her head into the pillow and smiled at Emma. Her skin seemed like it was made of diamonds in cream, and she smelled like jasmine and honeyed cloves.

"You're too pretty, Maude," Emma said. She couldn't help it. Some stupid, hyper-girlie, baby part of her worried that Joe would fall hopelessly in love with Maude as soon as he saw her, their Soulmate thing or not.

"I feel different," Maude admitted. "Turned inside out, or peeled open. I feel utterly unprotected. I don't have anything around me to shield me."

"I'll protect you," Emma said. "And Turner will."

"Not like that," Maude said. "I feel entirely…revealed." Maude bit her cheek and blushed, and Emma was surprised they'd choose the same word to describe her state. "Like I'm wearing my soul outside my body and everyone can see it or touch it, and I can't do anything about that."

The door opened and Turner walked in. "What's a Mask?" he asked.

CHAPTER TWENTY

"Were you listening?" Emma asked.

"I wanted to see if Maude was okay. Are you?"

Maude nodded.

Turner sat in Maude's white and gold painted desk chair. "What's a Mask?"

Neither Maude nor Emma said anything.

Turner took what looked like a flat rock out of his pocket and began tossing it back and forth between his hands. "Mom and Dad were relieved that Rachel had an abortion," he said, avoiding Emma's and Maude's eyes, and taking a long, shuddering breath, "because we"—he faced both of them now—"are not human. We're from another world. Mom and Dad won't tell me why they left."

"What did they tell you?" Maude asked.

"That the world is called Saceres or the Commonworld," he said. "That almost everyone there has some kind of power. That we can't go back. And that nothing is more important to a Commonworlder than his or her Eynosyndeo. His Soulmate."

Turner shuddered and sat down, and Emma and Maude listened while he explained everything he'd learned from their parents since he broke up with Rachel a month ago. And since he was Turner, at this point he could teach a class on Sacerian studies. He told them that in the Commonworld people called *Theama*, or Revealers, visually and aurally disseminated information the way television and the Internet did in this world. Theama chose what to reveal and how to reveal it. And what to keep secret.

"The images are physically projected from the Revealer," Turner said, sitting straight as a pencil on the edge of Maude's bed, "who in something similar to sending positive or negative feelings or energy out into the world releases visible energy that's been specifically...shaped. But controlled projection has to be learned."

"How do they learn to control it?" Maude asked, and Emma knew she was thinking about Gryphon and how he'd learned to control his power.

"The Commonworld school day is separated into halves," her brother said in his very Turnerish, school-loving way, and Emma knew he needed to concentrate on something so he wouldn't think about Rachel. Turner felt like he was bleeding on the inside whenever his ex's face flashed in his head.

"Oooh, a whole new kind of school," Emma said. "Calm down, big brother, you don't want to alarm the neighbors. You're probably levitating their bushes in your excitement."

"You're hilarious, Emma."

"Well?" she prompted. "Aren't you going to tell us about the Commonworld educational system? I know you want to."

Turner exhaled and smiled at her. "Half the day is devoted to learning about culture, history, reading, writing, math, and science. The second half, the kids are separated by their individual powers in order to learn to control and better use them."

Because she felt regretful about not paying enough attention to Turner when he'd first told her about Rachel, Emma sat back and semi-patiently listened to him talk. She guessed it was Dad who'd told Turner everything about the Commonworld and Turner drank it in like the information sponge he was.

"There are two political parties in the Commonworld," her brother said, his amber eyes glittering. "The *Aythentia* and the *Eleytheria*. The Eleytheria choose one leader. Right now that leader is Fen Elos. Incidentally, Fen Elos was a teacher of Mom's and she was his favorite student." Being every Dearborn teacher's favorite student, he blushed saying this.

"Anyway," he continued. "The Aythentia rule with the *Sosta Arithmos*, the Three Leaders. The current Sosta Arithmos are a female *Elafra*...that's a Lucent in English. Elafra are humanized energy, a visible manifestation of the energy that is part of everything; they can connect to the energy fabric. The second of the current Three Leaders is a female *Thoryba Exocho*—that's a telepath like you, Emma, but much more powerful and proficient."

"Thanks, Mr. Kochenderfer," Emma interjected. She threw Maude's stuffed rabbit at her brother, but Turner stopped the fluffy toy midflight and made it march through the air and then hit Emma on the head with its floppy ears.

"Show off!" she gasped.

He grinned. "May I continue?"

"Go ahead," Emma said, smiling back. She could keep listening. Talking about all this was making Turner feel better. And maybe something he said would help her understand something about the terrible thing that happened to Joe when he was little.

"The last of the current Three Leaders is a male *Dimiorg*. A Transformist. They...can make things out of other things."

"What are the differences between the two political parties?" Maude spoke up. "Aythentia and the Eleytheria, you said? Is it kind of like here, conservative and liberal?"

Emma gave Maude a *What the hell are you thinking?* look. Turner loved politics the way Emma loved The Smiths. A little too much. This was bound to go on longer than it needed to.

"The Aythentia believe in the necessity of ultimate authority," Turner said. "They believe there are people who are superior in strength, intellect, power and compassion, and those are the people who should rule the others. They reject the idea of community rule. Mom and Dad—but Mom especially—hate the Aythentia."

"So that's the same as here I guess," Emma said. "It's more about hating the other side rather than trying to make things work."

"Well, I don't know if everyone hates the opposite party the way Mom does," Turner said. "I'm sure there are radical thinkers and more moderate thinkers in the Commonworld just like there are here."

"Why does Mom hate the Aythentia?" Maude asked, as if the answer was important to her.

"The Aythentia believe that the end always justifies the means, and whatever they—as incontrovertibly superior creatures—choose to do in order to make the world safe and prosperous for all Commonworlders is right."

"What do the Eleytheria believe?" Maude asked.

"The Eleytheria acknowledge that there are varying degrees of strength, intellect, power and compassion among all Commonworlders," Turner said. "But they also believe that people are complex and not so easily sorted. The Eleytheria believe in argument, discussion and dissent. They believe a society that lacks or doesn't allow for free and honorable dissent becomes brittle and eventually chaotic."

"Who's in charge now?" Emma asked, and Turner beamed, recognizing that she and Maude were both genuinely interested. "Okay, okay," Emma allowed, "I want you to keep going, but not for too much longer. I'm starting to have test anxiety."

"I bet you are," Turner said. "Unsurprisingly, you're not taking notes."

Her brother grinned, and Emma sucked back a joke about not believing Rachel actually liked him because he'd always been such an old man. She glanced at Turner with concern, but it seemed she was the only one of them who could hear thoughts—for now, anyway. And she couldn't do it all the time.

He definitely hadn't heard what she'd almost said, because he continued: "The ruling political party is called the *Moklu Dynami,* or the Ones in Power, and the out-of-power party is called the *Perimena,* or the Resisters. Right now, the Aythentia are the Ones in Power and the Eleytheria are the Resisters."

"Do you think that's why Mom and Dad left?" Emma asked.

"No." Turner shook his head. "Mom and Dad are Eleytheria, but they didn't leave the only world they'd ever known because their political party fell out of power. Would you leave the United States just because whoever you wanted to be president lost the election?"

"If they didn't leave because of whoever is or isn't in power, why did they leave?" Emma asked. "And why did they keep our real identities a secret?"

"Gryphon told me Mom and Dad are fugitives," Maude spoke up, "and that we're all wearing identity shields called *emai fylakas.* Mom and Dad put them on us and on themselves. Identity shields make it difficult for other Commonworlders to detect your Commonworld identity or even to be able to tell that you are a Commonworlder at all."

"What?" Emma said. "Why are they fugitives? What did they do?"

"He wouldn't tell me," Maude said. "Gryphon is a Gatherer, a *Masevo*. He graduated from school last year as soon as he turned fifteen. A Masevo is like a policeman or an FBI agent. A lot of Masks are Masevo. Gryphon was sent here because something gave us away. He wouldn't tell me what it was, but he was sent here to investigate."

"Who's Gryphon?" Turner asked. "Is he the guy who kidnapped you?"

"Gryphon didn't kidnap me," Maude said. "He asked me if I wanted to go with him."

"Is he the guy you were talking about when I came in?" Turner said. "The Mask? The Teknasma? Why the hell are you taking his word against Mom and Dad? How do you know he didn't trick you or fool you? Commonworlders have powers we don't have. Remember—"

"We're from the Commonworld," Maude interrupted, standing up. "Mom and Dad took us away and hid us here."

"They must have had a good reason," Turner snapped.

"I'm sure they did," Maude agreed.

Turner swore and started pacing. Emma gazed at Maude, who stood still and watched him.

"Wait," Turner said, stopping to face Maude. "You don't think he's your Soulmate, do you?"

Maude set her jaw. "If Mom and Dad told you that the Eynosyndeo connection is the most sacred, protected thing in the Commonworld, then they told you that Soulmates are always true."

"They also told me that you cannot meet your Soulmate or know who he or she is until you're fifteen," Turner said, his face red.

"I am fifteen," Maude said. "Did you forget my birthday?"

"No," Turner admitted in a strained voice. He sat on the bed next to Emma. Now he couldn't stop thinking about Rachel. How hard she had cried when he told her he couldn't be with her anymore. How he still felt physically torn in half. How he couldn't breathe when he thought of her.

Maude sat on his other side and took his hand, but he pulled it away. "I'm going to go to bed," he growled, rising unsteadily to his feet. "Here." He threw the rock he'd been holding to Maude. "I took it out of Gryphon's car yesterday."

Emma worried that her brother might collapse. He was so pale and tremulous. "Sit down, Turner," she said. "Talk with us. We'll listen."

Turner ignored her, addressing Maude. "I think it's some kind of reading thing. If you run your finger down the central crevice it opens like a book. There's some kind of writing inside."

Emma watched as Maude ran her finger over the stone. It opened as Turner said it would. The writing was unfamiliar.

"What do you think it says?" Emma asked, but Turner had already left.

After a minute the stone closed itself.

"Separation from a Soulmate is devastatingly painful," Maude said in a hollow voice. "Gryphon said that there are people in either world, but primarily in Pali, the Otherworld, *this world*," she stressed, "who never connect with their Soulmate. These people suffer under a permanent state of disconnection. Love is real, as real as sunlight, as real as breath. And hideously painful if broken. He is my Soulmate, Emma. I know he is. And Rachel must be Turner's. God, poor Turner."

Emma closed her eyes. She wished she could call Joe.

"I'm going to go to bed," Maude said.

"Okay," Emma replied, and she slipped out of her sister's room.

Mom and Dad were holding hands and waiting in the hall. Mom's real hair and Dad's real skin color shivered just inside them like anguished faces held under dirty water. Emma wondered if the kids at school could see what her family looked like now or if it was only them.

"Mom and I want to talk with you," Dad said, squeezing Mom's hand before letting go of it.

"All right," Emma said, crossing her arms over her chest.

Dad sighed, and Mom ran her fingers through her changeable hair.

"I know you and Turner and Maude have been talking," Dad said.

"You should have told us a long time ago," Emma replied.

"I know," Dad said. "You're right. We should have."

"Well, what do you want to tell me?" Emma asked. "Are there more secrets? Does Maude have some kind of power she doesn't know about?"

A shiver of green undulated over Mom's face.

"Some Commonworlders," Dad began, "can wear their souls outside their bodies, just at the surface of the skin."

"Is that why Maude looked crazy beautiful tonight?" Emma asked.

"Yes. The Gatherer who tried to take her gave Maude a dress made of a material that dissolves the protections Mom and I put on Maude when she was a baby so that her soul wouldn't be visible on her skin."

"Will she be okay?" Emma asked.

"Yes," Mom said.

"When Commonworlders like Maude are born," Dad said, "everyone wants to touch them. When Mom and I were young, a man named Gelon Lira believed that the ashes of cremated *Syche Katharos*, Soulskins— that's what Commonworlders like Maude are called, Soulskins—" Dad looked to Mom for support. She didn't look back at him but stared straight ahead.

"Gelon Lira believed that the ashes of cremated Soulskins contained healing powers. He murdered seven people before someone stopped him. One of Mom's friends was almost killed."

"But Gryphon is Maude's Soulmate," Emma said. "He would never try to hurt her."

"Gryphon is not Maude's Soulmate, Emma," Mom spoke up. "He's a Mask, a Teknasma. A Mask tricks people into believing in something that isn't really there."

"I know what a Mask is," Emma said. "Maude told me. Gryphon told her he was a Mask."

A disagreement rose in the air between Mom and Dad.

"It isn't possible, Peter," Mom said. "Have you forgotten what he is? Have you forgotten he's Aythentia? Can you think of anyone in either of our families or any of our friends who are Eynosyndeo with an Aythentia?"

"I'm sure there are, Gwen," Dad said.

"Name one."

"I didn't know the names of every Soulmate when we lived in Saceres," Dad said. "And I certainly don't know the names of all the Soulmates who've met since we left home."

Mom would have none of it. "Can you imagine anyone less likely to be Maude's Soulmate? She won't even kill spiders in the greenhouse. She picks them up and puts them outside. It's not possible. He's Aythentia. She's young. He fooled her."

"Gwen," Dad pleaded.

"No," Mom said. "I should have made the protections stronger. I should have concealed everything permanently. I should have severed us. I'm going to bed." She left Emma and Dad alone in the hall.

"Is that it?" Emma said. "That's all you're going to tell me?"

"Try not to be angry with Mom," Dad said. "She's afraid for you, for all of you. And she hates feeling out of control. You know that."

"That's no excuse, Dad," Emma said. "I'm sorry she feels likes she's lost control of something, and I'm sorry she's a hothead, but that's no excuse. The truth is this is your fault. You guys should have told us. You should have told us. *Something.*"

CHAPTER TWENTY-ONE

Dad rubbed his hands over his hair. That didn't change, but his skin did. He was cartoon-sky blue. Then his hair disappeared. He didn't have any hair at all. For a second a flood of relief washed over his face, as if he could finally breathe, as if he'd been wearing itchy, uncomfortable clothes for days and finally he could take them off, but the arrow-shot of sorrow returned almost immediately to his expression.

Emma sat on the chair under the window. Sandy called it "the lonely chair" because no one ever sat in it.

"You and Turner and Maude weren't born in Portsmouth," Dad said. "Mommy and I didn't leave the Commonworld until you were two and Maude was a baby."

"That means Turner was three," Emma said. "He'd remember something."

"We erased it."

"What?" Emma said, standing up. "You can't do that. Those memories were his. They weren't yours to take."

Dad opened his mouth to protest then held up his wrist and opened the face of his watch. Inside two silver balls spun like infant planets. "I never threw them away," he said, carefully closing the watch. "Mom doesn't know. She was terrified that any trace would reveal us."

Emma stared down at the dark lawn outside the window.

"Mom and I took you, Turner and Maude, said goodbye to our friends and families, and left."

Emma picked up her head. "There are more people in our family?"

Dad nodded. "Mom has a brother. He has a daughter almost exactly your age. You were born two months apart. Isohel is her name. We kept in contact at first. But Claudeo's wife, his Soulmate, died five years after we moved here. Mom's brother couldn't forgive her for not coming home to be with him. We haven't spoken to him since."

"How could you have kept all of this a secret for so long?" Emma asked, grateful for the fierce release of justifiable fury.

"We couldn't risk being discovered."

"Why?" Emma demanded.

Dad stood up. His blue skin throbbed like a song in the weak light from the window. "Leaving the Commonworld without permission is a death-punishable offense," Dad said.

Emma sank back into the chair. "Turner didn't tell me that."

"We didn't tell him," Dad said. "Mom and I didn't want to frighten any of you."

Emma tucked her feet under her thighs. "Why did you leave?"

"There were a lot of reasons," Dad explained. "In the Commonworld, the Ones in Power keep track of everyone. Where they are. What they think. We wanted you to grow up in a place where the government had less power, where your every move wasn't monitored and recorded. And your every choice wasn't analyzed. Even though there is some of that here, it's nothing compared to what goes on in the Commonworld. Here the government and corporations gather a great deal of information, but they're only just now learning how to process it and what to do with it. We wanted some freedom for you."

Emma sat up straighter. Dad was leaving something out. She didn't know what it was but she could feel him holding back. He looked at her, and Emma realized that he knew what she was thinking. He sighed and rubbed both hands over his face.

"When you were three years old and we were already living here, there was a man, a very close friend of Mom and me, whom the Ones in Power wanted to capture. When they learned where he was hiding, the Ones in Power eliminated nearly every person in the area in an attempt to find him."

"Why?" Emma said. "And how did you know about it if you already lived here?"

"There are always a few Sacerians living here in Pali," Dad said. "Agatha Moore was Sacerian. She told us."

"Our old babysitter?"

Dad nodded. "Agatha was so helpful to us. I don't know that we would have been as successful at hiding without her advice. And lovely Mr. Norway provided the necessary connection to the humans here."

"Mr. Norway is a Commonworlder, too!" Emma said.

"No," Dad shook his head. "And he doesn't know about the Commonworld. But he was Agatha's very good friend for a very long time. And he's the kindest human I know."

"So what happened?" Emma said. "You still haven't told me why you guys left."

"The Ones in Power believed—as they still do—that capturing our friend was worth any price," Dad said. "They killed everyone in the area where he was hiding in order to flush him out. But they failed."

"Why were those people called the Worthless?" Emma asked, having heard her father's thoughts as clearly as if he'd spoken. "You called it the Massacre of the Worthless."

Dad flushed. "*Anaxio*, the Worthless, are Commonworlders who have no powers," he said. "They can't contribute to society, so they're separated and forbidden to work. Food, clothes, and shelter are provided by the *Kena*, the Refuge. Except for the Soulmate connection, Commonworlders value contribution and participation more than anything."

The hairs on the back of Emma's neck stood up as she heard Dad's next question before he asked it.

"Sandy said you have a boyfriend," he said. "Is that true?"

Emma's cheeks burned. She'd forgotten Sandy somehow knew about Joe.

"Well, if every Commonworlder can read thoughts," she said. "You know I do."

"Soulmates are always true," Dad said. "Commonworlders don't make false matches or bad alliances in love. We can certainly screw up a relationship. Or die. But united couples are always Soulmates. And Soulmates are always true. If this boy is important to you, if he *is* your Soulmate—and only you and he will know initially," Dad continued. "Only the pair knows at first. It's impossible for anyone else to access Soulmate information until the *Kiryx Eynosyndeo*, the Soulmate Revelation."

"What's that?" Emma said, terrified that there would be some huge, embarrassing display of affection that she wouldn't be able to control and that would happen in public. Was all of this somehow related to the panic attacks plaguing her in the middle of March? But she hadn't even known Joe then.

"It's a powerful release of energy," Dad said reassuringly. "It's not embarrassing, and once the pair acknowledges it, it's usually celebrated like an engagement party or a wedding. But the energy release would give us away unless we contained it. We think that's what happened with Turner and Rachel."

He took another breath and shuddered. "Mom and I were profoundly stupid not to have prepared. We had no idea Turner was so serious about Rachel until the night he told us she was pregnant. Their Kiryx must have already occurred and we didn't know about it. We think the energy release alerted the Ones in Power and that's why that Gryphon youth was sent to investigate."

"Well, what are you going to do now?" Emma said. "Gryphon obviously found us. And if leaving the Commonworld without permission is a death-punishable offense, what are you going to do?" She realized she was almost yelling and tried to calm down.

Dad laid his hands on her shoulders. "Mom fooled Gryphon before she let him go tonight," he said. "She planted a different reason in his mind for the energy release. Mom is very powerful and very skilled. And despite our mistake with not preparing soon enough for Turner's Soulmate Revelation, she and I have done a very good job protecting all our identities and the house. We're all wearing nearly impenetrable identity shields. And the house is covered with deflective protections that prevent the Ones in Power from sensing our presence here."

"But they know now," Emma protested.

"No," Dad said. "When Gryphon left, Mom had completely convinced him that he'd been mistaken."

"About the energy release and who we are?" Emma said. "Or about Maude?"

"About the energy release," Dad said. "Mom believes Gryphon manipulated Maude into thinking they're Eynosyndeo. As soon as Mom implanted a different reality explaining the energy release, all the information Gryphon collected about Maude would change as well."

"Do you think Gryphon fooled Maude?" Emma asked.

Dad exhaled. "Maude is fragile and susceptible to romantic fantasy. It would certainly complicate things if Gryphon was her Soulmate."

"Complicate things?" Emma echoed.

"Yes," Dad said.

Emma swore under her breath and stood up.

"Listen, honey," Dad said. "Mom is probably right. She almost always is. You know that. Maude is delicate and Gryphon is a manipulator. Right now, he's returning to the Commonworld with irrefutable-seeming information that the Ones in Power were wrong about the reason for the energy release. And Mom and I have increased and reapplied every protection. They won't find us. And if this boy Sandy told us about is your Soulmate…and when Elizabeth and Sandy meet theirs, we'll set up protections to hide the Kiryx energy release."

"How?" Emma asked, shocked that her father was being so stupid.

"We'll set up the protections for everyone you go out with, just in case."

"Is that practical?" Emma asked, exasperated.

"It's not difficult," he said.

She sat back on the chair and pressed her bare toes into the itchy green carpet. She didn't know what to say. Wasn't that their damned job, to *be prepared*? How could they have been so stupid? How could they continue to be so stupid? At least when kids fucked up they lived in some kind of private terror of getting caught. It seemed like adults—and not just her parents, but adults everywhere—fucked up majorly and somehow insanely thought that nothing would happen, that there would be no consequences, that they wouldn't get caught.

"I'm sorry," Dad said, clearly reading her thoughts. "You're right, we should have been more prepared. But I promise you we'll be better prepared from now on. Nothing bad is going to happen again."

Emma did not feel reassured, and she didn't pretend. Dad stepped closer and kissed the top of her head. "It's really important that you introduce us to the boy you like," he said.

Emma shivered and moved away from him a little.

"I'm not trying to embarrass you," he said.

Emma stared straight ahead at the scuffed wall at the end of the hall and concentrated on not crying. There used to be a painting of the ocean hanging at the end of the hall, but Sandy drew on it with a marker when he was three and Mom and Dad threw it away. She was exhausted. She just wanted to go bed, but she had no idea how she would ever fall asleep.

"Okay," Dad said softly. "We're finished. Go to bed. It's almost morning, and Mom will let you sleep in and go in late, but she won't let you skip school."

The weird splash of normal inside all the strangeness unnerved Emma. It was as if someone she knew had sprouted a second head, which disappeared and reappeared without warning, and nobody cared. Maybe living here had always felt something like that for her parents.

Dad hugged her. She didn't hug him back.

He walked down the hall. Before he reached his bedroom door, Dad turned and gazed at her. In an instant Emma saw—like she was simultaneously watching and being herself—flashes of memories from when she was little. She saw her sixth birthday party when no one showed up because Dad had put the wrong date on the invitations, and Mom had made extra presents appear seemingly out of nowhere. She saw Scott Baker tell her he didn't like her anymore in fourth grade. She'd cried in her room all afternoon, and Dad brought Fudgesicles from Mr. McShane's. And then she saw herself as a baby. Her skin was pink, like pale, pale strawberry ice cream, and her short hair looked like snow in the sun.

Dad smiled at her. "That's what I remember," he said, opening his watch face.

He peeled off the slender gold hour hand and pointed it at one of the silvery, spinning balls. The tiny sphere rose into the air, and Dad directed it to Emma's temple. It sank into her with a noise like a sigh.

"This is what *you* remember." He gazed at Emma as if he could see her at every stage of her life from birth to old woman. "Good night, *chi Erama*."

Erama was her real name, Emma realized. And Turner and Maude, and probably Elizabeth and Sandy had Sacerian names, too. And Mom and Dad. Peter and Gwen weren't their real names.

Emma watched her father go into his room then she climbed into bed. Softening morning light swam in her windows. She lay back and closed her eyes. She saw baby Turner throw a toy rabbit at her every time Mom looked away. But he wasn't throwing it, and it didn't always hit her. Sometimes it wiggled its tail in her face and she laughed. Sometimes it messed up her hair or knocked over the block tower she was building. Emma smelled her mom's hair, which smelled like the ocean and looked like moonlight. It fell over Emma's face as her mom put baby clothes on her. Mom was singing in a very pretty voice, in a language Emma almost but not quite remembered. Then Dad was throwing her in the air and Turner was yelling, "Me too!"

Safe and warm under her blankets, Emma watched the movie of her earliest life until she fell asleep.

CHAPTER TWENTY-TWO

After what felt like five minutes or several hours Emma woke up sweating. She got out of bed and went into the kitchen. It was almost six o'clock in the morning. She turned on the light. Turner would be up in a few minutes to take a shower.

Maybe she should unload the dishwasher. That would help Mom. That would be nice. The dishwasher was filled with beautiful pink and gold dishes trimmed with butterflies and flowers. The glasses on the top rack were all cut crystal, shimmering in the light from the chandelier and still a little wet.

A glass broke as Emma picked it up, stinging her palm. She pulled out a long, skinny shard of crystal, a drop of blood at the tip. Suddenly she felt sick. She sat down on the floor. Was the glass poisoned? Had she sliced an artery? Did you have arteries in your hands? Feeling sicker, she lay down and pressed her cheek to the cold floor.

Turner's shower went on upstairs. Maybe Mom would be down in a minute—

Turner's shower went on next to her room, and Emma pressed her cheek to her pillow. Her hand wasn't cut and she didn't feel sick. Joe got in bed beside her. He was naked. He was gorgeous. He lay on top of her and wrapped his arms around her. His skin was smooth and warm.

Oh my God. She was going to have sex for the first time and everyone was home. She tried to protest but nothing came out of her mouth. Joe kissed her softly and she thought of nothing else.

Turner's shower came on and he started singing. Emma blushed and rolled over. Joe wasn't there. She sat up. That was an awesome dream, she thought, smiling. She crossed her legs and tucked her feet under her thighs. Her arm hurt like someone was squeezing it. Ow. It *really* hurt. She was having a heart attack. Or a stroke in her arm. She screamed but no one came. What if no one heard her? What if she died here, alone?

Turner's shower came on and Emma started to panic. She was never going to actually wake up. Maybe the Ones in Power wanted her, too. Maybe she was somewhere Mom and Dad couldn't find her.

She tried to get out of bed but something held her down. Four hands pressed hard on her chest and she couldn't breathe. Something stabbed into the bottoms of her feet, and her shoulder blades burned as if someone was slicing into them. She screamed and no one came. One of the hands hit her hard in the face.

Turner's shower came on and Emma burst into tears. Mom and Dad's door opened and Mom went downstairs. Emma fell back on her pillow and stopped crying. She lay impossibly still in case everything changed again. The dull violet sky slowly turned pink, and the incoming sun shone through the dust floating above her messy desk. Emma shuddered and pulled her quilt around her.

* * *

Joe woke up with a huge headache. He pulled the pillow onto his head and rolled over. His back hurt. His feet hurt. His stomach felt sick. Maybe he had the flu. He knew that his mom would let him skip school without questioning him if he was still in bed when she woke up.

Joe shivered under his blanket. His head really, really hurt. When his mom came in he'd ask her for some Advil. He couldn't imagine getting out of bed or even opening his eyes.

* * *

Emma got dressed and went downstairs.

"Are you okay?" Mom asked, turning away from the waffle iron.

"I had a bad dream," Emma said, sinking into her chair. "Did you make waffles?" she asked stupidly.

"Yes," Mom said.

"I love waffles," Emma said.

"I know." Mom peeled a crispy, golden square from the iron and put it on a plate for her. "I heated the syrup."

"Yay," Emma whispered.

"Are you sure you're okay?" Mom asked. "You look sick."

"I'm just tired," Emma said, pouring syrup into every waffle square.

The waffles were delicious. Emma ate slowly. Maude and Sandy came in and sat down. Maude read the book of Shelley's poetry she'd gotten for her birthday. Sandy talked to himself about Marcus, his Play-Doh alien, whom he kept in a crumbling handful on his lap.

Food is great, Emma thought. Waffles with hot syrup are awesome. Her heart rate increased, and her scalp and fingertips started to sweat. She sat perfectly still in that way when you think there's a monster under your bed, but if you don't move, if you don't *breathe*, he won't stab through the mattress and kill you.

Emma watched Sandy whisper to Marcus. A stinging thread tore through her chest then the kitchen and Mom and Maude and Sandy receded. Everything softened, as if she'd mistakenly rubbed moisturizer into her eyes. She heard a noise like a metal-footed chair scraping across a stone floor.

Someone sat next to her. Every other loss-of-place vision had been her own or someone else's memory. This was the first time she'd lost her sense of place and remained in the present moment. She could hear two places at the same time, and inside both rooms.

A low and menacing hum murmured quietly like flower-scented poison.

Emma looked out of the corner of her eye. Maude was eating waffles and reading, Sandy was making a jagged waffle tower out of the bites he didn't want to finish. No chair. No stranger.

More chair noises, and the sound of feet on a floor. Emma moved her head. No response. Whoever they were, they didn't realize she could hear them.

"The Three Leaders have asked for my recommendation on what to do with the boy," said a cool, matter-of-fact female voice. "If Eury Vatic does not come to save his son within forty-eight hours, my recommendation is execution. Without his father the boy is no use to us. He doesn't know anything. He doesn't know Eury is his father. He doesn't know anything about him. We can't extract any more information from him at this point, and his continued presence here will open us up to infiltration by the Resisters."

"We don't know yet if he can be of any use to us," interrupted a raspy, masculine voice.

Emma felt the woman turn, saying smoothly, "I do. Without Eury Vatic, the boy is of no use. If he doesn't attempt to rescue his son within forty-eight hours we can safely depend that he will not come at all. We have to kill the boy before the Resisters find out he's alive."

"The Resisters will know he's alive, Selini," the male voice interrupted again. "They'll have had their own filters set to catch any memories of the little girl's death. They knew the boy was still alive as soon as we did. The difference was, *as it always is*, that we were better prepared to act."

Emma felt a chilly silence as another presence, one she recognized, rose to speak.

"Selini is right," Gryphon Venti said in a voice with more genuine emotion than Emma had heard from him before. "If this trap fails, and it seems already that it has, execution is the only option. Eury Vatic knew the moment Selini made the recommendation for execution and still he's made no move to come for his son. We've been preparing for this moment for a dozen years. The filters would have caught the slightest shift in the energy surrounding the boy's chamber. Eury Vatic sealed his son's fate when he chose, *again*, to save his own life over the boy's."

Emma felt a wave of admiration and envy circle the room. Gryphon Venti was the youngest of the Masevo but he was accorded the same power and responsibility as the others, and Emma felt him sense the conflicting emotions in the room. He waited until they dissipated before continuing.

"I'll agree to the forty-eight hours, but if nothing changes in that time then killing the boy is necessary. His presence brings us no closer to capturing Eury Vatic and makes us more vulnerable to the Resisters."

Emma felt a sickening trace of the pleasure she'd experienced every other time she'd seen Gryphon or heard his voice, but it was overpowered by a spike of terror.

"Any of us," Gryphon continued. "Any of us in this room would lay down our lives for what's right. That Eury Vatic's son Sfodro can't choose for himself is tragic. We have to acknowledge that. More than anyone, *we* cannot take lightly the loss of life."

Emma froze. They were talking about *Joe*. Gryphon had asked Joe if he was Sfodro Vatic when he met Joe on the street in town. She'd heard it in Joe's head. But Emma couldn't move while she could still hear the people in the Commonworld. They would notice her. Something had to break the connection.

Turner walked into the kitchen.

"I borrowed your graphing calculator without asking and I can't find it," Emma said as calmly as she could. "Sorry."

"What!" Turner shouted. "How many times have I asked you not to do that?"

The other room silenced, and Emma jumped out of her chair.

"Emma!" her brother said.

"I didn't take your calculator," Emma said. "It's in your desk."

"What?" Turner asked. "What's wrong with you?"

"Turner and Emma," Dad said, coming into the kitchen. "Stop fighting."

For the briefest second that seemed to extend into half of eternity, Emma held everything still. If she told them, they'd know she'd want to rescue Joe and they might try to stop her. But if she didn't leave now it might not matter. And she didn't know where he was or how to get there. That knowledge opened her mouth.

"Gryphon and the rest of the Masevo took Joe to the Commonworld," Emma said. *I'm sorry, Maude,* she mouthed to her sister.

"Who is Joe?" Dad said. "Is he your friend? How would Gryphon Venti know who Joe is?"

"Yes, Joe is my friend," Emma said. "And he almost got into a fight with Gryphon outside French's after school yesterday. Gryphon did something. He touched my mouth and Joe thought I was flirting with him."

Mom turned away from the waffle iron. "Maude, take Sandy out of the kitchen," she said. "And keep Elizabeth out as well when she comes downstairs."

"No," Maude protested, but Mom looked so severely at her she backed down and exhaling heavily said, "Come on, Sandy, you can show me your new comic book."

"It's not finished yet," Sandy said, following Maude through the swinging door.

"That's okay," Maude said, and the door closed.

"Let me see your face, Emma," Mom said. She ran her fingers over Emma's lips without touching them. She looked at her hand, swore under her breath, and showed it to Dad.

"What?" Emma asked.

"Gryphon made you an *Omilia*—a Betrayer," Mom said. "By touching your mouth he made you reveal secrets. You must have said something about Maude. He didn't see through the identity shields, Peter," she said, turning to Dad. "He suspected something after getting information from Emma and then just tried to access more through Maude."

CHAPTER TWENTY-THREE

Emma remembered thinking about Maude when Gryphon was in the store, but it was more like she was scrolling through family pictures or watching a home video about her sister. She didn't remember saying anything out loud.

"Will I still do that?" she asked, terrified that she could have done something without knowing. "Will I still tell people's secrets?"

"No," Mom said. She opened her hand in front of Emma's mouth. A silver tongue appeared. Mom grabbed and crushed it, and a wet groan filled the air. She wiped her hand on the side of her thigh and turned immediately to Dad. "Do you see, Peter? Nothing's changed. They're still manipulative and brutal, willing to justify anything to get what they want."

"We can't hide forever, Gwen," Dad said. "It will only get more complicated as the kids grow up."

"The Aythentia don't negotiate," Mom said.

"They will if it's in their best interest."

"We don't have anything to offer!" Mom said.

"Stop!" Emma said. "They want to kill Joe. I heard them."

Mom turned impatiently to Emma. "Why would the Aythentia want to kill your friend? They have no interest in powerless Otherworlders, Emma. Don't be dramatic."

"I'm not being dramatic," Emma snapped, suddenly not wanting to tell her mother anything. "They were arguing about it. They didn't say his name but—"

"Did they know you were listening?" Dad asked, alarmed. "And how did you hear them?"

"I don't know," Emma said. "I just did. And they didn't know I was listening. Turner yelled at me and the connection broke."

"Thank God," Dad breathed.

"Tell them," Turner said to Emma.

She took a deep breath. "Joe can fly. He must be from the Commonworld too."

Mom made a terrible noise and fell into her chair. Red light pulsed in the table under her hands.

Dad stood behind her and laid his hands on her shoulders. After a minute he said gently, "It's not possible, *Gwynaias*. Sofia and Eury's children are dead. Everyone saw it. Agatha showed us every available image."

"Everyone saw the images of Edoro's death," Mom said. "The images of Sfodro's death could never be verified. Fen Elos always believed they were false. Emma must be Sfodro Vatic's Soulmate. That's the only way she could have heard the Masevo without their knowledge. Eury must have made it possible for her to hear them." Mom briefly pressed her hands to her eyes then turned to Emma. "What else did they say?"

"They said that execution was the only option," Emma replied, her throat dry. "That Eury Vatic knew they'd made the made the decision to do it, and still he made no move to come for his son. Is Eury Vatic Joe's father? Would he just let Joe die?"

"No," Mom said emphatically. "No. If Eury didn't come to save Sfodro—*Joe*—it's because he couldn't. Eury loved his children..." Mom stopped and held hand over her mouth.

Dad sat beside her. Blue throbbed under his haggard face like drowned skin. After a long minute he took Mom's hands and kissed them. She stared hard at the floor and then gazed back up at him, her face hard and bright.

"I have to go, chi Gwynaias," he said. "You know I do. We promised Eury."

Mom nodded.

"You're far more skilled at protecting the house and the kids than I am," he said. "I'll be able to hide my traces."

"I know," Mom said, her voice thin.

Dad ran his hand across his chest and pulled out what looked like a clear balloon filled with blue smoke. He handed it to Mom, who rubbed it into her own chest with an expression of gratitude and fear.

"I will come back," Dad said.

Mom nodded again and closed her eyes.

"I'm coming with you," Emma said.

"I am too," Turner said.

"Petros," Mom begged, shaking her head.

Dad glanced at Emma. "Sfodro Vatic is Emma's Soulmate. You said it yourself. He must be. Joe's identity must have been revealed through her. The filters must have been set up to catch him through the Soulmate Revelation."

"But you haven't had one, have you, Emma?" Mom asked a little desperately. "I didn't sense it."

"We didn't sense Turner's," Dad said.

"*Misos*, Peter!" Mom said. "The emai fylakas. Sfodro would have been wearing an identity shield, too. Misos! God! What if they were incompatible?"

Mom suddenly grabbed Emma's face. "Why didn't you tell me you were feeling sick? Why did you lie to me in the kitchen last month when I asked if something happened in school? Why did you lie, chi Erama? Do you realize what could have happened? To you? To Sfodro?"

"Why did I lie to *you?"* Emma said, incensed. "What do you mean the identity shields were incompatible? What could have happened?"

No one spoke.

"Someone answer me!" Emma demanded.

Dad slumped into a chair with his head in his hands. When he raised his head again he said, "An identity shield works by affecting a harmless chemical change in the wearer. But if the shields are worn by a Soulmate pair who haven't met yet, and both wearers are older than fifteen, if *these* shields are incompatible, then they *negatively* interact like a powerful chemical reaction."

Dad looked like he was going to throw up. "If the negative interaction is strong enough," he continued, "and if the pair continues to be physically and emotionally separated while in close proximity, the incompatibility can cause a something like a drug overdose. Or madness from wildly swinging, uncontrollable emotions. Or death."

"Death?" Emma said. "I could have *died*? Joe..." She started to cry. "Joe could have died?" She felt Maude's arms around her, and Emma squeezed her sister's hand and stood up. "How could you guys have been so stupid? How could you not have prepared for this?"

"Chi Erama," Mom said, her voice cracking.

"What's Turner's real name?" Emma snarled. "What's Maude's real name? And Elizabeth's? And Sandy's? Tell us who we really are!"

Mom stood up. She took Turner's face in her hands and kissed his forehead.

"Tranos," she said. "It means Great One."

Mom held Maude's beautiful face, kissed her forehead and stroked her cheek. *"Psalla,"* she said. "Music Follows Her."

Mom sat down again and stared into the center of the room.

"Elizabeth is *Efkolas*," Dad said. "Laughing Flower. And Sandy is *Tharros*, A Well of Courage at the Heart." He took Mom's hand. "We are all *Mattah*, Mathews. Gifts to the Deserving."

"They can't go with you, Peter," Mom decided, letting go of Dad's hand. "They won't know what to expect or what to avoid. Go yourself. I know you have to. You have to, for Sofia and for Eury, but you can't take Turner and Emma. You can't."

Dad took her hand again. "If something happens to Sfodro—to Joe," Dad said, "think of what will happen to Emma. Think of what happened to Eury when Sofia died. You have to let her try to find him. And Turner can help look after her."

Mom gazed at Emma, who had never seen her mother look so scared. "Okay," she whispered. "Go. Go."

CHAPTER TWENTY-FOUR

Emma and Turner walked in silence behind Dad. Emma felt as though her feet weren't making actual contact with the ground, that she was only half-present.

Dad stopped walking and rubbed his hand over his head, which reverted to its natural bald blue state. "Follow me."

Emma and Turner followed Dad up Ozymandias, the climbing tree, until the branches got too thin. "Hold on," Dad said quietly. "This is *dentropyli*, a portal tree. All you have to do is concentrate on moving through it. Think yourself through."

Emma clasped a swaying branch in each hand and saw Turner do the same. She imagined herself passing through the tree and then, without anything, without sound or flashing light or a change in the air, Emma felt herself melt into it. Her skin smelled like maple syrup. Her arms and legs felt hard and porous and woody, and her fingers spread wide like pliant young leaves.

Then Emma opened her eyes and climbed out of a different tree in a small walled garden filled with sculptures. Some were beautiful, abstract, humanlike forms lit from within, but most looked like crushed spheres. The spheres were silver, unlit, and made to appear broken.

Turner and Dad were waiting for her at the bottom of the tree.

"Where are we?" she whispered.

"Mom's brother Claudeo's house," Dad said, his voice raw.

The light in a large round window grew brighter, and a man opened a door Emma hadn't seen before.

"What the hell are you doing here, Petros?" the man asked in a cold voice. "Is Gwynaias all right?"

"Gwen's fine," Dad said, walking forward. The man looked angrier the nearer Dad got. "We need your help, Claudeo."

Emma and Turner stepped closer. Claudeo's face softened.

"Misos," he said, gazing at them, and a small cry escaped his mouth. Emma had an out-of-body sense of being kissed on the forehead then tossed in the air.

"I still can't believe you refused to come home," Claudeo said, his voice thick.

"I'm sorry," Dad answered after an uncomfortable silence.

"Whatever you need, I can't help you," Claudeo said, leaning back into the white brightness coming from the window. "I won't endanger Isohel. I'm sorry. You have to leave."

"You could have come to us," Dad said. "You and Isohel might have been happy in Pali. Gwen missed you. We both did. And Isohel would have grown up with her whole family."

Claudeo looked exactly like Mom, the same tiny, sharp features, the same thin, light-filled hair, but he had no strength in his face. It was as if Mom had gotten all the blood and fire and he'd gotten what was left. Now he was shaking, white fury narrowing his eyes to grey slits.

"I'm sorry," Dad said. "I didn't mean..."

"You have *no idea*," Claudeo said, his voice tight like a rope was around his throat. He smashed his pale lips together and shook his head. "Get rid of your traces and get out." He walked into the house. The inside light clicked off.

Dad turned.

"What are we going to do?" Emma asked. "What about Joe? Where is he?"

A soft thud sounded near the tree they'd traveled through. Emma spun to see a green-haired girl about her age coming toward them.

The expression on her face was fierce. She was thin and pretty, and carrying a cute, sparkly bag. Emma thought of Elizabeth.

The girl glanced quickly from face to face as if memorizing something. "I'm Isohel Arismapsi," she said. "Claudeo's daughter."

Dad stared at the girl with the same heartbroken happiness that had been on Claudeo's face when he saw Emma and Turner.

"Gwen told me the Ones in Power have your friend," the girl said to Emma.

Emma looked at Dad. Mom must have contacted Isohel as soon as they left.

"Did you ask my dad for help and he refused?" the girl asked, barely concealed disgust in her voice.

"He doesn't want to put you in danger," Dad replied.

Isohel rolled her eyes and swore in a language Emma almost recognized. "Yeah," she sneered. She shifted on the spot. "You're Turner and you're a *Knino*, a Telekinetic, right?"

Turner nodded.

"And you're Emma and you're a *Thoryba*, a Telepath?"

"Yeah," Emma said. "But my mom said everyone in this world can hear thoughts."

Isohel smiled. "Not the way you can. Or the way you'll be able when you're here long enough. You'll be able to hear thoughts from a distance. Not everyone can do that. You're a *Thoryba Exocho*, a Super Telepath. Your mom told me." She glanced at the house. "We should go. Zino—that means Dad, Daddy, Father, Papa, whatever. Anyway, he thinks I already left for school."

"Where are we going?" Turner asked.

"The Detainee Tower," Isohel said to Dad. "We can take the train from *Dysikalloni*—Westfair."

"The train?" Turner said.

"Yeah." Isohel grinned. "We've actually copied some things from the Otherworld. You guys are good at efficiently moving large numbers of people. Too bad you don't take more advantage of it. Come on."

Within twenty minutes, Emma, Turner, and Dad followed Isohel into what looked like someone's fantasy of a subway tunnel: clean, bright, and efficient as a hospital, minus patients and disease.

"Here," Isohel said, handing each of them a strange but vaguely familiar object. "I put some minor deflective protections on these. Just give them back to me later. When the *metakan*—the train— comes in, blend into the crowd and think benign thoughts. Don't think anything about your friend or the tower."

"But we speak English," Turner said. "We think in English. It'll give us away."

"I speak English," Isohel said, scrunching her pretty face impatiently. "You understand me, right? We speak Sacerian—our ancient language—and English pretty interchangeably here. This part of the Commonworld is nearest to English-speaking parts of the Otherworld and the languages are constantly informed by each other. We all spring from the same source, right?" she added brightly. "Seriously, no worries. No one will think anything about words you do or don't know.

"Oh," the girl added, handing them tiny discs that looked like glass candy. "I almost forgot. You pay for the train with these. They all have 10 trips on them, so you should be okay. Unless you get really lost." She grinned.

The train glided into the station. They all got on after a fat woman and her three sleepy-eyed children, all with freshly cut, glittery-ended hair. The door closed with a squeaky whisper. Emma climbed over a pink-haired old man and sat in the window seat. The air smelled good, like clean hair and warm pajamas.

The pink-haired old man stroked the center of a stone similar to the one Turner had given Maude last night; it opened and he fell into sleepily half-reading. Emma couldn't read any of it. She kept her fear for Joe at the back of her head and stared at her knees. The object Isohel gave her sat in her palm. It looked like a cross between a phone and a tiny lunchbox. Emma turned it over then closed her fingers and leaned her head on the cool window and tried hard to think of nothing.

An announcer's voice came clearly through a speaker. Sacerian seemed similar to the language she'd made up with Izzy. Emma started whenever she heard a familiar-sounding word. A sharply angular woman with lush purple hair and gorgeous eyes stared unkindly. Emma shoved her hands under her legs and grimaced, making her best I-don't-care-about-anything face. The woman returned her attention to the illuminated rock in her hand, and Emma crushed the panic rising in her chest.

"This is our stop," Isohel whispered, standing up as the train slowed. "Keep your heads filled with inconsequential thoughts. My friend Tyrian's dad works for the Resisters. He interrupted the *prosechol*, the recording sphere, and he'll let us in, but don't look at him. We'll only have a few minutes to find your friend before the Ones in Power restart it."

CHAPTER TWENTY-FIVE

Emma, Turner and Dad silently followed Isohel through the cool, smooth-walled building up inside the tower. Isohel stopped.

"Tyrian told me the door would be here," she said to Dad. "Can you see it?"

Dad moved his hand in front of the blank wall, as if he were drawing the outline of a door, and an opening formed to reveal a large room with perpetually changing walls. Stone melted into cloudy nothingness then appeared to be made of colored glass then polished wood, and then something Emma didn't recognize. The group entered, and Dad closed the opening with a hush like drawn blood.

Inside, in the center of the shifting, borderless space, Joe lay quietly moaning, his legs curled into his chest.

Dad put his hand on Emma's shoulder. *Wait*, he thought. Emma looked at him in despair. *Can you sense anyone else in the room?*

Emma closed her eyes. The room was empty except for Joe and the four of them. Someone, or something, had been outside watching but it was gone.

She turned to Dad and shook her head no. Dad nodded, and all four of them ran to Joe. The ten feet between where they stood and where Joe lay was filled with echoing visual remnants of what had happened to him. How he'd had been pulled from his bed while dreaming of Emma. How it took four people to hold him down. How they injected something into the soles of his feet and opened the scars on his shoulder blades to search for hidden wings. How they made him believe he was home in bed, so the execution itself, when it came, would seem like sleep. Emma had dreamt this. She had dreamt this when it was happening.

She knelt beside Joe and laid her hand on his shoulder. "He's freezing."

Dad took off his jacket and gave it to her. Emma draped it over Joe. He tucked it around himself.

"Joe," she whispered, gently shaking him. "We have to go."

"I can't," he said. "I'm sick."

"I know," Emma murmured. "But we have to go."

"I don't want to," Joe said, pulling Dad's jacket more tightly around him.

Dad moved to pull Joe to his feet.

"No," Emma said. "Wait."

She didn't know what to do. Panic fluttered in her chest. She closed her eyes and opened herself up to what Joe was feeling. Pain shot into her head and she reeled back from a wave of nausea and weakness. But Turner held her shoulders she felt stronger.

Joe, Emma thought, teetering between wanting to throw up and run away. *The people who tried to take Maude have taken you. If you don't get up now they're going to come back and kill you.*

Joe shuddered and groaned in pain. He opened his eyes and looked at Emma. "How did you get here?" he asked, clutching his head.

"The same way you did," Dad said, gently helping Joe to his feet.

"Your skin, Emma," Joe said, shivering violently in Dad's jacket. "Is it pink?"

Emma glanced at her arms. They were a pale luminous pink, like the underside of a wet rose petal. "Yeah," she said. "I guess it is."

"It's pretty," he said.

Emma bit her cheek so she wouldn't cry.

"Who's she?" Joe asked, nodding.

"I'm Isohel. Emma's cousin. We have to get out of here. Now. How strong are you? Usually, I mean; not how strong you feel right now."

"Pretty strong, I guess," he said, still shaking.

"Do you think you could fly carrying Emma and her dad?" Isohel asked.

"I don't know," Joe said.

"It's not just happiness that helps you fly," Isohel continued. "It's a kind of adrenaline. Take hold of Emma and her dad and stand near the opening. Can you see it?"

Joe shook his head.

Isohel looked at Dad, who walked to a section of the cloudy wall and opened a hidden window, revealing their height in the tower and the grey sunlight on the city below. "I'm going to draw your adrenaline up," Isohel said to Joe, standing behind him at the opening. "Fly south. The sun's in the west right now. I'll catch up, and then you can follow me."

"Can you fly?" Joe asked.

The girl reached behind herself and pulled bright green wings out of her shoulder blades. "Ow!" She took a second to catch her breath. "I've never flown before, but I don't think it's that hard." She bit her cheek and breathed heavily through her nose as she opened the wings. "Dad said Turner had exceptionally strong telekinetic ability even as a baby. I hope he can propel us a little."

Emma felt the blood drain from her face. "They're coming."

Isohel pressed her hand to the middle of Joe's chest. He gave a strangled cry. "Go!" she whispered fiercely, grabbing Turner and clasping him around the waist.

Emma, her dad and Joe flew out the opening in the wall. She could barely hold on.

After a few minutes, Isohel passed them. "Follow me," she whispered in a strained voice. Emma's heart sank. Turner's face was scraped and bloody, and his teeth were clenched.

Joe flew below Isohel and took some of Turner's weight. Hair-thin blue lights streamed overhead.

They landed on a soft forest floor. Isohel pressed her hand to Joe's chest, and Joe groaned and sucked in a huge mouthful of air. "Try to calm down," she told him. "Breathe more slowly. Are you okay? I shouldn't have done that so quickly, but I had no choice."

"I'm okay," Joe said, catching his breath and seeming like himself again. "What happened to Turner? Is he all right?"

Dad was leaning over Turner, who sat on the ground breathing heavily.

"What happened?" Emma asked.

"They came in as soon as you left," Turner said quietly. "I had to fight them off."

"You were great," Isohel said. "They obviously underestimated you. No surprise there."

Dad looked around and swore through his teeth. "We're not far enough away. They'll have more than enough time to find us."

The streams of light, which had formed a mesh pattern above the trees, disintegrated and began to fall like tiny drops of pale blue fire.

"Run," Dad said.

Isohel led them into a cave.

"What are you *thinking*?" Dad asked, looking around at the grey, crystal-embedded walls. "This will give us away faster than anything else."

"They'll check the light pattern fall first," Isohel said, indifferent to Dad's anger. "They don't question their initial judgments, because they never make mistakes. The Aythentia are arrogant as fuck, remember? No questions or dissent because they're always right," she added spitefully. "The light grid is the most efficient way to find us, and until they realize it didn't work they won't try anything else."

"But we can't leave," Dad said. "Sooner or later someone will notice the degree of life-energy in here. There are too many of us, and all this quartz will clarify it more quickly."

Isohel frowned. "Do you think you can avoid every trace of light?" she demanded, pointing to sparks like dew on every surface outside the cave. "You can't."

"Can't we just fly over it?" Joe asked.

"No," she said. "The light leaves traces everywhere it moved. The whole area from the sky to the ground will reveal us."

"Can't we fight them off?" Joe asked.

Isohel smiled. "No. Not now. They underestimated Turner when they thought he was a powerless Otherworlder. They won't do that again. And there will be more of them than we can handle. Your identity shields are great, by the way. I never would have known who you were if Gwen hadn't told me."

A vehicle like a car but sleeker pulled up to the opening of the cave. The lights bounced off it like drops of water right after a car's been waxed. The door opened and Claudeo said in a frigid voice, "Get in. I've sealed off the *kima*."

That's the Sacerian word for car, Isohel mouthed then made a face and pulled a necklace with a stone pendant out of her shirt. She glanced at it and swore in what had to be Sacerian.

"Get in," Claudeo repeated fiercely.

"I didn't know this was a *konameta*," Isohel said, holding the pendant out to her father.

"Get in the car!" he shouted.

They all climbed in and the car sped off, leaving the light-studded forest behind.

"Thank you, Claudeo," Dad said.

Claudeo glared at Isohel and said nothing.

"They never would have gotten away without me," Emma's cousin said fiercely to her father. She really looked like Elizabeth, Emma thought, except for her smooth, green hair. "The Aythentia were going to kill him. He was in the death chamber."

"You could have been captured."

"Where's your sense of justice?" Isohel hissed between her teeth. "Where's your sense of loyalty?"

"With you," Claudeo answered, equally ferocious. "You. You're my responsibility and you're all I have. Your safety and your well-being come first. Above everything."

Isohel exhaled and stared out the window.

"I don't know if you remember my father's forest house," Claudeo said to Dad, calmly glancing over at him as if nothing happened. "Did Gwen ever take you? It's off the grid, so it should be safe."

"Once," Dad answered. "Before we were married."

"That's where we're going. It's too dangerous for you to stay with Isohel and me. You'll have to find a dentropyli on your own. My father knew about an unregistered portal tree, but he refused to tell Gwen or me the location, even right before he died."

"We're grateful for any help you can give us," Dad said.

"I've packed enough food for a few days," Claudeo said, turning the car, which Emma just realized was hovering a little above the ground, onto a smaller pathway. "I wouldn't stay any longer than that. The Ones in Power will eventually figure out who you really are. Even Gwen can't make a perfect identity shield. Try to remind her that she is not invincible." Claudeo rubbed his hand over his mouth. "Do you remember how to cook?"

Dad nodded.

"Once I drop you off I'm wiping every trace from the car, and from Isohel's and my memory," Claudeo said.

Isohel jumped. Claudeo shot her a forbidding glare. She sank back into the feather-soft seat, fuming.

Claudeo glanced back at Emma and Turner. "I'm sorry."

Emma felt Isohel's sharp elbow in her side. She turned to say something. Isohel put her finger to her lips and handed Emma a thin piece of silver in the shape of a dragonfly. A hair-thin stripe of blood crossed Isohel's palm. Isohel stared straight ahead with a mask of fake surrender on her face.

"Cut your hand like I did," she whispered without looking at Emma, "then hold mine."

"What!" Emma whispered back, a thousand blood-and-germ-and-bodily-fluid disease lectures running through her head.

"It's not what you think," Isohel murmured, almost too quietly for Emma to hear. "We get sick in other ways. This will keep me connected to you in a way my dad won't think to erase. I've already made a note on my reading stone to come to my grandfather's house tomorrow. When I see you," she said, turning her hand palm-up on her thigh so Emma could see the blood line, "the scar will help me remember you. So I won't actually forget you, and you won't forget anything." She turned to Emma. "You'll need me."

Emma glanced at the front of the car where Dad and Claudeo were quietly talking. "Won't your dad notice?" she asked. "Can't he read your thoughts?"

"He *can* do it, but he's not always doing it," Isohel said. "We all have access to other gemynd's thoughts, but we're not constantly listening. Even the Aythentia—the Ones in Power," she clarified with a sneer, "aren't constantly viewing the thoughts they access; they're constantly recording them to view later. And we, whether we support the Eleytheria or the Aythentia, are constantly trying to block their access. Every gemynd believes he or she has a right to reasonable privacy."

"What's a gemynd?" Emma whispered.

"You are," Isohel said. "We are. Commonworlders are not quite human, we're *gemynd*, humanlike beings gifted with powers of the mind. All of our powers are things we can do by thinking. Even flying is a kind of telekinesis. That's why Joe can fly without wings. Although it's really hard to do." Isohel smiled and nodded at the dragonfly.

Emma took a deep breath and slid the silver dragonfly's tail across her skin. It was cooling, not painful. Isohel took that hand and pressed it to her own. Emma felt a jolt of connection and the sense that a little bit of Isohel flowed through her.

Her cousin smiled. "We're all connected anyway. This just reinforces it. The Commonworld and the Otherworld are sister worlds. You should ask your dad to tell you the *Idrysi*, the Creation Story. It's pretty sweet."

Isohel smiled quickly again at Emma then opened her jeweled bag, pulled out a crystal cylinder, shoved it in her ear and closed her eyes. Emma could hear faint music coming from the glassy thing, kind of recognizable and kind of not. She considered Isohel's musical disconnect with envy. She wished she had her iPod. Music made everything better.

"Thanks for coming to get me," Joe said, taking Emma's hand in the dark car. Fireflies flew to Emma's fingertips.

"You're welcome," she whispered back.

CHAPTER TWENTY-SIX

Joe tucked his hand between Emma's legs and stared out the window at the passing blackness of the trees. He thought of his little sister dying when she was still a baby, and he thought of his mothers: the one he knew, the one he'd never know. Somewhere his father was alive. Had the man ever tried to find him? Did he even know his son was alive? Did he care?

Emma laid her hand on Joe's thigh. Blades of heat spread through the muscles of his legs and his stomach. He sensed Emma's struggle not to turn and kiss him. Something was changing between them; he could feel it. He dropped his free hand and clung to the underside of the seat, and Isohel's dad Claudeo glanced at him in the mirror.

"Are you okay, Turner?" Isohel asked, breaking the silence in the car.

Claudeo's eyes shot to Turner, who was sitting on Joe's other side.

"Turner fought them off," Isohel said defiantly. "He threw all four of them against the barrier, knocking two of them unconsciousness."

"How did they retaliate?" Claudeo asked.

"He's okay," Isohel snipped.

"I *am* okay," Turner agreed. "I was surprised. Next time I'll be prepared."

"Next time?" Claudeo said angrily to Emma's Dad. "What does that mean? I thought you were leaving."

"We are," Dad said.

Turner stared straight ahead. Joe looked at him.

"What?" Emma whispered, squeezing Joe's thigh.

He hadn't gotten used to the rose-petal pink color of Emma's skin. In the moonlit car she looked like a fairy. Joe wanted to kiss her forever. She wrapped her hand around his leg and tucked her soft fingers under his thigh. His heart thundered in his chest and he clung to the seat.

"I want to stay," Joe said, feeling Emma's sharp intake of air as if her breath was in his mouth. "I want to find my dad."

* * *

Joe held her hand but didn't say anything more. His skin touching hers made Emma aware that she was part of a world at once enormous and tiny. The two of them together made a small universe. What was she to do if he left? What would he do without her?

Mortifyingly, girlie tears sprang up. Emma wished her eyelids had teeth. She hated to feel weak.

She clenched her jaw and stared at the back of her father's blue head. Dad's thoughts were threaded with a dark happiness shot with guilt. He was so grateful to be home after almost fifteen years. He couldn't stop looking at the trees. They were older, and huge with curling branches that reached toward the road and each other. Dad wanted to suck in the air like a dog with its head out a car window. He couldn't look at everything hard enough.

Joe shifted his weight, and his legs and shoulders rubbed against Emma's. Sparks of fire rained underneath her skin. She sighed and gazed at the beautiful mystery sitting next to her on the leather seat. If it was leather. Maybe people in the Commonworld didn't sit on dead animal skins.

Joe grinned, still staring straight ahead. Emma blushed and shut her eyes. Had he heard her random dead animal skins question? Had he heard anything else?

Joe leaned in and kissed the top of her head.

"So I'm a *beautiful mystery*, huh?" he whispered.

"I was thinking of something else," Emma said.

"Uh-huh," Joe said. He laughed quietly and threaded his warm fingers through hers. Happiness flooded Emma's arms and legs.

See? That was it. How could she ever, *ever* be without the sense of him? And of herself? How could *he* ever be without it? How could anyone?

For the first time since Emma was really little, when the idea of her birthday made it impossible to sleep, when she ran everywhere, when she was never painfully aware of herself as something separated from the world around her, for the first time since then Emma felt her own aliveness. And she didn't want to let that feeling go.

"We're here."

Isohel's dad stopped the car, which Emma had just realized was soundless except for the suddenly slamming door.

"Why can't we just go home now?" she asked, helping to unload the contents of the car into the tall stone house. Before Joe *really* decides stay, she thought.

"The Masevo will be looking for us," Dad said. "It's too dangerous." He moved out of the way to let Claudeo pass.

"Who are the Masevo?" Joe asked, waiting while Turner manfully grabbed the heaviest bag. Emma's heart swelled. Joe didn't have to prove anything to anyone.

"They're the enforcement arm of the Ones in Power," Isohel said, grabbing a bag of colored fruit and swinging it while she walked. "They're the ones who set up the light grid and who chased us. They're arrogant pricks."

Claudeo raised his silvery eyebrows. Isohel grinned mockingly. Claudeo ignored her and glared at Dad like Isohel's smart mouth was his fault.

"Why is he mad at you?" Emma whispered to her father after Claudeo disappeared into the house.

Dad stared at the empty doorway then out into the cooling woods. "I don't know."

"Yes, you do."

"Not now, Emma. Okay?" Her father slung a bag of something brown and lumpy over his shoulder and walked into the house.

Joe sat on a rock, away from the car and bright late afternoon sunlight. "She's dangerous," he said, cocking his head in Isohel's direction.

"What?" Emma said. "No, she isn't. She's nice."

"She's impulsive and she doesn't question herself," Joe said. "And she's pissed at her dad."

"Who isn't pissed at their father when they're seventeen?" Emma snapped without thinking.

Joe's face darkened.

"Sorry," Emma said, taking her hand out of his and staring into the dark green forest.

"I'm just saying we have to be careful," Joe said.

"Fine," Emma agreed. She slid her hand under her legs. The rock was cold and pitted. "I'm afraid," she said.

Joe looked at her: The sensation that he flew into her and then back out again was so sudden and intense Emma thought she might lose her balance. Then Joe kissed her, clinging fiercely, his skin hot. Leaves brushed Emma's face as they floated up into the canopy of branches.

"We should get down," she said, pulling away from him a little after a moment.

"You want to get down?" Joe asked, out of breath.

"No," she said. "I don't."

Emma kissed him and ran her fingers through his hair. The blue roots were softer than the dyed sections, and Joe noticed more when she touched it. He made a rough sound in his throat that found an echo deep inside Emma. She tugged him closer.

"You're right," Joe said, breathing hard. "We should get back."

Emma nodded.

With a sigh of frustration, Joe kissed Emma's forehead and they drifted to the ground.

"Don't do that again," Dad said, dragging Emma to her feet and away.

"No worries," Isohel called out, standing between Dad and the door. "The Ones in Power don't know he can still fly."

"They must suspect it," Dad asked. "They dug into the scars."

Emma felt Joe's stomach tighten. She took his hand.

"Hardly anyone can fly after their wings are *cut*," Isohel remarked. "I told Emma. It's really hard."

"How did you know Joe had wings, anyway?" Emma asked.

"Your mom told me his wings must have been cut off when he was a baby but he could still fly." She put down a bag of food. "When we left I made it seem like Turner could fly. The less they know, the better off we are."

"Not *we*," Claudeo said, coming out of the house. Isohel jumped at the sight of him. He shut the car trunk. "We are not part of this anymore. I'm sorry, Peter."

"I understand," Dad said, and he sounded like he meant it.

Claudeo took Turner's hand and shook it. After a brief silence he pulled Turner close and hugged him tightly then did the same to Emma. Claudeo gazed at both of them for a long minute.

Turner hated to be stared at. His jaw was twitching but his eyes were sympathetic. Maybe Turner remembered more of their life in the Commonworld than Emma realized.

"Get rid of your *leronas* before you leave," Claudeo said to Dad. "Traces," he explained to Turner and Emma. "Leronas are the energy traces everyone leaves behind. You look like your grandmother, chi Erama." He stroked Emma's cheek then turned away. "Get in the car, Isohel."

"Thank you," Dad said, squeezing Isohel's hand briefly as she passed him. "We couldn't have done it without you."

She blushed and murmured, "Bye," before climbing into the car.

Claudeo looked at them for a moment then got in and drove away. Dad watched the car disappear into the woods.

"Let's go inside," he said huskily.

Inside, after the door was locked Dad said, "Turner, help me make a fire. This part of the forest gets cold at night." He stopped. "That's one of the reasons your grandfather loved it. He hated hot weather."

It was unsettling for Emma to learn she resembled a grandmother she'd never met or seen, and to know suddenly about a grandfather with likes and dislikes and an old stone house in the middle of a cold forest.

"I can make a fire," Joe said, shifting his weight from foot to foot. "Maybe you could make something to eat," he added softly. From the expression on his face Emma realized he hadn't eaten anything since yesterday. Dad saw it, too.

"Sure," Dad said. "Thanks, Joe. Turner, you and Emma go upstairs and make up the beds. And take this," he added, tossing a blue stick at his son.

"What is it?" Turner asked.

"It's like a flashlight," Dad said. "It will light up in the dark. I don't think Claudeo ever uses this house and there might be animals in the closets."

* * *

Hours later, after dinner, Turner and Dad went to bed and Joe and Emma stayed downstairs. Two enormous, cherry-red chairs faced the stone fireplace. Emma tucked her feet under her legs. The fire felt hot on her face. She undid her ponytail and pulled her now snow-white hair across her chest.

"What are you going to do?" she asked Joe.

Joe paced the room, being careful to stay near the fire. Away, it felt like January with the furnace off.

"I'm going to stay," he said. "I want to find my dad."

Emma's heart sank.

"What about your mom? What about school?" *What about me?* She stood up, and cold air swirled around her ankles and blew through her clothes. "What makes you think you can find your dad, anyway? The Ones in Power have been looking for him since you disappeared. What makes you think *you* can find him? How do you know he's still alive?"

Joe sat on the chair again and stared into the fire.

"You can't change anything," Emma said quietly. "You can't save your sister and you can't change what happened to you."

"You're right," Joe agreed. "I can't. But I don't want to run away."

"They were going to kill you," Emma said.

"Then I should stay and fight, shouldn't I?" Joe said. "Otherwise I'll spend my life looking behind me. What's to keep me in freaking New Hampshire anyway?"

Emma opened her mouth then closed it again.

"Forget it," Joe said. "I don't know what I'm going to do. I'm tired."

"Vengeance is stupid," Emma said. "Nothing good ever comes of it. *Ever*. No matter what anyone says."

Joe stared at her. "I'm not talking about vengeance, Emma. Jeez, what the hell do you think I am? I'm not talking about vengeance—"

"Then what *are* you talking about?"

"I'm talking about not running away. I'm talking about fighting for the chance to know myself and be myself and not…"

"What?" Emma prompted.

"I'm tired of feeling like no one else is anything like me," Joe said.

"We're like you," Emma pointed out.

Joe stood tall and wiry, and so beautiful in the half-light of the fire. His blue roots pushed up like indigo flowers through his lush dark hair.

"*I'm* like you," Emma added.

She watched Joe's face fall apart and then reform as if he'd been wearing a ceramic mask until now.

"We're part of the same thing," Emma went on. "The same single thing."

Joe crossed the room in one stride, pulled Emma into his arms and kissed her fiercely. She wanted to take a piece of him inside her and hold it forever. Emma slid her hands inside his sweater. He unbuttoned her shirt.

She didn't know how much longer she could resist, or how much longer she should resist. Sex was a big deal, but love was bigger. And if Joe Castlellaw wasn't her Soulmate, she didn't have one. Joe's warm hand was inside her bra, and Emma lost her train of thought. Her exposed back scraped against the gritty stone ceiling.

"I know you're not ready," Joe said, out of breath, his rough voice swallowing almost all of Emma's resistance.

"How do you know?" Emma asked, pulling him tight against her.

He cried out and sucked in a hard breath. "I just do."

Emma kissed him slow and soft, drinking the sweet sound of his voice through her skin. "I will be ready someday," she promised, breaking the kiss just to look at him.

Joe grinned.

Her legs and stomach were blazing. Maybe she was kidding herself about how long she could wait.

"And I'll be ready for you," he said, smiling against her throat. "But until then…"

They kissed for a long, long time.

Her shirt was all the way unbuttoned and Joe's sweater was pushed up. His hot, hard stomach moved against hers. Emma decided to say *yes*. Now, right now. She heard Joe hum sweetly as if he knew what she'd decided the instant she decided it. Then Turner or Dad opened a door upstairs and started coming down the stone steps.

Emma swore.

Joe whispered, "We'd better stop."

He held her so tightly Emma thought he might explode right there on the ceiling. She kissed his hot forehead. "Okay," she said.

They floated down to the floor.

"I'll go up first," she said.

"Thanks," he murmured, out of breath and pacing in the coldest part of the room. "Good night."

"Good night," Emma said, smiling because she couldn't help it.

CHAPTER TWENTY-SEVEN

"Are you in love with Emma?" Turner asked as soon as Joe shut the bedroom door.

"What?" Joe said. It had been a little while, and he had calmed down. It felt as if someone had ripped out all his muscles and then stretched them so now they didn't quite fit, though. And his feet and his shoulder blades hurt from where the Ones in Power cut into him.

"My sister. Emma," Turner said. "Are you in love with her?"

Joe sat on the narrow bed. "I know who you meant. Yes. I am," he said, realizing it was true. "But I don't know why it's any of your business."

"She's my sister."

"You said that." Joe kicked off his shoes. The soles of his feet stung in the cold air. "What do you want?"

Turner's eyes flashed.

"Sorry," Joe said. "I don't mean to be a dick."

"Were you ever in love with anyone else?" Turner asked. "Before Emma?"

"No," Joe said, easing himself onto the bed, burying his face in the soft pillow.

"Don't do anything to hurt her," Turner warned.

Lying down, Joe felt the past twenty-four hours pull at him. Turner's protective-brother shit pissed him off, and he wanted Emma so badly he could feel her in the space between his muscles and skin. Joe took a shallow breath and stretched his feet to the bottom of the chilly sheets. By now his mother would be going crazy. She didn't have anyone to talk to, and he had no way of getting in touch with her. What the hell would he tell her, anyway?

"Do you remember anything about your Commonworld parents?" Turner asked.

"What?" Joe said. The jolt of exhausted fury made him feel dizzy. "No."

"You must have remembered something, or Emma wouldn't have been able to see what happened to your sister."

"I don't remember anything about them," Joe said. His heart pounded and his arms and legs trembled with exhaustion. "Emma thinks she saw my dad that day in your house when I..." He drew in a long breath and felt a little sick. "When I had that vision that she saw too."

Turner got out of bed and opened a drawer in a carved cabinet near the door.

"What are you doing?" Joe asked.

Turner didn't answer.

"I have to go to sleep," Joe said, rolling over. The blanket was soft and smelled like snow. "I'll see you in the morning."

"I think this is a picture of your parents," Turner said. "They look like you."

Joe opened his eyes but he didn't turn around.

"Don't you want to see it?" Turner asked.

"No," Joe said, staring at the marshmallow-colored wall. "I don't. I just want to go to sleep."

If it was a picture of his parents, his real parents, he didn't want to see them for the first time when Turner was watching. Joe tugged the blanket more tightly around him and squeezed his eyes shut. Like a sudden downpour, he wanted Emma intensely again. There was a moment when they were kissing, when her back was against the ceiling and her nearly naked breasts were crushed against his burning skin that Joe thought she'd decided to say *yes*. Finally, yes.

"It's the only thing in the drawer," Turner said, getting back into bed.

"Thanks," Joe said. But he didn't move. Not until later.

After Turner fell asleep, Joe got out of bed and opened the drawer. The picture was three-dimensional and encased in a chunk of glass or clear stone. The figures didn't move or look at him. The woman's face was similar to his but her hair was black. The man had Joe's brown skin and an expression of fierce concentration in his eyes. Their hands were laced tightly together, as if someone or something was trying to tear them apart.

Joe held the glass up to the moonlight coming through the window and turned it over in his hand. He felt nothing. He should feel something, shouldn't he? Something big? Some smack of recognition? Some thrill of longing? Some resounding *yes*?

He put the thing back into the drawer then immediately took it out again. If he was going to stay it would help to know what his father looked like.

What the hell was he thinking? How could he stay here? Where would he even begin to look? This wasn't a movie, and he wasn't a superhero. And his father, if he was even alive, obviously had no interest in finding him.

Joe sat on the windowsill. The moon was still bright but the sky was lightening. He couldn't go back to New Hampshire and pretend nothing had happened. If his dad was still alive Joe couldn't do nothing.

The windowsill was as wide and as deep as a couch. Joe stretched out his legs and pressed his toes into the chilly, stone frame. The bottoms of his feet really hurt.

Nothing ever turned out to be what you thought.

* * *

After breakfast Emma and Joe cleared the plates and wiped the table. Dad and Turner were upstairs discussing how and when to leave. Joe hadn't told anyone but Emma that he wanted to stay.

Without knocking on the door or anything Isohel waltzed in, her sleek green hair swinging. The wings she had pulled out of her shoulder blades yesterday were gone. She looked at Emma strangely for a moment then smiled and said, "It worked!"

"What worked?" Joe asked.

"Before Dad erased my memory I wrote a note to myself to cut my morning classes, come here, and make sure to be nice to the girl with white hair." Isohel flopped onto one of the puffy red chairs in the sitting room and kicked off her shoes. "I made the connector scar super carefully so my memories of Emma would be almost impossible to erase. Brilliant, huh?"

"How did you give yourself wings yesterday?" Joe asked, sitting down on the broad stone hearth.

"I'm a *Dimiorg*, a Transformist," Isohel said. "I can transform anything tangible into something else. But I have to use properties of the original object. I made those wings out of my own skin and bone and muscle. Your mom is a Transformist," she said to Emma.

"Is it magic?" Joe asked.

"There's no such thing as magic," Isohel said. "Not the way you mean, anyway. The Commonworld is on a separate plane from the Otherworld, but everything is part of the same whole, the same universe. There is nothing super, or separate, or extra."

"How do you know?" Joe asked.

"Everyone knows," Isohel said. "We learn it in school."

Joe smiled at her, and Emma realized that for the first time he felt like he might belong somewhere.

"This isn't a different world, exactly," Isohel said. She peeled ice-green layers of polish from her fingernails and kicked the rose petal-thin flakes across the floor with her toe. "It's on a different plane but in the same space. That's why we call it the Commonworld. The ancient name, the one that's still used at festivals and in rituals, is Saceres. We are Sacerians. And you are, too, because you were born here. Pali is the ancient name for the Otherworld. Pali and Saceres and any other worlds we don't know about yet are part of the same whole. There's one universe with an infinite number of parts."

Joe didn't say anything.

Isohel continued, "Okay, well, some of your *lexingenia*—"

"What?" Joe said.

"Uh"—Isohel thought for a second—"physicists, sorry. Anyway, we learned in elementary knowledge classes that Otherworld physicists are coming to understand the nature of infinite parts. They call them multiverses, which means, obviously, countless universes, all of them with different natural laws but all of them part of the big whole. I think they call the big whole 'the landscape.'"

"Okay," Joe said, nodding, "I read something about that last year in *The Guardian*. A newspaper," he explained after Isohel made a face. "But this is a different world. Nobody in our world knows anything about this."

"Not nobody," Isohel interrupted. "Otherworlders have known about us for as long as they've been conscious of themselves." She sat up straight and tossed her emerald hair. "When Otherworlders sense something true that they can't explain, they make it into mythology because it's too important to abandon or disregard." She leaned forward and smiled. "We're your 'There must be something else.' We're the source of your fairy tales. We're your vampires and fairies and witches."

Joe took a deep breath. "Well, very few people *know* anything about it," he said. "I'd never heard anything, and if I told anyone about it now, no one would believe me."

"That's not relevant," Isohel said. "You're completely missing the point."

"Why are you angry?" Joe asked.

"Because this…," Isohel said, hissing through her teeth. "This is the problem." She leaned toward him, her long white fingers draped over her elegant knees. "We all *feel* separate. We believe we're not connected so what we do doesn't matter. What I do doesn't matter to you, and what you do doesn't matter to me. Except it does. Every action has a consequence, negative or positive."

Emma sat on a white chair near the wall and tucked her fingers under her thighs. "Well, of course, but how does that help explain who and what we are?" she said. "And Joe's right. Just because you say it's not a different world doesn't mean it doesn't seem that way to us."

Isohel stood up and moved to sit on the windowsill. "What do you want me to say?"

"I want to understand where we are." Joe spoke calmly, but Emma could feel his heart pounding. "I want to know what we are."

"Misos," Isohel said to Emma. "You parents really told you nothing, huh?"

"They were starting to," Emma began, feeling defensive. "Before the Aythentia took Joe."

Isohel nodded. "Well, like I told Emma last night in the kima, the car," Isohel said, "we're gemynd, humanlike creatures gifted with mind powers. All our powers, even yours, Joe, all our powers come from thinking. Flying is a kind of telekinesis."

"That's why I can fly without wings?"

"Yeah," Isohel said. "But just so you know, it's really hard. Most gemynd whose wings are missing can't fly."

Joe blushed, and Emma wanted to squeeze his hand.

Isohel leaned back and drew her knees up to her chest. "The source of the universe is a mystery to us just like it is to you. Your parents never told you the creation myth, the Idrysi?"

Emma shook her head.

"It's pretty sweet," Isohel said. "The Idrysi tells the story of twin sister goddesses with two souls and one body who disagreed over how to make a world. One sister believed that obstacles and misfortune would strengthen her creatures and gift them with the ability to care for themselves and the world around them. Pali, the old Sacerian name for the Otherworld, means struggle. Anyway, the other sister believed that tremendous powers of understanding and knowledge would give her creatures the capacity to truly care for themselves and the world around them. This, incidentally, is I think why your fairy tales warn of the danger of too many gifts or squandered gifts. Anyway, the sisters each created their own world, which they contained within themselves, and then they physically separated, but not entirely."

"That sounds like a fairy tale," Joe said.

"I told you it was our creation myth," Isohel replied, a little hotly.

Emma felt a contraction inside Joe's chest. She shoved her hands farther under her thighs then pulled them out again.

"It doesn't make sense," Joe said. "How could the sister-worlds have 'physically separated but not entirely?'"

"It's the portal trees, isn't it?" Emma said.

Isohel nodded, grateful. "Portal trees grow over the places where the veil between the worlds is the thinnest, the seams where the sisters are still connected. But travel is possible only by thought; you think yourself through a portal."

Joe got up and walked over to a glass cabinet filled with scrolls. He sat on the floor and leaned against the cabinet. Emma sat next to him. He took her hand without saying anything. Emma moved closer and laid her head on his warm shoulder for a second.

Isohel cocked her head and considered them. "I won't fall in love," she said.

"Of course you will," Emma said reassuringly. Like everyone else who has ever been seventeen, Isohel probably believed no one would ever fall in love with her. "My dad said Soulmates are always true," Emma added, smiling, "so you don't have to worry about it. That's one of the cool things about the Commonworld."

"Your dad didn't say *everyone* had a Soulmate," Isohel pointed out. "Did he?"

"No," Emma said. "I guess he didn't."

Isohel jumped off the windowsill. She crossed the room without looking at either Emma or Joe and leaned against the doorframe. "I'm a *Xeri*, a Loveless. I don't have a Soulmate."

"How...?" Joe began.

"I'm a freak," Isohel said, shaking her head in a crazy way like a monster in cartoon.

Emma couldn't believe someone as pretty as Isohel would never fall in love. In New Hampshire, if Isohel's hair weren't green—and maybe even if it was—guys would fall all over her, even if she didn't seem interested. Or maybe because of it. "I don't understand," she said.

"A Loveless means just that," Isohel said. "We don't have Soulmates. We can have sex if we want to, and we love other gemynd as friends and family. But all our love relationships are platonic."

"How do you know?" Emma said. "Are you sure? Maybe you just haven't met your Soulmate yet."

Isohel sighed. "I know. Loveless have something like a Kiryx Eynosyndeo, except ours is a revelation of aloneness. It's called a

Kiryx Xere. Just like a Soulmate Revelation, it can happen anytime after a gemynd turns fifteen. I'm seventeen. I had mine last year."

"But what about the Soulmate connection being the most sacred element in the Commonworld?" Joe asked.

"What," Isohel said, folding her arms across her chest and staring at Joe. "You have no genetic flukes in your messed up world? No freaks of nature there?"

Emma felt Joe's chest tighten again as he stood up to face Isohel.

"How can the Soulmate connection be irrefutable or real if some Commonworlders don't have one?" Emma asked.

"It is real," Isohel said. "It's what defines us. It's what created us."

"How?" Joe said.

Isohel gazed at both of them for a minute, her pretty face embarrassed and defiant, and then, sounding just like Elizabeth when Sandy had pushed her too far, Isohel growled and crossed back to the window, her bare feet slapping the floor like falling water. She took a deep breath.

"The asteroid that killed all your dinosaurs," Isohel said, "affected our world too. And the animals that escaped the mass extinctions—some ocean species and small scavengers—were devastated in a different way."

Isohel nestled herself back into the alcove of the window, and Joe sat next to Emma and took her hand onto his lap. Isohel's attention shot to their joined hands and rested there for a second. She drew in another deep breath and continued.

"Up until the impact of the asteroid," she said, "all the animal life forms in Saceres were dual creatures physically joined together. Both same sex and different sex wholes. Soulmate pairs."

Joe leaned forward, keeping Emma's hand in his. "Like the Aristophanes story in the *Symposium*?"

"And the 'Origin of Love' song from *Hedwig*," Emma added.

Joe smiled at her. She squeezed his hand and grinned back.

Isohel sighed. "Yeah, I guess." She drew her knees up to her chest and wrapped her long arms around them. "Anyway, after the asteroid all the remaining animals were split from their partners. One theory is that something like acid rain in the atmosphere caused a mutation. Eventually all the animals that survived were separated from their other halves."

Joe leaned back and stared at the ceiling. The heat from his body warmed Emma and she leaned into him. Isohel looked at her. Emma felt so sorry for her pretty cousin. What was the point of being alive if you never fell in love?

"I won't miss it," Isohel said, reading Emma's thoughts. "I feel bad, being different in such a major way, but…"

She took a deep breath and looked meaningfully at both Emma and Joe, and Emma had the sense that Isohel didn't have too many opportunities to talk about how she felt about things. She leaned forward so her cousin would know she was interested in what she had to say.

Isohel smiled for the first time since they'd started talking about this and continued. "It's like wanting something you can't quite identify, something you can't entirely comprehend. It's the not being able to understand something that pisses me off. I don't need to possess it, but I *hate* not knowing something."

"Me too," Joe said.

Isohel sat cross-legged on the floor in front of them. Emma smiled. She really liked Isohel. And this was real affection, not the fake swoon she'd fallen into over Gryphon Venti when he made her think he was hotter than young Morrissey. She ran her thumb over the scar on her palm, and her cousin smiled back.

"So," Joe said, sitting up straighter and thinking out loud. "After the devastation and mass extinctions there was an 'evolutionary burst' here like we had." He waited while Isohel nodded in affirmation. "The remaining animals developed primitive connective-thought abilities to stay connected with their other halves. But in people—*gemynd*," he corrected himself. "In gemynd these abilities evolved and developed into all the powers, each a different way to find the Soulmate, the literal other half."

"Yes," Isohel said, jumping up to slap Joe on the shoulder. "You're pretty smart for someone raised to believe he was a powerless Otherworlder."

"Just because we can't read minds doesn't mean we're all idiots," he grumped, but Emma saw he was blushing from Isohel's enthusiastic praise. He stared down at the floor and Emma wanted to kiss him. She took a shallow breath instead.

Isohel shook her head and murmured to Emma, "I don't know that I'd like it. It's too distracting. It infiltrates everything."

"What?" Joe asked.

"Nothing," Emma and Isohel said together.

Joe growled.

Isohel laughed.

"Not everything you have is better," Emma said.

"Our syntax is clearer."

"Funny," Emma said.

"You're right," Isohel admitted, smiling. "Your music is better. It evolved much earlier and faster than ours. When J. S. Bach was born we hardly had music at all. And your poetry is better."

Emma laughed. "Make sure you tell Maude that when you meet her. She'll be your friend forever."

"Okay, I will," Isohel said, grinning back. "Your food is better, too. Our food is super-efficient and pure, but yours has an aesthetic component we never thought of until recently."

"So we're sensualists," Joe said, still blushing. "And you're enlightened thinkers free from..." He stopped.

"No," Isohel said. "But except for the Soulmate connection we are ruled by what we think while you are ruled entirely by what you feel."

"That's not true," Emma said.

Joe glanced at her. Again, she wanted to kiss him. Isohel raised an eyebrow and smirked.

"I'm not saying we're not ruled by what we feel," Emma said. "But you are too. And it's not just the Soulmate connection. You just don't notice it. Or maybe you don't acknowledge it."

"That makes no sense," Isohel said.

"Part of the reason you came to save us is how mad you are at your dad for not letting you grow up, for watching over you like you're an expensive toy he loves more than anything," Emma said.

Isohel opened her mouth to speak.

"I'm not finished," Emma said. "Our system of government and justice is bound by reason. Yours must be as well. But nearly everything is fueled by emotional responses."

Emma never spoke up like this in school. She almost never said what she thought or felt about anything unless she was cornered—or unless she couldn't stop herself. But she didn't think things through. She just waited for things to happen. Until she met Joe, Emma had relied on her family and on Izzy for everything. No wonder Izzy felt suffocated.

From now on, Emma thought, she would think more about what she wanted to say and why she wanted to say it. And she would listen better, especially to people whose perspective was different from hers. From now on, Emma thought, she would trust herself.

Joe kissed her neck. "You are awesome, chi Erama."

Liquid heat danced again through Emma's blood.

Isohel rolled her eyes and crossed the room.

"You asked me to explain it," she said to Joe. "I told you what I know. I don't know what else to say."

Joe slid his warm hand under Emma's thigh. "It's not your fault," he said to Isohel. "I just hate not understanding something."

Isohel sighed and smiled. "Right," she said softly. "Hey." She turned to Emma, saying brightly, "do you mind if I look around? My dad never let me come here, even when our grandfather was alive."

"Sure," Emma said, hearing Dad and Turner come downstairs and walk into the kitchen. "You should talk with Turner. He woke up early so he could read the scrolls in that cabinet. He was so excited they were in English. But be careful, he might talk your ear off. I'm not kidding. Don't ask him too many questions or you'll be there all day."

Isohel grinned and bounced out of the room, her green hair flying behind her, reflecting the sunlight from the window like an emerald pool in a dark forest.

Joe turned to Emma and smiled.

"What?" she said.

"We're alone," he replied, shifting closer. "Isohel and Turner *both* love to talk. Your dad will be stuck with them for a while." He pushed Emma's hair over her shoulder and kissed her neck.

She closed her eyes and listened to her father, Turner and Isohel's thoughts to make sure Joe was right. Turner was predictably thrilled as Isohel started to explain Sacerian political history, how the political parties came into being and how the government functioned.

Joe kissed Emma's ear. She slid an arm around his waist. He sighed her name.

Dad wasn't paying any attention to Turner or Isohel. He was trying to figure out where the unregistered portal was.

Emma turned completely to Joe. He pulled away and gazed down at her, still softly breathing her name.

"You're right," she said. "Isohel and Turner are not going to stop talking until my Dad makes them. And he's busy trying to figure out where the unregistered portal tree is."

Joe grinned and made a sound that hummed through Emma's body like he was singing inside her. She leaned in and kissed him. He held her closer and ran his warm hands over her back and then under her shirt. Pulling away, he sucked air sharply through his teeth and Emma climbed onto his lap. They floated to the ceiling.

"I love you, Emma Mathews," Joe whispered into her hair.

Oh my God, Emma thought. She loved him too. She loved Joe Castlellaw and he loved her back. It seemed like real magic. Not that Joe could fly, and that they were from a different world where everyone had special powers, but that Joe loved her and she loved him back. Maybe that seemed crazy, but anyone who had ever been in love, really in love, would know it wasn't crazy at all. What every singer and poet tries to catch and re-reveal was suddenly clear as light to Emma in the dusty air of her grandfather's house.

"I love you, Joe Castellaw."

Joe kissed her again, long and slow. Emma was standing on his feet, her head inches from the high, arched ceiling. Joe broke the kiss to smile almost wickedly at her.

"Hold on," he said, clinging tightly to her as they dove toward the floor. Joe flipped around in the air so Emma lay on top of him. They stopped and hovered just above the surface of the floor. She kissed him and felt him respond beneath her. It was just like her dream, except he wasn't naked, though she wished he was. She wished she could feel his warm skin against hers.

Joe groaned in happiness and frustration, and slowly, as if they were underwater, or floating in zero gravity, he spun them both around again. As gently as if he were lying her down on a bed in a fairy tale they landed on the floor. His weight and his hard muscle and his hard everything else pressed into her.

"I know you're not ready," he said, but it sounded more like a question that was trying to answer itself.

"You seem like you think I am ready," she said, smiling against his skin. "Maybe I am."

"Are you?" he asked with so much naked hope in his voice that Emma hesitated. He arched his hips into her and Emma forgot to breathe.

She *was* ready. She couldn't believe she'd ever want Joe more than she did right now. Even with Dad and Turner right in the next room.

"Oh," she said, opening her eyes as she heard the front door open. Maybe Claudeo had figured out what Isohel did and came to get her.

"What?" Joe said, raising his head.

Emma turned to the doorway. Two tall winged creatures, a man and woman, flew at Emma and Joe so quickly she didn't have time to scream.

Part Two

Thy thunder, conscious of the new command,
Rumbles reluctant o'er our fallen house;
And thy sharp lightening in unpractis'd hands
Scorches and burns our once serene domain.
O aching time! O moments big as years!
All as ye pass swell out the monstrous truth,
And press it so upon our weary griefs
That unbelief has not a space to breathe.
—John Keats

CHAPTER TWENTY-EIGHT

When Emma woke up she was in a room like the one they'd rescued Joe from. Nothing hurt her they way it had Joe. She leapt to her feet and ran at the amorphous shifting wall. The cloudy surface was soft and yielding but she couldn't penetrate it.

She closed her eyes and concentrated, but her thoughts bounced back like a ball thrown against a playground wall. She couldn't hear anything, and she couldn't see anything except her own body and the changing, swirling surface of the walls. The light in the room seemed to have no place of origin.

For the first time since she met Joe, Emma heard nothing inside her head except her own thoughts. Instead of feeling relief, she felt scared and broken. Naked. As if a part of her was missing. She felt alone and utterly disconnected. She tried different ways to contact or hear someone, but always her thoughts came back to her, solitary and singular as an echo.

Emma had no idea what time it was or how long she had been there. The light in the room never changed. Her hair didn't feel dirty and her mouth didn't feel too gross, so it couldn't have been that long.

Without a sound or a shift in the level of light or a change in the swirling surface of the walls, a tray of food appeared. Steam and a somewhat pleasant scent rose from the surface of a bowl, and with a pang of desire Emma realized she was hungry. She went to look at what was in the bowl. It was a yellowish-brown, smooth liquid, but it smelled good, like vegetable soup in a Chinese restaurant. Emma touched her fingertip to the hot surface and tasted it. She thought of

Persephone and the pomegranate seeds. If she ate the soup would she be transformed, or brainwashed, or dead? She wasn't hungry enough to find out.

As soon as Emma made the decision not to eat, the food disappeared, which meant someone or something could hear her, even if she couldn't hear them. Isohel had said that the Ones in Power constantly recorded thoughts but didn't constantly view them. Here in this room it seemed to Emma that her thoughts were being constantly recorded *and* constantly viewed. What they hell were they looking for? What did they want from her? She had to be careful not to think anything that might endanger anyone else.

She sat on the floor in despair. She had no idea what had happened. Had the winged people taken Dad, Turner and Isohel as well? And what about Mom, Elizabeth and Sandy? Were they still home? Were they still safe? Would these thoughts give anything away or put anyone in danger?

Emma stood up and swore as loudly as she could. "What do you want?" The cloudy walls turned purple. "What do you want from me?" she screamed again, louder.

The walls turned black.

Emma remembered that Dad had cut away the cloudy shifting surface to reveal a window when they rescued Joe. This surface was an illusion of some kind. Emma tried to see a door or a window anywhere around her. She ran to the place where the food had appeared and jumped up and down furiously. The walls flickered and darkened but no door or opening appeared.

But, Emma knew, if people could move through trees and come into another world, if Joe could fly and Isohel could pull wings out of her shoulder blades, there had to be a way out of this room.

* * *

Joe sat against the wall in a room with no light and no sound and wondered why he wasn't dead. They'd meant to kill him before. Why hadn't they done it yet? He walked along the wall and felt for an opening, or a door, or a change in the surface. It was smooth as glass with no corners and seemingly no end.

He stopped and put his hands into his pockets. The picture of his parents was still there. He could feel it though he couldn't see anything. He was glad he had it with him. They hadn't taken it.

The darkness in the room was solid and complete. If Joe wasn't careful, he might become disoriented. He remembered a story he'd read about a man standing at the edge of a lake at midnight. There was no light except for the stars, and as the man lingered at the water's edge the lake became the night sky and the sky became the black lake. The man stepped back before he fell into the starry water and drowned.

Again Joe walked along the wall, never coming to any change in the surface or any sense he had traveled any distance at all but instead simply walked the circumference of a subtle circle. He pushed against it. The surface wasn't warm or cold. The only discernible sensory difference between wall and the air was the smooth solidity of the wall.

Joe closed his eyes. When he opened them again there was light. His eyes adjusted and he saw Emma standing in her room, trying on a sweater. He just missed her breasts disappearing beneath the blue fabric.

Joe closed and opened his eyes again, and he was in a forest, not one he recognized. He stepped up to a tree and touched it. It felt like a real tree, cool and rough with a sense of wet life at the core. The air smelled like spring. He could smell water and mossy rocks, and damp earth where he saw crawling insects.

Joe's eyes closed by themselves. Now he was in school. The teacher was speaking but no sound came out of her mouth.

This jumping of place to place, sometimes with sound and scent, sometimes with people he knew, sometimes with something he could touch, went on and on without any effort from him. It was like being inside a giant television with constantly changing channels. He took out the picture of his parents and looked at them, their tightly clasped hands white at the knuckles.

The visions slowed then evaporated, and Joe was back in darkness. The image of his parents' joined hands hung in the air for a minute like a visual echo.

* * *

Emma concentrated on the place where, she hoped, she remembered the food appearing. She ran her hands all over the floor and reached around for secret buttons or levers but found none. She sat down for a minute, scared and defeated. Then she stood back up and closed her eyes.

As hard as she could—and as calmly as she could—she concentrated on an image of the food, the shape of the bowl, the glistening brown surface, the good smell. She thought about it until she wasn't thinking of anything else, except a vague feeling of hunger and a slight desire to taste whatever was in that bowl. It worked. And as soon as she felt its reappearance, Emma shifted her desire from eating the food to changing places with the bowl itself, to going where it came from. She made sure the desire to be where the bowl had been was pure and untouched by any other thought or emotion…and with a sense of being squished through a crowded hallway, Emma suddenly found herself in a kitchen filled with steaming vessels of food, and piles of fruits and vegetables separated by color: orange, green yellow. The few workers in the long room gaped at Emma in astonishment.

"I'm lost," Emma said. "I came to visit my dad and I think I went the wrong way." She smiled sheepishly, her heart and mind calm.

"How did you get here?" The woman who spoke had a lavender face and a nose as narrow as the thorax of a wasp.

"I don't know," Emma said. "I told my dad I could do it by myself but I guess I didn't know how."

"What department were you trying to go to?" the woman asked.

"My dad's," Emma said.

The woman rolled her eyes. "Come on," she said. "I'll take you to the directory."

"Thanks," Emma said. "I hope he's not mad."

The woman smiled and opened a door. Emma stared at the floor and thought of her pretend dad.

"The directory is at the end of this hall," the woman said. "Femius is at the desk today. He'll help you."

"Thanks," Emma said cheerily, and waved.

She waited until the woman went back into the kitchen and then followed a group of gemynd who were walking together and chatting about lunch. Emma prayed they were going outside the building and not to some ugly-food cafeteria inside.

The sight of sunshine coming through a suddenly present glass door made Emma's heart leap. She swallowed that feeling, hid herself in the middle of the crowd, and walked outside. As she followed them into the fresh warm air she thought blandly about lunch and school. The glass door closed and the gemynd dispersed in small groups and different directions.

An alarm sounded inside the building. Steel wrapped itself around the place where the door had been. Along with a few of the gemynd in the lunch crowd, Emma glanced at the humming structure. She turned away casually and walked toward what she prayed was a train station. The only place she knew how to get to was Isohel's house.

* * *

Joe picked up his head. A faint throbbing sound wailed somewhere outside the room. Had something happened? Were they coming to get him now? To kill him? He would be ready if and when they got here.

A blinding light went on, boring into Joe's brain and making him feel sick. He burrowed his palms into his eye sockets and breathed deeply. When he moved his hands slightly the glare had softened, but it was still brighter than sunshine.

From what Joe could see through the cracks in his fingers he was in a smallish room with bare, watery-smooth walls and a gleaming white floor. The alarm, if that's what it was, continued to sound in the distance. It couldn't have been for him. Someone would have been here already.

What about Emma? Or her family? Or his mom? Had they been taken, too? The idea of anyone getting hurt made him feel sicker. It was him they wanted. He hoped the Masevo had taken him and left everyone else alone.

The picture of his parents in his pocket vibrated like a phone. He took it out and looked at it. Nothing had changed. His parents were still clasping hands and gazing slightly defensively at the camera. Then suddenly Joe felt a softening sensation like he was disintegrating and expanding at the same time. It wasn't unpleasant. When he could see again he found himself in a small room. Through a filthy window he could see a forest but no buildings or people.

For a very long time Joe stood completely still. Nothing changed or appeared. He tentatively touched the top of a stone table. Dust stuck to his fingertip. He watched the door, or the place where a door must have once been. There was nothing there now but strips of torn metal and spiderwebs littered with dead leaves and insect carcasses.

Joe stepped outside and breathed in what smelled like genuine fresh air. He squeezed his eyes shut then opened them again. The scene was the same: trees, rocks, new green leaves and tiny white flowers growing out of crevices in rotting logs. He walked farther into the woods then shut and opened his eyes again. The same trees and rocks waited in front of him. He turned. The ruined house stood unchanged and silent behind him.

Joe waited for a second then ran as fast as he could into the woods.

CHAPTER TWENTY-NINE

Emma got onto the train when it arrived. Had the Masevo let her go? That escape was too easy, she thought before remembering not to think anything. She found a seat next to a cute boy around her age with a quartzy-looking reading stone in his palm. He grinned at Emma and she smiled back.

"Did you cut school today, too?" he asked, pulling out of his ear the same glassy music thing Isohel had worn.

"What?" Emma asked, temporarily shocked at being addressed. "Yeah."

The boy grinned again. "I hate Information Day. I try to cut it every year."

"This is my first year cutting," Emma said, hoping that something near the truth would arouse less suspicion.

The boy closed the reading stone and put it in his pocket. "Do you think it's true?"

"What?" Emma asked.

The boy leaned closer. His mouth moved as if he was asking her whether she had finished her History of the Fourth Revolution homework, and Emma even heard that question faintly uttered, but when she looked at his pale gold eyes she heard the real question: "Do you think the Ones in Power really have Eury Vatic's son?"

Emma leaned back on the soft train seat. For the first time since she'd left the building she couldn't stop her heart from pounding or her feelings from screaming inside her.

"Yes," she said truthfully. "I think they do."

The boy smiled. He rested his head on the attached pillow behind him and closed his eyes. "Then it must be true that Eury Vatic is still alive." He turned to Emma and grinned slyly at her, as if they shared some powerful secret.

Emma smiled back, filling her heart with an echo of the boy's happiness so that he couldn't read the real thoughts and fears in her head.

"Is your partner okay?" he said after a minute, pointing to the scar on Emma's palm.

"Who?" Emma asked, closing her fingers over the suddenly throbbing red line.

"Whoever you're connecting with," the boy said, indicating Emma's hand again with a nod of his head. "The scar looks like that when something bad happens," he added. "Didn't you know?"

Emma opened her hand and examined the scar. "I didn't even notice," she gasped. "I was so worried about getting caught for cutting." She made this true in her head. It helped that she really was worried about Isohel now.

The boy looked concerned. "You should try to contact him. Her?"

"Her," Emma said.

"Something's happened," the boy said.

"I know," Emma replied. She stared at her hand. "Does this train stop at Westfair? I think I might have gotten on the wrong train."

The boy laughed. "Dysikalloni? Were you asleep when you got on? We're heading in the opposite direction on a totally different line."

"This is only my second time in the city," Emma said.

The boy narrowed his golden eyes. Emma had the impression of sunlight glinting through shuttered blinds.

"My parents are Eleytheria and they're afraid of the Ones in Power," she said, hoping it didn't sound too ridiculous.

The boy nodded his head. "Oh."

"So, how do I get to Westfair?" Emma asked.

The boy told her. "I get off here," he added when the train stopped again. "I'm Tyrian."

"Emma," Emma said, taking his hand. "Nice to meet you."

He smiled and got off the train.

Emma followed his directions and changed trains. At Dysikalloni she walked out of the train station and into the sweet-smelling sunlight. It looked to be around two or three o'clock in the afternoon. The street was quiet except for a few gemynd walking in and out of stores and laughing with one another. For another world it seemed remarkably similar.

A wildly gesticulating woman with bright white hair and a hard face was talking loudly to an absent listener or into an invisible cell phone-like thing. She bumped into Emma and threw her a biting look. Emma brushed off her shirt and was about to shout something equally nasty back when two or three silver-suited gemynd emerged from the train station, their eyes searching every face, so Emma walked into the first door she saw.

Reading stones of every size and color lined white wood shelves. Tightly rolled scrolls stood together in glass cabinets locked with dragonfly clasps. Emma touched the tip of a shining silver tail. Someone waited next to her. She cleared her head before looking up.

A very tall man with a helmet of grey hair streaked with gold gazed down at her. His face seemed relatively young for an old man. He looked somewhere around fifty or sixty, but his eyes, which were green with sharp spots of silver, seemed ancient.

"Did you come to buy something?" he asked.

"No," Emma said. "I came to hide from someone." Shit. What had she said that for? She curled her toes inside her sneakers.

The man's face opened into a beautiful smile, like God or Santa Claus.

"Well," he said. "Come back here to the Other and Ancient section. It's not visible from the street."

Emma followed the man through the bright aisles into a darker room paneled with honey-colored wood and thickly polished shelves lined with books. Real books with leather bindings and paper covers, titles and author names on the spines. Maude would be in heaven. Emma sucked in short breath. She couldn't think about Maude in here. Even if the man did have a nice smile.

"Do you like Otherworld poetry?" he asked, a thread of boyish hopefulness in his voice.

"A little," Emma said. "But my sister loves it. She's obsessed with something about St. Agnes and her doomed boyfriend." What the hell was wrong with her? Why couldn't she just shut up?

The man's sea green eyes blazed with brightness. "Ah," he said, pulling a red leather volume from the shelf. "'The Eve of St. Agnes' by John Keats. Does your sister believe the boy, Porphyro, is doomed?"

"Uh," Emma replied, feeling a bit sweaty. "I don't know. She said the girl's family hated him."

"Mmmm," the man said, reading a verse to himself. He sighed and returned the book to the shelf. He could be Maude's soulmate if he wasn't a thousand years old.

"Do you think you still need to hide from your friends?" he asked.

Emma suddenly felt like crying. "I don't know."

A light hum sounded. Glad to be distracted, Emma glanced up to see where the song was coming from. The old man gaped. He seemed surprised she heard it.

"Wait here," he said, and left through a door hidden in the bookcase.

Emma didn't know what to do. He seemed trustworthy, but she wasn't sure. She gazed at the hundreds of books on the shelves.

Some titles were familiar and in English. Some were in different Otherworld languages. A few were in Sacerian. A copy of *The Green Mile* by Stephen King glowed between something that looked like Sanskrit and a huge illuminated edition of the King James Bible.

The man's voice floated into Emma's head. She didn't know if he was speaking or thinking, or whether or not he knew she could hear him.

If they had him and he escaped it was with their help. They wouldn't let him go a second time.

Was he talking about Joe?

Another voice sounded, but it was too far off to understand.

They are desperate, Odym, the man replied to that distant voice.

Once more, incoherent bursts of sound.

That only proves their desperation, the man was saying when Emma could again hear. *Any remaining traces were collected and processed long ago. The house will have no resonance for him. He'll simply run once he realizes he's free. I would. Anyone would.*

The undulating almost-words broke in again. The man waited.

No, he said. *He'll do more harm than good. His presence will only draw the Ones in Power closer to us.*

The sound came again, the gentle hum Emma heard before the man left. It went on lightly, like background music in a store. Inside the hum, so faintly she wasn't sure if she heard it, a human-seeming voice occasionally whispered. The rasping, musical sound belonged to neither the white-haired man nor his distant counterpart. Emma listened closely to see if she could hear what the voice said. She couldn't, but as soon as she forgot about it the voice was clear again, like those books where you can only see the secret picture when you squish your eyes and half-stare at the page.

The airy language sounded like disconnected lines of poetry or spoken songs, or bits of speeches and unconnected conversations: questions and answers that didn't originally belong to one another.

Emma listened without trying, and the words blended together to form a single idea.

Surrender.

CHAPTER THIRTY

Joe ran through the forest without ever having the sense that he was being followed or that anyone knew where he was. When he finally stopped to catch his breath, no one materialized to question or capture him. Where was he? How had he escaped? Did they let him go? He certainly didn't transport himself to that ruin of a house.

He wished he had a bottle of water. His throat was so dry he could hardly breathe. There had to be a stream somewhere nearby.

Joe thought about taking his parents' picture out of his pocket but he didn't want to be transported back to that house again. Was it his parents' house? Did looking at the picture take him there?

The forest was ridged and hilly but not nearly as steep as the hills of the waterfall trail in Richardson Park. His heart swelled as he thought of Emma. Was she okay? Did they have her, too? Was she foolishly trying to find him?

He sprinted up a hill to see what was on the other side. A lake with a surface like blue glass, trimmed with a narrow margin of pale green sand, lay at the bottom of the slope. Tables and fire pits were scattered among the surrounding trees. Pockets of red columbine and white foam flowers sprouted like cinnamon hearts and rock candy between grey stones and ropy tree roots. Joe glanced around to make sure the area was deserted then ran down to the lake.

He drank, praying the water was safe. When his stomach was bursting with its cool refreshment, Joe lay on his back on the soft green sand. He couldn't stay here much longer, but where else could he go? Back to the city? Where was it? And where would he go when he got there? If Emma and her family were taken as well, he had to go back and find a way to free them.

The sun on his chest and the warm sand beneath his back started to make Joe feel sleepy. He stood and brushed the grit off his legs. Near one of the fire pits two flat rocks lay together like a stone sandwich. Joe walked over. He ran his finger slowly down a central crevice in the top rock, and the stone opened and a kind of trail map appeared. The blue glass lake was in the middle. It was the only independent body of water. Other streams and rivers snaked like black veins over the landscape. There were four entrances with no indication of where they came from or led to.

To avoid retracing his steps, Joe ran his finger over the stone map, atop the hill and in the direction of the place where he thought the house stood. The surface was lined and rough. Joe's fingertip caught on tiny ridges and grooves. Although he had seen very little of the city and the surrounding land, he didn't remember any distant hills or views to indicate that the city itself stood at any great height. The forest they'd landed in after Emma came to rescue him was flat. The trees stood at the same height. Joe decided to head in the direction of the entrance on the other side of the lake. No mountains or hills stood beyond, and it seemed in the opposite direction of the ruined house.

His finger stopped at the place where he remembered the house to be. The tiny spot was worn smooth like the noses of bronze saints rubbed for good fortune. It felt cooler than the rest of the map, too, as if there was a vent or an opening beneath the smooth stone.

Joe took a deep breath. Maybe he could fly. Isohel had thought— and Emma's dad had thought so, too—that he would be in danger if the Ones in Power knew he could fly. But that seemed irrelevant now.

Joe took his hand off the reading stone map. After a moment it closed itself.

Except for the escape, when Isohel had helped him, Joe had never flown for an extended period without Emma in his arms. Emma alone made him happy enough to fly.

Joe shut his eyes. He thought about Emma's sweet face after he'd spilled her jelly beans all over the street. Of her soft smile when she realized he liked her back. And this morning...

Joe's feet lifted from the ground and his heart roared like a muscle car engine.

Emma was definitely ready to have sex with him. Even though they were interrupted and then kidnapped by flying people, he didn't have to wait anymore. Emma was ready. More importantly, she wanted to make love with him as much as he wanted to make love with her.

Joe soared into the air, but his happiness faltered as soon as he remembered he didn't know where Emma was. If she was in danger, it was his fault. His feet hit the ground and he stood there, surprised.

It's not just happiness that helps you fly. It's a kind of adrenaline.

Joe climbed to the swaying top of the tallest tree, closed his eyes, and jumped off. Terror shrunk his chest as he plummeted toward the ground. He took a huge breath—and rose toward the forest ceiling. Leaves and branches scratched his face as he broke out of the woven green and into the open sky. Joe flew faster than he ever had before. The blue glass lake shimmered beneath him, but there were no cities or houses in the distance. Beyond the lake, an arboreal ocean spread out as far as he could see.

Spinning in the air, thrilling to the exhilarating freedom, Joe turned back to look in the direction of the ruined house and saw the end of the forest with a city in the distance. He wished Emma was with him. The sense of her absence plunged him toward the water but he told himself that he was going to find her. And his father. Joe rose into the air again, as effortlessly as floating up from the bottom of a pool.

Beyond the scalloped edge of trees, the skyline of the city made a jagged shadow. Joe recognized the central tower. His heart fell but his courage didn't. He soared in the direction of the city, his eyes on the tower and his thoughts on Emma.

* * *

Emma listened, lulled by the airy sound of the humming voice. She felt herself smile as the grey-haired man came back in through the bookcase door.

"What are you doing?" he asked, a look of horror in his penetrating eyes.

"Nothing," Emma said, instantly guilty. The airy voice cracked like ice and she couldn't hear it anymore.

"Where did you come from?" the man growled, his eyes green slits. "Why aren't you in school?"

"I'm cutting," Emma said, trying to grab hold of a sense of inner nothing. "I hate Information Day."

The man sighed but didn't take his eyes off her. Emma felt him trying to read her thoughts. She imagined an orange. She concentrated on the shining, dimpled surface, and the removable, red-rimmed sticker that read FLORIDA and ORGANIC. She envisioned cutting the orange into eighths, clear juice spilling out. She tasted it. Cold, tart, and sweet. She imagined biting into a slippery, bitter seed and then spitting it out.

The man stepped back. Emma swallowed a victorious grin. He hadn't seen anything but the orange.

"Thanks for giving me a place to hide," she said cheerily.

The man didn't respond.

"Bye," she said, walking toward the door.

The sunlight streaming though the round windows disappeared as a wall dropped down and covered the front of the store. Emma whipped around. "Who are you?" she asked. "Are you trying to help me or hurt me? You'd better decide right now, because you can't do both."

The man laughed. It wasn't an entirely unpleasant sound.

"The two are often, regrettably, interdependent," he said. "I don't want to hurt you."

"Let me go," Emma said, moving toward the wall where the door used to be. "You don't need me. And I can't help you."

"I want to help you," the man said. His voice sounded kind yet scary. Not one but both. "But first you must help me."

Emma kept the orange at the front of her brain, careful not to replace it with a face or an idea.

"What were you doing when I came back from my conversation?" he said.

"Nothing," Emma answered, relieved to be truthful.

"What were you listening to?"

Maybe there were no oranges in the Commonworld, but even if there were they probably didn't get them from Florida. *Florida*, Emma thought and tried not to cringe. *He knows I'm from the Otherworld.* She thought of loud music. "Shakespeare's Sister" always made her feel like she could move storms, so Emma concentrated on the driving percussion and frenetic, sweet guitar.

Something happened to the man's face. His expression aged and fell, but the light in his eyes didn't dim. "I'm not going to hurt you," he said.

"Nobody says that unless they intend to hurt someone," Emma answered, backing up and keeping the song blasting in her head.

"What were you listening to?" the man asked again, a note of desperation in his voice. "I can't help you until I know for certain. Please tell me, and I promise I will do everything in my power to make sure you and your family and friends are safe, but now, please, please tell me what you were listening to."

"Nothing," Emma repeated, stepping away from the wall and looking for another way out of the room.

In that instant, the wall in front of the window slid open and sunlight splashed across the man's deeply creased face. Emma turned to run. A line of silver-suited men and women blocked the door. A very young man stepped out in front.

"Hello, Fen," he said to the grey-haired man.

"Hello, Gryphon," the grey-haired man replied.

Gryphon Venti gave no indication that he saw or recognized Emma. "You know better than to lock your door when an alarm's been sounded," he said.

A man with skin like trout scales and glowing blond hair came up to Emma. The grey-haired man gazed intently at her, and suddenly Emma wished more than anything she'd told him what she'd heard, and who she was, and that she knew Joe was Eury Vatic's son.

The pale wood floor vibrated beneath her feet. Before she disappeared Emma saw the all the reading stones burst open. *I'm sorry*, replaced every word, and wrote itself all over the walls and ceiling.

Later Emma learned that the floor covered an unregistered portal and was made of wood from a portal tree. As Emma moved through it she heard Gryphon shout, "No!"

There was a smell of smoke and burning hair or skin, and then Emma emerged from a gnarled tree in a quiet walled garden in the center of the city. Flowering trees lined the walls, and grey statues of winged men and women stood watch in the corners.

A beautiful silver-faced man came out from behind a white rose vine. "Come with me," he whispered, holding out a glowing hand. "I'm Odym Chadia. Fen Elos, the man in the reading store, sent me to help you." Upon speaking Fen Elos's name, the man's silver face darkened for a moment.

Emma took his hand.

He opened a bronze gate. Still holding his hand Emma followed the man into a dusty, cold room filled with garden tools and trays of fresh-smelling dirt. Before Emma could stop it, Maude's face appeared, happy and anxious, filling little flower plots and staring at a quivering shaft of light outside the greenhouse. A beautiful memory.

"Don't think," the man said.

A wide floor stone moved to reveal stairs and a dark tunnel. Never letting go of Emma's hand, the man led her down and in and replaced the stone.

The tunnel was lit by Odym Chadia's luminous skin and hair. He looked like he was made of moonlight. They walked in silence, Emma unwilling to let go of his hand.

She slowed her steps and listened. He stopped. The tunnel was filled with noise, but it wasn't words or voices that Emma heard. It was a leftover sound, like the stink of fish or smoke in the kitchen the next day, the idea or memory of voices. Then Odym tugged her hand gently and they kept walking. The aural space in the hall stagnated with the leftover sound until Emma could practically see it hanging like a ghost in front of her.

"What is that noise?" Emma said.

"*Theama peritta,*" he said. "The detritus of Revelation voices." He pulled harder, and Emma nearly tripped keeping up.

"What does that mean?" she asked.

He made an exasperated sound. "In the Commonworld information is disseminated visually and aurally by Revealers. Did your parents tell you nothing?"

"I know what a Revealer is," Emma said. "But this is just incoherent noise."

"Images dissipate," he said, glancing back at her. "But sounds from Revealed images seep into the ground to rot." The man stopped at a pool of black water hardly wider than a grown woman. "You have to jump in," he directed.

"What?" Emma asked.

"I can't," he said.

Emma stared at him.

"It only looks like water," he explained.

Emma didn't know what to do.

"The portal pool leads to a house," Odym said, turning to glance behind him. "The gemynd inside will help you find your family."

"What happened to my family?" Emma said. "Are they all right? What happened?"

"The gemynd inside are *Perimena*, Resisters. They'll help you," the man insisted. "I must go." He turned around. "Try to contact the boy," he added.

"What boy?" Emma asked.

"Eury Vatic's son."

Then Odym Chadia left. Emma watched him and the light he produced disappear into the tunnel. She was now in complete darkness. Nothing was reflected in the pool. The noise had stopped, but the tunnel was filled with distant sounds of shifting rock and falling water.

Emma closed her eyes—though why she should she didn't know—and thought of Joe. His image came so hard and crashing that she lost her balance and almost fell into the pool. He was flying away from an endless forest and toward the city. He must have felt her call him, because he dropped a little and struggled to right himself.

I'm okay, Emma thought to him. *I'm okay.*

CHAPTER THIRTY-ONE

Joe struggled to catch his breath, his heart beating madly as he fought to rise up to where he'd been flying. The sound of Emma's voice, her real voice, made him feel for a moment as if he'd been bathed in honey.

Are you okay? she asked.

Yes, Joe said. *Where are you?*

I'm in a tunnel in the city, Emma said. *I'm going to meet Resisters who can help find my family.*

Was your family captured? Joe asked.

I don't know, Emma said.

Can't you try to hear them? Joe asked.

I tried, Emma said, *when I was in the tower. My thoughts kept bouncing back. Were you in the tower, too? How did you get out?*

I think they let me out. Where is the tunnel?

The entrance is in the shed of a walled garden, Emma said. *There are white roses and winged statues.*

I'm coming to find you, Joe said.

The grey-haired man's stricken face flashed in Emma's head. He'd known what she was listening to, and he'd been afraid. It had something to do with Joe and his father. And a trap.

No, Emma said. *Wait until I meet the Resisters.*

No, Joe said. *We have no idea what's going on or what happened to your family.*

Please, Emma said. *Please wait until I talk to the Resisters.*

Emma, Joe said. *I can see the tower. I won't get lost. I'll be able to find the tunnel.*

No, Emma begged.

What do you want me to do? Joe asked. *Fly around waiting for the Masevo to capture me?*

I thought you said they let you go.

I don't know what happened, Joe said, *I heard an alarm and then I was in an old house in the woods.*

They must have let you go for a reason, Emma said. She suddenly remembered what the grey-haired man had said to his inaudible listener: If they had him and he escaped it was with their help. They wouldn't let him go a second time. Which probably meant the Ones in Power were trying to use Joe as bait to trap his father.

Before Emma could beg Joe to stay out of the city, a streak of light and energy shot down the tunnel and pushed her into the narrow black pool.

* * *

A ragged thrashing in Joe's chest swung him toward the trees. He fought against it and managed to land in a clearing.

"Emma!" he called aloud, rubbing his chest like he had held her there and she'd been torn from him. "Emma! Are you okay? Emma!" He listened to the silence then cursed loudly and threw a stone hard against a tree. The stone cracked against the bark and bounced to the soft ground.

He swore again, and a squirrel-like thing leapt from one slender branch to another. The city was still miles away. He didn't think he could fly again. Emma was stuck somewhere alone. His mom was terrified wherever she was. And something must have happened to Emma's family. All because of him. Why had they let him go? What was Emma trying to tell him?

Joe started walking toward the city, desperate to get there faster than his feet could take him. He was exhausted.

The rushing song of a stream or a brook roared ahead. The lake water hadn't hurt him and he was thirsty again. Over a ridge, a broad stream fell wildly between rocky banks studded with trailing red flowers, and Joe climbed down. He knelt at the edge of the water and drank. Wiping his mouth he stood up.

There were no places where the stream was narrow enough to jump across, so Joe stepped into the water. The swift current made it hard to cross. Twice Joe nearly slipped on a slick rock. He walked carefully, trying to wedge his feet between stones rather than step on them, but the opposite bank remained at the same distance no matter how far or long he walked. Joe turned around. The bank where he'd come in from was the same distance as the one he was trying to reach. He walked back toward it. The bank moved away, matching his pace and traveled space. He turned around again. The other side was farther. It seemed he could increase but not close the space between him and either bank of the rushing stream.

Joe tried to run. His shoes stuck in the mud of the streambed. He pulled his feet out, and his socks rose from his shoes and floated away. Plunging his head into the cold water, Joe reached down to retrieve his shoes. Something swam around his ankles and bit into the soles of both of his bare feet. Jumping back and hoping it wasn't a snake or a snapping turtle, Joe saw nothing in the water but a shiver of light that glowed brighter and then disappeared. He slipped his feet back into his shoes and started walking again.

The cold, rushing water made his legs ache. He tried to think amazing thoughts of Emma. Of kissing. Laughing. Sex. He rose from the streambed but the water pulled him back down like gentle, determined hands.

Joe's ruined shoes were weighted with mud, and his jeans clung heavily to him. He stopped to catch his breath. A replica of the city glittered from the bottom of the stream. Joe dunked his head under the water and opened his eyes. Small figures moved in and out of buildings and cars. It looked like one of those Victorian village scenes in expensive shop windows in tourist towns. His mom had worked in one once when they lived on the Cape.

Joe picked up his head and grabbed a mouthful of breath then got down on his hands and knees to look closer. The city had disappeared, replaced by an interior view of two rooms separated by a closed door. One of the rooms was filled with old-fashioned furniture and lit with fat candles in cut glass jars. The other was harshly lit and empty except for a large table. Emma was alone in the empty room. Her family was in the other, clustered together and talking. Emma stood with her head in her hands, crying. Her mother called out to her, but Emma didn't hear. The walls and the ceiling of the empty room began to collapse inward.

Joe leapt out of the stream but was pulled back down again. He fought against its draw and the strength of the current, slipping on rocks and trying not to swallow too much water. Panting and desperate he stood in the center of the stream. He couldn't fly out and he couldn't cross.

Laughing voices sounded in the distance. Joe dropped to his knees and hid in the water. The rooms and Emma and her family were gone. Sunfish and silvery trout darted past. Crawling on his hands and knees, his fingers sinking into the silky mud at the bottom of the stream, Joe followed the fish, occasionally raising his head for air. He didn't see the gemynd whose voices he'd heard.

CHAPTER THIRTY-TWO

Emma heard herself screaming, so she couldn't be drowning. The silver man was right. It wasn't water. It felt like silk, like floating through an endless closet filled with dresses.

She emerged onto a wood-framed bed in a room lit by huge candles set in glittering jars the size of Halloween pumpkins. Emma jumped off the bed and ran for the door. It opened before she touched the handle.

"Emma!" her dad said, grabbing her and hugging her tightly. "Misos. Are you all right?" He held her at arm's length, looked at her and hugged her again.

"What happened?" Emma said. "Are Turner and Isohel okay?"

Before her dad had time to answer Emma's mom came into the room.

"Mom," Emma said. "What are you doing here? What is going on?"

Her mother contracted her face like she was trying not to breathe. She kissed the top of Emma's head. "Thank God."

Past her mom's shoulder Emma saw Sandy sleeping on a bench, a satiny blue cloth crumpled in his hand and his thumb in his mouth. Elizabeth peeked her head around the doorway and came in.

"Please tell me what is going on?" Emma begged her father.

"I'm glad you're okay," Elizabeth said.

Emma gave her little sister a huge hug.

"Why are you pink?" Elizabeth asked, picking up Emma's arm.

Emma glanced at her parents. "Because I am pink."

Elizabeth turned to Mom and Dad. "Am I going to be a different color? Am I going to look weird?" She touched her hair. "I don't want to be different. I want to be just like I am. What will my friends say if I look like a weirdo? I won't have any friends. And what about Sandy?"

"Calm down, honey," Mom said, stroking Elizabeth's head. "You and Sandy don't ever have to look different until you want to."

"I'll never want to."

"Okay," Mom agreed. "Let's not worry about that right now. Let Daddy answer Emma's question." She nodded at him.

Dad turned to Emma. "We didn't realize you and Joe were taken," he said. "The Masevo who took you hid their traces and left a sense of your sneaking off to..." He hesitated, and Emma felt herself blush as her father began again. "They left behind a sense of your sneaking off to hook up," he said. "By your expression, I see that wasn't far from the truth."

"We didn't leave the room," Emma said in a small voice.

Dad shook his head. "By the time I realized you and Joe were gone, Claudeo showed up to get Isohel. He brought three Resisters with him."

"I thought the Resisters were the good guys," Emma said.

"There are no good guys or bad guys," Dad said.

Mom snorted.

"Resisters means the 'out of power political party,' whichever it is," Dad continued. "As we told you, right now the Eleytheria are the Resisters. At other times the Aythentia are the Resisters and the Eleytheria are the Ones in Power. Mom and I are Eleytheria, but..."

"Why is Mom here?" Emma asked.

"The Ones in Power want to capture Joe's father," Dad said. "We believe that...well, as soon as they realized you might be Joe's Soulmate they decided to use you and us to get to Eury through Joe."

"But how did you guys *get* here?" Emma said.

"Gryphon helped us," Maude replied, coming into the room with Turner.

"Maude!" Emma ran over and hugged her.

Turner hugged Emma, too. "I'm glad you're okay, Em."

"Where are we?" Emma asked, smiling at her brother. "And how did Gryphon help you?"

"This is a safehouse," Dad said. "I sent for Mom and everyone else as soon as I realized you and Joe were taken. We've all been hiding here since then."

"Fen Elos, the gemynd who saved you…," Mom said. Her voice cracked. She took a deep breath. "Fen Elos was the Eleytheria leader. As soon as he understood who you were he sent a message to Odym Chadia who led you to the passageway to this place."

"Was that why all the books read, 'I'm sorry'?" Emma asked.

Her mother turned away. "Yes," she said. "That passageway was an unregistered portal that connected to the Otherworld and to protected places in this world," she added, turning around again. "The Ones in Power didn't know about it. Now they do, and they've taken it over. They followed you."

"Not right away," Maude said.

"Because of Fen's sacrifice," Mom insisted, her voice hard.

"Because Gryphon stopped them," Maude corrected.

"Gwen," Dad spoke up. "You don't know what happened."

"I know what Maude wants to believe," Mom replied.

"I'm right here!" Maude said. "Do you think I can't hear you when you talk? I don't *want* to believe it. Whether I believe it or not doesn't matter. It happened. Gryphon held them back long enough for Emma to escape."

Mom tightened her mouth.

"Come on," Dad said softly. "Hyllus and Aurelia will want to talk to Emma. Are you hungry, Elizabeth? Do you want to take a nap with Sandy?"

Elizabeth shook her head. Emma had never seen her little sister look scared.

"Did you meet our cousin Isohel?" she asked, brushing Elizabeth's curls over her tiny shoulders. "She looks just like you with green hair. She's really pretty."

"We won't be able to see Isohel for a while," Dad said.

"Why?" Emma asked. With a jolt to her chest she remembered her scar. It was still raised and shiny.

"The Masevo caught Claudeo on his way home," Dad said. "They opened Isohel's scar to find out what she knew about you. Isohel fought against them and they hurt her. She's in the hospital. Claudeo is devastated."

"Is she okay?" Emma asked, closing her fingers over her own scar as if she could protect it somehow.

"I think so," Dad said. "Claudeo refuses to speak with us. We got our information from Hyllus and Aurelia—they're the Resisters who are here helping us now. Do you know where Joe is?"

"He's flying toward the city," Emma said.

"Wasn't he captured, too?" Turner asked.

"He was," Emma said. "But they let him go. I think they must have let me go as well. What happened to Joe's mom?" she asked, looking around. "Is she here too?"

"Mom convinced Odym to let Joe's mom stay in the Otherworld," Dad said. "At first Odym wanted to put an identity shield on her. He didn't know Joe's adoptive mother was an Otherworlder. I don't think anyone knew. An identity shield, even a permanent one, is useless on an Otherworlder."

"Why aren't we wearing permanent identity shields?" Emma said. "Why isn't Joe wearing one?"

Mom glared at Dad in disbelief before speaking. "After a permanent identity shield, a gemynd can only know his or her Soulmate. They won't recognize anyone they knew before, and can never be reacquainted with former relationships. You don't recognize your parents or your brothers and sisters or your friends ever again. And they will never recognize you. But everyone involved feels the loss like pain from a phantom limb. It's illegal and it's barbaric."

"But sometimes," Dad said, "it is the only way to save someone. When a permanent shield is applied, even the most powerful gemynd cannot identify a fellow Commonworlder."

A glance passed between Mom and Dad.

"Come on," he said, and he took Elizabeth's hand. Mom kissed Sandy on the head and followed Dad out of the room.

"A permanent identity shield can only be applied to an adult by a Soulmate," Turner said, "or to a child by a parent. And it cannot be applied to any gemynd without his or her cooperation."

"How do you know?" Emma asked.

"I read about them in the scrolls," Turner said. "At different times in Sacerian history, permanent identity shields *were* the only way to save loved ones from death or unspeakable cruelty. Gemynd were willing to sacrifice relationships to save a child's life."

Emma watched Maude stare unseeingly out the window.

"Why did they let Joe go?" Turner asked Emma.

"I don't know," she said, still looking at Maude. "I think Dad's right. I think they want to use him as bait to trap his father."

"No one knows where Eury Vatic is," Turner said. "Dad told me both the Resisters and the Ones in Power have been looking for him since he disappeared. That was right after Joe's little sister Edoro was killed and Joe vanished. Joe's real name is Sfodro. Did you know that? It means Ruled by Love."

Emma nodded. "I didn't know that's what it meant. Was there anything about Joe's father in the scrolls you read?"

"No," Turner said. "They were Sacerian history scrolls. But I did find a picture of Joe's parents."

"Where?"

"In the room where we were sleeping," Turner said. "I think he took it with him."

"What did they look like?" Emma asked.

"Kind of like Joe," Turner answered. "His dad looked intense. He and Joe's mom were holding hands."

Emma remembered Maude. "How did you know about Gryphon?" she asked.

Maude gazed defensively at her but said nothing.

"Before I moved through the floor I heard Gryphon shout, 'No,'" Emma said, and her sister's eyes filled with tears.

"Maude," Turner said, very gently. "I know it feels like Gryphon is your Soulmate, but he can't be. He never would have done the things he did, put you in danger, put the ones you love in danger, if he was. I think the pressure of all this is getting to you and you're latching on to a fantasy of true love as a way out. He's not your Soulmate, Maude. He can't be."

Maude said, "You don't understand."

"Of course I understand," Turner said. "Don't forget," he added, his face turning red, "I *broke up* with Rachel to keep her safe from all this. Don't tell me I don't freaking understand!" He clenched his jaw and was silent.

"We should go," Maude said. "Mom and Dad are waiting."

"What do the Resisters want to ask me about?" Emma asked, following her siblings into the next room.

"About Joe," Maude said. "And about his dad."

CHAPTER THIRTY-THREE

The stream narrowed and grew shallower. The water wouldn't hide Joe anymore. He stood up, dreamed awake of Emma's face, and floated out of the water to the other side. He shouted happily and flew into the forest canopy.

Fast-moving air streaked over Joe's wet skin and hair, making him shiver as he flew toward the city. He could fly faster than he could walk but it still seemed to take forever to get there. He flew and flew but the buildings stayed the same size and distance away. For a minute Joe panicked that what had happened in the water was happening in the sky, but he looked down and saw the trees and ground change beneath him so he knew he was moving.

After what felt like an hour he landed near a busy road just outside the city. He leapt over scrubby grass and bright purple flowers to the footpath. The few pedestrians glanced at him and went back to their business. One narrow man with grey skin and peach fuzz hair was singing softly, a glassy thing just visible in his huge ear. His black, shining eyes were half-closed and his ugly face was softened with a sweet grin. The song must have been about love, though Joe couldn't understand the words.

The orange sun burst between two buildings, blinding Joe for a second. He shaded his eyes and looked around. The detainee tower was straight ahead, just to the right of the setting sun. If he stayed reasonably clear of it he'd be able to avoid the Masevo, he hoped, and if he kept it in his sightline he wouldn't get lost. Emma was somewhere in the city. He was sure of it. And he was sure the vision in the water meant he had to reunite her with her family, wherever they were. He just had to find the tunnel and Emma before the Masevo.

Joe's clothes and shoes had dried in the wind and his jeans had shrunk until they were uncomfortably tight. The air was getting cooler as the sun sank lower. He wished he had a jacket.

The outskirts of the city were dotted with small houses fronted by little walled gardens. The architecture was a strangely appealing mix of modern and medieval, as if Frank Gehry had designed house-sized castles made of steel and stone. A few gardens had flowering vines that climbed over white walls. Joe heard laughing. He saw a few winged kids flying and playing above their yards.

Joe walked with his head down so as not to be noticed, but he couldn't help looking up as gemynd coming home from work or going out for the night filled the stone footpaths between buildings. There were almost no cars in this part of the city and the footpath was clean and smooth. Every few minutes a thick crowd of rainbow-skinned figures emerged from a train tunnel. A very pretty young woman with green skin and hair like rushing water smiled seductively at him. He kept walking.

On nearly every block images hung in the air. Some were advertisements that seemed like short movies. These images shifted subtly depending on who was looking, constantly adjusting to the viewer's needs and desires and idea of himself or herself. When Joe watched he knew without a doubt that he needed whatever the product was, but he had to keep walking. He made a mental note to investigate how to get it later.

Some images were stories about gemynd, some were desperate requests for money or help. As the buildings got taller and the gardens disappeared, the footpaths grew darker and dirtier. Here most of the images were of Emma and her family:

OTHERWORLDERS HELD CAPTIVE BY **PARANOMO**
RESISTERS, AND IN DANGER.

PLEASE CONTACT THE OFFICE OF INFORMATION.
TIROFORA, **OBSERVE AND INFORM**.

The images were utterly convincing. Emma and her family were begging unseen Resisters to let them go, and her dad was defending the rightness of the Ones in Power like a brilliant, underdog hero. Intensely affecting music scored the whole scene. If Joe didn't know better he would have believed the whole thing. He had a hard time not believing it now.

A group of silver-suited men appeared at the top of the block. Joe turned onto a narrow street flanked by walls of windowless buildings. He walked swiftly, hoping the men wouldn't notice him. At the end of the alley the street was dirtier and the buildings uglier and falling apart. Here the floating images were more lurid but less contrived. The images of Emma and her family were grainy and there was no mention of being held by the Resisters.

Other images, jagged and flickering, hardly stayed in the air long enough to see. They disappeared and reappeared with such rapidity that Joe felt sick looking at them. These flashing pictures were of him when he was little, and of a laughing baby girl with a white dress and tiny red shoes. She must have been his murdered sister Edoro. A dark-skinned man, tall and thin, with sections of his body torn out and light pouring from the empty places, hung in the air, replacing Joe and Edoro. The man's mouth was moving constantly but Joe couldn't figure out what he was saying. He recognized the gaunt face from the picture in his pocket. It was his father's.

Someone came up behind Joe and pushed him against a wall. Two boys searched his pockets.

"What's this?" one of them said, tossing the picture of Joe's parents to the other. "You and your pretty Soulmate?"

Joe remembered that his thoughts were not his own. *Yeah*, he thought blankly, *me and my Soulmate*. There were two of them and

Joe didn't know if they had any weapons he couldn't defend himself against. They could have the picture if that was all they wanted.

A siren wailed from the other end of the alley. It couldn't have been a curfew because it seemed to surprise the boys. The bigger one cursed and dropped Joe's picture. The noise sounded more like the alarm Joe heard in the tower before he escaped today; it must have been some kind of law enforcement siren. Both boys listened for an instant and then ran, apparently deciding that whatever Joe had, it wasn't worth being taken to the detainee tower. Joe picked up the picture of his mom and dad and ran in the same direction. They weren't interested in him anymore, and kids like these would know where to hide.

As the boys disappeared down a flight of stairs, Joe went into a filthy room that looked like a restaurant. Someone pushed him out. He ran farther down the street. If he wasn't careful he'd lose his way and be too far from the tower. He stopped to find the sun and walked again in that direction, joining a crowd that had stopped for the siren but now continued with whatever they were doing. A little girl, maybe about seven years old, her bouncing brown hair in pigtails, walked unevenly ahead of him, talking to a stuffed blue tiger.

"You should be at home," a sweet-voiced old man with fiery red curls said to the girl. "Where is your *genna, chichi*?"

The girl glanced up. "My mommy's inside," she said, indicating a store window filled with bright white clothes and sharp metallic shoes. She wrinkled her nose. "It's hot in there."

The man peered in and saw a thin young woman with serious features that matched the girl's. He smiled. "Don't let Genna shop too long," he said. "An alarm's been sounded."

"Okay," the girl said. "Bye."

The man smiled again and walked away.

As Joe moved past the girl, her face changed for an instant. It was pale and bloody and belonged to a boy about his age. Joe thought he heard his own name, but when he looked again the girl was whispering to her tiger.

The orange sun split into sheets of pink light that would soon dissolve into indigo darkness. Joe stood for a moment then turned around. The little girl looked at him then ran. After a few feet she fell onto the stone footpath. Splotches of blood and dirt appeared and disappeared on her skin. Joe knelt beside her.

"Go away," she whispered in the ferocious voice of a teenage boy. "You'll lead them right to me."

Joe didn't move. The voice sounded like someone he knew, but he couldn't think who it was.

"Leave!" the girl said, pushing him away, the strength of someone Joe's size in her tiny hands.

"Why are they looking for you?" Joe asked, standing up. "And what do I have to do with it?"

"Leave," the child whispered again.

The alarm shrieked. The figure in front of Joe vacillated between a bruised, bloody boy and an unharmed little girl. "Leave," she said a third time.

Joe ran.

The alarm screamed louder. The neighborhood changed again. The wide-windowed shops were replaced with decrepit buildings and dirty streets. Ragged images of a teenage boy hung briefly and disappeared. He'd worked for the Ones in Power but did something wrong. Now they were after him.

Joe stopped to catch his breath. He leaned against a noisy, darkened building that reeked of fruity smoke and dulling wine. The girl with the watery hair he'd seen at the entrance to the train stumbled out and stood unsteadily in front of him. She grinned, something akin to drunkenness animating her pretty face.

"Hey," she said, moving toward him. "I remember you."

Joe felt suddenly dizzy. Everything about this girl—her face, her body, the way she moved, and the light in her dark brown eyes—made him want to kiss her. The closer she came to him, the more Joe forgot about everything but the idea of her mouth and every inch of her skin.

"What are you looking at?" she asked in a lazy growl. "Never needed a Fallwell before? Already found your Soulmate, have you?"

Joe didn't know what to say. Kissing this girl, and maybe more than that, seemed increasingly necessary.

"What's a Fallwell?" he asked, unable to move away.

"You're funny," she said, leaning closer. "I'm a Fallwell. A *Xerienati*," she added, whispering in his ear.

The blurred image of the fugitive boy suddenly popped like a dirty bubble between them. Unable to help himself despite breathing in the intoxicating scent of the Fallwell girl, Joe asked, "Who is that kid?"

"Don't worry about him," she said. "No one from either side will help him now. Never fuck with the Aythentia. They'll hunt you forever."

The boy's sober expression flashed in front of them again. It looked familiar.

"What did he do?" Joe asked, desire leaching from him as he remembered the pig-tailed little girl he'd seen earlier and the bloody boy's face that had appeared for a moment inside hers.

"He tried to stop the Masevo from killing Fen Elos," the Fallwell replied, the seductive edge gone from her voice. "And he let a prisoner get away. An Otherworld girl." She breathed in and out, and Joe felt instantly hot and dizzy again. She ran her finger up his chest. Her breasts were practically touching him. Joe felt like his legs, like his whole lower body was on fire. Whatever a Fallwell was, and he thought he had a pretty good idea at this point, he *needed* her.

"Why?" Joe said, gazing down at the girl's outrageous body. "Why do the Ones in Power care about an Otherworld girl?"

"Forget about her," the hot girl whispered.

She kissed him.

It was bad. He knew it was bad to kiss her, but hadn't he had a terrible day? Didn't he deserve something good? She ran her hands down his chest to his stomach. Joe wrapped his arms around her. She felt amazing. He did deserve something good. He deserved this. He kissed her back. Her hands were warm against his skin. She pulled him closer, running her fingers across his shoulder blades. Joe thought of Emma. He didn't feel guilty exactly. Kissing this Fallwell made Joe want Emma more. The girl pressed her hips into his, and Joe imagined Emma naked and sweet beneath him. Emma was ready to say yes. They would have done it this morning in her grandfather's house if they hadn't been captured.

"Wait," Joe said, out of breath and burning. "Wait. Why do they care about an Otherworld girl?"

The girl opened her soft mouth on his neck, and his legs melted.

"I don't know," she whispered, her hot tongue in his ear. Joe leaned back, feeling desperate to cool his head. "What else could it be?" she said, plunging her hand down the front of his jeans. "What do they think about except Eury Vatic? They captured his son, you know." She grabbed him gently and Joe's head spun. "But I heard he got away."

The Fallwell took Joe's hand and put it on her magnificent breasts.

At the last possible moment for escape, Joe realized who the angry little girl with the tiger really was. With a tremendous effort Joe pushed away from the lovely Fallwell and ran back to find the little girl bleeding invisibly on the street.

CHAPTER THIRTY-FOUR

"I said get away from me!" the little girl whispered, standing up but holding on to the building when Joe ran up to her. He'd realized who this little girl had to be. Emma had explained what a Mask was that morning in her grandfather's house. Joe just had to make certain he was right about who the little girl really was.

She clung to the building, her legs shaking. The tiger lay abandoned on the footpath. "Go away!"

"Shut up," Joe said. He picked her up and groaned. "Jeez, you're heavy."

The girl grimaced. "Of course I'm heavy. I'm the same size as you are. Ow," he added very quietly. "Please don't try to carry me."

Joe put the child down.

"Well," the kid said. "Do you have a plan? Or did you come back to learn the laws of physics?"

"Is there some sort of hospital or doctor you could go to?" Joe asked, keeping an eye on the street.

"No," the kid said. "Because of the alarm, they take every patient to a room for clarification. They wouldn't even treat me." The child winced. "They would just turn me in."

"How come there's no blood on the sidewalk?" Joe asked. "When I first saw you, for a second you seemed pretty bloody."

"Clever, huh?" the child said, eyebrows raised. "I'm the best Teknasma anyone's seen in more than twenty years. Not that it matters anymore." He began to reach down but thought better of it. "Can you hand me that tiger?"

Joe picked it up. "Here."

"Hello," an outrageously tall, jewel-covered woman said. "What are you two doing out?"

"My sister's afraid of the siren," Joe said, taking her hand.

The little girl started crying. Joe's heart clenched. Terrible pain and real fear were in the small, sobbing voice.

"Where do you live?" the woman asked, digging around in her bright orange bag.

"Dysikalloni," Joe said. "Westfair."

The girl glanced up for a second.

"Here you go, chichi," the woman said. "This will make you feel better."

She handed over an object, and the little girl unwrapped a thumb-shaped, white candy. "Thanks," she said, putting it in her mouth.

"I'm headed for the train, too," the woman said. "Do you want to walk with me? You can tell me about your tiger. What's his name?" She started walking at a brisk pace.

"Maude. She's a girl."

"Maude," the woman repeated slowly, like she was tasting it. "Not a very tiger-ish name, is it?"

"She's named for the Otherworld empress," the little girl said, pain aerating her voice.

"Can we slow down?" Joe said, taking her hand again. "My sister can't walk this fast."

"Oh. Sure," the woman said. "I'm not much of a slow walker." Her voice was light and musical, and the colored stones around her neck threw small rainbows on the buildings as they passed.

"Thanks," Joe said.

As she slowed her pace, the woman increased her volubility. She chatted rapidly about the weather: Good but could be better. And the upcoming holiday: Glorious! If only she could go on holiday every day. And something about a swimming dog and a Volucris dancer. Joe stopped listening. He held the Mask's hand.

"I can't go any further," the child whispered to Joe. Blue eyes burned through the little girl's brown ones.

"Uh," Joe said, pulling her closer so she could lean on him. He had to be careful not to lose his balance; she was so much heavier than she looked. "I think we're just going to wait here and call—"

"I have to pee," the Mask interrupted.

"Okay," Joe said, looking down at her. "Thanks," he added to the woman. "We'll get home all right."

"Are you certain?" the woman asked.

"Yeah," Joe said, lying easily. "I have to take care of her a lot. Our parents are really busy."

The woman smiled sympathetically. "Well, I'll run then." And despite her size she glided away as swiftly as if she'd been wearing ice skates.

Breathing heavily, the Mask sank onto the footpath.

"You're Gryphon Venti, aren't you?" Joe asked.

Gryphon nodded, his little-girl pigtails bouncing. "Have you heard…?" He stopped and took several long breaths. "Have you heard anything about Maude? Is she okay?" He glanced up at Joe with a strangely vulnerable expression on his little girl face and took another halting breath. "She'll know something happened to me. Soulmates always know when their other half is…when their other half is in some kind of serious danger. I just don't want her to feel upset, or to be in any kind of pain about it. I can't access her thoughts from here, but she…" He turned away from Joe. "She will feel something of what I'm feeling."

"I don't know how Maude is," Joe said, kneeling next to Gryphon. "Emma hadn't found them yet, but she was going to talk with someone who could help her."

Gryphon had stopped paying attention.

"Don't you have anyone?" Joe asked. "Family? Friends?"

Gryphon shook his head, bruises and dried blood appearing below his little-girl skin like stains at the bottom of a pool. "My parents are dead. I live alone. My friends all work for the Registry of Information and Observation, the *Plirolexis*. They would turn me in." He winced and swore quietly. "I would have turned them in."

"Why did you do it?" Joe asked.

"What do you think I did?" Gryphon asked, his real face framed by the girl's hair.

"I think you helped Emma escape."

Gryphon nodded.

"I thought...," he said, panting again. "I thought the Resisters would help her. And that she would make sure nothing bad happened to Maude."

"Why would the Resisters help Emma?" Joe asked.

Gryphon looked up. "Because of you. The Resisters want to find Eury Vatic before we do. Hell," he added, spitting blood on the footpath. "Sorry." He wiped his hand over the spot and it disappeared. "It's still there," he said, noticing Joe's face. "You just think you can't see it."

"Wow," Joe whispered. "If you can make people believe anything—"

"Not anything," Gryphon corrected.

"Well, almost anything," Joe said. "No wonder your side is the Ones in Power."

"Not every Aythentia is a Teknasma," Gryphon reminded him. "And not all Masks are on our side. No Teknasma has been as gifted as I am for a very long time. The Ones in Power didn't know what to do with me at first. They still don't. Not really." He leaned against the building and made a small noise.

"What were you going to say before?" Joe asked.

Gryphon looked at him like he'd forgotten he was there. Then: "That if you did find your father, I'd turn you both in. I could have my life back and Maude would still be safe." He winced again and breathed slowly. Joe stared at him.

"I'm serious," Gryphon said. "I just don't think you'll find him. You can leave," he added. "I would." Blood and bruises flashed like a neon sign on his chest. Joe leaned against the building. Gryphon moaned softly.

"Fuck it," Joe said. "Come on."

"I told you," Gryphon said. "I can't go any farther."

"Where are the Resisters?" Joe asked.

"Everywhere," Gryphon said, closing his eyes.

"But where do you think they took Emma?"

"I don't know," Gryphon said, cradling his chest with his arms.

"Can I...?" Joe asked. "Can you contact Emma? Or Maude?"

"The Resisters will have all access blocked or encrypted," Gryphon said. "I might be able to find whether we—whether the Ones in Power—know anything, but then they'd reach them before you and I could anyway."

"What about a Revelation?" Joe asked.

"What?" Gryphon said, smiling a little.

"A Revealer," Joe said. "Those images that hang in the air. They're different in different neighborhoods."

"I know," Gryphon said, a thread of derision in his voice.

"Well, maybe a Revealer in a Resister neighborhood will know something," Joe said.

"They won't publicly reveal anything," Gryphon snapped. "Don't be stupid."

"I'm trying to help you," Joe said.

"You're trying to help yourself," Gryphon argued. "And you'll feel guilty if you leave me."

"Fuck you," Joe said.

Gryphon smiled. "You're only angry because I'm right." He sucked in a mouthful of air. "Ow."

Joe cursed again.

"How did you get rid of the tracking light?" Gryphon asked.

"What?" Joe said.

"The *fostrochia*, the tracking light," Gryphon repeated. "Didn't your feet hurt? We injected a tracking light into the soles of your feet in case your father tried to bring you to him."

Joe remembered the mysterious bite in the stream after he lost his shoes, and the light flashing and disappearing in the water. "I cut my feet on a rock."

"Oh," Gryphon said weakly. He pressed the heels of his hands to his eyes and exhaled unsteadily.

"Wait," Joe said. "God, I'm such an idiot. Emma said something about a walled garden with winged statues."

"That's helpful," Gryphon drawled. "There are ten thousand gardens in the city, almost all of them with walls and statues." He sat up straighter, groaning. "Did she say anything else?"

"No… Wait! She said the tool shed in the garden was an entrance to a tunnel."

Gryphon thought for a minute, and Joe stared at him. He knew this kid would tell the Ones in Power about the tunnel's location if he figured out where it was and thought telling them would help him. And the Resisters would probably turn Gryphon in or keep him prisoner if he showed up, even if Joe was with him. But Joe couldn't leave Gryphon here. It went against his nature to abandon someone in trouble. He couldn't do it.

Gryphon closed his eyes. "Can you fly?"

"Yes," Joe said. Lying at this point seemed useless.

Painfully, Gryphon stood up. Joe watched in amazement as the little girl disappeared and a girl his own age stood in her place, laughing and smiling and playing with her hair. She blew a silver bubble in Joe's face and laughed. She was *so* hot.

"That is awesome," Joe said.

The girl smiled adorably, but Gryphon's exhausted voice came bizarrely out of her mouth. "Thanks." He grabbed the side of the building, grinning at Joe as a group of gemynd passed. He closed his beautiful eyes and frowned. "We have to move fast. The Masevo are using clarifiers. If they shine one on us they'll see me."

"Where are we going?" Joe asked.

Gryphon popped another bubble at Joe.

"Is that gum?" Joe asked.

"What else would it be?" Gryphon said, shaking his pretty head at Joe before sucking the gum back. "There are old tunnels we thought abandoned. One of them leads to a garden attached to the Library of Useless Information. I hope the entrance is there. If not, I don't know."

Joe stared. "Why would anyone need a Library of Useless Information?"

"The information is filed as useless now," Gryphon explained. "But no information is really useless. The Ones in Power might need it someday." He took in a shuddering breath. "Ow. Misos." He exhaled. "Okay. We'll be less suspicious if we're *katavolus*."

"What?" Joe asked.

"Other half of my soul," Gryphon explained. "We say Misos when there are no words big enough to express something."

"Thanks," Joe said, "but I meant the other word. What does katavolus mean?"

"Oh," Gryphon said. "Kissing and flying. *Volucris* is the Sacerian word for a winged gemynd. And *kata* is kissing."

"I don't want to kiss you," Joe said.

Gryphon grinned. "You don't sound very convincing." He popped another bubble. "No one is supposed to be out after the alarm, but they're not going to bother with young *katavolucris*."

Joe was still staring at him.

"Because of the sacredness of Soulmates," Gryphon said. "Love is protected. You're going to have to support me. I can't help at all. You don't have to kiss me on the mouth, but you'll have to kiss me on the forehead or something. And you can't be an Otherworld weakling and worry about it or we'll fall out of the sky. Think of Emma. Think of winning. Think of finding your dad."

A sense of freedom blossomed in Joe's chest. "Stand on my feet," he said, wrapping his arms around Gryphon's gorgeous girl-body. He took a deep breath and kissed Gryphon's smooth forehead. They shot up into the sky.

"I'll tell you where to go," Gryphon said, his arms around Joe.

The higher they flew, the freer Joe felt. Strips of worry and fear, about what other people thought or felt about him, it all fell away like dead skin.

CHAPTER THIRTY-FIVE

Isohel was right about Commonworld food. It seemed totally healthy, but it was not very exciting. During dinner Mom kept raving about how nutritious it was, and didn't everything taste better without artificial ingredients or unnecessary processing. There was the same vegetable soup Emma had seen in the tower, and some dark, grainy bread. And wine. Dad said they could all taste it, even Sandy. The tiny glass of wine Emma had was good. When Turner and Maude finished eating they went into the adjacent candlelit room. Elizabeth and Sandy stayed with Mom and Dad. Emma had to go into another room and talk to the Resisters.

"God," Emma said, closing the door behind her after the polite but intense interrogation was over. "That sucked. I think they regret helping us, and especially me. I couldn't tell them anything they didn't already know. It's *creepy* how much they knew about all of us."

Turner and Maude were silent.

"What happened?" Emma asked. "Is something else wrong?"

Maude stood up and walked over to a narrow window.

"Is it dark yet?" Emma asked, following her.

"Almost," Maude said.

"Are you mad at me?" Emma whispered.

"Not everything is about you," her sister said carefully.

Emma turned and looked at Turner. He shrugged his shoulders and mouthed, *I think she's worried about Gryphon.*

"Why?" Emma whispered.

Turner shrugged again and stood up. "I'm going to see if Mom and Dad need any help."

"Okay," Emma said, and her brother left.

Maude stood at the window. Her eyes were distant and her pale skin was luminous against her black hair.

"Maude," Emma said.

"Couldn't you just figure it out?" Maude complained. "Couldn't you just read my thoughts?"

"No," Emma said. "I can't hear anything in here. I think the Resisters emptied my brain. I feel like I've been puking up thoughts."

Maude wrinkled her nose. "Gross."

"That's what it felt like," Emma said quietly.

Maude clearly wanted to do something with her hands. At home, whenever she was upset she could always repot some plant or water flowers. Lumps of honey-colored wax piled at the bottoms of the huge candles, and Emma lifted one of the glass jars and scooped up a soft, warm handful.

"Here," she said.

"What's that for?" Maude asked.

"I thought maybe you could make something."

Maude bit her lip and took the squishy lump out of Emma's hand. "It's beeswax," she said, lifting her hands to her face and breathing in the fragrance. "And I think it's scented with mignonette, too." She pulled a small table over to the bed, sat down and rolled the wax onto the tabletop.

Emma lay on the bed, her attention half on the white ceiling, half on the wax in Maude's hands. For a while neither of them said anything. Maude sculpted a rose. Sharp-eyed thorns stuck out along the stem, and a perfectly formed but closed bud sat at the top.

"Wow, Maude," Emma said, sitting up. "That's awesome." She took the wax rose out of her sister's hand.

Tears ran down Maude's cheeks. She bit her lip like she wanted to chew it off.

"I'll listen," Emma said quietly.

Maude rolled her eyes and stood up, an extra piece of wax thin and translucent between her fingers.

"Are you worried that I don't believe you?" Emma asked. "About Gryphon, I mean. Turner just can't bear the thought of anything painful or bad happening to you. That's why he tells himself that Gryphon can't be your Soulmate."

Maude kept squeezing and reshaping the wax in her fingers.

"What is it?" Emma asked. "You can trust me."

Maude sealed her mouth shut but a sob shook her narrow chest.

"Something's happened," she said, her voice in pieces. "Someone hurt him. I think…I think he got away, but he's hurt. He's really hurt, and I don't know where he is, and I don't know how to find him. I don't *know* him," she said, sobbing. "I know that. I know I'm only fifteen. I know I don't know anything about him, but…" She stopped. "But I've known him forever. I've known him my whole life. I knew him before I was born and I'll know him after I die. I would know him if he were something else: a tree, a flower, an old man, a baby. Whatever I'm made of, he's made of. We're part of the same thing, the same single thing. And something's happened. He's hurt, he's really hurt, and I can't do anything." She turned to the window again and caught her breath.

Emma opened her mouth to speak.

"And," Maude said, turning on her heel, her eyes burning. "No one here will help him. If he came, somehow, to find me, someone would turn him in."

Although she instantly chastised herself for being a selfish baby, Emma worried that she didn't feel anything so strong about Joe. Then she realized that Joe was okay. She didn't feel anything so powerful because Joe was safe.

Neither she nor her sister spoke for a time. Night fell. Emma got off the bed and walked over to the window. The sky was littered with stars. Could there be more stars in this world? Could that be possible? She heard Maude sit on the bed behind her.

"Maybe I can help," Emma said.

"You can't help," Maude snapped. "If the Resisters hear you, they'll get to him first."

"I told Joe about the entrance in the garden," Emma said.

"I know." Maude nodded. "Turner and I heard you answering questions."

"Weren't they intense?" Emma asked.

A light of sorrow flickered across Maude's face.

"Sorry," Emma said. She sucked in a huge breath—and staggered as an image burst into her head. *Gryphon was with Joe.* Emma held the realization at the edge of her brain like an imminent sneeze at the wrong time.

"What?" Maude asked.

Emma delicately suspended the thought, afraid to breathe.

"What?" Maude asked again.

Emma concentrated on speaking casually and emotionlessly. "I have to figure out how to tell you without anyone hearing."

* * *

"Stop," Gryphon said. "Stop."

Joe stopped flying forward. They hung suspended in the air above the city, rocking back and forth on the wind.

"What?" Joe asked, his arms still wrapped around Gryphon's slender girl frame.

"The tunnel's been blocked," Gryphon said. "Guards are positioned all around it."

"How do you know?" Joe asked. "Are we close enough to see?"

"No," Gryphon said. "But I just saw a first-level guy from the Registry trying to impress a pretty Gatherer, and I listened to their conversation."

"How could you see any faces clearly from up here?" Joe asked.

"I see differently than you do," Gryphon said. "And this guy is impossible to miss."

"Well, what should we do?" Joe said. "We can't just hang here."

Gryphon nodded. Joe kissed his cheek and played with the ends of his soft hair in case people were looking.

"Let's fly toward the garden," Joe suggested. "Try to think about where the tunnel went and we'll head in that direction."

"We could only record half the length," Gryphon said. "The rest was impossible to detect."

"I'm going to fly a little lower," Joe said. He dropped gently. Gryphon made a small pained noise.

They glided slowly, weaving in and out of rooftops and manicured branches. Occasionally someone would glance out a window and smile at them. Gryphon's eyes were closed and his head rested on Joe's broad chest.

"Why is my dad so important?" Joe asked as he gently stroked Gryphon's head, careful not to touch the patches of dried blood and open wounds he could feel but not see.

"You don't know anything," Gryphon said not unkindly, "do you?"

"No," Joe answered.

"Your father is an *Oloklira*, a Whole Listener," Gryphon said. "He hears and sees everything that happens in both worlds as it's happening, all the time. And no gemynd can access the thoughts of a Whole Listener without his or her permission. Even I can't access your father's thoughts. An Oloklira is completely connected to everyone, and no one can connect to him or her without permission. It is a *terrible*, burdensome power." Gryphon exhaled painfully.

"Whole Listeners deteriorate faster than other gemynd. If your father did try to contact you at this point it would come in the form of images in a vision. You probably wouldn't realize the message was from him or even understand what it meant."

"I have a picture of him," Joe said.

Gryphon tensed. Joe regretted mentioning the picture.

"We have to get inside," Gryphon said. "There's no one out anymore."

CHAPTER THIRTY-SIX

Joe dropped silently to the ground and landed on his feet, still holding hot-girl Gryphon in his arms. "Where are we going to go?" he asked.

"No one will let us in anywhere without checking us out first," Gryphon said. "We have to break into an abandoned space."

"When that woman was talking about going on vacation, she mentioned someone at her job who was lucky enough to be away already," Joe said. "Could you figure out where that guy lives?"

"Yes," Gryphon said, smiling for the first time in a long while. "I'd forgotten that. Her thoughts were so insistent and loud, and so dull I tried to block them out, but I remember her image of the guy on vacation. I know him. I just have to remember where he lives."

Joe watched Gryphon stare blankly at a slender tree surrounded by tiny orange flowers shooting up between glittering stones. Then: "Okay." Gryphon exhaled in relief. "I remember. The apartment's near here." As he spoke, his hot-girl image transformed into a middle-aged man with shocks of fluffy blue hair, laughing eyes, and a thick body stuffed into clothes that had fit better a decade earlier. "Let's go."

They reached the apartment building and waited in the shadows for someone who could let them in. After a few minutes a breathless young woman with soft, indistinct features and long legs approached the building.

"Oh!" she said, seeing them. "I'm so happy you're still out, too. The alarm at work isn't functioning or something. I don't know. I've been in a panic trying to get home before someone sees me." She ran her hand over the slippery lock. It hissed open.

Gryphon beamed, his blue locks quivering in the breeze from the opening door. "We're out of danger now," he reassured the woman. He held the door open for Joe.

"Is this your nephew?" the young woman asked.

"Yes," Gryphon replied, closing the door.

"He looks like you," she said, smiling, and Joe smiled back.

"Thank you." Gryphon spoke grandly, matching his tone with his ridiculous hair. Then he and Joe started walking.

"Where are you going?" the woman asked.

Gryphon closed his eyes and shook his head in embarrassment. "My own panic, I suppose, from fear of being out too long." He ruffled Joe's hair. "It would be my head if anything happened to him."

He followed the woman down the hall. She stopped and smiled and opened a door. Light streamed into the hall from every interior surface before she stepped through and became transparent. "See you," she said, and closed the door.

Gryphon and Joe walked slowly down the corridor, pausing at every door so Gryphon could tell if anyone was inside. The undulating walls were made of something like brushed steel, and the floor was highly polished black stone.

Gryphon stopped. "This is it."

"How do we get in?" Joe asked.

"I don't know," Gryphon said.

"What?"

Gryphon glared at him. "I can't fool the lock," he said. "And someone will be around eventually to check for anyone in the halls." He ran his hand over his puffy blue hair. "I don't know what to do."

"How does the door open?" Joe asked.

"It responds to an identification code."

"Can't we try to figure it out?"

"It's not that kind of code," Gryphon said. "It's formulated to recognize unique physical characteristics."

"Like a retinal scan," Joe guessed.

"Yes," Gryphon said. "But not so primitive."

"What does it run on?" Joe asked.

"What do you mean?" Gryphon turned to look at him.

"What is the energy source?" Joe clarified. "How does it operate? Every machine can malfunction. Everything has a weakness."

Gryphon thought for a minute. "We'd have to break it and repair it almost immediately. And we'd have to cause some bigger disturbance so the lock glitch wouldn't be noticed until later. But not too big. We only want the house security, not any city patrol. The house will report but only after they've taken care of it themselves. House security is absurdly territorial.

"Bite off part of your fingernail and give it to me."

"Why?" Joe asked.

"Sometimes you can jam a key-reader with unfamiliar animal matter," Gryphon replied. "It doesn't know what to do and the lock pops open. When I was a kid, my friends and I used to break into the big apartments in our neighborhood and reprogram all the readers in the house." He smiled and then shook himself. "Make sure the piece of your fingernail is big enough so I can get it out again."

Joe did.

"Fly to the front door as fast as you can," Gryphon said. "Fly face down, so your image will be harder to identify. Hit the door hard with your feet. Be back here as soon as I open the door. We'll only have a few seconds before it will seem like anything more than a minor malfunction."

Joe flew to the door and kicked it. An alarm, more insistent but less terrifying than the city-wide wail, went off. Joe shot back just as

Gryphon jammed and un-jammed the key-reader. They went in the apartment together and closed the door.

Gryphon stumbled to the kitchen and drank some green liquid, moved to a corner of the biggest room and slumped painfully to the floor. "Most gemynd create a place in their houses that the filters and readers can't access," he said as his real face emerged from the smiling blue-haired man. "You can tell because it's the coldest spot in a wall. It's legal, unbelievably. The Eleytheria created that brilliant freedom-of-privacy law. We haven't revoked it yet. It's too popular, even among the Aythentia." He let out a long strained breath. "Everyone has secrets."

Joe gasped. One of Gryphon's eyes was swollen shut. His mouth was bruised and caked with dried blood and dirt. His straight brown hair was matted, spread apart where a crusted gash split his scalp. Around his ribs his clothes were torn open, and his skin was bruised and burned in places. He was trembling.

Joe grabbed a puffy red blanket from a giant bed and gave it to him. Carefully Gryphon wrapped it around him.

"Show me the picture of your father," he said.

* * *

Elizabeth, Turner and Sandy came in from the other room. Mom and Dad's fighting voices reached a crescendo and quieted as the door opened and closed.

"Sandy wants to go home," Elizabeth said.

"No, I don't," Sandy said. "I want to stay."

"Here?" Elizabeth said. "Where we don't know anyone? Where there are no phones or Internet or TV? Where everyone looks weird?"

"Mom and Dad are not going to stay here," Turner said.

"That's what they're fighting about," Elizabeth remarked.

"No, they're not," Sandy argued. "They're fighting about bad-guy singers."

Elizabeth sighed. "I heard them, Sandy," she said importantly. "They're fighting about when and how to leave."

"I heard them too," Sandy replied. "And that's what they *said*, but it isn't what they meant. Mommy is worried about bad-guy singers and Daddy doesn't believe her." He wiggled a newly loose tooth with his tongue and made a face at Elizabeth. "But Mommy is right."

Everyone looked at him.

"How do you know?" Emma asked.

"It's part of the story," Sandy said. "It's part of what happens."

"What else happens?" Turner said.

"I don't know." Sandy turned. "Hey! Who made that flower?" He picked up Maude's wax rose. "Can I make something?"

"No," Turner said.

Emma snorted. "Of course you can. Sit on the bed." She grabbed two handfuls of wax, which was piled like honey-colored whipped cream at the bottom of the candle jars. She laid the soft mess on the table and smiled at Elizabeth, who frowned and blushed but still came over.

"I'm going to make a monster," Sandy said.

"I'm going to make a butterfly for Maude's flower," Elizabeth decided.

Sandy changed his mind. "I'm going to make a bee for Maude's flower."

"I'm still hungry," Emma said. "Is there any food left?"

Turner grimaced. "I think there's more of that soup that looked like vomit."

"It tasted okay, though," Emma said. She was keeping what she knew about Gryphon and Joe at the back of her mind. She had to find a way to be alone with Maude without drawing any attention to them.

"I ate it with my eyes closed," Elizabeth remarked, spreading open a waxen wing with her thumb.

"Do you think we're stuck here?" Emma asked Turner in a half-whisper.

Sandy concentrated on his bee, frustrated that the thin stinger kept falling off. "I can't make it stick," he complained to Elizabeth. She rolled her eyes but fastened the stinger to the fluffy back end of his wax insect.

"I don't know," Turner said to Emma. "Dad says there's a portal tree in the back of a restaurant on the corner. He worked there when he was a kid and used to sneak into the Otherworld to watch girls."

Emma wrinkled her nose. "I don't want to think about that. Do the Resisters know about the tree?"

"I don't think so," Turner said. "But I don't know if it's still there. Apparently it was an illegal tree. The restaurant owner didn't know Dad knew about it. But I think it leads somewhere near where we live. It's part of the reason Mom and Dad moved there."

"Wait," Emma said, sudden panic flooding her chest. "Can the Resisters hear everything we're thinking?"

"I think they can," Turner said, "but they're only listening for certain words or phrases. Mom said they're recording everything we're thinking and then they'll analyze it later."

Emma sat next to Elizabeth. She smiled at her sister's fragile gold butterfly. "Awesome," she whispered, then stood up again. She hated feeling trapped in this room. And she couldn't think about anything important. She couldn't think about Joe.

His name in her head raised the hairs on her arms. The Resisters had heard.

"How's Isohel?" Emma asked Turner more loudly than she meant.

"I think she's okay, but Mom's brother won't talk to us so I don't know for sure."

"So we are stuck here," Emma said.

Maude walked over to the window.

"Are we all supposed to sleep in that bed?" Emma asked, searching for a distraction.

"There are other a lot of other rooms," Turner said. "This place is huge."

Emma felt a wave of dizziness. "Come on, Maude," she said.

"Where are you going?" Turner demanded.

"I want to see the rest of the house."

"Tell Mom and Dad," Turner said.

Emma made a face. "I'm not an idiot."

CHAPTER THIRTY-SEVEN

Maude followed Emma into the other room. Mom and Dad stopped talking and turned, their argument suspended like a paused TV show.

"Are you guys all right?" Dad asked.

"Would it be okay if we walked around the house?" Emma asked.

"No," Mom said.

"Please," Maude begged. "I need to move around a little."

Mom scrutinized both of them. Emma kept her head filled with characteristic restlessness and benign curiosity. She hoped Maude was doing the same.

"Don't take too long," Mom said. "I'll tell Hyllus and Aurelia that you're exploring a little."

"Thanks," Emma said, and walked into the hall with Maude behind her.

"Don't say anything yet," Emma whispered. "Just follow me. And don't think about anything."

Maude nodded.

They walked down halls and stairs, and in and out of rooms that seemed both familiar and foreign. Emma kept her head open to anything in the air and walls. She pulled Maude into a corner of a ground-floor room. Emma pressed her back against a frigid spot in a smooth wall. She motioned for Maude to do the same.

"I heard Gryphon tell Joe that every house has a place the filters can't access," Emma said. "No one can hear us here."

"Is he okay?" Maude asked.

"I don't know yet," Emma said. "After I realized they were together, I only heard that one thing. I'm going to try to hear more."

Maude nodded.

"Wherever they are," Emma said, "I think they're in a similarly safe place for now."

* * *

Joe held the picture in his hand.

Gryphon ignored his obvious distrust. "Every image of your father was destroyed," he said. "Except for the ones in the Plirolexis, and no one has seen those for years."

Joe stared at him.

"Revealers are blocked from revealing memory images from anyone who knew your father and remembers what he looks like," Gryphon added, answering Joe's unspoken question.

"Can the Ones in Power do that?" Joe asked.

"Of course they can," Gryphon grunted. He closed his eyes for a second.

"What was that green stuff you drank?" Joe asked.

"A restorative," Gryphon said. "But I don't think it will help. Where did you get the picture?"

Joe didn't say anything. Gryphon rested his head on the wall. Neither of them spoke for a moment.

"Why would you want to help someone who hurt you?" Joe asked. "It seems like the Ones in Power would have killed you."

"I would have done the same thing to anyone else," Gryphon said fiercely. "I believe in what they're doing. I'm only trying to save myself because that's what everyone does. Everyone fights to save his or her own life no matter what they've done. Even the worst tyrants weep for mercy. But," he added, "except for Maude, nothing is as important to me as the beliefs of the Aythentia and keeping them in power. Without absolute authority enforced by superior gemynd, society falls to corruption, decay and eventually ruin. Ask Emma's parents about the end of the last period of Eleytheria rule. Ask them to defend the precious, naïve freedom that allowed Gelon Lira to murder and burn to ashes seven Syche Katharos. Seven *children*. To prevent atrocities like the ones committed by Gelon Lira, the Aythentia have to find your father before the Resisters do. So give me that picture."

"No," Joe said, backing away, preparing to fight Gryphon even in his debilitated state.

Gryphon closed his eyes. He drew in a breath that seemed to take all his strength and transformed again. His battered visage melted and in its place Emma's face appeared, as pretty as the day she dropped the candy on the sidewalk, her eyes as bright, her expression as open and loving as the first time Joe kissed her.

You're not Emma, Joe repeated to himself. But, God, Gryphon looked so much like her, so exactly like her.

Emma smiled, and before he could stop himself Joe smiled back. Then her eyes filled with terror. She screamed as invisible hands pushed her to the ground and hit her. Pleas for help poured from her mouth, followed by so much blood she started to choke.

"Stop it!" Joe said, shaking her.

"Joe," Emma screamed.

"Stop it," Joe said.

Emma pulled away, crying for someone to help her.

Joe! Emma's real voice called out alongside the screaming like a ribbon of sound. *Joe,* the voice repeated. *It's me.*

Gryphon stopped screaming. Emma's face dripped off his like rain-battered mud.

Joe, Emma's voice said again.

"Can you hear her?" Gryphon whispered, clearly exhausted by the last transformation.

"You can't?" Joe said.

Gryphon shook his head. "I only know that you can. I can hear you respond."

"Emma?" Joe said.

"You don't have to talk," Gryphon said. "She'll hear you." The fight had left him and he lay on the floor. For a second Joe thought he was crying.

Emma, Joe repeated in his head.

Joe! Are you okay? Where are you? Is Gryphon with you?

We're in an empty apartment, Joe said. *Right now no one knows we're here. Gryphon is with me. He's hurt. Pretty badly.* An image of Sean Bolton bleeding on the floor flashed in Joe's head and he felt sick. *Where are you?*

We're in the house that the tunnel led to, Emma said. *Mom and Dad and everyone else are here.*

What about my mom? Joe asked.

She's still in the Otherworld. The Resisters put some kind of protective shield around her. And they also implanted a story in her head about you being away at some leadership conference so she wouldn't worry about you. My mom said she'll be safe.

Joe sighed. *We can't come to you,* he said.

Yeah, I know, Emma replied. *The Resisters would take Gryphon.*

He would turn us in to the Ones in Power if he could, Joe said.

I'm sure he would, Emma agreed. *But that doesn't matter, does it? It's not about winning. It's about fighting to do the right thing.*

Joe felt a flash of fierce love. *I wish I could see you,* he said.

Emma smiled inside his chest.

Before Joe knew what was happening, Gryphon plunged his hand into Joe's pocket, pulled out the picture and disappeared.

* * *

Maude sank to the floor. Emma's connection with Joe snapped. Footsteps sounded on the stairs in the hall.

Emma grabbed Maude's hand. "Let's go."

The door opened.

"Come with me," Hyllus said.

Maude and Emma followed without a word.

Mom and Dad sat motionless at a bright white table. A Resister Emma hadn't met before sat between them.

Emma glared defiantly at her mother, expecting a disapproving, I-told-you-so look. Instead she felt a huge wave of empathy. The strange Resister immediately turned to Mom. Hyllus laid his hand on the table. Emma could see a flat, smooth rock under his palm.

"Sit down," Hyllus said.

Maude sat.

"Sit down, Emma," Dad said.

"Where are Turner, Elizabeth and Sandy?" Emma asked.

"They're fine," Dad said. "Sandy's asleep and Turner is reading to Elizabeth."

"How is he reading?" Maude asked in a high voice. "There aren't any books or reading stones in this house, are there?"

"He isn't reading, he's reciting," Emma said softly. "Remember he memorized all those little kid books when Sandy was a baby?"

"Oh," Maude said. "Of course." Her skin was like skim milk, translucent and drained of color.

"Please sit down, Emma," Dad said.

Emma looked at her feet. The faces Joe had drawn on her sneakers smiled up at her, and Turner's voice floated into her head: *Don't try anything stupid. Mom and Dad know what they're doing. Just do what the Resisters ask you to do.*

"Your brother is right," Hyllus said.

"We don't want to hurt you," Aurelia added. "As soon as we have Eury Vatic we'll help you find a safe place here or in the Otherworld. By not cooperating you're putting your family and Eury's son in danger."

Emma didn't know what to do. And she couldn't think through anything safely because the Resisters were listening to her every thought. Her heart pounded in her chest. She felt sweaty.

"Please sit down," Dad said. She ignored him.

"You know I'm not going to sit down," Emma said to Hyllus, "so you might as well do what you want."

"Have it your way," Hyllus said.

Emma's heart beat so hard she could feel it in her teeth. *There had to be something she could do. There had to be a way out.*

"There is no way out," Hyllus said calmly, placing three stones on the table.

"What are those?" Emma asked.

"Recording stones," Aurelia said. "To document what you think and say."

Emma closed her eyes and emptied her head. Izzy Peccant's face the day she told Emma about Stacy drifted in, followed in airy succession by Izzy's cute shoes, the rock, the crushed magnolia, the bench and the plaque… As she formulated a thought about that day and Izzy and the plaque, and whose name was on it, Emma heard her mother's voice.

Go, Mom shouted into Emma's head. *Now.*

CHAPTER THIRTY-EIGHT

Emma ran. She went to the room where Turner, Elizabeth and Sandy were and locked the door.

"Take Elizabeth and Sandy to Agatha Moore's old house," Emma instructed Turner as a wall of sound rose up in the room where the Resisters had been sitting with Mom and Dad and Maude. "She was a Commonworlder. Her house will be safe. Ask Mr. Norway where it is. They were best friends. Break in if you have to. Go to that portal tree Dad told you about. Move yourself, Elizabeth and Sandy."

"How do you know all that?" Turner said.

"Mom thought it to me," Emma said. "Just now. Go!"

Emma opened the window as Turner concentrated fiercely on his sister and brother. As if tossed by giant, invisible hands, Elizabeth and Sandy were propelled clumsily but swiftly out of the room. Turner followed. He grabbed their hands and the three of them ran to the corner of the street where the tree was.

The roar from the other room silenced. Aurelia and the strange Resister burst into the room.

"The window," the Resister barked, and Aurelia leapt through it. Emma prayed she didn't know about the illegal portal tree. She thought Mom might be trying to block the Resisters from hearing their thoughts but didn't know if it was working. Grabbing a huge candle jar, Emma threw it as hard as she could at the strange Resister and ran back into the first room.

Dad held Maude behind his back while Mom, who was now made entirely of silvery light, fought with Hyllus who was formed of the same fire. Emma stood behind Dad's back and gripped Maude's hand.

Hyllus tried to slice at Mom's face with the white light from his fingers, but she held him off with a ferocious shell of energy that surrounded her. He broke the shell. Mom pierced him through the eye and he fell to the floor. She draped what looked like a blanket of green liquid over him then reached behind her back and pulled out silver wings. She did the same to Dad, Maude, and Emma, running her hands over their shoulder blades, painfully expanding existing bone and muscle in order to drag out wings. Maude bit her lip and Emma screamed.

Mom shifted something in the air around them, and Emma felt a wave of shelter like closing the door after coming from freezing rain. "Think of Joe," her mom said. "Tell him to stand outside and we'll meet him wherever he is."

Emma envisioned where Joe was and told her mother.

Mom flew out the window and they all followed, clumsily at first but then more easily. It was like flapping your arms in the playground and actually rising off the ground. If things hadn't been so scary it would have been the second most awesome experience of Emma's life.

* * *

Joe stood in the safe spot of the strange apartment, his thigh still tingling from when the picture vibrated seconds before Gryphon took it. Gryphon must have thought—and he was probably right—that the Ones in Power had used the picture as a transporting device to let Joe escape. And now Gryphon had used it. But why? Did Gryphon think he could use the picture to find Joe's dad? He must have thought he could do something like that or why would he have risked moving and exposing himself to the Masevo when he was so injured?

Emma's voice came into Joe's head. *Meet us outside your building. Be ready to fly. Don't think of anything else.*

Joe flew to the front door and kicked it open. The alarm shrieked again. As he went outside, Emma and her family—all winged—landed around him.

He grabbed Emma and held her, inhaling the scent of her hair, but her mom said, "There's no time for that," pulling Emma away and moving her hands in the air around Joe's head. He felt absurdly safe. "That's the *fylakas ilizo*. It's a filter shield. The Masevo will have to break through it. That should give us enough time to get to a safer location." Then Emma's mom shouted over the thundering alarm, "Follow me!"

Dad, Maude, Emma, and Joe rose into the air behind her.

* * *

They flew silently through the darkness above the city.

After a while Mom thought to Emma, *It's safe to talk now. The filter shields will hold for a little while. The Resisters don't know where Turner took Elizabeth and Sandy. As soon as that garden club plaque came into your head I blocked Hyllus from accessing your thoughts. That's what the terrible noise was.* As Dad flew next to Mom and squeezed her hand she added, *You can talk to Joe now if you want.*

Where are we going? Emma thought to her mother.

We're going to the house where Sfodro—where Joe—was born.

Emma flew closer to Joe and took his hand. He rose higher than the others and kissed her.

"I'm so glad you're okay," he said, his arms wrapped around her.

Emma held the thrill of Joe's kiss for a second then whispered, "I'm so glad you're okay, too. Where's Gryphon?"

Joe told her what happened, how Gryphon used the picture to transport himself somewhere, and how it was probably for nothing. "How's Maude?" he asked.

"Terrible." Emma shuddered. "She knows he's hurt, and she can't do anything."

"He's really hurt, Em," Joe said. "And he still wants to help them."

Emma laced her fingers through his. "My mom said we're going to the house where you were born."

"I think I've already been there," Joe said. "I think that's where the picture took me when I left the tower. Why are we going there?"

"I don't know," Emma said. "You should have seen my mom fight. She was kind of awesome."

"Where are Turner, Elizabeth and Sandy?" Joe asked.

"There was an old lady in town," Emma said. "Agatha Moore. She was a Commonworlder and friends with Mr. Norway and my parents. I was thinking of Izzy sitting on a bench with me the other day and I saw a plaque on the bench honoring Agatha Moore. Mom saw the plaque in my head. She blocked my thoughts from the Resisters while I told Turner that Agatha Moore's house would be a safe place for him to hide with Elizabeth and Sandy. Turner moved the three of them out the window, and they ran to a portal tree before the Resisters broke in."

"How did you know where the portal tree led?" Joe asked.

"My dad used it when he was a kid. It's an illegal tree, so hopefully the Resisters won't know where it is until Turner and everyone else are safe." Emma's heart clenched. What if the Resisters found Elizabeth and Sandy anyway? Would Turner be able to fight them off by himself? Would the Resisters be as ruthless as the Ones in Power were supposed to be? Why had Mom decided they should run?

Joe took her hand and kissed it. The lights of the city below had disappeared. They were flying over a forest.

"Does this look familiar?" Emma asked.

"It's dark," Joe said. "I don't know. I guess so."

A long beam of silent light erupted from the direction of the city. Mom shouted at Joe and opened her hands toward Maude and Emma. Their wings vanished. Emma and Maude plummeted toward the forest, but Joe caught each of them by the hand, slowing their descent. They landed hard but safely.

"What the hell is that?" Emma said, pointing up to where Mom and Dad still were. The thick arm of light stayed fighting in the sky with them—then a strip branched off like an unexpected river and dropped toward Emma, Joe and Maude.

"Run!" Joe said.

They stayed close together as the light trailed them, slowing suddenly as if something or someone had diminished its power source.

"Over there!" Maude pointed in another direction. "A portal tree."

Joe and Emma kept running straight ahead.

"*Trust* me," Maude panted. "There's a distinctive pattern to the bark of any portal tree. You wouldn't notice it, but I did. Come on."

The three of them ran for the huge evergreen and climbed its sticky branches. Emma felt a pull on her foot as the light reached the tree, but she jumped down and landed on the ground in the Otherworld. *Earth.* They were home. Well, sort of.

The tall pine tree burst into purple flames and disintegrated into a pile of sparking ash. She watched in astonishment with Maude and Joe; then Emma reached for her foot. It was scratched and bleeding.

"My shoe is gone."

Maude took off her own shoes and tossed her socks at Emma. "Put my socks and your other sock on your foot. It will be like a slipper, and your foot won't get cut any more than it already is."

Emma did as she was told. "Thanks. Good idea."

Her sister smiled as Emma stood and brushed the dirt off her jeans. "That was stupid," she remarked, looking at the pile of smoking ash where the portal tree had been. "Now they won't be able to follow us."

"Do you think Mom and Dad are okay?" Emma asked.

"I don't know," Maude said.

Joe looked around. "Where do you think we are?"

Maude stepped forward into a shaft of moonlight and examined a nearby tree. "I think we're in New England," she said. "The leaves are still young and shaped like they are at home. And here," she said, kneeling beside a clump of pink flowers with heavy pouch-like petals that made Emma think of a dog's tongue. "These moccasin flowers are blooming in the woods near our house."

"We should try to sleep while we can," Joe pointed out.

"Where?" Maude asked.

"In a tree," Joe said, looking around for trees with wide, smooth branches. "I'll help you guys up."

"I can get up by myself," Emma said.

Joe grinned. "Okay. I'll just help your sister."

They both turned smiling to Maude, but she was staring unseeingly into the woods.

Joe took Emma's hand. "Gryphon looked terrible," he whispered—low, but Maude gasped anyway. "You should talk with her."

"I've tried," Emma said. "I don't think she can talk about it."

They walked and scouted until Joe said, "This tree is good."

Maude turned her head.

"Do you want to go first?" Joe asked.

"Okay," Maude said, but she didn't move to climb the tree or ask for help.

Joe glanced at Emma, then back. "Do you need me to help you up?"

"No. Thanks. I can do it." And Maude climbed up the tree. Emma followed, climbing just a bit higher.

"I'll be back in few minutes," Joe said from the ground.

"Okay," Emma replied.

"Where is he going?" Maude asked.

"Probably to pee," Emma said, thankful Joe was giving them a chance to talk alone. She turned to lie on her stomach on the thick branch, and her arms and legs draped over the sides, her hair falling on her hands, fluttering like a hippie skirt in the slight breeze. "Maybe you'll feel better if you talk about it," she suggested to her sister. "You couldn't feel worse."

Maude gazed up at her with such a stricken expression that Emma wished she hadn't said anything at all.

Maude climbed to a higher branch, and Emma rolled onto her back so she could see her sister's face.

"Be careful you don't fall," Maude said.

"I won't," Emma replied. "This branch is really wide."

"This is kind of like the bunk beds we never had," Maude remarked in a flat voice.

"Yeah, it is," Emma agreed. "Except for the bugs."

"Remember when we used to let black ants crawl up our arms?" Maude said.

"Remember when I tried it with a red ant because I thought they were cuter?"

"I was glad you tried it first," Maude said, smiling slightly.

"Thanks," Emma said, and threw a leaf at her.

Maude dropped the leaf back down. "You missed."

"Seriously," Emma said. "Whenever you want to, if you want to, I'm here to listen."

"Thanks." Maude flipped her hair in front of her, and her face shone through it like the moon between rain clouds. "I've already told you everything. I can't say it out loud again."

More than anything Emma wanted to say that Gryphon would be okay, but she didn't know if that was true. And it seemed too horrible to pretend.

"I really hope he's okay," Emma said at last, because she couldn't say nothing.

"Me, too," Maude said in a small voice.

Emma closed her eyes and prayed Gryphon would be all right.

"Em," Maude said after a few quiet minutes.

"Yeah?"

"I'm going to tell you something, but I don't want you to ask me any questions about it."

"Okay," Emma said, sitting up.

"And I don't want you to tell Turner or Mom and Dad."

"Okay," Emma said. "I won't. I promise."

"You can tell Joe if you want."

"All right," Emma said.

Maude inhaled, and Emma felt her sister's sorrow slice through her chest.

"Oh, *Maude,*" Emma began.

"Shhh," Maude said. "Please. Don't interrupt me. It's hard enough. I just want to say it. Out loud. Just once. Otherwise I'm afraid somehow it won't be real."

CHAPTER THIRTY-NINE

Emma nodded in the dark, confident her sister sensed her intent to listen without speaking or interrupting.

"He called me Psalla," Maude said. "He knew my real name and said that he heard me reciting poetry in his dreams but didn't realize who I was at first. I know it was terrifying for you and Mom and Dad and everyone, but I am so, *so* glad I went away with Gryphon that night. If I hadn't, I don't know…"

Maude stopped talking and Emma waited, listening helplessly as her sweet, fierce sister wept in the darkness.

After a long time Maude spoke again. "If I hadn't gone with Gryphon that night," she said, her voice hollow, "I don't know if I ever would have gotten the chance to kiss him." She climbed down to Emma's branch and sat beside her. She laid her head on Emma's shoulder, and Emma took her hand. Maude squeezed it in return.

"For years after Keats died, people thought he was weak," Maude said. Emma smiled in the dark at Maude's adorable habit of explaining things through poetry or stories about poets.

"They thought he was a soft-minded, too-feminine sensualist," Maude continued, "who died because he couldn't handle bad reviews." Maude's voice was angry now, as if Keats were someone she actually knew and loved, who had been grievously and recently wronged. "The truth is, Keats is the greatest of the Romantic poets—Wordsworth included—and he wasn't weak at all. He was a ferocious fighter for the people and ideas that were important to him. And for himself."

Emma knew it was easier for Maude to talk about Keats than it was for her to continue with whatever was breaking her heart about Gryphon. She kept her promise not to interrupt.

"When Keats died in Rome, he was twenty-five years old," Maude said. "The coroner who examined his body said he had never seen lungs as destroyed as Keats's lungs were and that he couldn't believe anyone could have survive so long with lungs in that condition." Maude picked up her head and looked directly at Emma.

"He didn't want to die," she continued. "He wasn't destroyed by bad reviews from idiotic men who had no idea what real poetry is. Keats knew he had greatness in him. He had so many poems to write; his brain was teeming with unwritten poetry. And he loved Fanny Brawne. He *really* loved her, not as a phantom or a figure of fancy, like some shrivelly brained critics think, but as a woman—the way Fanny loved him, as a real man and not as a poem or a novel."

Emma squeezed her sister's hand. Maude smiled so sadly.

"Keats got to kiss Fanny," Maude remarked. "And maybe a little more than that. I don't know. But he never got to sleep with her. He would have married her. When Keats was dying in that little coffin-shaped room in Rome, he clung to a piece of carnelian Fanny gave him but he couldn't bear to hear the letters she wrote. He wouldn't let his sweet friend Joseph Severn read them to him."

Maude suddenly kissed Emma on the cheek and climbed back up to her branch. "I slept with Gryphon," she said, her soft voice falling between the branches. "It was beautiful and amazing—even the parts that hurt a little, or were messy and embarrassing. And for the rest of my life I'll be grateful that I did."

"Maude," Emma said, looking up at her sister lying on a wide branch.

"You promised," Maude said. "No questions."

"That's not fair and you know it," Emma said. "I never would have promised if I knew *this* was what you were going to tell me."

Maude didn't say anything.

"You're only *fifteen*," Emma said in a pleading voice as if she could undo what her little sister had done. "And before you get all romantic poetry on me and tell me that 'Juliet was only fourteen,' let me remind you what happened to her."

Maude swore viciously at Emma and nearly fell out of the tree. In her whole life Maude had never uttered a curse word, and now she was directing a violent one at Emma?

"Gryphon didn't kidnap me," Maude said, the light from her soul blazing like fire from her skin. "He asked me—*asked* me—if I wanted him to talk to Mom and Dad, to tell them together that we were Eynosyndeo. Even though he knew how much Mom hates Aythentia. Even though he knew he might lose his position for falsely reporting who our family is and where we are. He was protecting me and all of us from being discovered. And look what happened! Look what happened to him."

"Maude," Emma said.

"No!" Maude said. "You listen to me." She hesitated, and Emma worried she was crying or falling apart, but instead her fierce younger sister climbed down and sat beside her. Emma felt a wave of awe and a little envy at the power and strength of Maude's unwavering belief in herself.

"After I told Gryphon I didn't want to talk to Mom and Dad yet," Maude said, "—and not because I was unsure about how I felt, but because I didn't think I would be able to stand hearing Mom insult him—"

And Emma began to understand. Maude might only be fifteen but she wasn't like any fifteen-year-old Emma knew. She wasn't even like very many adults. Maude *knew* herself. She was strong and passionate and smart, and she could take care of herself. It was incredible.

"After I told him that," Maude continued, gazing directly at Emma, waiting until she was sure she had Emma's complete attention.

Emma took her sister's hand. "I'm listening, Maude."

Maude smiled and took Emma's other hand.

"After that," she said. "He asked me if I wanted to come live with him in the Commonworld now or stay in New Hampshire until I finished school. Asked me. Not forced me. Not fooled me. Asked me. I said I wanted to go with him that night, but I couldn't leave for good without telling Mom and Dad. Without saying goodbye to Sandy, Elizabeth, and Turner. Without talking to you and making sure you'd be okay without me. I know there are things about being with Joe that you're still confused about, and I wanted to be there for you if you needed me."

"What?" Emma whispered. "How do you know that?"

"How could you not be confused—or at least conflicted about it, Em?" Maude said in her steady, clear voice. "You're still hiding from yourself a little, aren't you? From your strengths and your weaknesses? From who you really are?"

"Can you hear that in my head?" Emma asked.

"No." Maude laughed. "I've just watched you forever." She squeezed Emma's hand. "Like you've watched me."

Emma turned away. Maude waited until she looked back.

"You're the only one who ever knew I was strong, Em. You're the only one who didn't judge me because of how I look or because of the things I like."

Emma gazed in the darkness at her beloved sister. She said nothing. There was nothing to say.

"So," Maude continued, leaning back against the trunk of the tree, "I went to Saceres with Gryphon that night. Before we left, he Masked my whole room with a long, complex series of false images of him and me so Mom and Dad wouldn't and couldn't follow us.

He said he made the images using a 'sticky resonance,' and that it was very hard to do successfully. I'd say he was showing off, but he doesn't have to. He really is the best Teknasma in a super-long time. Anyway," Maude went on, sorrow bleeding through her softening voice. "We went to his apartment. He made me dinner. And then..." She sighed and smiled so beautifully and so sadly. "For the rest of my life, Emma, I will be so, *so* grateful for those few hours with me and Gryphon alone."

Maude kissed Emma on the forehead and climbed back up to her branch.

"Hey," Joe said from the bottom of the tree. "Is it okay if I come up now?"

"Yeah," Emma said, in shock from Maude's revelation. "Sure."

"Is Maude okay?" Joe whispered, sitting on the branch beside her.

"I think so," Emma said. "She's afraid for Gryphon."

Joe tucked his hand under Emma's hair and slung his arm around her shoulder, drawing her closer. "I'm sure she is," he said. "Gryphon told me Maude would feel something of what he felt and that it would be painful for her. All he wanted was for Maude to be okay."

Emma stared straight ahead, and Joe kissed her cheek.

"Are you all right?" he asked.

"Yeah," Emma said. "I guess."

"Did Maude say something that upset you?" Joe asked.

"Why do you say that?" Emma said, turning swiftly to him.

He leaned back. "You seem distracted or something."

"It's just so much to take in," Emma said, looking into the dark woods again.

"I know," Joe agreed. "I'm glad we're together," he added. "I feel terrible for Maude. And for Gryphon. But I'm so glad you're here with me."

"Me, too," Emma said. And she kissed him.

Joe hummed into her mouth and pulled her onto his lap. Emma wound her legs around his waist, grabbed the tree trunk with her feet and tugged Joe more tightly against her.

"God, Emma," he gasped, taking off his shirt and sliding a hot hand to the cool skin under her bra. He raised his hips into hers and Emma gasped. He whispered her name again and again, quietly enough that she hoped Maude wouldn't hear.

He kissed her mouth and the sweet place between her ear and her jaw; then he took her hand and gazed as if it were something particularly amazing, although it had always seemed like a perfectly ordinary extremity to Emma. Joe smiled at her and then ran kisses from her palm to the inside of her wrist. Emma couldn't catch her breath.

Joe grabbed her hips and repositioned her on his lap, making such sweet sounds that Emma lost her place in the world, living for a moment inside the low, rough hum singing in his throat. He rocked against her and Emma felt dizzy. This went on for a very nice, very long time.

Joe unbuttoned and then unzipped her jeans.

"Wait," Emma gasped, out of breath, her hand on Joe's strong wrist. "Wait."

"It's okay," he said soothingly. "Maude's asleep. If she wasn't, you would hear her thoughts as she tried to ignore us. You don't, do you?"

"No," Emma said. "But…"

Joe kissed along Emma's throat and up to her ear. "I have a condom," he said. "I've had them in my pockets every day since we met. Just in case."

"Wait," Emma said. "Wait a minute. I'm serious."

"What is it?" Joe said. "Are you afraid we'll fall?" He kissed her collarbone and moved his hand back under her bra. "That's the great benefit of a flying boyfriend. Even if we fall, we'll just fly back up again."

"I mean *I want to wait,*" Emma said. "I'm not ready."

"Wait?" Joe echoed. "What do you mean? I thought you decided this morning that you were ready. I heard it. I *felt* it. God, please, Emma, no. Don't say wait. Don't change your mind."

"I'm sorry," Emma said. "I'm just not ready yet."

Joe growled in frustration. "Why did you wait until this moment to tell me? Couldn't you have said something when I first got back? Before I kissed you? Before *you* kissed *me*?"

"I didn't know until this minute," Emma said.

"You didn't know until I said I had a condom and it seemed there was no going back? Do you have any idea how unfair that is?"

"I didn't realize it was a...competition," Emma said, mind muddled.

"It's not a competition," Joe said, "but it's also not just about you. You're not the only player in this game. Why do you get to make all the rules?"

"Because I'm the one who can get pregnant!" Emma said.

"I have a condom," Joe said. "I have a bunch!"

"Turner's girlfriend got pregnant when they were using a condom," Emma retorted angrily. "She had to have an abortion. They broke up!"

Joe smashed his head back into the tree and swore. "I'm sorry," he said, still out of breath and still very ready beneath her. "I didn't know."

Neither of them spoke for a few minutes while they both calmed down. An owl hooted in a nearby tree then flew off.

"Is that really the reason?" Joe asked. "You're afraid you'll get pregnant?"

Emma didn't know if Joe could hear her thoughts when she didn't want him to, but she didn't want to lie to him anyway. "No," she said. "It isn't. I am a little afraid of getting pregnant, but Turner was careless. And then he didn't tell Rachel until it was too late and she was already pregnant. That's why they broke up."

"So what's the real reason?" Joe said, his voice still tense.

"I've never done anything before," Emma said.

"I know," he said. "I know that." He grinned sweetly and brushed her hair over her shoulder. "I'm a virgin, too, remember?" He rested his head against the tree and said jokingly, "Maybe it will suck. Maybe it will be incredibly messy or embarrassing. Maybe the noises will draw owls and bears. Maybe we won't be able to figure out how the whole thing works and what goes where, and we'll need to find a library so we can check out an instruction manual."

"Ha-ha," Emma said, leaning her cheek into his warm, strong palm.

"But even if all those things happen," Joe said, kissing her forehead. "Even if owls and bears and snakes come running—"

"Only the bears would run," Emma said. "The owls would fly and the snakes would slither."

"Okay." Joe laughed, smiling against her skin. "Even if owls, bears and snakes come flying, running, and slithering, I still want, more than anything, to be with you, really be with you, right now, tonight."

Emma's heart clenched. "I want to be with you, too," she said.

"Don't say 'but,'" Joe begged. "Please don't say anything but yes."

"Just not yet," Emma said.

Joe smashed his head against the tree again.

"When I said I've never done anything before," Emma said. "I didn't mean sex. Although that's true. I meant that I've spent too much time in the shadows of my life, watching but not doing. Running away from things that I didn't understand or that scared me."

"You're killing me, Emma," Joe said. "You're killing me. I'm not kidding."

"I want to test myself," Emma said. "I want to try things. I want to experience something of myself before I give myself to you. Before I let you give yourself to me."

"Did you read this on a freaking blog?" he said unkindly.

"No," she said. "And just because it sounds like a platitude doesn't mean it's not true. You know who you are, Joe. I don't. Not really."

"How the fuck can you say that to me?" he growled. He lifted Emma roughly off his lap and climbed to another branch. "You have a normal family," he said. "A normal life. A normal mom. A dad who loves you. A house. Brothers and sisters. I don't have any of that. I didn't even know my real name until a few days ago. And it's in a language I didn't know existed."

"It means Ruled by Love," Emma said. "Sfodro. Turner told me. Do you want me to call you Sfodro?"

"No!" Joe said, crashing down to a lower branch. "I want you to love me as much as I love you!"

"I do," Emma said.

"I don't think so," Joe said. "You obviously don't trust me."

"Why is it so important to have sex right now?" Emma said.

"I don't even understand that question!"

"This morning I really, *really* wanted you," Emma said. "And I really wanted you tonight."

Joe made a screeching noise like animals fighting. Emma prayed Maude wouldn't wake up.

"I still want you," she said. "But I want to wait until I *want* to sleep with you, not just because you're so hot, but because I'm ready to give myself to you and to feel you give yourself to me. Not just your hot body, but your whole complicated self."

"I have to take a walk," Joe said.

"Maude had sex with Gryphon," Emma said.

"Maude had sex with Gryphon so you don't want to have sex with me?" Joe asked.

"Maude had sex with Gryphon for a million good reasons," Emma said. "As if they were already married. As if they already knew everything about each other. You're right, I did decide to have sex with you this morning in my grandfather's house, but only because you're so hot. Only because I wanted you so much I thought it might kill me not to have sex with you."

"And that's a bad reason?" Joe asked, his deep voice high and strained.

"It's not a good enough reason," Emma said. "Not for me."

"I'm taking a walk," Joe repeated, and he jumped out of the tree.

CHAPTER FORTY

He did go back and sleep, but Joe left the tree again the next morning before Emma and Maude woke up. At least, he hoped they were asleep. He was still upset about the fight and didn't want talk about it again. Certainly not in front of poor Maude.

At first, Joe had been angry. He knew Emma wasn't teasing him on purpose, but that minor freaking detail didn't make him feel any better. He felt like a fucking clogged drain, especially when it seemed Emma couldn't make up her mind, telling him she wanted him *so much* but wasn't ready. And then she was all, "I want to try new things, just not this, and not with you. Not now anyway."

Joe grabbed a rock and threw it as hard as he could. The thing that had kept him up half the night was her stupid, stupid question, why it was so important to have sex right now. It *was* important. He kicked a rotten log down the hill, and a million ants ran out from under it. He wanted her desperately and definitely. And *now.*

He had assumed—and he was probably still right and Emma just fucked up his logic about the whole thing—that he wanted Emma now because…well, just because he *wanted* her. Because it was sex and she was beautiful. And because she wanted him. But Emma would say yes someday. Joe knew she would. And it would be sooner rather than later. She was being honest last night, even if she did sound like a blog or a freaking daytime talk show. And she did want him. He could feel it. It was a question of *when,* not *if,* so why did he feel like tearing out his hair? Why did this urgency feel more like desperation than pleasure?

Joe turned around to see if Emma was awake yet and coming down the hill. He was both relieved and disappointed when she wasn't.

He made his way down to the stream he'd found last night and threw cold water on his face. Emma's shitty question gnawed at him. He didn't know the answer, and he *really* didn't feel like figuring it out. But he missed her and loved her and hoped she wasn't angry when she woke up.

After he'd drunk some water, leaning back against a tree above the brook Joe thought about the task before him that had nothing to do with sex or anger or uncomfortable questions. Last night all they'd had to do was find a safe place to sleep. Now, the enormity of not knowing where they were exactly or what they were going to do next weighed upon him. Joe felt responsible for taking care of Emma and Maude, for somehow leading them to safety before he started back to look for his father.

The sound of the two sisters talking and coming out of the tree broke into his thoughts.

He stood up and called out, "I'm over here! I found a stream. And the water's clean."

Maude appeared first, over the slight lift in the ground. The fully risen sun shone on her face and teased out red and brown highlights hidden in her black hair. Emma was right; she was unbelievably beautiful.

"Hey," she said and walked down to the water.

Emma came second, and although she wasn't as beautiful as Maude Joe felt the air being sucked from his lungs when she looked at him. She grabbed his hand and squeezed it as she passed, and Joe stood there just watching her.

"You have to leave so we can pee," Emma said, turning around and grinning.

Joe felt his face go scarlet. "Oh. Sure."

He ran up the hill to look for something to eat. It was too early in the spring for berries. If he had his lighter he'd look for eggs or dig up crayfish, but he had no idea how build a fire from nothing.

He was kneeling on the ground picking edible violets when Maude screamed.

"What is it?" he called, running down the hill to where she sat on the ground, Emma kneeling beside her. Maude buried her face in Emma's shoulder.

Emma shook her head. "I don't know what happened," she said, her arms around her sister. "We were just talking about how much it sucks to be a girl and pee outside, because it goes into your socks, when she screamed."

"Did something bite her?" Joe asked, looking around for a snake or a snapping turtle.

"No," Emma said.

Joe stood up. He didn't see anything dangerous or frightening anywhere.

Maude picked up her head. "Gryphon's here," she said.

"Here?" Emma repeated.

"Where?" Joe asked.

"In the woods," Maude said, out of breath. "Someplace near us."

"Where?" Joe repeated.

"Close," Maude said. "I don't know."

"Why did you scream?" Emma asked.

Maude started to cry.

Joe gazed at Emma, who asked her sister quietly, "Is he okay?"

Maude didn't answer.

"Well, let's not just stand here," Joe said. "Let's find him."

"What if the Masevo or something worse is with him?" Emma said. "We have to be prepared."

"I know," Joe murmured.

Maude still didn't say anything.

"Come on," Emma coaxed. "Joe's right. We can't just stand here."

Maude stood up. She looked more beautiful, unreal, and older somehow, as if she'd passed through something and it changed her.

Joe felt Emma notice him. He waited for a wave of jealousy he'd have to defend himself against, but it didn't come. Emma turned her attention back to Maude. From the sorrow on her face, Joe realized Emma saw what Maude was seeing.

"What?" Joe whispered.

"We have to go," Emma said.

"Where?" Joe asked. "Can you figure out where he is?"

"Maude," Emma said gently. "Try to see where Gryphon is."

Maude swallowed a shuddering breath and stared into the woods. Emma took her hand, shivering.

"Okay," she whispered to Joe, letting go of Maude's hand. "Follow me."

She led Joe and Maude through the woods. They crossed the brook where it narrowed, stepping easily from stone to stone, but a swipe of fear ran through Joe.

"Are you okay?" Emma asked.

"Yeah," Joe said. "I just had a hard time crossing a river when I was trying to get back to the city."

"That was in the Commonworld," Maude said in a hollow voice. "The brook can't change itself here."

"How did you know what happened in the river?" Joe asked.

"I saw what you thought," Maude said.

"Can *you* hear or see what people are thinking?" Emma asked.

"Sometimes," Maude answered. Her voice was thin and reedy. "Since Gryphon came to the house."

"How come I can't do it?" Joe asked, cracking a stick under his foot.

"You can hear me," Emma pointed out, taking his hand.

"I know," Joe said. He kissed Emma's hand.

Ahead Gryphon lay in a ball on the ground. A tall, gaunt man stood over him, and the sun behind him cast a ragged pattern on Gryphon's crumpled form. As Emma, Maude, and Joe approached, the man disappeared, folding into the light around him like mud disappearing into itself, or wet sand instantly filling a footprint under the waves.

Maude ran to Gryphon and threw her arms around him. This time, Joe knew Gryphon was crying. He and Emma turned away for a second.

"That man was your father," Emma said.

A jolt of terror and relief rocked Joe. "Are you sure? How do you know?"

"I heard him thinking when he saw you."

"When did he see me?" Joe asked. "I didn't see his face. He was looking at Gryphon the whole time." How could he not have known his own father?

"He left as soon as we saw him," Emma said. "But he knew it was you. He wanted to see you, if only for a second."

Maude turned, her face full of despair, and Joe and Emma ran over.

"What's wrong with him?" Maude asked them, looking at Gryphon. "Can we do something?"

Joe felt utterly helpless. What could they do except stay with him? "We should wash the blood off his face and try to clean that cut on his head."

"I don't think we should use the brook water for the cut, but we could wash his face," Emma suggested.

Maude pulled off the flowery cotton ribbon she used as a belt. "This is clean," she said, handing it to Joe.

He threw the belt around his neck and ran back to the brook. When he reached it, he knelt down and scrubbed his hands then dried them on the cleanest part of his shirt before he soaked the wide ribbon in the running water. For the first time in his life he wished he'd been a Boy Scout, at least long enough to learn something about first aid. Maybe Emma could mentally contact an emergency room or something and ask questions. It was a stupid idea, but it was clear they shouldn't move Gryphon.

What had his father been doing there? And why had he left? Had he hurt Gryphon further? Joe wrung out the ribbon and ran back.

"Do you know what's wrong with you?" Joe heard Emma ask Gryphon gently.

Gryphon shook his head.

"Someone—it had to have been more than one person—from the Ones in Power attacked him," Joe said. "I don't know how he got away. Maybe his ribs are broken, maybe he's bleeding internally, I don't know, but he was beaten pretty severely."

Maude took Gryphon's hand and kissed it. "Masevo attacked him," she said, gazing at Gryphon and reading his thoughts.

"I thought Gryphon was a Masevo," Emma said.

"He is," Maude said. "But he committed a death-punishable offense when he interfered with the capture of Fen Elos. The Masevo who attacked him were jealous and felt that no matter how talented or powerful Gryphon was, he was too young to be assigned that much responsibility. That the risk of the volatility of not yet knowing his Soulmate was too great no matter what possibilities his powers afforded. And he was arrogant and disdainful." She took the ribbon from Joe and wiped the dirt and blood from Gryphon's face. He made such sad noises when she tried to clean his torso she stopped and kissed him then gently wiped his hands, whispering sweetly, too quietly for Joe or Emma to hear.

"I don't know how to figure out exactly what's wrong with him," Emma remarked to Joe. "And even if we did know, what could we do?"

Suddenly, Maude's gaze shot to Emma. "Dad did something before you guys left to rescue Joe," she said. "What was it?"

"What are you talking about?" Emma asked.

"Before he left," Maude said. "At breakfast, remember? They were fighting and Dad took something out of his chest—"

"Don't," Gryphon said, his voice dry.

"Get him some water to drink," Emma said to Joe.

"I don't want any water," Gryphon said.

"What would I carry it in?" Joe asked. "This belt is filthy now. Do you have something clean?"

"Don't do it, Maude," Gryphon said, his voice stronger.

Maude kissed his forehead. He shuddered and she lay down beside him. He smiled at her.

"What was Maude talking about?" Joe asked Emma.

"Before we left to rescue you, my dad pulled something out of his chest," Emma said. "It was like a squishy, transparent balloon filled with blue smoke the color of Dad's skin. He gave it to Mom and she rubbed it into her own chest. I don't know what it was, but it made her happy. But how did you know about it?" she asked Maude. "You weren't in the kitchen."

"I was watching from the hall," Maude said, keeping her attention on Gryphon. "Sandy was scared. He asked me to peek in."

"Don't let Maude do it," Gryphon told Emma, his eyes fixed on Maude's face as if he would sketch it onto the skin of his heart. "It's dangerous. Even if you knew how." He stopped to take a shattering breath. "And she's young. That makes a difference, too."

Joe could see that Gryphon wanted to close his eyes but he didn't want to stop looking at Maude. As this occurred to Joe, Maude kissed both of Gryphon's eyes closed and pressed her lips to his forehead.

"Why?" Emma asked. "It didn't look dangerous."

"Maude wants to remove too much," Gryphon said, his breathing shallow. "She could accidentally leave an opening." His eyes opened and his gaze moved to the spot where Eury Vatic had stood a moment before.

"Remove what?" Joe asked. "What are you talking about?"

"It's a part of your life force," Maude said, stroking Gryphon's cheek. "It's a way of protecting your Soulmate when you're separated or in danger. Mom gave it back to Dad when we were with the Resisters."

Gryphon's face clouded with pain again. "Please don't."

"But I'm not going to take mine back," Maude declared, impossibly sweetly, like she was singing to a baby in a dream.

"Maude," Emma whispered in horror, seeming to understand at last. She looked at Joe, who understood too.

"Please don't," Gryphon repeated.

"Try to remember exactly what Mom and Dad looked like," Maude said to Emma. "And put your hand on my back."

CHAPTER FORTY-ONE

"Maude," Emma begged.

Her sister looked fiercely at her, and Emma realized Maude would do it whether she helped or not. In her own way, Maude was as much a warrior as Mom.

With her hand on Maude's back, Emma thought of Dad's face and what his hand had looked like when he touched his chest. She tried to catch what he was thinking when he did it. When she softened her concentration and didn't try too hard, she could hear what he'd been thinking when he did it, as if his thoughts had left behind an echo only she could hear. Emma let Dad's thoughts float through her and into Maude.

Maude sat up. Emma sat back. Joe took her hand, and she was grateful.

Maude unbuttoned the top of her shirt. Tears streamed down Gryphon's face, making wet tracks where the dirt and blood had been.

"Please. Please, don't," he said. "I didn't do all this so you would sacrifice yourself."

Maude ignored him. She opened her slender hand and pressed it to her chest, and Gryphon closed his eyes. With a sound like a thousand breathing rosebuds, Maude pulled a huge, balloon-like thing out of her chest. Sweat poured off her skin. Emma could see her pulse throbbing in her neck.

Maude held the balloon thing delicately in both hands. Instead of blue smoke, Maude's visible life force was made of light and breath, a mélange of flowers and a melody Emma couldn't quite hear but knew was there. She felt it brush her skin as Maude laid the thing on Gryphon's bare chest.

Almost instantly, the gossamer sphere sank into Gryphon's bruised skin. He sucked in air like someone who had been underwater too long. Maude fell back. Joe caught her.

No one spoke. Gryphon's breathing grew steadier. He pulled himself to a sitting position with less physical pain than he had previously shown, but his grief-stricken face was furious. He took Maude from Joe's arms and held her like a baby in his lap.

"How could you have expected," Maude asked, her voice dry, "that I would do less for you?"

Gryphon held his teeth together as if speaking would crack him in half. "It's not what I wanted," he said after a long silence.

Maude took a deep breath and closed her eyes. "I'll be fine."

Gryphon took her hand and kissed her fingers, and Maude fell asleep. Slowly the color returned to her face, though it was not as vivid as before.

"What's going to happen to her?" Emma asked.

Gryphon looked at Emma as if he'd forgotten she and Joe were there. "I told you," he said angrily, as if Emma and Joe could have done something to stop her. "She took too much. She took years off her life." He brushed his hand across her forehead. "She'll die earlier than she was meant to. I don't know how much." He turned his gaze again to Maude, but he was thinking of something else.

He's still thinking of turning you in, Emma thought to Joe.

"Joe knows that," Gryphon growled. "He doesn't need you to tell him."

"How could you be so cold?" Joe spat, his face full of fury.

"Softness helps nothing," Gryphon replied. "You have to know that. Do you see?" he asked. "Do you see what my soft feelings for Maude...?" His voice broke and he roared in fury to restore it. "Do you see what happened because of it? If I'd let things unfold as they were meant to, if I'd let the Masevo take Emma…" He stopped and straightened his posture. "Maude would have the full life allotted to her."

"Why did you, then?" Emma asked, her anger equal to Joe's. "Why did you help me? You have no idea what would have happened to Maude. Maybe the Masevo would have would have decided it would be better for everyone—*for the safety and the security of the community*—to get rid of all of us, despite the protected Soulmate connection. They certainly didn't think to protect the Soulmate connection of all those Worthless they murdered when they wanted to catch Joe's dad."

"The Anaxio are different," Gryphon sneered. "And I do know Maude would have her whole life. She couldn't have given her *Nevma* to anyone but me."

"You don't know what else might have happened to her," Emma shouted, disgusted by his attitude about the Worthless and frustrated by his arrogance. "You can't predict the future, you can only tap in to what's going on right now in this moment. But the future…the future is volatile and unfixed. So don't blame the one good thing about you for causing this. Maude would have helped you no matter what you did. And you, or me, or my parents, or the fucking Resisters or the fucking Ones in Power couldn't have done anything to stop her."

"Shrieking your opinions doesn't make them facts," Gryphon snapped, his hand on Maude's hair.

"It doesn't make them fantasy, either," Emma replied. "You did what you thought was right at the time in order to protect her. And you can't change it."

"Where's the picture of my parents?" Joe asked.

Gryphon's eyes narrowed. "You think now's the time to find your father? The picture won't transport you unless he wants it to.

He used it to bring you to him. I made him think I was you. That's how I got away."

Joe stepped back.

"You must have figured that out," Gryphon said coldly.

"I guess I hadn't thought it through," Joe muttered.

"Clearly." Gryphon gently stroked Maude's pale cheek.

"If he was so curious to see what I looked like, why didn't I see my father when I got to the house?" Joe asked Emma.

"He wanted to see you," she replied. "He didn't want you to see him."

"What house?" Gryphon asked.

Emma and Joe stared at him.

Maude made a small sound and shifted on Gryphon's lap. His face was instantly soft and kind and full of concern.

"How can you love her and hate everything else?" Joe asked.

"How can you love *her*," Gryphon echoed, "and not understand anything else?" He ran his fingers gently through Maude's hair and she fell back to sleep. He rubbed his forehead.

"Where are your parents?" he asked Emma. "And your brothers and sister?"

"I'm not going to tell you," Emma said indignantly. When Gryphon's gaze dropped to Maude's sleeping face she added, "And don't you dare ask Maude."

Gryphon glared at Emma as if he would kill her, and then his face changed. In terror he stared at the empty air in front of him. Without speaking he gently handed Maude to Emma and stood up. Eury Vatic had appeared at the foot of a tree near the brook.

Joe moved to stand beside Gryphon. Emma stayed on the ground, her arms around the still-sleeping Maude.

"What do you want?" Joe asked his father, ready to push Gryphon out of the way if he tried anything. *Why didn't you try to find me? Why didn't you look for me?* pushed against the inside of Joe's mouth like a hand banging on a locked basement door.

"The Three Leaders have asked for my recommendation on what to do with the boy," Eury Vatic said, in a voice that didn't seem to come from his mouth or even belong to him, though Joe hadn't heard his father's voice since he was a baby. "My recommendation is execution."

"No," Joe said. He felt disdain run though Gryphon, and he turned, thinking, *Fuck you*, and grinning slightly. Gryphon glared back, clearly not amused.

Gryphon moved to pick up the picture of Joe's parents, but Eury Vatic opened his huge hand. The glassy thing flew to him. He crushed it between two rocks.

"Hey!" Joe said, running toward the broken glass now smoking with torn images. "That wasn't yours."

His father gazed darkly down at him then looked to Emma.

Joe leapt to his feet and placed himself between his father and the others. "I don't know what you want," he said, the darkness in his voice matching the bleakness in his father's eyes. "But if you're planning to hurt any of them, you'll have to hurt me first."

* * *

Emma stared, while Gryphon made a sound of disgust.

"Do you think you're some sort of superhero, Joe?" he sneered, though he never took his eyes from Eury Vatic's towering form. "Or whatever it is you call those men who make sinewy proclamations, convinced they can save the day by force of will and lack of thought." Gryphon shifted his weight, clearly ready to fight. "It's no wonder your ridiculous world is perpetually of the verge of self-destruction."

Eury Vatic kept his clear eyes on his son. "The boy is of no use. We have to kill him." He spoke in twin voices: one raw, one smooth. Emma recognized the smooth female voice, but she couldn't place it.

"The boy is of no use," Eury Vatic repeated, the clear female voice dominating the striving male one. "We have to kill him."

A strange look crossed Gryphon's cocky face, and the confidence leached from his skin like body heat in frigid water. Still on Emma's lap, Maude opened her eyes. Gryphon turned to her.

"'I've known him my whole life,'" Eury Vatic said, following Gryphon's gaze. Lightness mingled with the heavy rasp of his voice. "'I knew him before I was born. And I'll know him after I die. I would know him if he was something else: a tree, a flower, an old man, a baby. Whatever I'm made of, he's made of. We're part of the same thing, the same single thing.'"

Gryphon ran to Maude, who got up and stood unsteadily beside him. Eury Vatic smiled with a mix of sympathy and menace that terrified Emma.

"'Porphyro grew faint,'" he said to Gryphon with the same strange lightness as before, the same knot of empathy and malice. "'She knelt so pure a thing. So free from mortal taint.'"

"Use your own words," Emma commanded, her voice stronger than she felt. "Not Maude's. What do you want?" She stood beside Joe. "And what did you do that everyone is hunting you?"

Eury turned for a second to Joe. "You look like your mother," he said, the sweet thickness of an old woman's happy tremor cracking his voice in half. "Just like your mother."

Joe squeezed Emma's hand as she repeated, "What do you want?"

Light burst through Eury Vatic's flesh in dancing chunks like the sun through trees. The whole image of him flickered in and out like a dying light bulb. Sometimes, for an instant, he appeared whole and bright and human then he dimmed and shrank back to a figure of a man marked with openings where solid flesh should be.

A noise like voices swimming together in the same aural pool emerged simultaneously from a distance and from beneath Emma's feet. She drew in a breath of ice. Eury Vatic gazed directly at her, despair glowing on his half-face.

"'The air was filled with phantoms,'" he said, the liquid tenor of an actor's voice smothering his own.

The sound Emma had heard in Fen Elos's store, twisting like a beautiful poisonous vine around Fen's conversation about Joe, the voice she'd heard softly piercing everything, was suddenly present and overwhelming. She looked at Joe and Gryphon and Maude. None of them heard it.

Joe's face, or something like it, hid in the light of his father's broken features.

The voices came together like harmonies in a song. *Listen*, they breathed, beautifully, as one. Yet still no one heard. Just her.

Who is speaking? Emma heard herself want to say. The question jumped from the bottom of her stomach, trying to climb out of her mouth, but the walls of her throat were slick and the question waited, anxious and unexpressed.

Who is speaking? she breathed, moving the question to the air in her head where it hung unspoken.

"Who is speaking?" she asked, the softly uttered words peeled of their power and urgency. She felt calm and sleepy. Everything was going to be okay. Nothing mattered. Nothing was real anyway. Or if it was real, it wasn't important or necessary.

A word—the word *surrender*, a collection of swaying syllables—soared around her head and through her heart like a butterfly. The voices surrounded Eury Vatic and poured from his mouth like music. Maude and Joe were listening now. Emma could tell Gryphon wasn't, but he would soon. She sank into herself.

Everybody wanted to feel like this, to know—to really *know*, like you know there's blood in your veins—that everything would be okay.

Who is speaking? The question cracked at the bottom of Emma's stomach, and the broken words felt sharp and dangerous. She turned to look at Maude. *But I know he's there*, Maude had said in the woods near their house the day Gryphon had taken her. *Like I know there's air in my lungs and blood in my veins. Like I know there's a real world even when I'm asleep.*

Maude's mouth was moving. She was whispering something. Emma couldn't hear her but Eury Vatic could. He repeated Maude's words a second after she said them, whispering them back in a seemingly harmless echo that took the life from Maude's voice.

"Stop!" Emma shouted, the ice in her stomach bleeding into fire that finally opened her mouth.

CHAPTER FORTY-TWO

Eury Vatic turned to Emma. "'But here there is no light,'" he said, "'save what from heaven is with the breezes blown through verdurous glooms and winding mossy ways.'" As before, he sounded threatening and apologizing, as if he wanted to save and destroy with every breath.

Emma threw a rock that struck him. She was stunned when he winced.

The idea of the pleasure and relief of surrendering, of giving in and giving up, circled sweetly around her again. Emma turned her head and saw the back of Joe's neck where his hair dusted the top of his collar. The muscles of his arms and back filled his shirt, and his strong hands fell beautifully to his sides. Emma took one in her own. Joe shivered and gazed at her.

"Stop listening," she whispered.

"Stop listening," Gryphon whispered to Maude.

"Don't give up, chi Sfodro," Eury Vatic said in a pure, woman's voice. Then he disappeared.

Emma let go of Joe's hand. "That was your mother's voice," she said.

"Help me," Gryphon asked suddenly, Maude falling into his arms.

Emma and Joe ran to him.

"Maude hasn't had anything to eat or drink since yesterday," Emma said.

Gryphon shuddered, the grey pallor returning to his skin. "Do you know where we are?"

"No," Joe said. "Except that we're in our world now, the Otherworld." Emma knew he was reeling from seeing his father and whatever his father was.

"Portal trees are never far from a populated area," Gryphon remarked, straining to hold Maude. Joe moved to take her but was stopped by a glance of fury. "I'll stay here with her. You and Emma find a path or a road and figure out how we can get her out of here."

"No way," Emma said. "You'll just leave with her."

"I would," Gryphon said without apology, "if I didn't think it would hurt her." He rubbed his hand on his forehead and grimaced. "Just find a way out," he barked. "We'll be here when you get back."

Joe flew like an arrow to the treetops. Emma felt a rush of pride that she blushed away when Gryphon sneered at her.

"There's a road not far from here," Joe said, coming back down. "I saw a diner or something at an intersection. Maybe there's a phone. You could try to call Turner, Emma."

"Well, get out of here then," Gryphon growled. He sat on the chilly ground, Maude's head on his lap. He gazed down at her.

Joe wrapped his arms around Emma, and she stood on his feet. A familiar, pleasing jolt unfolded in her stomach as they rose into the air, but Joe didn't kiss her. He held her tightly and stared straight ahead to a boxy grey building sitting at the crossroads.

Hidden in the soft air between the treetops, Emma and Joe didn't speak. She knew he was thinking about his father, trying to understand what he was. He was angry that after a lifetime of dreaming of a monster or a hero, he'd found a broken mystery.

"Thank God," Joe said, dropping gently to the ground just at the inside edge of the forest. "It is a diner, and it looks open."

"Do you have any money?" Emma asked, thinking of food for Maude.

"I only have three dollars," Joe said. "I'll steal tips off the tables while you ask about a phone and a bathroom."

Emma felt her eyes widen.

"Ask for a takeout menu," Joe said, smoothing his hair and his shirt. "We'll mail the money back as soon as we can."

Emma smiled at him, relieved. For some reason she hadn't wanted to think of him as a thief.

"You have dirt on your face," he said, brushing her cheek. "And your hair's a mess." Gently he ran his fingers through her hair, and Emma felt guilty for wanting to kiss him. Then he grinned and kissed her on the nose, took her hand, and they walked out of the woods and onto the road.

Stealing the money in the crowded diner turned out to be depressingly easy. Joe ordered a vanilla milkshake and a grilled cheese sandwich for Maude. Emma chatted with the cashier and glanced at the address at the bottom of the takeout menu.

"We're in the Catskills?" she asked, louder than she meant.

The woman at the cash register laughed. "Where'd you think you were?"

"I guess I forgot," Emma said easily. "We've been driving so long I forgot where we were. I thought it would look more like the book. Rip Van Winkle," she added. "You know. This looks just like New Hampshire."

The woman nodded, but she was only half-listening as she counted the money in the drawer. Joe sat at the counter and waited for Maude's food, raising his eyebrows at Emma to tell her to stop talking so much.

"Can I have some quarters?" Emma asked him.

Joe handed her the money. "Why?"

"I want to call Mr. Norway, but I don't know his number. The Resisters took our phones," she added in a whisper. "And there's an old pay phone on the wall." Emma hadn't seen a real pay phone since the library in town had theirs removed a few years ago. She hoped this one was the kind that accepted calls.

"What could Mr. Norway do?" Joe asked.

"He and my parents are friends," Emma said. "And more importantly, Mr. Norway and Agatha Moore were friends. I think he'll know how I can contact Turner. And Turner probably would have contacted Mr. Norway about missed schoolwork."

"Here's your food." The cashier, who was not super old, smiled at Joe.

"Thanks," he said, taking the white paper bag already dotted with grease from the sandwich. He paid her and dropped the change in the tip jar. She grinned at him again.

Emma got Mr. Norway's number from information and called him collect.

"Emma," the guidance counselor said, his voice noticeably frightened through the sticky, bright yellow phone. "What's going on? Are you all right? Where are you?"

Emma bit her lip so she wouldn't cry with relief at the familiar voice. "I'm okay," she said. "I'm with Joe Castlellaw and Maude." She almost added Gryphon's name. "We're all okay. Did Turner call you?"

Emma curled her toes, afraid of his answer. She'd forgotten she was only wearing one shoe. Quickly she glanced around the diner to see if anyone noticed. People were eating and talking, not looking at her. The cashier was spinning a rag in a circle like a lasso behind her back and chatting with the man at the kitchen window.

"Yes," Mr. Norway said. "Turner called me. He and your brother Sandy and your sister Elizabeth are staying with Mr. Spencer until your parents get back. I offered my house but Mr. Spencer has more room and thought it would be easier for the younger kids."

Emma didn't ask about Agatha Moore. That seemed like an insane idea now anyway. Surely there were other people living in her house.

"Do you have Mr. Spencer's phone number?" she asked. "Wait. No. I'm at a pay phone and I don't have any money. Can I give you this number and he can call me?"

"Where are you?" Mr. Norway asked.

"We're in the Catskills."

She gave him the phone number. He repeated it back to her as he wrote it down then paused. Emma waited. "Is everything all right?" he asked again. "Where are your parents?"

Emma bit her lip again and glanced at the cashier, who was taking a long order over the restaurant phone.

"My parents are fine," she said. She rubbed her socked toe in a circle on the dirty floor. "I don't know how to explain what's going on."

"Are you in trouble?" Mr. Norway asked. "Whatever it is, I can help you, Emma. If you and Joe have done something, if you're afraid to tell your parents, if you've gotten into some sort of trouble that you don't know how to get out of, tell me. Let me help you. I'm old, but I've seen a lot more of the ugliness of the world than you have."

Emma had a sudden rush of terrifying images from Mr. Norway's life. "My mom and dad know what's going on," she said, trying to swallow the guidance counselor's past traumas so she could concentrate on her present situation. "And you helped a lot when you helped Turner. Will you please give this number to Mr. Spencer so I can talk to Turner, and tell him that Maude and me and Joe are okay?"

"Are you coming home?" Mr. Norway asked.

"Yes," Emma said, hoping it was true. "As soon as I talk to Turner. Thanks, Mr. Norway," she added and hung up the phone.

Joe leaned against the notice-plastered wall nearby. A lost cat flyer sat above his head near posters advertising an antique car show and massage therapy for horses. Joe held the bag of food as if it were a baby, his hand supporting the heavy bottom in case it broke.

The phone chimed suddenly, in thick notes like dropping coins. Emma jumped. Joe shifted the bag to his other hand.

"Emma." Mr. Spencer's quiet voice surprised her. "Listen to me."

"Let me talk to Turner first," she said. "Please."

"Em," Turner said a moment later. "What's going on? What the hell are you doing in the Catskills?"

Emma told Turner the whole story. She held the phone away from her ear when he swore about what Maude had done.

"Fuck," Turner shouted. "Fuck. She thinks he's her Soulmate, doesn't she? Well, he isn't. He can't be. Why didn't you talk to her, Emma? She's too young. She's too vulnerable. She can't have a Soulmate yet." Turner swore again. "Did he fool her? Did he trick her into believing he was her Soulmate? That's his job, remember, making people see what they want to see. I should have stayed with Maude, and you should have come here with Elizabeth and Sandy."

A big-eyed woman with wormy lips frowned at Turner's bad language sparking out of the phone.

"Stop," Emma said quietly. "He didn't fool her. And don't shout. People can hear you. I'll talk with you about it later. Are Elizabeth and Sandy okay?"

"They're fine," Turner said. "Elizabeth is complaining about not being able to talk to her friends. And Sandy is making a new comic book."

"How are we going to get home?" Emma asked.

Turner was quiet for a second. "Talk to Mr. Spencer," he said.

"What?" Emma whispered. "Why? Wait. No."

But Turner wasn't on the phone anymore. Emma groaned. Why the hell did she need to talk to her science teacher? As smart and cool as Mr. Spencer was, this situation was beyond anything he could know about.

"Emma," Mr. Spencer said. "Listen to me carefully, and make sure Joe can hear you."

"He's standing right next to me," Emma said, scared and pissed that Turner handed her off to Mr. Spencer at a time like this.

"That's not what I mean," Mr. Spencer said. "Make sure he hears what you're *hearing*."

A shiver ran from Emma's cold feet to her throat. Mr. Spencer knew about the Commonworld—or he was a Commonworlder himself.

Listen, she thought to Joe, who nodded.

"The portal tree you used to escape has been destroyed," Mr. Spencer said.

"How did you know—?" Emma began.

"Don't interrupt. I'll explain later. The trees only act as portals to Saceres, inside Saceres or from Saceres to here. You can't use them to travel within this world. I'm going to go to Saceres and find the tree nearest to where you are, and then I'll come get you and take you home, but it could take me a little while. I don't have time to search for an unregistered tree and I'll have to be very careful that the Ones in Power don't follow me."

"Why don't you just drive?" Emma said.

"Traveling to the Commonworld and back will be much faster than driving. You're at least eight hours from here." He took a long breath. "How is the boy?"

She could tell he meant Gryphon. "How did you know—? Never mind," Emma said. "I don't know how he is." She looked at Joe. He squeezed her hand. "Maude helped him."

Emma felt Mr. Spencer shudder through the phone. "Of course she did," he whispered. For an instant, Emma saw a lovely woman's face. She had dark eyes with thick lashes and brown hair prettily wrapped around her head like she was in an old movie or a painting. Then Mr. Spencer said, "Listen to me carefully. The Ones in Power and the Resisters are both looking for you."

"What about my mom and dad?" Emma asked. "Do you know anything about them?"

"Your mother destroyed that tree before the Masevo light could follow you," the science teacher said. "Other than that, I don't know. But," he added in a kind voice, "if anything difficult happened I would have heard. Now, you have to go to a safer place. Can Maude and Gryphon be moved?"

"I think so," Emma said.

"Good. There's a state park not far from where you are. It's an estate that belonged to an Otherworld nature writer named John Burroughs."

"I think my dad has books by him," Emma said, and she saw Mr. Spencer smile.

"I'm sure he does. Go to the park. Go to the cabin. It's called Slabsides. John Burroughs wrote there. Agatha Moore was a friend and admirer of his. She put protections on the land and around the cabin. You'll be safe there, at least until I can come get you."

John Burroughs lived almost hundred years ago, Joe thought to Emma. *How could she have known him?*

"Hello, Joe," Mr. Spencer said. "I'm glad you're all right. I'll explain about Agatha, I'll explain about a lot of things later. Right now, just get to that park."

"We'll leave now," Emma said. "I'll ask the woman behind the counter how—"

"Don't ask anyone," Mr. Spencer said. "As soon as you're back with Maude and Gryphon, think of me and I'll tell you how to get there."

CHAPTER FORTY-THREE

"We should have gotten water," Emma said when she and Joe were flying though the trees toward Gryphon and Maude.

"Do you think your mom and dad know Mr. Spencer is a Commonworlder?" Joe said. "And don't worry. I stole two bottles of water when you were on the phone."

He swerved to avoid a fallen tree hidden in the branches of another. Emma clung to him so she wouldn't lose her balance.

"When?" she asked. "I didn't see you."

"You weren't paying attention," he replied. Then Joe's face fell.

"What?" Emma asked, turning around.

"Gryphon," Joe said, nodding toward the tree where the Commonworlder and Maude were sitting. "He looks terrible."

Emma's heart clenched, and Joe brought them down near the tree. Maude was sitting up. She must be feeling better. Gryphon was leaning against her, his eyes closed. Emma didn't want to think about what might have happened to Gryphon if her sister hadn't helped him.

"Did you talk to Turner?" Maude asked quietly, careful not to wake Gryphon.

"Yes," Emma said, kneeling on the ground and opening the bag. She gave a bottle of water to Joe and one to Maude. Maude put aside the water for Gryphon and ate the sandwich.

"Thanks," she said to Joe. "This is the best grilled cheese I've ever had in my life."

Joe grinned.

"Can I have a sip of your milkshake?" Emma asked. There'd been only enough money for one sandwich and one milkshake. She and Joe agreed that Maude should have both, but the smell of the grilled cheese made Emma realize how starving she was, and the milkshake was bigger.

"Sure," Maude said, handing her the cup. And as Emma took a long drink of the vanilla shake, her sister broke half of the grilled cheese into two pieces. She gave one to Emma and one to Joe.

"No," Joe said, handing it back. "You need it more than I do."

Maude just looked at him.

"Thanks," Joe said.

He ate the sandwich slowly. Emma ate hers in two bites.

"You've never been really hungry, have you?" he asked, eating his half.

"No," Emma said. "I guess not."

Gryphon shivered, and Maude said, "I wish we had a blanket."

Emma asked, "Do you think Gryphon can walk?"

"I don't know," Maude said.

"I'll carry him," Joe suggested, standing up. "Think of Mr. Spencer," he said to Emma.

Joe told Maude all about the phone call while Emma contacted Mr. Spencer.

What took so long? the science teacher asked.

We were eating.

He sighed. *Move quickly.*

"We have to move quickly," Emma repeated aloud.

Joe picked up Gryphon, who moaned and insisted he could walk. "Shut up," Joe said. "Hold on." Then he flew, holding Gryphon just a little above the ground as Mr. Spencer guided Emma and she led everyone to the park in the forest.

"Put me down," Gryphon said at the entrance to the trail that led to the cabin. He took several short breaths. "There are people up ahead."

Joe came down gently near a green metal fence and an old wooden arrow that read SLABSIDES. Gryphon panted for a few more seconds then smiled at Maude. She smiled back and kissed him. He wrapped his arms slowly around her, leaning a little of his weight onto her slender frame.

Two hikers—a youngish man and a younger woman—appeared on the gravel path, led by a bouncing, dusty, chocolate-brown dog.

"He's friendly," the woman shouted as the dog bounded down the path, mouth open, drool flying.

Joe knelt and petted the dog's head. His tail wagged so violently his whole body wiggled back and forth.

"Hey," Joe said, scratching the dog's shoulders. "*Hey.* How are you, boy?"

"Great day, huh?" the male hiker said. "Oscar, come. He doesn't want to marry you."

The dog ran back. Emma saw a dirty yellow tennis ball in the man's hand. He threw it, and the dog took off like a shot.

"Are you guys going to the cabin?" the woman asked.

"Yeah," Emma said. "Our dad loves John Burroughs. We promised him we'd go when we were here."

The man smiled. "What does your dad do?"

"He's an environmental sciences professor," Maude said.

"Cool," the woman remarked. "Where does he teach?"

Gryphon gazed at the woman, and she began animatedly talking about herself. The man just grinned in affectionate curiosity.

"I'm in the graduate program at the University of Vermont," she revealed excitedly. "I think I want to teach, but I really want to write. The cabin, Slabsides, is amazing. It's like a shrine. Or a cathedral. I've never felt so safe or peaceful anywhere else in my life."

"We've got to go," Joe said, glancing at Gryphon's strained face. "Her parents want us back soon."

"Have fun," the man said, tossing the ball for the dog a third time. "Don't forget to write something in the notebook. It's in a wooden box in front of the house."

"We won't forget," Maude said. "Bye."

A short time later they reached the cabin. Old hippies, young environmentalists and tourists wearing tee shirts that listed destinations presumably now crossed off their list walked into and around a cabin made of rounded slabs of wood. Two kids of about eight and ten years old played with a hand pump that inflated balloons which then rocketed into the air, noisily rising and then diving as they deflated.

"Don't leave those balloons on the ground," a young woman in shorts and hiking sandals warned. The little girl frowned at being spoken to by a stranger, but the boy ran to pick up the colored strips.

We're here, Emma thought to Mr. Spencer.

Good, the science teacher said. *Get inside the cabin. I'll be there in an hour. Maybe a little longer.*

How are we supposed to wait inside the cabin for an hour? Emma thought to Mr. Spencer. *There are four of us and it's pretty small.*

Just get inside, Mr. Spencer said. *And wait for me.*

He broke the connection.

The interior walls of the cabin were the same as the exterior. Inside, a stone fireplace smelled faintly of long dead fires. Books and framed pictures flanked the windows near and opposite the hearth. The rustic furniture was made of roots and tree trunks. A straw hat hung patiently on a wall as if the writer had just left. The girl hiker was right. The place did feel like a sanctuary.

Gryphon held tightly to Maude's hand. "I can make us less apparent.

"I'll be fine," he whispered when she gazed worriedly at him, and he kissed her head. "Sit on the floor with me," he ordered everyone, indicating a stretch of wall near a window.

Emma waited to see herself disappear. Nothing happened. She looked at Joe. He was still there too. And Maude and Gryphon. But the next group of people coming in didn't notice them. They walked around the cabin, reading book titles and gazing at pictures on the wooden walls.

Gryphon gazed at Joe as if trying to figure something out. "How long did you have that picture of your parents?" he asked.

"Emma's brother found it in their grandfather's house," Joe said.

"So, you had it almost right after they rescued you initially," Gryphon said in disbelief.

Joe nodded.

Gryphon stared back into space, still trying to understand something.

After a minute he sighed and looked at Maude. "One of the Three Leaders is a Thoryba Exocho, a Super Telepath," he said. "She must have known about you as soon as we met that night in the Otherworld." He smiled at her. "Our Soulmate revelation was almost instantaneous."

Maude kissed him. Joe and Emma were silent.

"The Ones in Power had already stopped trusting me," Gryphon revealed to Joe after a few minutes. "That's why I didn't know about the picture or your father's house. They'd stopped trusting me to do my job because they believed I would put Maude first." He glanced at her again, this time without smiling but with so much love and longing in his expression Joe and Emma both had to look away. "Capturing Emma was a test, and I failed."

No one said anything for a while. Gryphon rested his head on Maude's shoulder, and Emma leaned against Joe. It was a relief just to sit and be quiet.

A young couple came in, laughing. They looked around then kissed for an uncomfortably long time. Emma worried that Maude would be embarrassed, especially because the kisses were spitty and noisy, like on a TV show, but Maude just stared ahead, lost in her own thoughts.

Later, a little boy who had come in with his mother picked up something from the bookshelf and put it in his pocket.

"Don't say anything," Gryphon whispered to Maude, who had sat up in shock. He glanced at the boy's mother, and a few minutes later she turned around.

"What's in your pocket?" she asked the boy.

"Nothing," he said.

"Give it to me," she said.

"I don't have anything."

"Give it to me," she ordered, "or I'll ask the park ranger to ask you."

The boy wrinkled his face and pulled the thing out of his pocket and handed it over.

"Where did you get it?"

He pointed to the shelf.

She put it back. "No ice cream."

"But—" he protested.

"No ice cream," she repeated, and pulled him out of the cabin.

Gryphon exhaled and leaned against the wall. Maude laced her fingers through his.

"My butt is falling asleep," Emma remarked.

"Nice," Gryphon whispered, his eyes closed.

"Do you think I could walk around a little?" Emma asked. "Inside the cabin, I mean."

"Is anyone else close by?" Gryphon asked, his voice dry. Maude handed him a half-empty bottle of water and he drank a little. "We're only hard to see near the wall."

"No one's outside," Emma said.

"Go ahead," Gryphon allowed. "But don't touch anything."

"Thanks, Dad," Emma said.

Maude kissed Gryphon's cheek. Emma walked over to a table covered with notebooks and rocks and something that looked like an old bird's nest.

CHAPTER FORTY-FOUR

Emma glanced back to see if Gryphon was watching then paged through a book called *The Summit of the Years*. On the last page, heavier writing shone through. She turned it over. The writing wasn't on the back of the book; it was on the table. It shimmered just beneath the surface of the wood, and Emma could hardly see it now that she'd uncovered it. Neither could she immediately read what it said.

"What is it?" Gryphon asked, sitting up straighter. "Ow."

Maude rested her hand on his thigh.

"Nothing," Emma said. "Someone wrote something on the table. I'm trying to read it." She glanced at Joe, who stood up and brushed the dirt off his jeans.

"Lie down," Maude whispered to Gryphon, taking his head in her lap. He made a soft noise and obeyed. She stroked his hair with one hand and held his hand with the other.

Joe watched the pair for a second then walked over to Emma. "What is it?" he whispered.

"This," she said, pointing to the half-visible writing. "On the table. Can you see it?"

Joe bent close. "It looks like insect trails."

"It's not," Emma said. "It's Sacerian."

"How can you read it?" Joe asked.

"I can't," Emma said. "But I know what it says. I can hear what the man was thinking. And if I don't try too hard, I can understand him."

"What does it say?" Joe asked.

The door opened and a park ranger came in. "The cabin is closing, you two," he said, cocking his head toward the door.

"Do you mind if I finish reading the book titles?" Emma asked. "I promised my dad I would try to remember all the books in the cabin. It will only take a minute."

The man glanced at the watch on his belt. "Two minutes."

"Thanks," Emma said, smiling.

When the ranger closed the door, she and Joe sat next to Gryphon and Maude.

* * *

The sun was fading and the air was turning cooler when Mr. Spencer walked in. He breathed a sigh of relief but looked worried at the sight of Gryphon and Maude.

"I'm sorry," he said. "I had a little trouble in the Commonworld. The alarm is still sounded and the security is fierce." He knelt in front of Gryphon. "I'm Will Spencer," he said, reaching out his hand.

Gryphon's eyes widened. "Gryphon Venti," he said, briefly taking the science teacher's hand.

Mr. Spencer touched Gryphon's forehead and felt his pulse. A shiver of displeasure flashed in his expression. He glanced from Maude to Joe to Emma then ran his hand over his face.

"We didn't know you were in the Otherworld again," Gryphon said.

"I registered."

"I didn't see your name on the list," Gryphon remarked.

Mr. Spencer colored a little. "I saw it myself," he said. "I reregistered two years ago."

"Once you've been arrested you're required to reregister every year," Gryphon said. "I would have thought you'd know that law."

"The law must have changed," Mr. Spencer said, keeping the story of his arrest hidden from Emma, who was trying to read his thoughts. "It was every two years when I last registered, which means I'm still in compliance." His voice was firm, but his expression was filled with concern. Emma realized the concern was not for himself but Gryphon.

Gryphon sat up. "Ow," he muttered under his breath. Maude made a soft sound.

"I didn't think…," Mr. Spencer said to Emma, but he didn't finish his thought. "I don't know how we're going to get him out of here and then into Saceres and then back to my house in the Otherworld again. We'll have to move too quickly. It was hard for me to do by myself. But we can't stay here forever either."

"I can change—" Gryphon began.

"No," Mr. Spencer said, squeezing his shoulder. "Save your strength. I'll think of something."

But Mr. Spencer didn't have any ideas, Emma realized. The portal trees through the Commonworld were the fastest way home, but Gryphon was too injured to move quickly and the security had increased substantially since they'd escaped.

Mr. Spencer stood up and walked to the darkening window.

"Maybe there's another way," Emma said.

Mr. Spencer shook his head. "I searched every map."

"Maybe there's a way that's not on a map," Emma said.

"What are you trying to say?" Mr. Spencer turned to Emma then immediately faced the window again.

"Someone," Emma said, "a Commonworlder, wrote a story and left it here."

"What?" Mr. Spencer gasped. "Where?"

"Here," Emma said. "On the table. It's hard to see unless you half look at it."

Mr. Spencer walked to the table and ran his finger over the hidden text.

"What is it?" Emma asked when the science teacher didn't say anything.

He sat on a chair, but Maude said softly, "You're not supposed to sit on the furniture," so Mr. Spencer smiled a little and stood up again.

"Can you read it?" Emma asked. "Don't be embarrassed if you can't. I know what it says."

Mr. Spencer stared without answering into the diminishing light of the cabin.

"You're a Commonworlder, aren't you?" Emma said. "I mean, you have to be. Otherwise how could you have known about portal trees and registering and other stuff."

"Yes," Mr. Spencer said. "And I read the story."

"I read, it too," Emma said. "Well, I didn't read it. I looked at it and I heard his voice."

Mr. Spencer gazed at her. "You heard his voice?"

"Yeah," Emma said. "I knew it was Sacerian, but I can't read it."

She watched Gryphon watch Mr. Spencer pace the small room and sit on the chair again. "I won't break the chair," Mr. Spencer said to Maude. "I promise."

"What are you going to do?" Gryphon asked quietly.

"You know, I don't know," Mr. Spencer answered, his eyes on Gryphon's haggard face.

"What is going on?" Emma demanded.

"The story was a cryptic message from Eury Vatic," Gryphon said. "Mr. Spencer could use it to contact him but—"

"We've already seen my father," Joe said.

Mr. Spencer paled and stared at Emma. "Why didn't you tell me?"

"I forgot," she said. The teacher made a noise that sounded like disbelief, horror and laughter.

"I don't think he'll help us," Joe remarked. "I think he wanted me to kill Gryphon. He said something about killing the boy."

Gryphon half smiled. "Joe was too soft-hearted to oblige."

"He asked you to kill Gryphon?" Mr. Spencer said. "Are you sure that's what he meant?"

"You still believe Eury Vatic's Eleytheria?" Gryphon asked mockingly. He shifted his weight with Maude's help. "He fights for himself and no one else. He doesn't believe in anything." Deep disdain filled his exhausted voice.

"Why did he have holes in his body?" Maude asked.

"What?" Mr. Spencer looked utterly preoccupied.

"He had holes in his body," Maude said. "As if parts of him had rotted and fallen off. You could see through him."

"He spoke with other voices," Joe added. "And I think in other people's words. Emma thought he didn't use his own words at all." He shoved his hands in his pockets. "Once she thought he used my mother's voice."

Mr. Spencer stood up.

"Did you know my parents?" Joe asked. "Before this happened to my dad?"

Mr. Spencer looked at Joe as if he'd only half-heard the question, and then in a distraught voice he said, "Your dad and I were very good friends. I knew him before he met your mother."

"How can that be?" Emma said. "Aren't you, like, thirty? You would have been, like, eight years old when Joe's dad was already an adult."

Mr. Spencer ignored her question. "Sofia," he said to Joe. "Your mother's name was Sofia. She wanted to save your dad, and he wanted to spare her having to watch him diminish. In the end neither of them got what they wanted."

"Yes, they did," Maude said, her voice fierce. "They didn't give up. They fought to stay with each other as long as they could. And they did, didn't they?"

Mr. Spencer's jaw flexed for a second. "You're right. They did."

"But what happened to him?" Joe asked. "What is he? Why doesn't he speak with his own voice? How can he disappear, or exist with part of his body missing? And what did he do that everyone wants to find him? Did he kill my sister? Did he try to kill me?"

"No," Mr. Spencer said. "No. He tried to save you. After your mother died he sent you and Edoro away. He knew the Ones in Power wanted to capture him, and he was terrified that they would use you and Edoro as kind of ransom. I don't think he realized the Resisters would come after him as well as the Ones in Power."

"Only the weak surrender," Gryphon said.

Something clutched at Emma's throat. The room softened and the edges of every object and every face blurred. The story on the table rose into the air and the voice and voices inside blended together to form a beautiful chorus, so beautiful, so achingly perfect and lovely Emma wondered if real angels were singing.

Joe made a face like he was frightened. Emma glanced away from him. The wooden walls seemed soft and amorphous; if she wanted to, Emma could push her hand right through. Nothing was real. Nothing mattered. Whatever was left of Eury Vatic's cryptic story willingly surrendered to the sublime chorus.

CHAPTER FORTY-FIVE

Gryphon jumped to his feet and stared hard at Emma, who fell.

Joe caught her before she smashed her head on the floor. "What the hell did you do to her?" he shouted.

"I helped her, you idiot," Gryphon snarled, sinking into Maude's arms.

Joe turned on Mr. Spencer. "What's going on?"

"I don't know," Mr. Spencer said.

The door opened, and Emma's parents came in. Mr. Mathews ran to Emma. "What happened?" he asked.

"I don't know," Mr. Spencer repeated. "Eury left a *glyf charasso*, a kind of engraving," he explained. "In the table. Something about a ruined home, a broken house, a severed girl. I don't understand what he was trying to say." He shuddered. "The kids saw him. His deterioration is almost complete. I don't know how much of his real self is left."

"What happened to Emma?" Mr. Mathews asked, glancing at his daughter in Joe's arms.

"She made a weird face and then..." Joe decided not to mention what Gryphon did. Maybe he was telling the truth about helping her. Maude obviously thought so. "She fainted."

Her mom took Emma out of Joe's arms. "We have to get out now," she said. "Will, take Maude back to—"

"No," Maude interrupted. "I'm staying with Gryphon."

The grateful expression in Gryphon's eyes made Joe happy he hadn't said anything. He really was Maude's Soulmate.

"We don't have time for this, Maude," Mrs. Mathews warned.

"I won't leave without him." Maude spoke softly, but Joe realized that Emma was right. Maude was as strong as her warrior mother.

Mrs. Mathews muttered something that sounded like a Sacerian curse. "Have it your way," she said through her teeth. "Will, go back and stay with Turner, Elizabeth, and Sandy." The science teacher nodded, and Mrs. Mathews placed protections over all of them, hesitating for a moment before shielding Gryphon. "These protections haven't been used since before the power shift twenty years ago," she said to Mr. Mathews and Mr. Spencer. "The Masevo won't check for them. We'll be able to move through the portal trees without detection. They don't last long, though. That's why they fell out of favor. We'll have to travel swiftly. Petros, carry Gryphon and help him through the portal tree."

"I can move by myself," Gryphon protested.

"Don't disobey me," Mrs. Mathews growled, and Gryphon backed down and let Emma's dad carry him.

Joe held Emma, and the seven of them left to return to the Commonworld.

* * *

When Emma woke, her mother was sitting at the edge of the bed, her hollow hair floating around her head as though she were under invisible water. For a second Emma didn't recognize her.

"Where are we?" Emma asked.

"We're in Sfodro's parents' house," Mom said.

"But the Ones in Power know it's here," Emma said, sitting up.

"I know," Mom agreed. "They've already checked it. But Daddy and I put deflective protections around the house before we brought you here. We're hiding in plain sight."

"Is everyone here?" Emma asked.

"Most everyone is here and everyone is okay," Mom said. "Mr. Spencer went back to the Otherworld to watch over Turner, Elizabeth, and Sandy."

"Did you know Mr. Spencer was a Commonworlder?" Emma asked.

"Yes," Mom said. "Daddy and I both knew. Now," she said, patting Emma's leg. "Get up and eat something."

"Why was I in bed?" Emma asked.

"You fainted," Mom said.

"When?" Emma asked.

"We'll talk about it after you eat," Mom said. "Come on."

* * *

Joe stood up when Emma came into the room.

"Hey," he said, taking her hand and squeezing it while her mom put food on a plate she'd created along with cooking utensils out of sticks and stones. It was amazing to watch. He smiled at Emma. "How are you?"

"Fine," Emma said, squeezing his hand back. "I guess. Where are Maude and Gryphon?"

"In the other room," Joe said. "Your dad is trying to help him."

"What about a doctor or a hospital?" Emma said.

"Your dad and Gryphon said the same thing," Joe explained. "That as soon as someone realized who he was they wouldn't treat him until he'd been turned in and interrogated. Even at a hospital. Everything is subordinate to what the Ones in Power want. Gryphon wouldn't have gotten special treatment."

Emma sat at the table and looked at the green mess her mom put in front of her. "What is that?" she asked.

"Wild greens and onion grass in a nut milk sauce," Mrs. Mathews said. "Joe helped me forage."

Joe smiled.

Emma took a bite. She made a face then swallowed. "I can't wait to eat real food again."

"You had some of Maude's milkshake and half of her grilled cheese this morning," Joe pointed out.

Emma stuck out her tongue at him then smiled, blushing. Joe felt undone and sat beside her. She pushed her leg near his, and he held her knee under the table. She laid her hand on top of his.

Mrs. Mathews sat across from them. She looked unreal, with her luminous skin and floating hair.

"Thanks for coming to get us," Joe said.

She leaned forward and gazed at him with flashing eyes. Joe had the distinct impression she was trying to read his thoughts.

"You could just ask me," he said.

Mrs. Mathews raised a silvery eyebrow. "I'm trying to gauge your readiness, not learn the secrets of your heart."

"I think they're probably connected," Joe said.

Emma moved her hand to his thigh. This was the only thing he was sure of, that Emma was a part of him and he was a part of her. Their connection seemed like the one true thing in a world where nothing was definite but change. Maybe that was the answer to Emma's question that had upset him so much. Maybe he just needed to physically connect with her. Like Gryphon had with Maude.

Mrs. Mathews sat up straighter. Her hair bounced in the air like strings on a bunch of helium balloons. "Your father is an Oloklira, a Whole Listener," she said to Joe.

"I know," he said. "Gryphon told me."

Mrs. Mathews paled to a translucent green. "Emma doesn't know what it is," she said. "And it's important that you both understand. What did Gryphon tell you?"

"That a Whole Listener hears and sees everything that's going on in both worlds as it's happening," Joe said. "That it's constant. And terrible."

Mrs. Mathews screwed up her face as if she couldn't stand the thought of Gryphon doing anything good. "That's right," she said. "Eventually it becomes overwhelming and the Whole Listener deteriorates, losing the sense of himself or herself inside that ocean of information. That's why your father has holes in his flesh. He is weakening and has less and less physical and mental capacity of his own. It is a kind of madness." She took a deep breath and said sympathetically, "Whole Listeners don't live much past thirty. The last one died in the terrible aftermath of the Fourth Revolution. They're born every two thousand years or so. It's an extremely uncommon power. More like a genetic fluke. No one knows why they exist at all. There have only been five."

"I don't care what my father is," Joe said, careful to keep the despair out of his voice. "Has he done something wrong? Why do the Ones in Power and the Resisters want to find him? Why was my sister murdered? Why didn't my dad ever come to find me?" The last question was out of Joe's mouth before he could stop it, but then he felt better, like after ripping off a Band-Aid or diving into a frigid pool.

"Your father hasn't done anything wrong," Mrs. Mathews said quietly.

"Then why would the Ones in Power do anything to find him?"

"A Whole Listener absorbs and acquires other powers," Mrs. Mathew's said. "He or she can be a Revealer, a Transformist, a Telekinetic, anything a Commonworlder can be. In theory every gemynd has the capacity to absorb other powers, but as far we know only your father has been able to do it. I think he's also absorbed the powers of a Lucent, an Elafra. That's why he can fold into the energy fabric like Odym Chadia. Odym Chadia was the Elafra who helped Emma after Fen Elos was killed."

"So they want him because he's more powerful than other Commonworlders?" Emma asked. "He seems more like a god than a person, even for a Commonworlder."

"Eury's not a god," Mrs. Mathews said. "He's a gemynd like all of us. But he feels and sees and knows everything that happens in his lifetime." She squeezed Joe's shoulder and something shielding washed through him like a drug. "It becomes an unbearable existence."

Joe walked to the jagged hole in the wall where a window used to block rain and let in light. He leaned into the cool air. It came in at his cuffs and through his collar, smelling of spring and the wet life at the core of everything. Emma stood beside him. She fixed her night-blue eyes on his. He held her gaze as if it were a blood-filled cord that kept them both alive.

"Do the Ones in Power want my father for his information?" Joe asked. "That's it, isn't it? They want to know everything about Commonworlders so they can control people more easily. Isohel was right. It's not a different world than ours at all."

"That is part of it, yes," Mrs. Mathews said.

"Well, what else is there?" Joe said, anguish clogging his throat. "They want to know everything. My father knows everything, what else is there? They have every other power in the Commonworld. They don't need him to learn how to fly, or move things, or read thoughts. They just need him to learn how to hear everything."

Joe staggered backward as the icy realization came to him. "That's it," he said quietly. "Isn't it? The Ones in Power and the Resisters want to learn *how* my father hears and sees everything. And each of them wants to be the sole possessor of that knowledge. Whoever learns first will be able to permanently connect to every living thing, to know every thought, every fear, every desire for all the time."

He looked at Emma's mom for validation. She nodded. He stepped away from the soothing cool of the window and continued, "Both sides believe that they alone know what's best for everyone, and that the power to know everything is too dangerous for anyone to possess but themselves. They both want to control and keep it. And both sides are willing to do anything to get it."

Mrs. Mathews walked over to Joe. He didn't want to see her sympathetic face. He didn't know her. He didn't want her to see him feeling like this. He felt like he couldn't breathe, and he folded his arms across his chest as Mrs. Mathews moved to speak.

"Your father is forty-two years old," she said. "His deterioration is almost complete. That's why he speaks in already-spoken or written or thought-of sentences. His voice is strangled by other voices. Both sides want to capture your father before he deteriorates completely." Mrs. Mathews stood up straighter, and her sympathetic expression vanished. She left him in the middle of the room, cleared away Emma's plate and rubbed it back into the stone from which it had been created. Joe felt that he would fall apart.

Emma walked past him and confronted her mother. "None of this is a secret, Mom," she said. "Gryphon knows all of this. He would have told Joe if Joe asked."

Joe glanced at her. Like his ability to fly, Emma's ability to read what other people thought had gotten stronger in the Commonworld. And, like him, she now had better control. She looked brave and strong, and inside this moment of chaos and fear, love swelled in his chest and he felt stronger. He smiled and felt Emma smile back in her heart, but her hard gaze was still fixed to her mother's wandering attention.

"What are you leaving out?" Emma asked. "What are you afraid to tell us?"

"The world is so *ugly*, Emma," her mom said, in the first vulnerable voice Joe had ever heard from her. "Both worlds. They always have been. The skin of civilization is as thin as rice paper. One tear at the surface and every aggressive, violent feature fights to get out, followed by desperation, sickness, humiliation, death, and despair. The dehumanization of every enemy and the reckless, ravenous consumption of every resource wreak havoc everywhere, all the time. Little things, big things. Loss of life after life after life."

"That isn't a secret either, Mom," Emma said, clearly annoyed. "Life can be bad. People can be brutal. What can be done? What aren't you saying? Stop trying to control an out-of-control situation!" she shouted when her mother turned away. "Stop trying to protect us. Tell us why neither the Ones in Power nor the Resisters should ever have access to Eury Vatic. It's not just about political control of some dangerous power. Control can always be wrested away, power and knowledge can be sold. What's the *real* reason? I know there's more going on!"

A wave of blue shock shivered over Mrs. Mathews's lighted skin.

"You can't hide everything from me," Emma said. "You're afraid. I can hear parts of what you're thinking."

Mrs. Mathews sat at the table, the light in her skin and hair faded to a dull grey, and Joe thought of Emma's dad's dull pallor when they first came to Emma's grandfather's house. "What did you hear right before Fen Elos died?" she asked Emma, who blushed with guilt.

"I heard a voice," Emma said. "Voices all together, like a chorus of whispers."

Mrs. Mathews didn't say anything.

"I heard them again after Mr. Spencer came to Slabsides," Emma added.

Her mother walked to the doorway and stared into the other room, which was empty of people and filled with spiderwebs. "Most Commonworlders—Dad included—wouldn't believe you if you told them what you heard," she said, "because Fen Elos turned those voices, the *Phylotelas*, the Singers of the Apocalypse, into a myth before they could inflict any damage in the Commonworld. He was less successful in the Otherworld. Humans are more susceptible to fantasy and magical thinking than gemynd are."

"I heard them, too," Joe said, to Mrs. Mathews's obvious horror. "The first time I saw my father. Emma and Gryphon broke the connection. What are they?"

"I can't believe you heard them too," Mrs. Mathews said, more to herself than anyone else.

"What are they?" Emma repeated.

"The first Singer of the Apocalypse came out of a failed agrarian utopia in the fifteenth century," her mother said. "One member of that community was an exceptionally beautiful Lucent who was the Soulmate of a Crossworlder."

"Is that someone who lives in both worlds?" Emma said.

"They often end up living in both worlds," Mrs. Mathews admitted. "*Pernatopa*, Crossworlders, age ten years for every three hundred. Will Spencer is a Pernatopa. So was Fen Elos." She sat down again.

Emma walked over to Joe and laced her fingers through his. He squeezed her hand, as always grateful to be connected with her.

"In order to reduce the pain of their separation when she eventually died, the Lucent gave her *Nevma*—her Spirit Sphere, what Maude gave to Gryphon and what Daddy gave to me—to her Crossworlder lover," Mrs. Mathews said. "A Crossworlder lives most of his or her very long life without a Soulmate. At the Lucent's untimely death, the Crossworlder tried to kill himself, but he couldn't because of the Spirit Sphere and his own powers of longevity, and instead he became part of the fabric of the life force, the energy that everything in every universe is a part of. The agrarian utopia fell apart for the reasons everything falls apart, and the

Crossworlder lover, wild with grief and cut off from life, turned his unbearable pain into fury at the irredeemable corruption of both worlds. He gave bits of himself, infused with the Lucent's powers of connection, to other similarly distraught Crossworlders…and they became the Phylotelas, the Singers of the Apocalypse."

"What? What does all this have to do with my father?" Joe asked.

"The Singers of the Apocalypse believe gemynd and humans are sick beyond repair and should be destroyed," Mrs. Mathews said. "They create an image of destruction so beautiful and perfect that people begin to long for and believe in the solution of death rather than the rightness of living."

"What does this have to do with my father?" Joe asked again. "He doesn't believe what they do, does he?"

"No," Mrs. Mathews said. "No, he doesn't. But they need him."

"Why?" Joe said.

"The Phylotelas can only connect with a few gemynd at a time," Mrs. Mathews replied. "Your father is simultaneously connected to everyone. Always." She took a deep breath. "The Phylotelas must believe that if he joins with them, his power will give them the power to instantaneously connect with everyone in both worlds. They could truly end human and gemynd life forever."

Joe looked at Emma to help him, and she asked, "Do you think Joe's dad really wants to join with them?"

"All Eury wants is to protect you, Sfodro," Mrs. Mathews said. She glanced at Emma. "And now that he knows Emma is your Soulmate, he believes the only way he can save you from the Ones in Power or the Resisters is to put a permanent identity shield on you, and to ask Emma's dad and me to put one on her. That's what that the glyf charasso, the engraved story, meant. That's what he was trying to tell you when he showed you the image in the water."

"How did you know about that?" Joe said. "And how do you know that's what he meant?"

"Are you going to put a permanent identity shield on me?" Emma said, her eyes aghast. "I won't know you anymore, or Dad or Maude or Sandy or anyone but Joe, right? And you won't know me?"

"But wait," Joe said. "What difference does any of it make if the Singers of the Apocalypse convince my dad to join them? How do we stop that from happening?"

"Your father won't give in to the Singers unless something happens to you," Mrs. Mathews said. "The Singers know that. I think that's why they've been targeting Emma. If they can get Emma to let go of her life, they believe you'll follow and your father will give in to despair. Gemynd don't have to do anything to commit suicide. We can simply let go of life and stop our own hearts from beating."

"Then put the permanent shield on me, Mom," Emma said, trying not to cry.

"The Singers of the Apocalypse are part of the life force," Mrs. Mathews said. "They can see through the shield."

"How long will the protections you put up hold?" Joe asked. Maybe his father would listen to him. Maybe he could stop Eury from joining the Singers of the Apocalypse. Then maybe no one else would get hurt.

"A few hours," Mrs. Mathews said.

"I've been here to this house before," Joe said. "The picture brought me here. And Gryphon took it and used it to find my father."

"What picture?" Mrs. Mathews asked, clearly stunned that she'd missed such a vital piece of information.

"The picture of my parents in a chunk of glass," Joe said. "Turner found it. It vibrated after the alarm went off when I was in the tower. Then it transported me here. I don't know where it took Gryphon."

"May I see it?" Mrs. Mathews asked.

"My father destroyed it."

Without saying anything, Mrs. Mathews left the room. Joe and Emma followed.

* * *

"What is it?" Dad asked, turning away from Gryphon.

Maude sat in a chair at Gryphon's feet. Emma couldn't look at her.

"Where did he get the blanket?" she whispered to Joe.

"Your mom made it from thistledown and milkweed," Joe said. "It was amazing. She made one for you too. Didn't you notice?"

"I guess not," Emma said. "Did I really faint?"

"Mr. Spencer was talking about my parents, and you started whispering to yourself," Joe said. "You looked wasted. Gryphon did something, and then you fainted and I caught you."

"I don't remember," Emma said. "I remember Mr. Spencer talking and I remember hearing the voices, but I don't remember anything else."

"How is he?" Mom asked, indicating Gryphon.

"I really don't know," Dad said. "His ribs are broken, and I think he has some internal bleeding, but I can't be sure."

"You were right," Mom said.

"About what?"

"About Eury and this house," Mom said. "He's been coming here since Edoro died and Joe disappeared. I don't know how he hid the traces but he's been coming here and using the house as a portal to the Otherworld."

"How do you know?"

"He brought Joe here," Mom said. "Using the konameta Sofia gave me just before she died. I brought it to my father's forest house. It must have escaped the filters somehow. Maybe Eury did something to it, or maybe it was because the house was off the grid. I don't know."

"What's a konameta?" Emma said.

"An image transport," Dad said. "It can transport the holder to the gemynd in the picture. Parents use it for kids whom they worry will stay out too late. Soulmates use it to see each other when they're forcibly separated. Claudeo has one of Isohel, that's how he was able to rescue us from the forest. An image transport isn't very powerful, though. It's an expensive toy."

"Once we find the portal," Mom said, "we'll be able to find Eury."

"I'm not going with you," Maude said. "I'm staying with Gryphon."

Mom's face froze.

"You can't change it, chi Gwynaias," Dad said. "Why do you persist in believing it's not true?"

"Maybe it isn't," Mom said. "Maybe he deceived her. He is a Teknasma. He fooled me. He fooled Emma. *He's Aythentia.*"

"Maude never would have been able to give him her Nevma if it wasn't true," Dad said. "It would have rejected him."

Mom closed her eyes. Her hair curled into itself like a burning leaf.

Maude laid her hand on Gryphon's thigh, and he made a sound of sad pleasure.

"She only just turned fifteen," Mom said.

"That's old enough," Dad remarked. "You know that."

"If you leave them here," Joe said, "they'll be vulnerable to the Ones in Power and the Resisters as soon as the protections wear off."

Gryphon squeezed Maude's hand. She leaned over and kissed him on the mouth. When she picked up her head, Emma saw Maude looked like she had that night in her room when the dress Gryphon gave her revealed her identity as a Soulskin.

"Chi Psalla," Mom said quietly, and Emma realized that when her parents saw Maude with her soul entirely revealed it was as if she were a newborn and they were seeing her for the first time.

"What about a restorative?" Joe said, breaking the silence in the room.

Mom looked at him.

"When Gryphon and I were hiding in the blue-haired guy's apartment, Gryphon drank a green liquid he called a restorative," Joe said. "What's in it? Maybe we could make it."

Maude stood up. Dad gazed at her and clearly knew what she was thinking.

"Come with me," he said. "The woods are full of medicinal plants. And Mom can make a restorative."

Maude left the room and Dad followed.

"You two stay here and watch Gryphon," Mom said. "I'm going to find that portal entrance. Eury had to have disguised it somehow." She went into the hall that led to a basement.

Gryphon lay quietly, half-asleep under the thistledown blanket. Emma took Joe's hand and together they sat at the table. Gryphon breathed more audibly, as if he was trying to concentrate his diminishing strength.

After a few minutes, he sucked in a huge mouthful of air and sat up. He stared hard at Emma. Joe protectively grabbed her hand. Gryphon smiled a little.

"I don't even need to read your thoughts, Joe," he said. "You're as predictable as spring. Where's Maude?"

"She's with my dad getting plants for medicine for you," Emma said.

Gryphon pressed the heels of his hands to his eyes for a second. He picked up the frothy white thistledown blanket. "Is your mother a Dimiorg?" he asked.

Emma nodded.

Gryphon frowned. "I should have known that. Why didn't I know that?"

"My parents have been hiding for a long time," Emma said. "They changed or deleted their records. And my mom is excellent at protecting secrets."

Gryphon smiled at her. "I think I would have liked you someday."

"What does that mean?" Emma asked.

Ignoring the question, Gryphon got out of bed, wincing and swaying for a moment as he stood.

"What are you doing?" Joe asked, running over to him.

"You make a fetching nurse, Joe," Gryphon said, "but I'm fine. Ask your mother to come here, Emma." He clenched his teeth and drew short breaths though his nose.

"She's looking for something," Emma said.

Gryphon smiled again. "I know. This won't take long."

Emma glanced at Joe. Gryphon must have determined that her mother was the leader of their small group, and he had connected to her thoughts with what remained of his energy. Unfortunately, Emma could not connect to Gryphon and learn what he planned to do.

"Ask her to come here," Gryphon repeated. "And then bring me a damp stick."

Emma frowned.

"Please," he said, and he flashed the face of young Morrissey.

Emma blushed and got her mother.

CHAPTER FORTY-SIX

"What the hell are you doing?" Joe asked.

"It's frustrating, I imagine," Gryphon said, holding the edge of the headboard. "Not being able to hear anyone's thoughts other than Emma's."

"Fuck you," Joe said.

"Thanks for helping me," Gryphon added, his voice sincere. "I wouldn't have helped you, and I can't admire your impulse or your sentiment, but I wouldn't have seen Maude again. So, thank you."

"You're welcome," Joe said warily. "But what are you doing?"

Mrs. Mathews came into the room with an irritated expression on her silvery face. Emma brought Gryphon the wet stick.

"Well?" Mrs. Mathews said.

Joe watched Gryphon struggle to decide whether or not to transform himself. He decided against it.

"Good choice," Mrs. Mathews said. "Now, what do you want?"

"I want you to make me a sheet of paper," he said, handing her the stick. "Several pages actually. And if you could you bind them prettily somehow..." He tore a strip of blue cloth from his shirt. "Maybe with this."

"Why?" Mrs. Mathews asked.

"For Maude."

Mrs. Mathews clenched her teeth and considered him, then sat down and silently pulled at the wet stick until six or seven sheets of textured paper the color of milky coffee were bound with a blue ribbon. She laid the little book on the table.

"Thank you," Gryphon said.

"You're welcome," Mrs. Mathews said, and she left the room.

Gryphon opened the book and eyed it lovingly, as if Maude herself gazed at him from the blank pages. Words appeared, filling each page until he closed it. "This is for your sister," he said, handing it to Emma. "Don't let anyone else have it."

"Okay," Emma said, slipping it carefully into her pocket.

"Tell her to write over the lines with real ink," he said. "The Masked words won't last forever."

"Why?" Emma asked.

"I can't impart words onto an object using thought alone like a Chronicler—an *Istografia*—can," Gryphon said, "but I can do something like it. I can leave a sticky resonance that has to be renewed, which is why Maude will have to write over the letters. It's not permanent but it's hard to detect." He smiled affectionately and almost mischievously at both of them. "If Eury wanted to hide something without anyone knowing, that might be the way he'd do it."

"Are you going somewhere?" Joe asked.

Gryphon smiled more broadly at him. "You're funnier than you seemed at first." He turned to Emma and said with a flourish, "A parting gift." Then he transformed into young Morrissey cocking his head adorably and singing the end of "This Charming Man." Swinging his gladiolas, Gryphon-as-Morrissey brushed the wilted flowers once across Emma's cheek, stared at a single spot on the wall and disappeared.

* * *

Mom ran in, but she was too late. "Where did he go?"

"Through that wall," Emma said, pointing.

Frantically Mom ran her hands over the rough wood. "I can't find any opening. What did he do? Did he do anything before he left?"

"He transformed into Morrissey singing 'This Charming Man,'" Emma said.

"What!" Mom said.

"I think he was trying to be funny," Joe suggested.

"Funny?" Mom said. "*Funny?* I asked you two to watch him. How could you let him get away?"

"It's disguised," Emma said, looking at the wall.

"I know it's disguised, Emma!" Mom snapped.

"Like a Mask," Emma said, realizing what Gryphon had meant when he'd said this was the way Eury might hide something. "Joe's father disguised the portal the same way a Mask disguises himself. You see but you don't realize it. You think you're seeing something else."

"That's absurd," Mom said. "Someone would have discovered it."

"Why?" Emma asked. "Why would you discover something you didn't know you were looking for? The portal was disguised to look like a tiny spot on the wall. Who would look for a tiny spot on the wall?"

"Gryphon said something about a clarifier when we were in the city," Joe remarked. "He said if the Masevo shined it on him they would be able to see him through his power."

"I don't have an *exetafi*—a clarifier," Mom said. "And I can't make one."

"Does Mr. Spencer have one?" Joe asked.

"No," Mom said. "Only the Ones in Power have them. The Resisters might have a few but they wouldn't give them up." She sat at the table and cursed in Sacerian. "Eury must be hiding on the other side of the portal. It could lead anywhere in Saceres or the Otherworld. And, Gryphon doesn't have to turn Eury in himself," she added in frustration and despair. "He doesn't have to fight him. He just has to call the Ones in Power to him before Eury realizes it."

"But if my father sees everything," Joe said. "He'll see Gryphon coming."

"Your father sees everything," Mom agreed, "but it takes enormous strength of mind to filter that. It's like taking single grains of salt from the ocean. All Gryphon has to do is lightly mask his approach."

"Why didn't he do that the first time?" Joe asked.

"He wasn't prepared. Now he is." She glanced up from the table and swore loudly again, then glanced at the visibly unchanged walls. "And now the protections are disintegrating. Wait here. I have to get Dad and Maude."

Mom ran through the door, and Emma looked at the wall. A mouth, open and murmuring, blossomed in the center. Red and silver light dripped onto the floor and sizzled into colored vapor. Something was drawing their attention there. On purpose.

Emma turned to Joe. He didn't see the light, but he saw the mouth and heard what it was whispering. The voice, soft and musical, opened its beautiful song in Emma's head. She felt better than she had when Joe kissed her, better than flying, better than knowing he loved her. That last thought tore insistently at the core of her heart but she ignored it.

"Let's go," she said, hearing her own voice seconds after it came out of her mouth. "Let's follow it."

Joe didn't notice her. He was already walking toward the whispering mouth.

They practically fell into the portal. Emma couldn't see anything but soft light. It was like breathing underwater. She felt weightless and formless. The voices whispered sweetly. The urge to let go nearly overwhelmed her. Eury Vatic's rasping tenor mixed rapturously with those other voices, sometimes Maude's voice reciting in the woods, sometimes Dad's reading to her at night when she was little, and sometimes a voice she couldn't identify but knew all the same:

I have been half in love with easeful Death,

Nothing mattered, Emma thought.

Call'd him soft names in many a mused rhyme,

This life was over.

To take into the air my quiet breath;

It was never real to begin with.

Now more than ever seems it rich to die,

It was wasted.

To cease upon the midnight with no pain,

And pointless.

While thou art pouring forth thy soul abroad/In such an ecstasy!

And over.

Then they landed. Well, she landed. Joe didn't matter. Did he? Was he ever really there? Had she been asleep for her whole life, as Sandy feared when he was really little, and she would only wake up at this, the easeful moment of her death?

She landed—*they* landed—near the tree where Gryphon had lain at Eury Vatic's feet that morning. Gryphon was floating, cradled in the air by invisible hands as a paralyzed insect numbed by compassionate venom sleeps in the thinnest of spiderwebs, a blissful expression of release on his face.

Emma heard Joe's voice. It sounded dirty and profane. He stood before his father, light pouring from that pierced and towering figure. What was Joe thinking? He was going to ruin things for everyone. Emma ran to stop him, but like running in water or a dream, she couldn't move fast enough.

* * *

Joe knelt on the ground, sweat pouring down his neck and chest. He'd managed to separate himself from the Singers when he landed—for that's what they were, he assured himself—but he could still hear their voices. The compulsion to give in, to let go, was so strong that the muscles in his arms and legs shook.

His father towered over him. Joe picked up a rock and dug a hole in the soft spring ground. He wanted to sense something real. He took a handful of dirt and breathed in the scent. His heart pounded in his throat and he felt dizzy.

"What are you doing?" Emma's voice tumbled slurred and ecstatic out of her mouth. She didn't move.

Joe shut his eyes. The cool, loose soil in his hands breathed with throbbing life and necessary decay. Joe stood up and faced his father.

"'I can't go on, I'll go on,'" Joe said, quoting Samuel Beckett. "'I can't go on. I'll go on. I can't go on. I'll go on.'"

His father's image breathed and diminished.

"'I can't go on,'" Joe repeated. "'I'll go on.'" He went to Gryphon, took Gryphon's face in his hands and turned it to face him.

"'This is no dream,'" Eury Vatic crooned in the singsong voice of a long-dead poet.

"'No dream,'" Gryphon answered back in recitation, his voice stripped of strength. "'Alas! Alas! And woe is mine! Porphyro will leave me here to fade and pine. Cruel! What traitor could thee hither bring?' *Help* me," he begged Joe.

Joe reached for Gryphon, but he was pushed back to Emma by the gentlest, most irresistible force. Was his dad trying to prevent him from helping Gryphon, or trying to help him free Emma from the Singers? He kissed her, thinking to break her away, but the connection didn't break. It was like kissing a toy, or a dead girl; Emma stayed passive in his arms.

Joe kissed her harder. She shifted slightly, her feet fixed to the ground, her torso swaying. No other effect could be seen.

Before Joe, still caught in his dream, Gryphon closed his eyes tightly and suddenly Maude's black hair draped from his head. Gryphon held it in his hands and laid his bruised cheek against it. For Gryphon the hair was a memory, a comfort, some last tie to Maude, and Joe almost wept at what was happening. He didn't want to think about what was happening.

No. He had to save Emma. The Voices' song of annihilation swirled with frantic seduction through his dizzy head, and his heart thundered in his chest at the effort of resisting. Concentrating on an image of Maude and what she'd once done, Joe unbuttoned Emma's shirt. Her head lolled aimlessly on her neck and her eyes were glazed with the empty expression of deep intoxication. Joe touched his own chest and pulled out a soft, balloon-like thing filled with fire and voices and books.

Eury Vatic cried out, and the voices stopped. Gryphon fell from the air and landed on the ground.

Joe didn't stop. He rubbed his Spirit Sphere into Emma's chest. It sank in like water down a drain. He felt weak, but not as weak as Maude had looked. He must have done it right.

"Joe," Emma gasped, sucking at the air. "Joe." Her chest rose and fell in an unsteady rhythm. She turned to Eury Vatic. "Don't give in," she said to him. "Don't let go."

Gryphon lay on the ground, breathing softly. He wasn't moaning or panting any longer.

CHAPTER FORTY-SEVEN

Emma knelt on the ground next to Gryphon. "There's nothing to be done," she said.

It wasn't pretty or romantic. He said nothing poignant or memorable. No music swelled. Nothing was revealed to make his death mean something, worth something. Sixteen-year-old Gryphon Venti just stopped breathing, and that was it. Emma touched his chest. He was empty. At the same time, a naming of losses, of life after life after life from every time and every culture and every religion, poured out of Eury Vatic's gaping, roaring mouth.

"Your father didn't kill Gryphon," Emma cried, realizing the truth. "He was trying to help him."

"It doesn't matter what killed him," Joe said. "We have to get out of here. If Gryphon contacted the Masevo they'll be here soon. My father will follow us." He picked up Gryphon's body and rose into the air. He beckoned to Emma. "Come on."

Emma couldn't move. Her feet stuck to the ground as if she wore the crust of the world for shoes.

Eury Vatic waved his hand, and the face of every name he spoke flashed into existence until the woven air was filled with a tapestry of faces. And in the center, ringed by images of children slaughtered by commission and omission, Edoro Vatic was torn in half again and again. Emma did not close her eyes.

"'And still she slept'," Eury Vatic hissed in furious accusation, the voices of grieving mothers and fathers twined inexorably around his own.

The cold of the earth seeped into Emma's sock-clad foot. She did not close her eyes.

With his mouth wide as the sky, Eury Vatic blew out his voice like the sacrificial winds:

> *Methinks I am a prophet new inspired,*
> *And thus expiring do foretell of him:*
> *His rash fierce blaze of riot cannot last,*
> *For violent fires soon burn out themselves;*
> *Small showers last long, but sudden storms are short;*
> *He tires betimes that spurs too fast betimes;*
> *With eager feeding food doth choke the feeder;*
> *Light vanity, insatiate cormorant,*
> *Consuming means, soon preys upon itself.*

Emma stood not moving. Eury Vatic's great, hard breath spread across her face. She felt the Voices waiting but they did not speak. And still she did not close her eyes.

Eury continued in a voice like consuming fire:

> *This royal throne of kings, this sceptered isle,*
> *This earth of majesty, this seat of Mars,*
> *This other Eden, demi-paradise,*
> *This fortress built by Nature for herself*
> *Against infection and the hand of war,*
> *This happy breed of men, this little world,*
> *This precious stone set in the silver sea,*
> *Which serves it in the office of a wall*
> *Or as a moat defensive to an house,*
> *Against the envy of less happier lands,*
> *This land of such dear souls, this dear dear land,*
> *Dear for her reputation through the world,*
> *Is now leased out...*

"'I can't go on,'" Emma said, her voice breaking. "'I'll go on.'"

The ground released her feet, and she ran after Joe.

* * *

As gently as he could, Joe laid Gryphon on the ground at the edge of the forest near the road. He had never seen a dead person before, and he was embarrassed how scared and heartbroken he felt. He leaned against a tree on the ground next to Gryphon and occasionally touched his hand, which grew colder and stiffer the longer Joe waited for Emma.

After what felt like an eternal instant, Emma ran up, out of breath. The echo of Joe's father's voice trailed like a kite behind her. Emma saw Gryphon, knelt beside him, and wept.

Joe dug his fingernails into his palms until he felt the rough skin split. He didn't want to cry in front of anyone, not even Emma. She leaned back on her heels and looked at him.

"He thought that if he brought your father to the Ones in Power, they wouldn't punish Maude or the rest of us," Emma said. "The power of Soulmates is honored, and I think he was right. I think we wouldn't have been punished if he had been the one to bring your father to them." She put her face in her hands and Joe sat next to her. "He thought he might die—that's why he made the book for Maude—but more than anything he wanted to save her."

Joe put his arms around Emma and buried his face in her hair.

After a few minutes he stood up. "I'm going to go to the diner and call Mr. Spencer," he said. Joe knew he'd have to stop the Singers by himself, and only Mr. Spencer could protect Emma now. "Do you remember the number?"

"No," Emma said, stroking Gryphon's hand. "He called me. Remember?"

"Well, can you contact him and tell him to meet us here?" Joe asked, fear and impatience bleeding into his voice.

Emma stared at Gryphon's face. Joe knew she couldn't believe he was actually dead.

"What are you going to do?" she asked Joe after a while.

"I'm going make sure my father doesn't join the Singers," Joe said. There was no point lying to her.

"I'm coming with you," Emma said, turning to look at him.

"No, you're not," Joe said.

"Yes," Emma said. "I am."

"Contact Mr. Spencer," Joe said.

Emma closed her eyes and nodded. *Listen,* she thought to Joe.

* * *

Apparently Mom and Dad had dropped Maude off at Mr. Spencer's house and then returned to the Commonworld to find Eury Vatic before the Ones in Power or the Resisters did. Emma told Mr. Spencer what had happened, and that Eury Vatic was in the Otherworld, and that she and Joe were here, too.

Get out now, Mr. Spencer thought. *Leave Gryphon and get out.*

No! Maude's anguished voice pierced Emma's heart like a hot scissors. Her sister already knew what had happened. She'd felt it.

Leave him, Mr. Spencer repeated. *I'll come get him as soon as it's safe.*

Please, Maude thought. *Please, Emma. Don't leave him.*

Do it, Mr. Spencer said.

Emma shut her eyes and envisioned Maude as completely as she could. She opened her eyes and looked at Gryphon's face.

Can you see him? she thought to Maude.

Yes, her sister said, that soft voice crushed into pieces.

Emma kissed Gryphon's icy forehead. She kept her eyes open.

Don't look away yet, Maude begged, her heart breaking inside Emma's chest.

I won't, Emma said.

Please, Mr. Spencer insisted. *Please leave.*

Emma took in all of Gryphon, his bruised and bloody face, his matted brown hair, his soft mouth, his closed eyes, his bruised chest, his pale hands.

Okay, Emma said to Maude, brushing her fingertips against Gryphon's cheek. *I'm going.*

She severed the connection with Maude and Mr. Spencer and then stood up, her own heart broken for Maude and for Gryphon.

"I'm not taking you with me," Joe said, following Emma as she walked away.

"I don't believe you can convince your father by yourself," she responded. "I think it will have to be two people, together, who stop him."

"No," Joe said. "I don't want anything to happen to you."

"Something already has happened to me."

A circle of winged Masevo dropped out of the sky and surrounded Joe and Emma. They both ran to Gryphon's body and stood to guard it.

"Get away from him," demanded a woman whose voice Emma recognized. "There is no need to protect him, we're not animals. He'll be brought home and memorialized."

"No," Emma said.

The woman locked her eyes on Emma's, and Emma muddied her thoughts with car commercials, ugly dogs, and awesome shoes.

"He was my friend," Joe began.

"He was not your friend," the woman interrupted. "He was my friend. And he would want to be memorialized in his own world, not here." She turned away from Joe. "Take Gryphon home," she said to a tall, black-haired Gatherer.

The man pushed Emma and Joe aside, picked Gryphon up, and flew away.

"I can't help you find my father," Joe said defiantly.

"Of course you can't," the woman responded. "We never thought you could. It is he who will come to you."

"No, he won't," Emma said.

The woman gazed again at her. "Your parents have been apprehended and processed. You won't be able to communicate with them anymore. Consider the welfare of your brothers and sisters."

She's lying, Emma thought desperately to Joe.

"I'm not lying," the woman said. "I have no reason to lie to you. Your brothers and sisters are at home. Take her to her mother's house," she said to another man.

During the borderless instant between the word *home* and the woman's command, Emma froze the muscles of her stomach and kept her thoughts on the underside of her consciousness. This woman thought that Turner, Elizabeth, and Sandy were at home. They didn't know about Mr. Spencer. He must have done something to disguise the house.

"You cannot escape, Erama," the woman said.

"Where is my cousin?" Emma asked.

"If you mean Isohel Arismapsi," the woman said, "she's recovering at home. You won't be able to see her. Her father has blocked you and anyone in your family from coming near her. With our permission and help."

"Isohel is Eleytheria," Emma said. "She'll never agree to cooperate with you."

"She already has," the woman said. "Take her," she repeated to the man.

Emma realized who the woman was. *Let's get out of here*, she thought to Joe.

CHAPTER FORTY-EIGHT

Joe grabbed Emma's waist. They shot into the air, pursued by the winged Masevo.

"That woman," Emma said quickly. "Her name is Selini Quaero. She's the Gatherer who killed your sister."

Joe dropped a little. The Masevo narrowed the distance.

Eury Vatic's devastated face, surrounded by repeating images of the death of his little girl rose in Emma's head. "I'm going to completely connect with everything inside your father's head," she said.

"No!" Joe cried. The muscles in his chest and legs contracted as he increased his speed. Emma leaned harder into him. Whoever was leading the Masevo shouted something. Joe tensed and flew faster.

"Your father wants me to," Emma said. "He wants me to listen inside his head. He's weakening. He doesn't want to give in to the Singers of the Apocalypse, but he can't resist them much longer."

"How do you know that?" Joe said. "You can't possibly know that." His hold on Emma slipped. She fell.

"Shit!" He grabbed her before she dropped to the ground. "Are you all right?"

"Your father held me back when you left with Gryphon," Emma said, ignoring Joe's question. "He is drowning and he can't hold on much longer. He wants me to connect with him so I'll understand how to help him."

"He can just tell you what he wants," Joe said, his voice desperate. "You can't connect with him, Emma. Even if you're right and he wants you to, you can't. You don't know what will happen.

Fuck, Emma, my dad has the noise of the fucking world in his head!"

"You heard him," she said. "He can't speak with his own words anymore. I think one of the Phylotelas is the only gemynd he's been able to communicate with in years. He doesn't have anyone else. I'm the only one."

"No," Joe said. "It's suicide. You can't. I won't let you."

"You can't stop me," she said. "And I have to. There is no one else. And even if there was, there's no time to figure out who that person would be!"

"What if you can't disconnect?" Joe said. "What if the Singers get to you and I can't stop them? Is that what happened to Gryphon?"

Emma shook her head. "Gryphon died because of his injuries. He wouldn't have given in to the Singers without a fight, and they didn't need him. But the struggle killed him anyway."

Joe wrapped his arm tightly around Emma's waist. "Please," he said. "Please. For me. Don't do this. Don't."

He held the back of her head and tilted her face so he could gaze directly into her eyes. He didn't look away. It felt as if he melted into her and then pulled himself out again, like they were part of the same thing, the same single thing.

"I love you," he said. "Please don't do this."

Maude's voice sang in Emma's head. *I've known him my whole life. I knew him before I was born. And I'll know him after I die. Whatever I'm made of, he's made of.*

"I love you, Emma," Joe repeated. "You're brave and beautiful and amazing, but this is stupid. It's dangerous, and you don't know what will happen."

He kissed her, and Emma's determination wavered. Maude loved Gryphon, and she would never see him again, never get married, never have a baby, never love anyone again. Now she might be doing the same thing to Joe.

"We'll think of something else," Joe whispered into her hair. "I promise. Just don't leave me."

An icy realization slowed Emma's heart. "There isn't anything else," she said, knowing it was true. "Your father is ready to surrender. He's depending on me to figure out how to save him. I have to connect with him. Let me go."

"No!" Joe said, falling slightly then shooting up again. Emma felt like she was on a broken amusement park ride, and she wrapped her arms tighter around Joe's strong body. How could she leave him, knowing something bad could happen to her? How could she let him go? Yet how the hell could she stay, knowing the possible consequences?

Emma pressed her head against his chest and clarified her thoughts. "Your father won't let the Masevo or the Singers get to you," she said. "But he's not strong enough to keep them away from me at the same time. Stay with him. I have to get away from the Singers and connect with your father without them knowing. The Masevo will go back to get your father. They won't notice or care right now that I've left, and he'll be able to hold them off for a while. You have to let me go."

Joe flew faster, and the wind burned Emma's eyes. "NO!" he shouted. "I'm stronger than you. And I won't let you go. I won't let you kill yourself."

Maybe that would happen. Maybe she would die. Whole Listening was Eury Vatic's power and it was killing him. Would she be able to stand it—knowing everything, hearing everything, even for a little while? Emma picked up her head, her throat thick, terrified about what might happen.

"Keep your head down," Joe barked. "I can fly faster when your head is against my chest."

She looked at him: his ridiculously long eyelashes, his soft mouth, his half-blue, half-brown hair, his dark skin, his long throat, his beautiful, beautiful, beautiful face filled with terror and fury. She loved him. Now and forever. *I'm sorry,* she thought. How could one choose oneself when so much else was at stake? *I'm sorry.*

"What are you thinking?" Joe screamed.

Emma crushed the lump in her throat and decided. She glanced behind Joe at the swiftly pursuing Masevo and said, "I'm going to give you the image of your sister Edoro's death. It's always at the center of your father's thoughts. Use Selini's presence as a way to begin to convince your father to separate from the Singers, because death, no matter what caused it, looks the same—*is* the same—for everyone. Every life is sacred," she added. "That's what Saceres means."

"Why are you telling me this?" Joe said, his voice shaking.

Emma didn't have time argue or explain. She was the only one who could connect to Eury Vatic. She knew that now. And she needed to be in the Commonworld, away from the Masevo, away from Joe and from the Singers of the Apocalypse to do it.

Maude's understanding of the distinct pattern on the bark of a portal tree flew into Emma's head as a broad-branched red maple appeared a little ahead of them. Emma closed her hands around Joe's head for an instant then thrust herself out of his arms—and into the portal tree below.

* * *

She'd left him.

The circle of Masevo closed around Joe and pulled him to the ground.

She'd left him. After he'd begged her to stay.

The Masevo stood in a tight circle around him.

Emma had left him to save his father. A man he never knew, who never came to find him or to check on him. A man who didn't care about Joe at all. He'd given Emma part of his life force, his Nevma, his Spirit Sphere, and she'd fucking *left him*. How could he stay with her now, Soulmate connection or not, when he'd begged her to stay and she left him? He couldn't ever trust Emma again.

Joe fell to his knees as his head slowly filled with repeating images of his sister's horrifying death.

"If your father hadn't broken his promise to turn himself over after your mother's death, nothing would have happened to the little girl," the woman named Selini said with calm conviction. "Her death was a regrettable accident brought on by your father's betrayal of his word."

Joe vomited violently on the ground. He supported his weight on his hands and tried to catch his breath.

Let go, a sweet voice whispered. *Let go.*

Of course, Joe thought, and the contracting steel in his stomach relaxed. Of course. He breathed slowly, letting the bliss of sleep and dreams come to him. He was tired. So tired. What was the use of fighting for anything? Everything sucked. And when it didn't suck, it disappeared. Look at Maude. Gryphon had loved her, really loved her, and she had loved him. And for what? He died at six-*fucking*-teen. And Maude lost her Soulmate.

Joe glanced up. The faces of all the Masevo, including Selini, the woman who had caused Edoro's death, had slackened into a blissful release. One by one they let go of their holds on life—a dirty, filthy, unholy thing—and fell to the unforgiving ground. Beautiful, soothing promises of eternal bliss swam in Joe's own head, and through his body, but the faces on the ground looked like Gryphon's had at the end. Empty, devoid of anything. Joe sucked at the soft air permeated with the tang of vomit.

"There is nothing else," he said, rising to his feet. Life, whatever it was, was all there was.

Joe felt his father swirl around him, listening for something. Joe wished he knew what his father needed. He said, "My mother wanted to save you."

The soothing, musical voices came closer, brushing Joe's cheek like a kiss of peach skin, soft as velvet but leaving behind threadlike needles stinging in his flesh.

"My mother thought she could save you," Joe continued to his father. "She loved you."

"'But here there is no light,'" his father's voice and the other voices uttered, "'Save what from heaven is with the breezes blown through verdurous glooms and winding mossy ways.'"

Emma's wild eyes shone for an instant in Eury Vatic's ragged face—and then Joe's father disappeared.

CHAPTER FORTY-NINE

The portal tree in the Commonworld was in a little yard attached to something like a church or a monastery. The general alarm still sounded, a throbbing pain inside the skin of the city. Revealer images hung everywhere. Doleful tributes to Gryphon and elaborate paeans to his sacrifice for the Ones in Power were interrupted by belligerent visual blasts from Eleytheria Revealers. These images told of the martyrdom of Fen Elos and were followed by grainy flashes of Mom and Dad's terrified faces as they were interrogated by the Ones in Power.

Emma froze. A thought blossomed in her head, a message implanted while back at the cabin, and she trembled at the sound of her mother's disembodied voice. *"Nothing is more important than preventing Eury Vatic from joining the Singers of the Apocalypse. If Daddy and I are captured or in trouble—and we are if you're hearing this—don't try to help us. Stop the Phylotelas. Stop the Singers of the Apocalypse. Help Dad and me later. I have faith in you, chi Erama. I always have. Daddy and I love you very much. Tell Maude I'm sorry, sorry about not trusting her, and so deeply sorry about Gryphon. Go. Now. Stop the Singers. I love you forever, my quiet, snow-haired little daughter."*

Please let my mom and dad be okay, she thought, then held her breath and glanced up at the building before her.

There were no windows on the first floor, but in the huge panes on the second Emma saw gemynd smiling and scurrying about, their faces calm and bright, seemingly untouched by everything outside. Emma searched for a door. Maybe this was some sort of embassy or sanctuary. Maybe she could connect Eury Vatic from inside. Maybe the Ones in Power couldn't find her here.

The exterior walls of the ground floor were of polished blue stone. There was no door. Not even to the well-kept garden. There was a pretty little wooden shed filled with oiled tools and shiny watering cans, but no trap door or secret tunnel. Emma walked around the building again, running her hand against the skin of the stone, hoping to feel some variation that would indicate a lock or opening mechanism.

Her palm itched. She touched the wall with her fingertip to see if something scratched it.

"I shouldn't be here." The familiar voice was soft.

"Isohel!" Emma said, turning around. "Oh my God, are you okay? I'm so sorry about what happened. Does your dad know you're here?"

"I left a *dydima*, a replica, of myself in my bed," Isohel said, almost too quietly for Emma to hear. "But it was so exhausting to make. I never did it before. I didn't think it would be so hard."

"Are you sure you're okay?" Emma said. "You sound weird."

"Maybe I took too much of myself to make the dydima," Isohel suggested. "I don't feel strong enough to keep standing. Still," she said, a little fire returning to her voice, "I had to get out. My dad tries to keep Revealer images from me but I have a secret place in the house where I can see them and he won't know. I made it when he wouldn't tell me anything about my mom."

"What are you doing here?" Emma asked.

"Looking for you," Isohel said.

"How did you know I was here?"

Isohel grinned and held up her hand. The scar was black and hollow, carved open and sewn shut again. Emma grimaced.

"It did hurt," Isohel said, glancing curiously at the serrated black stripe dividing her palm in half. "More than I thought it would. But I made this connector very carefully so my dad couldn't destroy it if he discovered it." She grinned. "The Ones in Power underestimated me."

Emma smiled back. "Where are we? What is this building?

Isohel glanced up. "Oh. The *Anagrafo*, the Record Keepers, live here. They never leave."

"What are Anagrafo?" Emma asked.

"They filter and categorize information as useful or useless," Isohel said. "Not like the Ones in Power. They don't want to use it to hurt anybody. They keep notes on all history, kind of like medieval monks in your world. They are born emotionally disconnected, except for a vague happiness that makes it possible to do their job. If a baby is born an Anagrafo, the parents can keep it until it's around two or three and then it comes here."

"How do you get in?" Emma asked.

"There's a place on the footpath that acts as a portal, but it can only transport Anagrafo," Isohel said. "Some parents try to fight it, but the kids come here anyway. They don't connect to any gemynd other than their Soulmates, who are also Anagrafo. Except for that, they only connect to information."

"Why is there a portal tree in the garden?" Emma asked.

Isohel's eyes widened. "I didn't know there was one," she said. "There isn't supposed to be."

"It's how I got here," Emma said. "It's connected to the Otherworld."

"Eury Vatic," Isohel guessed. "He must have Masked it."

"Do you know what he is?" Emma said.

"Of course I do," Isohel said. "Everyone knows. Eury Vatic is an Oloklira, a Whole Listener. He can connect with every living thing all the time."

"He can't just do it," Emma said. "He can't *not* do it. He hears every word and every thought, and sees every vision all the time. He can't stop it."

"I know," Isohel said. "It's sad. Eventually he'll deteriorate. They all do. Wait, did you see him?"

"Joe and Maude and I saw him," Emma said. "And Gryphon, too. And he is deteriorating."

"Why doesn't he just give himself to the Eleytheria before it's too late?" Isohel asked angrily. "If he has the way of listening, someone else will too someday, or someone will figure out how to create it. Why not just give it to the side that best understands how to help everyone? Isn't that better than letting the Aythentia get it? They'll only use it to hurt gemynd who don't do what they want or think what they think."

"The Eleytheria aren't any better," Emma said. "You just believe what they believe, so whatever they do is okay. It's always the ends justifying the means, no matter what side anyone is on."

Isohel slapped Emma's face. "Fen Elos died to save you."

"And Gryphon died to save Maude," Emma said, suddenly furious. "Every person, every *gemynd*, no matter what system of government they support, is willing to die for someone or something. And everyone is capable of good and bad."

"Profound," Isohel sneered. "It's dangerously naïve to think there is no difference between the two ways of thinking. Some systems and ideas are better than others."

"I'm not saying everything is equal," Emma snapped.

"Yes, you are," Isohel said. "You said everyone is the same."

"No, I didn't," Emma corrected. "I said everyone is capable of good and wicked acts. No one is immune from either."

"But one set of ideas is better," Isohel said. "You have to know that."

"Do you know what the Singers of the Apocalypse are?" Emma asked.

"The Phylotelas are a myth," Isohel said. "Only Otherworlders and desperate Commonworlders believe in the Singers of the Apocalypse."

"They're not a myth, and they want Eury Vatic to join with them," Emma said. "They want to use his way of listening to help them bring about the end of everything, or at least of human and gemynd life."

Isohel stepped back. "That's not true."

"Yes, it is," Emma said. "The Singers of the Apocalypse believe humans and gemynd are corrupt beyond redemption and should be destroyed. The easiest way to do that—besides convincing people and gemynd that everyone who isn't like them is evil and should be killed—is to seduce them into believing that this life is too hard and that there's something better and beautiful awaiting them as soon as they let go."

"That's not true," Isohel repeated.

"I've heard them," Emma said. "And you can't imagine how good it feels to listen. Like nothing you've ever felt in your life or ever expect to feel. Like the best food, or drug. Or the most perfect kiss. It is the best I've ever felt, perfect peace and happiness."

Isohel's eyes were wide but her mouth was tight and furious.

"Except it's not real," Emma said. "There's nothing on the other side but emptiness. It's a trick. A beautiful, seductive trick."

The Anagrafo in the rooms above their heads darted in and out of view like fireflies.

"It can't be true," Isohel said.

"It is," Emma warned. "So it doesn't matter whether the Ones in Power or the Resisters get to Eury Vatic first. What's the point of being able to hear every thought if there's no one to speak and no one to hear?"

Isohel stared up at the darkening sky.

"What made you think the portal tree was here because of Eury Vatic?" Emma asked. But she couldn't connect with him here. Isohel would try to turn him over to the Resisters. Her cousin still looked like she'd been the one slapped in the face.

"Because of the Anagrafo," Isohel said. "I thought he'd want to connect with them so he'd know more about history, and not just the last forty-two years and the present moment. I thought he'd want to know and understand history so he could help other gemynd learn from it and not keep making the same mistakes."

"The Singers of the Apocalypse don't want to learn from history," Emma said, trying to think of a way to get clear from Isohel so she could connect with Eury Vatic. "They want to erase it."

The leaves and branches shook once, as if someone important had come into the garden and everything had better stand straight. Pinpricks of light glittered like raindrops from crevices in the bark.

Isohel—and everything around her—began to disappear, or maybe Emma's ability to see the world in front of her was disappearing. The buildings, the footpath, and the grey sky behind Isohel's vanishing form disintegrated slowly, as if someone stood behind a tapestry of the world and pulled it apart thread by thread. The ground fell away and Emma felt her body dissolve like salt in water. Isohel called out a warning to run but Emma was already made of more emptiness than substance.

A thunder of voices hit Emma's ear like a thousand hammers, countless, incoherent threads of sound. She tried to move but was sucked further in as blindingly fast images exploded in front of her. She pressed her hands to her to eyes. When she opened them again, all was quiet. She was in the woods at the top of a hill, surrounded by huge, jutting grey stones spotted with drops of lichen like a spat-out green milkshake. Then the woods and the quiet disappeared and the light and sound came back, frantic and relentless.

Briefly, in flashes almost too quick to register, Emma saw the woods and listened to the quiet before the chaos of sound and images returned. She couldn't see her feet or her own body. Light poured out in stomachfuls beneath her.

Eury Vatic had taken her into himself. She couldn't close her eyes against the images or her ears against the noise. When the brief moments of peace came, Emma clung to them like a drowning girl.

CHAPTER FIFTY

One by one the dead Masevo disappeared. Someone in the Commonworld must have realized what had happened and was taking them home. Joe turned to his father, terrified that the Ones in Power would find him next, then secretly hoping that something would happen and this would all be over. A wave of self-loathing instantly followed. He had to be stronger. He couldn't give up.

For an instant Joe saw his biological mother's face replace his father's. She was smiling and saying something he didn't understand. Her hair was long and black and her eyes were dark and pretty. She smiled at him. Then his father turned away and spread wide until he was indistinguishable from the air around him. He was going to connect with Emma. Joe knew this as surely as if his father had told him, and maybe Eury had, in a way.

Two Masevo remained crumpled on the ground: Selini, the woman who had killed his sister, and a bald man with clear red skin. Joe ran toward the portal tree Emma had dropped into and transported himself back to the Commonworld.

"Isohel," he said, as he climbed down from the tree. "Are you all right?"

"I'm fine," Emma's cousin said, staring in front of her with a strange look on her face.

Joe didn't see Emma at first. She was almost invisible, standing a few feet from Isohel, shrouded in the shadow of the building. Emma stood—hung actually, although her feet were on the ground. Her eyes and her mouth were open and she was breathing.

"Emma," Joe said, grabbing her shoulders and shaking her. "What happened to her?" he asked Isohel when Emma didn't respond.

"I saw your father," Isohel said, staring at Emma and past her.

"Did my father do something to Emma?" Joe asked. "Is he here?"

"He came out of the portal tree and looked at her," Isohel said. "He didn't look anything like I thought he would."

"What did he do to Emma?" Joe asked slowly.

"He just looked at her," Isohel said. "My friend Tyrian would say, 'He fixed his gaze on her.' Emma opened her mouth like she wanted to tell me something, then she sort of froze. Disappeared into herself, actually, like she melted away inside her own body."

"Where is my father now?" Joe asked, hardly able to keep from shouting.

"He vanished," Isohel said.

A new city alarm shrieked, obliterating the under-throb that had hummed in fierce irritation all day. Isohel snapped out of her reverie.

"Shit," she said, listening for a second. "We have to get out of here." She grabbed Emma's hand and started to pull.

"I'll get her," Joe said, and he picked Emma up. Even if he wasn't going to be part of Emma's life anymore, he wouldn't abandon her.

"Hurry." Isohel's warning was unnecessary, as Revealer images of the dead Masevo filled the street, brutally murdered by a raving Eury Vatic wailing about the death of his daughter.

Joe soon followed Isohel between buildings and through alleyways that were disguised to look like walls or fences. "Wait," he said, putting Emma down as her cousin descended a narrow flight of stairs.

"Hurry," Isohel whispered.

Joe switched Emma to his other shoulder and rushed after her.

A lurid spectrum of light blazed from windows smeared with dirt. Candles and flowers and colored spheres floated alongside images of Fen Elos. Some of the images were torn and some candles broken, as if someone hadn't liked what they showed or honored.

"Where are we?" Joe asked.

"We're in the *Kena*, the Refuge of the Anaxio, the Worthless," Isohel said. "Gemynd who can't or won't do what they're supposed to do. Unless their Soulmates are valuable, they have to live here, in this segregated section of the city. They eat leftover food that's transported from houses and restaurants and offices. They breed like vermin but for some reason most of their kids are valuable. If the kids are lucky someone tells them their parents are dead, but I think they always know. Anaxio don't do anything," she added derisively. "My dad told me Eury Vatic hid here after you disappeared and your sister was killed. As soon as the Ones in Power found out, they cleared the area. They killed or imprisoned everyone, but they didn't find your dad or any of his traces. Now, fifteen years later, new Worthless have filled it up again. It's disgusting. They're disgusting. But we can hide here until I can get us out."

Joe felt eyes watching him, but when he turned he saw nothing. "Where is everyone?" he asked.

"Hiding," Isohel said. "Come on."

She took Joe's hand and led him down a long flight of stairs and into a filthy room that smelled like feces and garbage.

"God," he said, retching as he put Emma down, leaning her against him. "What is that?"

"What do you think it is?" Isohel asked, pushing through the garbage on the floor.

Joe tried not to vomit.

Isohel stood up and tore three pieces of fabric from her shirt. She pulled rapidly at them until she had three small masks. "Put one on yourself and one on Emma," she said. "It will help with the smell."

Joe did as he was told. It helped a little.

Muffled shouts came from the street above. Isohel glanced up and listened. "The Worthless hate the Aythentia," she said. "They hate Eleytheria, too, except for Fen Elos. They loved him. They'll tell the Masevo about us, but only when they want to or when they've gotten something in exchange. Lean Emma against a wall and help me."

"Help you what?" Joe asked.

"Search the piles, and give me any metal, rubber, circuitry, plastic, fiber, and rotten food," she said.

The shouts on the street grew louder.

"What are you doing?" Joe whispered, holding Emma stiffly on his lap as he dug through wet, stinking refuse.

"Don't talk to me," Isohel said, concentrating on the pile of junk in front of her.

The voices above snapped like gunshots. Isohel stopped.

"Shit," she said, digging through another hideous pile. She pulled something out. "Thank Misos." She sighed. "Okay."

Joe watched in amazement as a large cylinder emerged from where Isohel pulled at the garbage. But footsteps sounded in the room upstairs.

"They're here," Joe said.

"I know," Isohel said. "Shut up so I can concentrate."

There was a horrible shout, and the voices upstairs silenced.

"They know we're down here," Isohel said. "Put Emma in first." She had made what looked like a steel tube just big enough to fit three people inside. "Then get in yourself," she directed. "I have to do one more thing."

Joe pushed Emma into the silver cylinder then climbed in himself. Isohel pulled furiously at another pile of garbage.

"We have to go," she shouted, dropping a string of fire on the ground near the pile she'd just made.

The door opened, and Gatherer lights burst into the room. Isohel did something and the tube sealed itself shut and shot through the ceiling. Joe felt a slight lift, like going over a rise in the road, and he felt the heat of the explosion Isohel had created. They were going so fast he couldn't focus on anything streaking past the narrow windows.

"You're probably going to feel pretty sick in a minute," Isohel said. "Try not to puke on me." She leaned into the movement of the tube. "Misos, I hope all the Worthless upstairs were already dead."

CHAPTER FIFTY-ONE

Joe didn't know where to turn his head. The cylinder was narrow and Emma was leaning against him. He pushed her away in time to lean over and vomit on the floor of the tube.

"Where are we going?" he asked between concentrated breaths meant to calm his stomach. They didn't help.

"I don't know," Isohel answered. Joe continued to retch out nothing.

"What do you mean you don't know?" he asked, his stomach violently shaking and his head spinning.

"I don't know," Isohel repeated. "There's no place to hide. Everyone is looking for you now." She gazed at him with an expression of fear and admiration. "Did you kill those Masevo?"

"No," Joe said, closing his eyes and then opening them again. Nothing helped. Isohel turned the speeding contraption, and miraculously, with nothing in his stomach, Joe vomited again.

"Sorry," she said. "I've been flying for years. It's wretched until you get used to it."

He could only groan.

"I have an idea," Isohel said, rapidly turning again. Joe almost wept.

She landed the makeshift vehicle on a street lined with heavily scented, flowering trees, and anchored by a cylindrical windowless building made of pale pink stone. Joe fell, leaving Isohel to help Emma. He retched once more then lay down and pressed his forehead to the cool footpath.

The second alarm still screamed, and Revealer images of the dead Masevo hung everywhere. Isohel sat Emma next to Joe and rolled the machine to the middle of the footpath, far away from them.

This alarm must be different from the others, Joe thought. There was no one on the street and every window was shrouded. He watched Isohel move her hands over the cylinder. She jumped to her feet and ran back as the tube imploded with a puff of smoke.

"You can make anything out of garbage," she said, smiling, her silver eyes bright.

Joe nodded. He wished everything would stop spinning.

"Take Emma into that building," Isohel directed pointing to the pink stone structure. "Run her hand—the one with the scar on it—over the lock."

"Where are you going?" Joe asked, reluctant to open his mouth.

"I'll be back in a second," Isohel said, running down the street and leaping to peek into various gardens.

Trembling and sweating, Joe guided Emma to the door. He picked up her hand and waved her scarred palm in front of the lock. The door opened.

The building was a single room, several stories high, and filled with what looked like horizontal strings of gold light floating independently of one another all the way to the ceiling. Coming closer Joe saw that the ornately curled, gently swaying gold strings were illuminated names seemingly etched on the air, supported by nothing. Small enough to hold in your hand.

A beam of clear light passed through Emma and then through Joe. "Nyll Arismapsi," a female voice softly intoned. Joe whipped his head around then instinctively grabbed Emma for support as the dizziness overwhelmed him. "Edoro Vatic," the voice murmured. "Sofia Vatic."

Emma trembled slightly.

The door opened. Joe clutched Emma to him.

"It's just me," Isohel said, waiting for the light to pass through her.

"Nyll Arismapsi," the voice uttered.

"Where are we?" Joe asked.

"This is a Memorium," Isohel said. "When you're born, your identity marker— It's like DNA," she explained when Joe whispered something like a question. "Your identity marker is put into a nameplate along with the identity markers of your closest relatives. You add your friends and Soulmate later. When you die, your nameplate is suspended here and the sensor light calls out your name whenever any of those gemynd come to visit. Did the light reveal your mom's and your sister's names?" she asked brightly, as if the thought just occurred to her.

Joe nodded. His head was still swimming.

"Oh," Isohel said. "Sorry. I almost forgot." She knelt on the ground and made a small bowl out of a stone then mixed wet leaves and something that smelled like vinegar into a thick paste inside. "Take this," she said, handing the bowl to him. "It will help with the disorientation and the sickness."

"I can't eat that," Joe said, trying not to retch again.

"You don't eat it," Isohel said. "You rub it on your skin. Lift up your shirt."

Joe raised his shirt with trembling fingers. He was shaking from the chill on his exposed skin and sweating at the same time. Isohel scooped up a handful of the wet mess and smeared it on his chest. The acidic stench made him gag.

"You'll feel better in a minute," she said, standing back and wiping her hands on her jeans.

Joe held on to Emma for support, and Isohel was right; a few seconds later he felt better. His head stopped spinning and his stomach calmed. "Thanks," he said.

Isohel smiled.

"Now," she said. "What are you going to do about your dad?"

"What do you mean?" Joe asked.

"Are you going to hand him over to the Resisters, or are you going to let the Aythentia get to him first? And they will," she said. "They are better at getting what they want."

"The Singers of the Apocalypse want my dad to join them," Joe said.

"I know. Emma told me," Isohel said. "I don't care. The Ones in Power cannot find him first."

"The Singers of the Apocalypse easily killed those Masevo," Joe said.

"The Eleytheria will be able to reason with him," Isohel continued, unheeding. "He worked beside them for so long. He'll listen to what they have to say."

"No, he won't," Joe said. "He's already heard what they have to say. He can hear this. He can hear us. He doesn't care about anything anymore."

"You're wrong," Isohel said.

Joe.

Emma's thought-voice was so quiet Joe wasn't sure he'd heard or imagined it. He took her hand and thought back at her, *Emma?*

Nothing happened.

"What did my father do to her?" Joe asked, irrationally angry, as if it was Isohel's fault.

Isohel ran her hands over Emma's head. "I think he took her into himself," she said. "I think he took her mind into his. She's seeing and hearing everything he sees and hears."

Terror nearly stopped Joe's heart. She had done it, then. She had connected with his father. Now he was going to lose her.

He was furious. At himself for letting her go. At Emma for leaving.

Isohel swayed a little and grabbed his hand for a second then dropped it. "I made a replica of myself to fool my dad," she said with a spark of defiance before she sat on the floor. "It was exhausting. I need to sit down for a minute."

Joe held Emma, furious and despairing then furious again. He couldn't lose her. Why hadn't she listened to him?

"Nyll Arismapsi," Isohel said and held out her hands. One of the light strings turned in the air then dropped slowly until Isohel caught her mother's name and kissed it. A series of several Revealer images of a beautiful young woman blossomed for a few moments then vanished in front of her.

"Eury Vatic saved my mother's life," Isohel said.

Joe held Emma's unresponsive hands in his. "How?" he asked.

"My mom was a Syche Katharos, a Soulskin," Isohel said. "Like Emma's sister Maude. When my mom was little, around six or seven, an Eleytheria Transformist named Gelon Lira convinced gemynd that the ashes of encausted Soulskins, I think you say 'cremated'... Anyway"—Isohel sighed in the soft light of the huge room—"Gelon Lira convinced gemynd that Soulskin ashes could be made into a restorative that would eliminate every disease. And he was right. But the ashes couldn't be synthesized in a stable form even by the most skilled Transformists. In order to be effective the ashes had to come always from recently encausted Syche Katharos. Hundreds if not thousands of Soulskins would have to be killed to make enough of the restorative to really eliminate the threat of disease in the entire gemynd population. Gelon Lira believed, and the gemynd who followed him believed as well, that these Soulskins should be sacrificed for the good of everyone else. He invoked the *Nomos Apodektas*, the Acceptable Consequences Doctrine, and for a while he succeeded."

The names of the dead and the remembered swayed in the airy tower, and intricate threads of connected light flickered over

Emma's pale pink skin like glitter. Joe kissed her head and prayed she'd be okay. Isohel kept talking.

"The Eleytheria were the Ones in Power then," she said. "This was before the power shift. Most Eleytheria believe Gelon Lira's actions brought on the power shift. The Aythentia couldn't wait to use the reprehensible actions of Gelon Lira and a few Eleytheria to advance their own cause. Gelon Lira had Aythentia followers as well, but he was the leader and he was Eleytheria. So…"

Emma's soft hand was cold in Joe's. "What did my father do?" he asked.

"Before the Eleytheria caught Gelon Lira," Isohel said, "—it's very difficult to catch a gifted Transformist," she added with a flash of perverse pride. "He'd murdered and encausted seven Soulskins. All children. Someone who worked for him captured my mother. Eury Vatic was about your age then, maybe a little younger. No one knew he was an Oloklira then, everyone believed he was just a kid Transformist. But he saw what happened to my mom—just a flash, but he saw it. And he went to find her. And even though it might have revealed something about his greater powers, because there was no reason for him to see something completely unrelated to who he was, or his family, or where he lived, Eury Vatic saved my mother and returned her to my grandparents. And the Eleytheria caught Gelon Lira."

Isohel released her mother's name. It floated to the ceiling like the visible scent of flowers. She smiled softly at Joe.

The door opened, and Isohel jumped to her feet.

"Hellena Balzac," the disembodied Memorium voice murmured.

An ancient man with narrow eyes and thick gold hair echoed the words of the voice and raised his hands to receive the name. He cradled the air-etched letters in his palm and spoke lovingly to them. Revealer images of children and flowers appeared all around him.

Isohel gaped at him in silent, angry envy. "I hate not knowing what it feels like to love someone like that."

Joe had forgotten Isohel was a Loveless. He couldn't imagine what it would be like to know you didn't have a Soulmate. Joe gazed up at the thousands of etched names hanging in the air all the way to the high ceiling in the circular room.

Sofia Vatic, he thought. *Edoro Vatic*. And he held out his hands.

The Memorium voice echoed his thoughts aloud. The illuminated names floated, along with Revealer images of his mother and sister, into Joe's open hands like pennies dropped in a pool of water.

Emma turned, her empty gaze replaced with Eury Vatic's wild eyes, and his voice poured painfully from her puppet mouth. "'How shall the heart be reconciled to its feast of losses?'"

The door opened again. The names disappeared, and the light in the room vanished. The old man cried out. Emma fell into Joe's arms. Then a dozen Gatherer lights shot out, weaving strands of luminous blue into the darkness of the empty room.

Joe held tight to Emma as the light hit them.

CHAPTER FIFTY-TWO

The Gatherer lights must have acted like an image transport. Emma felt Joe's arms clutching her as they were swiftly transported from the Memorium. She screamed. Her voice, Joe's father's voice, and the aggregate chorus of despair poured from her mouth like blood. More than anything she wanted Mom to put hands over her ears and make everything disappear.

The voices and images quieted, curling in the back of her head like a throbbing seed that might blossom into a headache later in the day. The light shifted and the air cooled. She and Joe were still together, suspended gently in the center of a room. Emma didn't know where they were, or how far they had traveled from the Memorium. The room had no windows and there was no ambient sound.

Three women stood around them. Emma did not have any sense that they would be easy to defeat or outsmart.

"Where are my parents?" she shouted, relieved almost to the point of weeping to hear her own voice free of the others.

The women did not move or speak.

Joe held her tightly. The floor was three feet below them. Joe looked pale and exhausted. He gazed unsmiling at her, and Emma remembered when they first met and how she'd unknowingly recited the story from his mother's painting, the story of Edoro's death. He'd felt so betrayed, and he looked the same way now.

She touched his cheek. Joe closed his eyes for a moment but his expression didn't alter. What had happened while she was connected with his father?

Emma ran her hand over her chest and pulled out his Spirit Sphere. When he'd given it to her she was under the effect of the Singers and didn't care. Now she couldn't believe she'd ever felt like that. The Nevma felt weird leaving her, like watching someone drive away forever that you loved but never told. Joe's chest instantly absorbed the sphere. His skin was cool and damp. He shuddered and took a deep, shaking breath.

The three women stood motionless, and a tremor of realization opened a door in Emma's head.

"They're guarding us," she said. It seemed ridiculous to think anything to Joe; these women were Super Telepaths and connected completely with the one person they were guarding. "The Masevo haven't caught your father yet. You and I are the only links to him. If your father tries to contact you or disconnect from me, the Ones in Power hope one of these guards will be able to figure out where he is. Then the Masevo will catch him." Like a little kid, Emma glanced at one of the women for a sign of approval that she'd gotten it right. All three faces remained unchanged.

"Why are there three of them?" Joe asked.

"One for me, one for you and one for your dad," Emma said. "His thoughts are still in my head, waiting like a virus in my blood, but they can't access them."

"Can you hear anything they're thinking?" Joe asked.

"They're not thinking anything right now," Emma said. "They're like receptacles. They're only listening and collecting. Can you move us around?"

"No," Joe said. "I feel like I'm under thick water. Is that how you feel?"

"Yeah," Emma said. "Where's Isohel?"

"I don't know."

Emma looked at the scar on her hand. A shiver of energy passed between the three listeners, and then her palm turned over on its own. A knife point of blue light focused on it.

She and Joe dropped gently from the air. Their feet stuck to the floor.

"They're going to cut out this scar," Emma said, her heart pounding. She pressed her hand to her head, hoping to warn her cousin.

Two more women came into the room. One of them immobilized Emma and Joe. The other took Emma's hand and pulled out the scar. Emma couldn't scream except inside her own head. Her listening guard was in her sight line. A flash of empathy sprinted across the woman's face.

The first newcomer returned Emma and Joe's mobility and sent them back to hanging in the air, then both newcomers left. Emma groaned and held her throbbing hand to her chest but she refused to scream or cry. "Be ready," she said to Joe.

A wave of alarm passed through the three Super Telepaths.

"Don't let go." Emma held tightly to Joe's hand. Then she gazed at her listening guard and released the memories of everything she had seen today in Eury Vatic's consciousness.

Hanging in the air and holding Joe's hand made it easier; she didn't have to utilize energy for anything other than opening the chaos of love and cruelty, filth and sacred beauty to the guard. The woman staggered. The other two turned to their fallen colleague, and Emma and Joe fell to the floor. And now that their singular connections were broken, Emma turned to the other two and released more of the chaos that had been in Eury's head. The women dropped to their knees.

Joe picked up his stunned listener and waved her hand in front of the door, which opened with a hush of metal. He and Emma ran out.

"Isohel went to the Resisters," Emma said. "The Masevo didn't know to take her, and she fled the Memorium. I saw her before they took out the scar. The Resisters want to use me to get to your father. And Isohel is going to help them."

The narrow hall was dark and doorless.

"How are we going to get out of here?" Emma asked, struggling to keep up with Joe.

"I'm not sure we've escaped," Joe replied, slowing down. "No one has come after us, and no alarm has sounded."

"Let's fly to the ceiling," she suggested. "Remember when my dad cut away the wall to reveal an open window? Maybe there's an opening we can't see."

Joe took her into his arms and they flew, but there was no ceiling, just soft darkness and no substance. "We could get lost here," Joe said. "There aren't any boundaries."

"It has to exist somewhere," Emma said. "It has to begin and end *somewhere.*" She concentrated on understanding the building and who built it and why.

Joe flew swiftly, apparently hoping that acting decisively would make something happen.

Emma looked at him, though she could hardly see his face. "The endlessness is part of the impenetrable defense properties of the structure," she said. "It's meant to be slowly maddening and disorienting. The only path is back to the listening room. There is no way to find the door, no indication, no trace, nothing."

"Someone must know how to get out," Joe said. "Someone planned it. Someone built it."

"Your father would know," Emma whispered. "But I have to be able to contact him without alerting the filters or whoever was watching the listeners."

"Why hasn't an alarm sounded?" Joe asked, looking behind them and pulling Emma closer. "Why isn't anyone chasing us?"

"I don't know," Emma said, "but we have to get out of here."

She sucked in a breath and concentrated on an inconsequential image. She let Eury Vatic linger at the outside of her thinking. An image of Mr. Spencer's classroom popped into her head. His room was filled with posters. Some were magnified photographs of bacteria or elements. Some were portraits of scientists or poets. A few were beautiful advertisements for book fairs.

Joe held her tightly. Emma split her focus between a steady imagining of Mr. Spencer's classroom and the cluster of sound and vision trembling at the back of her head. Eury Vatic would know where the opening was. He would lead her to it.

In the center of a New England Antiquarian Book Fair poster was picture of an old book called *A Necklace of Flowers*. Inside a ring of red roses, a speck of darkness opened like the mouth of a spider. Emma bent Joe toward the poster in her head. The circle of flowers came closer, and at last they passed through it.

* * *

The air outside was thick with Revealer images of the dead Masevo, of Isohel and of Fen Elos. And now Joe's face and Emma's. The screaming siren hurt Joe's ears. Masevo stood on every corner.

A Gatherer light streaked toward them. Joe wrapped his arms around Emma and they shot toward the sky.

"The Resisters have your dad," Emma said.

"Are you sure?" Joe asked.

Emma nodded and held him tighter. "He's still connected with me, but that is fading. Try to hear what I'm thinking. Fly where I lead you."

Joe closed his eyes and concentrated but couldn't hear anything. The crush in his chest every time he thought of leaving Emma rose up like a poison. She loved him. He knew she did. But he couldn't trust her. She wouldn't stay with him. He had to let her go.

She stared at him.

"You left," he said, knowing she'd heard what he was thinking. "You could have died."

"Joe," she said.

"No," he said. "I begged you to stay and you pushed yourself out of my arms. The freaking fall to the portal tree could have killed you."

"I had to," Emma said.

"No, you didn't," Joe said. "You didn't know about this world or my father or any of this a few months ago. But you do know me. And you were willing to sacrifice yourself without any guarantee or any idea at all that it would help. You left me."

Emma tightened her grip around Joe's waist. Her hands felt cold against his skin. "I had to," she said again.

"I know," he said. "But I can't stay with you knowing you might leave at any time because you think you might be able to avert a disaster you have nothing to do with."

"Joe," she said, "this isn't you. You're the kid who got kicked out of school for helping someone being brutalized. You're the kid who stood up to douchebag Kyle Sparks and his band of merry assholes, as you called them, when they were picking on poor Phil Puccini. You always want to fight for what's right. Why is that not okay for me?"

He didn't know. He didn't fucking *know*. She was right. If the circumstances were reversed he would have done the same thing she did, even if she'd begged him to stay. All Joe knew was that something broke irrevocably and permanently inside his heart when Emma left him. And he couldn't stay with her if she was just going to disappear. He couldn't. Her soft sweet voice broke inside his head and Joe felt like crying. He closed his eyes and felt Emma's hands on his face and his shoulders and his heart.

"You're not making this any easier for me," he said, crying now. He didn't fucking care.

Shhh, she murmured low and gently in his head. *Shhh*.

And then he was in a small bed in a room he almost recognized. They were still flying, he felt the wind against his cheeks and the movement of the air, but he was also in a small bed and he was very young, maybe not quite three. A man's voice came through the walls. The sound of it made Sfodro feel safe and worried at the same time.

"It will be two months tomorrow." Zino's voice was so sad it made Sfodro feel sad, too.

"You will, of course, know why we've contacted you," another man said.

"Illuminate me," Zino replied.

"Very well," agreed the other man. "But don't think for a moment that forcing me to articulate it will weaken our resolve. We have no choice—"

"Of course you do," Zino said, very angry. Sfodro picked up his stuffed dragonfly and kissed it. Genna had given him the dragonfly and he loved it.

"This is your choice," Zino said, still angry. "Have the integrity to acknowledge it to me. And to yourselves. Or you are no better than your enemies."

They stopped talking and Sfodro felt happy.

"Say it," Zino said suddenly. "Say it out loud. Say it."

"Turn yourself in within twenty-four hours," the other man said. Sfodro's father gasped.

"So soon? I thought..."

"Your affairs have been in order for months," the other man said. "You knew this day was coming."

"But twenty-four hours. It's too soon. I can't. A few more days, at least. What difference would that make? A few more days when you've been waiting for three years?"

Then Zino closed off the voices and Sfodro couldn't hear anymore. He picked up his dragonfly.

"Genna is missing," he confided to the soft toy. "But I'm going to find her and bring her home so chi Edoro and Zino won't be sad anymore." Sfodro didn't tell the dragonfly how sad he was. "When my arms and legs and wings are big and strong I'm going to find chi Genna and bring her home."

He still felt sad, but Zino felt sadder. Sfodro felt his father's sadness pour through the walls of his bedroom the way the blue water, chased by the noisy wind, had run onto the green beach when Genna and Edafio had taken him swimming.

Sfodro sang the Idrysi song for his father. Like Genna sang to him when he was sad or scared in the night. His mother would come home someday. He knew she would. She wouldn't leave him alone when bad guys were always trying to come take Zino away.

Emma kissed Joe's mouth, but he couldn't kiss her back. Not yet.

"I won't leave you, Joe," she said. "Ever. But you can't expect me to do something you would never do. You can't ask me to stand by and do nothing while terrible things happen to people I love. It's who I am."

CHAPTER FIFTY-THREE

Emma slid her hands under the back of Joe's shirt and opened her palms against the jagged scars he'd never let anyone see. Joe shivered, and Emma kissed the skin over his heart.

"I love you, Joe," she said. "Forever and always. Whether you decide you can't stay with me because I left when you begged me not to. Whether the Soulmate thing is true or not. I love you and I choose you. Now and forever. I love you because you picked up jelly beans off the sidewalk when I dropped them. I love you because you stood up for a kid you didn't know to a porch full of football players. I love you because you're protective of your mom. I love you because you do the right thing even though that's not how the world has always treated you. I love you because you kept coming back to me even after you freaked out or said the wrong thing, or felt embarrassed. I love you because when you kiss me and when you touch me I feel the real magic of what it means to be happy and to be alive. You make me feel grateful to live in the world, as shitty as it is sometimes. And I love you because you waited—and you're still waiting—until I was ready, even though you were ready the day we met in the hall. Because you apparently have a thing for sweaty, awkward girls."

He laughed.

"Now you have to trust yourself," Emma went on. "And you have to trust me. Even if you want to leave when all this is over. You have to open yourself inside me now or we'll never be able to find your dad. Think of Maude and Gryphon. Do you think either of them would have given up what they had to avoid the pain of being separated?"

Oh. That's what he'd been doing, Joe thought, realizing at last. He'd been living his life with one foot out the door. Never trusting anything. Never trusting anyone to stick around. And then when he had someone, someone who loved him for who he was, who knew him and loved him anyway, he'd almost let her go. He'd tried to find ways to chain her to him, and then he'd manufactured reasons to leave.

He felt sick. They plummeted toward the ground.

Emma grabbed his face and kissed him hard on the mouth. She kissed him as if it didn't matter if they hit the ground and died or if they found his father. Emma kissed him because she loved him and she always would, no matter what else happened to them. Joe kissed Emma back and they shot into the sky.

She pulled away and smiled so brightly at him, Joe forgot to breathe.

"I'm sorry," he said. "I'm so sorry."

She kissed him.

Joe wrapped his arms tightly around Emma and pressed his forehead hard on hers. He took a huge breath that seemed to shatter all his being and let go of everything he knew. Everything he didn't know. He let go of worrying she would leave. Let go of worrying he wasn't good enough. Let go of blaming himself for what happened to his parents. Let go of being afraid.

Something happened. He sucked in a huge mouthful of gorgeous air. He felt the warm breeze brush over Emma's soft skin. He felt her boundless, unconditional love for him from inside her soul. He felt Emma's desire for him wash through her like incandescent music, and he forgot about himself and his father and the Singers. He was aware of nothing but being alive in this moment, with Emma pressed against him. Her breasts brushed the hardness of his chest and he realized her would wait forever for her, whatever she wanted, whenever she wanted it.

"I love you," he said. Sweaty and awkward. Funny and brave. Forever and always. He kissed her.

"When this is over, *yes*," Emma said. "A thousand times yes."

He crushed his hard hips against her softer flesh.

"I don't know if I can promise a *thousand* times," he said, grinning against her neck. She just laughed and kissed him again.

A steely thread of terror and exhaustion suddenly shivered at the back of Emma's neck, and a bright hum of the chaos suffocating his father pulsed faintly. Joe closed his eyes, kissed Emma's hair, and followed it.

They flew for an endless-seeming handful of minutes, and then an ocean of trees spread out in front of them. Joe recognized the green sand beach at the edge of the blue-glass lake.

They landed near the stone tables and cold fire pits. White flowers shone like tiny moons between black tree roots. His father stood unmoving, shrouded by an oscillating shell of energy. But Eury Vatic saw him and smiled.

Emma gasped and trembled violently as Joe's father separated his mind from hers. She sank into Joe's arms, and a pale echo of what she had seen, of what his father had seen and continued to see, resonated in Joe's head like a drug overdose. A dozen or more men and women, including Isohel, emerged from the trees and surrounded Eury.

Isohel saw Joe and Emma before the others. *Get out,* she thought, glancing nervously around. *It's too late. You can't help him. It's for the best. Get out before someone sees you.*

Joe heard Emma's realization of her cousin's fear for them.

This is the only way, Isohel thought at Joe. *You had to know. You had to know.*

One by one, the Eleytheria turned some kind of light on Eury Vatic, and Joe watched in horror as his father trembled in agony under their penetrating glare. The lights seemed to be extracting something, because they entered and exited his father's gaunt body in a seemingly endless loop of visible energy, emptying his father of everything. The Eleytheria indeed seemed to believe a portion of the information Eury carried inside him would be valuable, and more than that, that the secret to the power of Whole Listening was hidden somewhere within. The blades of light swelled as they continued to silently search and drain Joe's father, who shook uncontrollably, supported by the transparent shell surrounding him.

"This won't work," Emma whispered to Joe. "Those things, whatever they are, won't be able to hold what they draw from him."

Some of the Eleytheria came to the same conclusion, and they exchanged their swollen instruments with fresh ones and began again.

"It's over," Joe said, stunned that they could have come this far and it hadn't made a difference. He could have lost Emma. Maude had lost Gryphon and Gryphon lost his life. For nothing. Nothing. None of it made any difference. "The Eleytheria will learn the secret of Whole Listening," Joe said, "And the Singers of the Apocalypse will find out that they have it, if they don't already know, and then they'll choose the Eleytheria most likely to join them, the one with the softest heart and the fiercest convictions, the one most likely to die for what he believes, and they'll buy the knowledge from him with the promise of a perfect peace that doesn't exist. It doesn't matter that my father lasted as long as he did. It's over. *Over*."

Eury Vatic turned and gazed fiercely and passionately at his son, and a flood of images from Joe's earliest life slammed against the bubble of energy and then slid to the ground. Joe saw his beautiful mother and his laughing infant sister. He saw his father and mother dancing and kissing in an illuminated room filled with flowers and gemynd. Mr. Spencer and Emma's parents, years younger, were there too, dancing and playing a game with jewel-colored spheres that floated and were hard to catch. And Joe saw himself, blue-haired and tiny, smiling in the sunlight.

"Chi Sfodro," his father said in his own voice. "My son." Eury glanced at Emma and smiled. "I'm happy I got to see your strong and beautiful Eynosyndeo, Sfodro. And I am grateful I lived to see you grow into a man. I love you, chi Sfodro. I love you, my stout-hearted, sweet, courageous, singing boy. Every creature must die, but do not stop singing."

The light swelled to the point of bursting. Then Eury Vatic fell to the ground and the vibrating energy consumed him.

The Eleytheria emptied what they had taken into a large, flask-shaped receiving chamber. The scrubby patch of ground where Joe's father had stood blazed with an intense, bright green color, like grass in a dream. There was no body.

"Leave it." A short female Eleytheria stopped a man who was aiming a light at the emerald circle. "We have everything we need," she said.

"What about the kids?" the man said, looking over at Emma and Joe.

"We have the extrication lights," the woman said. "Nothing else matters. We have to leave before the Aythentia get here."

The Eleytheria, including Isohel, climbed into a snake-like train hovering silently above the ground. Joe hadn't seen it before. Maybe it hadn't been there.

"I'm sorry," Isohel whispered as she entered the hollow vehicle.

"What?" Emma asked. "Where are you going? Are you leaving us here?"

Isohel didn't answer. The door closed behind her. The machine disappeared so fast it was as if it had never existed.

Joe knelt at the edge of the bright grass and grabbed a handful.

"I don't think he's dead," Emma said. "I think…"

"Can you still hear what he's thinking?"

Emma shook her head.

"Then where is he?" Joe asked. He leaned back on his heels. "Do you think he joined them?"

"I don't know," Emma said.

She gazed at Joe, and he felt hot and cold at the same time. Heavy, as if a concrete foot stood on his chest.

"What are you thinking?" he asked, climbing to his feet.

"I saw what he saw," Emma said quietly. "Babies pulled from their mother's arms and beaten to death while the mothers ran to save their other children. Today. Not a hundred years ago. Today. Old people drowning in their attics. A guy hardly older than you, beaten so badly for breaking a supposedly moral law his eyes burst out of his head. Today. I saw Sean Bolton shoving that kid into the locker and smashing him in the face again and again. I saw you save that boy's life. And get punished for it. I saw Maude's heart break again."

She walked to the lake and knelt in the water, and Joe stood next to Emma and took off his shoes. The surface of the water was warm from the sun, but the sandy bottom was cool.

"I saw what he saw," Emma repeated. "What he sees. Everything else—money, celebrities, movies, who's popular, who has a car, who's straight-edge, who's a drunk—everything else is a joke."

"I'm a joke?" Joe said, as softly as the water retreated from the shore.

"No," Emma said in a small voice.

"My mother took me swimming here when I was little," Joe said. "I saw it. In the memory you gave me."

"I didn't give it to you," Emma said. "It was yours. I just helped you find it again."

He took her hand. "You helped me find a lot of things."

Emma smiled at him. "You helped me, too. I was kind of a cranky bitch when you first met me."

"I thought you were the hottest girl I'd ever seen. I had to play a word-find game with the dance poster so I wouldn't humiliate myself in front of you and Mr. Norway."

"I thought you were bored," Emma said, laughing.

"I was the opposite of bored," Joe said, grinning and leaning over to kiss her. He sat and dug his bare feet into the cool sand. "That's why I was so mad when I thought you were making fun of my mom's paintings. I thought you'd been pretending to like me so you could make fun of me. Because I didn't look like, or live like, anyone else in your school."

"Wow," Emma said, sitting beside him and digging her toes under the sand to touch his foot. He grinned at her and slid his foot underneath hers. "I guess I was a pretty shitty telepath, then. I thought you couldn't wait to get away from me that day."

"I couldn't," he said, leaning close and lifting a lock of her hair. "Because I could hardly stand to be that close to you and not kiss you. And since we'd just met, maybe I would have come off as kind of pervy."

Emma laughed. "You might have," she said, agreeing. "Except I would have kissed you back."

Joe looked at her and shivered.

"We have to leave," he said. "I can't stay her for one second longer and not touch you."

"I can't either," Emma said.

For the briefest moment Joe thought of staying. How long could it take? He'd been ready for weeks. But he didn't want to rush. And now didn't really seem like the right time.

"It *almost* is the right time," Emma whispered, reading his thoughts and kissing his cheek. "But you're right. We can't stay. We have to figure out what happened to your dad. Who loves you by the way."

"I know," Joe said. "And I never would have heard him say it if it wasn't for you."

CHAPTER FIFTY-FOUR

"Maybe your dad became part of the energy fabric," Emma said. "That's what the Singers did." Emma took a deep breath and remembered. "Fen Elos turned the Singers of the Apocalypse into a myth to try to neutralize their power, but he knew exactly what they were and what they wanted. Mom told me Odym Chadia became the leader of the Resisters after Fen Elos died."

"Who's Odym Chadia?" Joe asked.

"He helped me escape when the Masevo found me in Fen Elos's store," Emma said. "And he brought my family from the Otherworld before the Masevo could find them. He's a Lucent," she added. "Like the lover of the Crossworlder who created the Singers of the Apocalypse. A Lucent is humanized energy, a visible manifestation of the energy that is part of everything. If your dad can still be contacted, Odym Chadia would know how."

Joe took her hand. "Let's go," he said.

As they rose into the air above the trees he remarked, "The Ones in Power will know the Resisters have what they want. So we're safe for a little while. They won't do anything but try to capture that train."

"Isohel," Emma whispered.

"The Resisters must have some kind of plan," Joe said. "They'll protect her."

Emma said nothing. Joe leaned into the sharp wind, and they were silent for a long time. The forest passed like a bright green cloud beneath them. Daylight softened and the air cooled. The sky turned orange then pink then finally became a deep blue that made Joe think of Emma's eyes the first time he saw her.

The serrated outline of the city, pierced like a tin lantern with white and yellow light, rose in the distance. They flew closer and eventually landed on the same patch of scrubby grass where Joe had landed what seemed a lifetime ago. The alarms had stopped and the streets and footpaths were filled with gemynd hurrying and talking, oblivious to what had happened.

"Can you contact Odym Chadia?" Joe asked.

"I'll try," Emma said.

After a few minutes she shook her head. "His access must be blocked. I'll try to connect to the energy left in Fen Elos's store. If he's there, maybe he'll hear me."

Joe picked her up again, and they flew to the tiny store now ringed with flowers and floating candles. Reading stone tributes littered the footpath in front of the darkened windows.

"This is where I first heard the Singers of the Apocalypse," Emma said.

Joe's eyes widened.

"Fen Elos wanted me to tell him what I'd heard, but I was afraid of him so I lied." Emma's delicate face contracted.

"It isn't your fault," Joe said.

"Gryphon wouldn't have died if I'd trusted Fen Elos," Emma said in a hollow voice.

A soft glow, like that of a gargantuan firefly, blossomed then disappeared in an explosion visible in the narrow space between two high-rise buildings to the west. The footpath upon which they stood vibrated slightly, and Emma screamed, clutching her black, scarred palm. A terrifying alarm tore through the air. For a hanging moment everyone froze—then everybody ran.

"What happened?" Joe whispered, grabbing Emma's arm and pulling her to him.

"The Ones in Power must have taken the train," she said. "Or destroyed it."

The alarm shrieked, and the streets emptied of gemynd. Emma and Joe just stood in disbelief.

"Was the train destroyed?" Joe asked after a minute.

"I don't know," Emma whispered.

A shapeless mass of silver light like a fairy cloak moving though water floated over the flowers and candles and into Fen Elos's store.

Emma grabbed Joe's hand. "That was Odym Chadia," she said.

* * *

They followed the silver light into the dark store, past the Ancient and Otherworld section and into the room where Fen Elos disappeared when she first heard the Singers. The figure of a man emerged from the light. He knelt on the floor.

Emma breathed in and the man turned, glancing quickly from her face to Joe's. He stood up, the air around him luminous and bright, littered with incandescent dust.

"You're Sfodro Vatic, aren't you?" he asked in a voice like etched glass. He walked to Joe and clasped his hand, and Emma felt Joe's shock that Odym's illuminated flesh was solid and substantial.

"Your parents have been secreted," Odym said to Emma.

"What does that mean?" she whispered.

Odym shook his head, and light splashed Joe and Emma's faces. "I don't know if you'll ever be able to find them," he said. "I'm sorry." He squeezed her shoulder with a soothing hand.

Another message implanted by her mother rose in Emma's head, and she asked, "Can you find an invisible door? My dad could," she added, letting her voice fall.

"Yes," he said. "I can."

"There's a door in this room," Emma said, her mother's voice following her as if Gwynaias stood beside her. "It's been Masked.

Fen Elos renewed it a few days ago. There are three Mask resonances on it."

"I have an exetafi, a clarifier," Odym said, reaching into a pocket and pulling out a slender wand. It sat strange and dark in his bright, thin fingers.

He shone the clarifier around the room until it revealed three Masks in the same spot. A small, brown door appeared in the wall, and Odym gazed at Emma. She took Joe's hand and opened the door.

Thick reading stones were piled to the high ceiling. Odym came into the room. Light from his body illuminated what seemed to be a thousand Revealer images.

"The Chronicles and the Revealer images of the Singers of the Apocalypse are in here," Emma said.

"The Singers of the Apocalypse are a myth," Odym said.

"They're not," Joe argued. "They want my father to join them. If he does, they'll be able to simultaneously seduce every human and every gemynd into letting go of his or her life."

The light from Odym's body pulsed violently, dimming and brightening the reading stones.

"Do you know where my father is?" Joe asked.

"He's part of the energy fabric," Odym said. "I felt him connect to it. You can't communicate with him anymore. I don't think anyone can."

"I can hear what happened just before he connected to the energy fabric," Emma said to Odym. "If you'll let me."

"No one can access the thoughts of an Oloklira without his cooperation," Odym said.

"Eury Vatic let me connect with him," Emma said.

Odym's bright, shivering face contracted in disbelief.

"At least let me try," Emma said.

Odym nodded, and Emma pressed her hands to his luminous head. He closed his eyes. She stepped back.

"He did it," she said softly to Joe. "He let go without giving in to the Singers of the Apocalypse."

"How?" Joe said.

"Because he saw you," Emma said. "He saw you, and he saw that you were happy. He saw that we were Soulmates. He remembered your mom and sister, but he saw that he saved you. He couldn't risk anyone knowing you were alive, so he hadn't seen you, even telepathically, since he left you in the woods with your Otherworld mother. Now he got to tell you he loved you—which he did. Your dad let go without surrendering to the Singers. He let go, but he never gave in and he never gave up. He valued his life—and everyone else's—right up until the end of his own."

Joe sat on a reading stone and put his head in his hands. Emma sat beside him.

"So he is dead, then," Joe said. "But what about your brothers and sisters?" he added desperately. "What about my mom? What about Isohel?"

"I don't know," Emma said.

"You two have to get back to the Otherworld," Odym said. "Right now the Aythentia still don't know that the rest of your family is with Will Spencer, but they'll figure it out soon enough. Will was Eury's closest friend," he added. "The two of them would have formed a plan of how to protect you, Sfodro, when Eury died or if your identity was in danger of discovery. You probably only met Will very recently, but he's been watching over you since you came to the Otherworld." Odym squeezed Joe's shoulder. "Come on. I'll take you to an unregistered portal tree."

He led them to a portal tree in a park dedicated to the heroes of every revolution. Emma and Joe passed through the tree, and Joe took over from there. He flew them to Mr. Spencer's house with Emma guiding him.

CHAPTER FIFTY-FIVE

Mr. Spencer was waiting on the brick steps of a small, grey, Cape Cod house. He was holding Sandy's hand. Light from a streetlamp fell on the pair's faces. The moon hadn't risen yet.

Sandy was clutching his ratty, blue blanket. "I told you they'd be here," he said.

Mr. Spencer looked as though he'd spent the night at someone's bedside waiting for her to die. "Come inside," he said hoarsely to Joe and Emma.

Maude was sitting on a window seat with her arms around her knees.

Mr. Spencer closed the door behind him. "Give her some time," he said to Emma.

"Where are Turner and Elizabeth?" Emma asked.

"Elizabeth is with Mr. Norway," Mr. Spencer said. "She needed to connect with her friends. And I knew..." He sucked in a raw mouthful of air. "I knew we weren't in immediate danger anymore."

"What about Turner?" Emma asked.

"Turner is with Rachel," Mr. Spencer said. "He should be back any minute."

Maude got up and walked over to the three of them. Emma squeezed her hand and gave her Gryphon's book. Maude took it without speaking.

"Trace the letters with ink," Emma recited gently. "They're a special sticky resonance of his thoughts, but they won't last forever."

Maude nodded.

Mr. Spencer sat on a chair embroidered in an intricate pattern. He pressed the heels of his hands to his eyes.

"I lost a tooth," Sandy said to Joe, shoving his tongue through the empty space. "See?"

"Cool," Joe said.

Sandy smiled.

"Let me see," Emma said, stepping closer to her little brother.

"How did you know we were coming here?" Joe asked him.

"It's part of the story," Sandy said, showing Emma the place where his tooth had been.

Emma leaned closer to Sandy. "What is that?" she asked, pulling at his shirt collar so she could see his back.

"Hey," Sandy said. "What are you doing?" He pulled his shirt away.

"Wait a minute," Emma said. "What is that cut on your back?"

"It's a not a cut," he said. "It's my birthmark. Mommy calls it my stork-bite, remember?"

"It looks different," Emma said, picking up his shirt again. "It looks like a cut or something."

"What happened, Sandy?" Maude asked, coming over.

Sandy flushed. "I'm really sorry your friend died."

Maude paled and turned away.

"Who told him about Gryphon?" Emma whispered angrily to Mr. Spencer. "He's only seven."

"No one told me," Sandy said. "I just know. Like I know Mommy and Daddy love me and I love Captain Underpants."

Mr. Spencer sat up straighter. "Go get your comic book," he said to Sandy. "You can show it to Emma and Joe."

Sandy ran upstairs. Mr. Spencer covered his face with his hands and then ran his fingers through his hair.

"What?" Emma said, her heart thumping. Joe took her hand, and they moved to sit in the chairs beside Mr. Spencer.

"Every Whole Listener has a Whole Chronicler, an *Olografia*," Mr. Spencer said. "After the Whole Listener dies, the Whole Chronicler begins to absorb everything the Whole Listener heard."

"Okay," Emma said.

"I think Sandy is Eury's Olografia," Mr. Spencer said. "That birthmark is a receptor. It opens like that as soon as the Whole Listener dies. Until the receptor opens, no one knows who the Whole Chronicler is."

"What does that mean?" Emma hissed, leaping to her feet. "Will he go crazy? How will he handle it? I connected with Eury for a short time. It was horrible. What will happen to Sandy? He's so little."

"It's okay, calm down," Mr. Spencer said, standing up. "Calm down." He gave Emma a hug then sat down again. "Sandy will absorb Eury's energy and information, but it will come to him slowly, in stories or in songs he sings to himself, or in dreams. It will take the length of Sandy's life to absorb and chronicle everything Eury heard. When he's an old man and all the information has been recorded he'll turn it in to the Anagrafo. It will be the first time in Sacerian history that a Whole Chronicler will have been able to absorb the energy and information of a Whole Listener who lived as long as Eury did."

Emma sat next to Joe, and he took her hand.

"Sandy feels the story of what's going on," Mr. Spencer explained. "And because he's so young and his powers are so immature he is naturally drawn to events that concern him or the people he loves."

"Is the comic book part of the Chronicle?" Joe asked.

Mr. Spencer nodded.

"Wait," Emma said. "Odym told us that the Ones in Power destroyed the train that the Eleytheria lights were on, the lights that held all the information extracted from Joe's dad. How can Sandy absorb information that's been destroyed?"

"I think the information was transferred directly from my father," Joe said. "As soon as he died."

Mr. Spencer moaned and covered his face with his hands. Emma could see he was trying not to cry. He stood up and grabbed a glass of wine from the dining room table. He drank most of it, and then said, half to himself, "That kind of complete extraction is indescribably painful." Finishing the wine, he turned to Emma and Joe. "I never would have believed that the Eleytheria could be capable of that kind of cruelty," he said, "no matter what the possibility for good or avoidance of evil. There had to be another way."

Joe was shaking. Emma squeezed his hand.

"Is Sandy in danger?" she nearly whispered.

Mr. Spencer gazed at her as if he didn't see her for a minute.

"Not yet. I don't think," he said. "If Sandy's identity could be discovered immediately, I would have heard something. Odym would have known. He would have told me. He's the Eleytheria leader now."

"Have you seen the comic book?" Joe asked.

Mr. Spencer shook his head. "He hasn't shown anyone," he said. "I was surprised he was so ready to show you."

Sandy ran noisily down the stairs and opened the book on the dining room table. While Joe and Emma looked at it, Sandy grabbed red grapes from a silver bowl and ate them. Joe stood close to Emma as she paged through the drawings of Gryphon and Maude, and of Eury Vatic, and herself and Joe.

"Who's that?" Emma said, pointing to a pretty, brown-haired girl smiling and holding hands with a different gorgeous girl.

"That's your friend, Izzy," Sandy said. "And that's her girlfriend. Her name's Tess. She used to go to your school when I was a baby.

She moved, but she found Izzy on her computer and now they love each other."

"What?" Emma said. "How do you know? What about Stacy?"

Sandy rolled his eyes. "Stacy loves Doug." He took the figure of a knight out of his pocket. "Does he have a horse?" he asked Mr. Spencer.

Mr. Spencer opened a brass box and took out a silver horse with a foaming blue mane.

"Not that one," Sandy directed. "The pink one."

Mr. Spencer handed Sandy a pink horse with a snow-white mane. Sandy carefully put the knight on the horse, then took another grape and shoved it through the toothless gap in his mouth so red juice poured down his chin.

Emma turned the pages of the comic book as Sandy ran around the table, noisily galloping the horse and the knight. Between the childishly drawn pictures of the winged Masevo chasing her and Joe, and Eury Vatic taking her into his consciousness, there were three squares colored entirely black.

"What are those, Sandy?" Joe asked.

Sandy looked at the black squares then looked away. "I don't know." He shoved the knight and the white horse into his pocket. "I'm thirsty. Can I have some chocolate milk? Mr. Spencer has the kind of chocolate milk Mommy lets us have. The kind in the glass bottle with the red writing. I want some chocolate milk."

"I'll get it for you," Maude said, and Sandy pulled her through the swinging kitchen door.

"Your mom and dad have been apprehended and processed," Mr. Spencer said. "That must be what the black squares are."

"Odym told us," Emma said. "Do you think they're okay?"

"I don't know," Mr. Spencer said. "The justice system in the Commonworld is not the same as it is here. Innocence, not guilt, has to be proven. And your parents were fugitives."

The front door opened.

"Turner!" Emma said, running over to him.

"I'm so glad you're okay, Emma," he said, grabbing his sister and hugging her. "You too, Joe," he said and hugged Joe. "Is it over? What happened?"

Emma told Turner about the extrication lights and the train. Turner glanced sympathetically at Joe, who colored and turned away.

"So he didn't give in to the Singers, then, did he?" Turner asked Emma in a low voice.

She shook her head. "No, he didn't."

"I got back together with Rachel," Turner said, his eyes bright.

Emma smiled and hugged him again.

"I think I would have died without her," her brother whispered into her ear. "I don't know what is going to happen to Maude." He broke away and shook himself. "Did Mr. Spencer tell you about Mom and Dad? Did he tell you I'm going to go back and rescue them? Mr. Spencer said he'd make sure I could make up any schoolwork when I get back."

"I'm coming with you," Joe said.

"I am too," Emma said, taking Joe's hand and smiling at him.

* * *

Later, after Mr. Spencer put Sandy to bed, he told Joe that his mom was home and okay, and that the implanted memories of Joe being away at a youth leadership conference would hold until she saw him again. It was too late at night to call Elizabeth. Emma would get her in the morning.

Rachel came sometime after midnight. She'd been texting and calling Turner since he'd left her that afternoon. She and Turner went into another room and didn't come out again for the rest of the night.

Maude finished inking in the Masked letters, but she didn't leave the window seat or speak. The moon set, and the grey light of dawn splashed over her silent face. She was still desperately beautiful.

When Mr. Spencer went into his study to start planning how to rescue Mom and Dad, Joe took Emma's hand and kissed it. Turning it over in his hand he asked, "What's wrong with your scar?"

A tiny, silvery light shone from the interior of the blackened scar like a drop of water in a pool of mud.

Emma stood up, gazing at her palm as if she was reading a book. "Isohel survived that explosion," she said. "She made something to protect herself."

"Let's go outside," Joe said, and he took her hand.

Splintered early sunlight hung between new-leaved branches, black and spiky against the purple clouds. The air was thick with birdsong and the delicate scent of lilacs, and everything seemed beautiful and new. Perfect.

"We should wait," Joe said, brushing Emma's hair over her shoulders. "After everything that's happened and everything we don't know, it seems wrong to think so much about ourselves and do something just for us."

"We can wait if you want to," Emma said.

"Do you want to?" Joe asked. "Wait, I mean. I'll do whatever you want."

Emma smiled and kissed him softly on the mouth. He sighed and smiled back at her, pressing his forehead into hers.

"I love you," he said.

"I love you, too," Emma said. "And I don't want to wait any longer. I love you and I want to be with you exactly the way you want to be with me."

He kissed her. "You're sure?"

Emma laughed. "Yes. I'm sure."

She grinned at him and walked toward the backyard.

"Where are you going?" he said, following her through the wet grass.

She spun around, her hands clasped behind her back. "You're not even trying to hear my thoughts, are you?" Spinning on her heels again, she walked into the shade of a huge oak tree.

"I forgot I could," Joe said, running up to her. "But I am now."

Emma pulled Joe to her and kissed him long and hard on the mouth. She dropped her hands to his waist and tugged him closer. He sucked the cool, wet morning air between his teeth and held himself very still.

"Izzy Peccant lived in this house when she was little," she said.

"I *so* don't want to think about Izzy Peccant right now," Joe said, his gorgeous voice rough and strained. "Or little-girl you. All I want is *right-now* you."

Emma smiled and laid a hand on his chest, holding him back.

"You're killing me, chi Erama," he said, laughing and pushing against her hand.

"Izzy's dad is an amazing carpenter."

Joe made a noise like he was physically injured.

"Hush, silly," Emma said, kissing him lightly on the mouth. "You're making this harder than it needs to be."

"I don't think I'm the one doing that." He grinned.

She smiled, and she kissed him long and slow and sweet.

"Okay," Joe said. "Enough with Izzy Peccant and her amazing carpenter dad." He grabbed Emma by the waist, and they rose up into the tree, weaving in and out of the heavy branches until they came to a tree house with windows and a little door and a gabled roof. It surprised Joe, and Emma laughed.

"All I was going to say," she continued, "was that Izzy had a great treehouse. We could be alone. And take as long as we wanted. And I could give myself to you. And you could give yourself to me. For the whole day if we wanted."

Joe stared at the treehouse.

"Well?" Emma said.

"This isn't over," he said, kissing her. "And, yes. Yes. A thousand times, *yes*." Joe leaned back in the air let her sweet weight fall into his body.

They floated, kissing, into the treehouse. Emma shut the door with her foot.

They stayed inside the treehouse for half the day.

AUTHOR'S NOTE

By the time Joe meets his father again, Eury Vatic has deteriorated to the point that he can only communicate using phrases and sentences that have already been written (or spoken) by someone else. Here is a listing of the material quoted by Eury Vatic that appears in *everything you know*:

"The air was filled with phantoms," is from the "Marley's Ghost" chapter of *A Christmas Carol* by Charles Dickens.

From *Ode to a Nightingale* by John Keats:

> "But here there is no light,
> Save what from heaven is with the breezes blown
> Through verdurous glooms and winding mossy ways....
> I have been half in love with easeful Death,
> Call'd him soft names in many a mused rhyme,
> To take into the air my quiet breath;
> Now more than ever seems it rich to die,
> To cease upon the midnight with no pain,
> While thou art pouring forth thy soul abroad
> In such an ecstasy!"

John of Gaunt from Act II, Scene I of *Richard II* by William Shakespeare:

> "Methinks I am a prophet new inspired,
> And thus expiring do foretell of him:

His rash fierce blaze of riot cannot last,
For violent fires soon burn out themselves;
Small showers last long, but sudden storms are short;
He tires betimes that spurs too fast betimes;
With eager feeding food doth choke the feeder;
Light vanity, insatiate cormorant,
Consuming means, soon preys upon itself.
This royal throne of kings, this sceptered isle,
This earth of majesty, this seat of Mars,
This other Eden, demi-paradise,
This fortress built by Nature for herself
Against infection and the hand of war,
This happy breed of men, this little world,
This precious stone set in the silver sea,
Which serves it in the office of a wall
Or as a moat defensive to an house,
Against the envy of less happier lands,
This land of such dear souls, this dear dear land,
Dear for her reputation through the world,
Is now leased out…"

Lines from *The Eve of St. Agnes* by John Keats appear several times in the story. The poem is one of Maude's favorites. Lines include:

"She clos'd the door, she panted, all akin/To spirits of the air, and visions wide:"
"Porphyro grew faint:/She knelt, so pure a thing, so free from mortal taint."
"Hark! 'Tis an elfin-storm from faery land/ Of haggard seeming, but a boon indeed:"
"No dream, alas! alas! And woe is mine!/Porphyro will leave me here to fade and pine./Cruel! what traitor could thee hither bring?"

Joe and his father both recite a line from Stanley Kunitz's poem *The Layers*, "How shall the heart be reconciled to its feast of losses?"

When Emma is trying to assure Eury Vatic that she'll help him she quotes the last lines of Samuel Beckett's novel *The Unnamable*. "I can't go on. I'll go on."

Like everyone who really loves music, Emma often has lyrics running through her head. The lines "And if you don't know this, then what do you know? Life is a pigsty" are from the song "Life Is A Pigsty," written by Morrissey and Alain Whyte on the album *Ringleader of the Tormenters*.

As Emma's powers grow stronger she has access to things she's heard but wouldn't necessarily remember. The Ralph Waldo Emerson quote she remembers her father reading to her is from *Nature*:

"If the stars should appear one night in a thousand years, how would men believe and adore; and preserve for many generations the remembrance of the city of God which had been shown! But every night come out these envoys of beauty, and light the universe with their admonishing smile."

Slabsides, located in West Park, New York, eighty miles north of New York City, was built by American Naturalist John Burroughs in 1895. The 191 protected acres surrounding the cabin are open year round. Although Emma, Joe, Gryphon, and Maude visit the cabin in April, Slabsides is actually only open to visitors twice a year, in May and October.

For more information: http://research.amnh.org/burroughs

To hear some of these works, or to read more about them try:

Actor Benedict Cumberbatch reads Keats' *Ode to a Nightingale* (swoon!)
http://www.youtube.com/watch?v=HrAGCJJkNbE

The full text of *The Layers*, by Stanley Kunitz
http://www.poetryfoundation.org/poem/242450

And if you've never listened to Patrick Stewart read *A Christmas Carol* by Charles Dickens, I highly recommend it.

ABOUT THE AUTHOR

More than a little obsessed with Keats and *Moby Dick* and fueled by loud music and cold grey days, Mary Beth Bass is the author of young-adult fantasy and romantic women's fiction. Her debut paranormal women's fiction hybrid *Follow Me* received the Book Buyers Best Award for Time Travel, Fantasy, and Paranormal Romance.

An occasional travel writer, Mary Beth has written about Paris, Bordeaux, and Yorkshire, where she hiked the moors to the legendary setting for *Wuthering Heights* and stood breathless in the parsonage room where Charlotte, Anne, and Emily Bronte talked out their stories with each other.

She also loves octopuses.

You can learn more at:
www.marybethbass.com
https://twitter.com/marybethbass
https://www.facebook.com/pages/Mary-Beth-BassBooks/224291404385433
http://www.pinterest.com/marybethbooks

"Through astounding imagery and richly lyrical prose, Bass's memorable romantic fantasy is, at its heart, a tribute to the unconquerable spirit of first love."
—Laura Toffler-Corrie author of *My Totally Awkward Supernatural Crush*

"*Everything You Know* transcends worlds and challenges the imagination with a desperate tale of love and survival."
—Kassy Tayler, Award-Winning Author of *Ashes Of Twilight*

NO ONE KNOWS EVERYTHING FOREVER

Emma Mathews never believed she was like everyone else, but neither did she think herself crazy. Meeting Joe Castlellaw, Henry Dearborn High's newest student, was like waking on a cold rock in a strange place, the world bathed in liquid moonlight. Everything is different now...and fraught. Visions of a dark forest, a screaming woman and blood haunt Emma's dreams, and not only at night. But Joe's lonely beauty makes her float on air, and she would follow him anywhere: out of high school and through the great tree, to a world of poetry and political savagery, of magic and murder, to a life that is entirely theirs and yet unlike anything they have ever known.

Did you enjoy this book? Drop us a line and say so! We love to hear from readers, and so do our authors. To connect, visit www.boroughspublishinggroup.com online, send comments directly to info@boroughspublishinggroup.com, or friend us on Facebook and Twitter. And be sure to check back regularly for contests and new releases in your favorite subgenres of romance!

Are you an aspiring writer? Check out www.boroughspublishinggroup.com/submit and see if we can help you make your dreams come true.